# Preacher on the Run

© Copyright 2020 by Jayna Baas
Permission is given by the author to copy or quote portions of this work, not exceeding two chapters, so long as proper credit is given and the author's name or the book's title appears with the selected portion.
"The laborer is worthy of his reward" —1 Tim. 5:18 KJV
All other rights reserved.

This is a work of fiction. While historical accuracy has been maintained as far as possible, this work is not intended as an authority on any historical subject.

All Scripture references are from the King James Bible.

Cover design by Jayna Baas
Sky and flintlock "spark" from photographs by Bethany Baas
All other graphics (stone wall, stripes, silhouettes) by Jayna Baas
Part I/Part II title page design and NC Piedmont map by Jayna Baas
(Accents from German map of Bethabara, NC, 1766)
Author photo by Bethany Baas

Typeset in Imprint MT Shadow and Poor Richard (headings) and Book Antiqua (body)

## www.booksbyjayna.com
P.O. Box 173
McBain, MI 49657


**Publisher's Summary**
    (provided by Jayna Baas)

Baas, Jayna (1999- )
    Preacher on the run: a novel of the Regulator Uprising
    ISBN: 978-1-7347175-0-1 (pbk.)

Summary: A North Carolina preacher must get his family and church to safety after he is outlawed in an uprising on the eve of the American Revolution.

1. United States—History—Revolution, 1775-1783—Fiction
2. Preachers—Fiction
3. Baptists—United States—History—Fiction
4. North Carolina—History—Regulator Insurrection, 1766-1771—Fiction

Printed in the United States of America

For Liberty & Conscience ⚔ 1

# Jayna Baas

# Preacher on the Run

### A Novel of the Regulator Uprising

*For Mom and Dad,
who believed I could.*

*And for Pastor Ben.
Wow.*

# Acknowledgments

All gratitude to Jesus Christ, the author and finisher of my faith, who opens doors and closes them, and who is the same today as He was in 1771. "Thanks be unto God for his unspeakable gift."

Further thanks to:
-Dad, Mom, Katelyn, Bethany, and Maralee—the people who love me whether I'm lovable or not. You've all been such a support and blessing to me, whether by reading and critiquing, enduring countless research reports, or patiently waiting for my mind to come back to twenty-first-century Michigan. Mom deserves special thanks for being my Chief Brainstorming Consultant (a.k.a. "sounding board").
-Dr. Ben Townsend, the one who taught me why I believe what I believe, my fellow writer and my friend. I doubt this book would have happened without you.
-Pastor Keith Hoover, who has forgotten more Baptist history than I'll ever know. Your review and critique gave me a major dose of confidence. Thanks for passing our heritage on to the next generation.

A big thank-you to my beta readers:
-Jennifer and Leona Griesbach—your attention to detail was a blessing, but not as much a blessing as your friendship and encouragement.
-Steve Smith—you took time not only to read this book, but to share it as well. Thanks for encouraging me to keep using my gift. I hope someday I can tell in 300 pages the stories you tell in three minutes.
-Rob Siedenburg—you were an answer to a prayer I hadn't even prayed. The help God sent through you gave me faith for the next step.
-Adallie and Mattea Bricker—fellow book-lovers make the best friends.

Extra thanks to everyone who let me recount in great detail everything I planned to write (before, while, and after I wrote it). You know who you are. You can come out of hiding until the next book.

Last but not least: Emma. Thank you for all of the above and more. You're the best.

This book is a tribute to all the brave Christians who have stood for both political freedom and religious freedom. Someday I'll meet them in heaven, but by then we'll all be too busy praising Christ to worry about it.

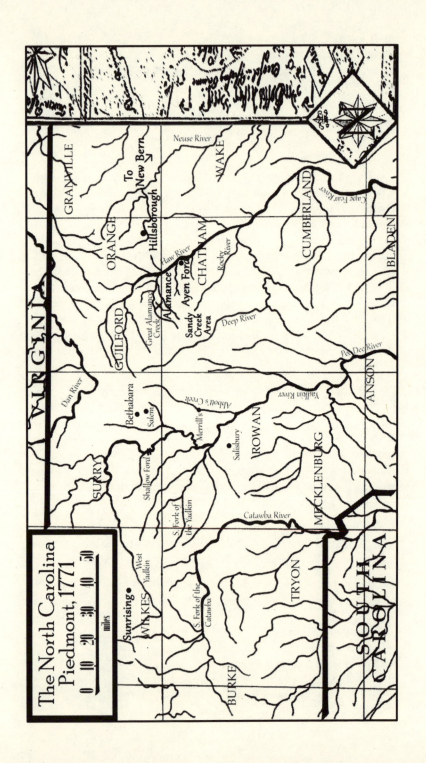

MARCH 22, 1767
SANDY CREEK,
NORTH CAROLINA

# Prologue

"YOU BOYS ARE *CERTAIN* YOU WANT ME TO BE A leader in this." Robert Boothe searched the faces of the men around him. "It's not just a few men here and there anymore. It's—" He picked up the paper in front of him and read, "'*An association to assemble ourselves for conferences for regulating public grievances and abuses of power.*'" He let the page drop. "It's a mighty big responsibility, leading a thing like that."

"If we trust you enough to write it, we trust you enough to lead us in standing by it," one of the men said.

John Woodbridge clapped Robert on the shoulder. "You've been leading folks for years, Pastor. We trust you. And whoever *don't* trust you—knoweth nothing yet as he ought to know, ain't that what the Bible says?"

"I don't think the Bible was talking about my leadership skills," Robert said. His drawl was quiet in the big meetinghouse. Too quiet. But he was not a man given to raising his voice.

"What was it you wrote in that pledge?" This from a rangy, angular man Robert knew only as Perry. "Right near the end, there. 'In cases of differences in judgment we will submit to the majority of our body.' So submit."

Robert glanced up and looked around at that "majority of the body," what part of it was present. So many men, all sick and tired of government corruption. Just like Robert.

All he had ever wanted was to be a preacher. A circuit rider, at that. Living life for the Lord, for the lost, for the wind in his face. Now he was "regulating public grievances and abuses of power." And still shy of thirty-five.

He took the pen Woodbridge handed him and ran his eye down the page one last time.

"*That we will pay no taxes until we are satisfied they are agreeable to law . . .*"

"*That we will pay no officer any more fees than the law allows . . .*"

"*That we will attend our meetings of conference as often as we conveniently can or is necessary . . .*"

"*That we will contribute to collections for defraying necessary expenses . . .*"

"*That in cases of differences in judgment we will submit to the majority of our body.*"

Signing the pledge did not force him to act as a leader. But Robert would not feel right joining anything he wasn't willing to take through to the very end. Once he signed it, there was no turning back. Not that there was any turning back, even now. Not after eleven years of preaching freedom.

"'To all of which we do solemnly swear,'" he read slowly, out loud.

He signed the pledge. Robert Boothe was a Regulator.

No turning back.

# PART I

## Resistance
March 22 – May 16, 1771

"If it be possible,
as much as lieth in you,
live peaceably with all men."
Romans 12:18

FOUR YEARS LATER
MARCH 22, 1771
AYEN FORD,
NORTH CAROLINA

# One

ROBERT BOOTHE HAD NEVER KNOWN COUNTY justice Geoffrey Sheridan to barge into a late-night Regulator meeting at the Ayen Ford Baptist meetinghouse. Other folks certainly had done just that. The sheriff, for instance. But not Geoffrey Sheridan. The moment his old friend came through the door, Robert knew those other folks weren't far behind.

"Sheriff Kendall on his way?" he asked in an undertone, stepping away from the men clustered in the back of the meetinghouse.

"Not only the sheriff this time," Sheridan said. He was in his mid-forties, only ten years older than Robert, but tonight he looked sixty. "One of the governor's men is with him. A new man, Colonel Charles Drake. I don't know what you and your men are meeting about tonight, and I don't want to know. But you've been preaching without a license for fifteen years, and you've been leading Regulators for nearly half that. Colonel Drake is looking for trouble. If he looks here—"

"I allow as he'll find it." Robert smiled grimly. "Thanks, Geoff. Now you'd best be getting out while you can."

The only warning was a sudden noise outside and the

crack of a musket butt against the door, and then it was too late. No time for Sheridan, or anyone else, to make it out the back way. Robert motioned Sheridan behind him an instant before the door crashed against the wall.

Robert had dealt with the wrong side of the law before. He'd dealt with it in his church building, too. But the last thing Ayen Ford needed was a new agent of Governor Tryon, and the stranger behind the sheriff wore a sword that branded him as a military man. No older than Robert, tall and trim, coal-black hair in a flawless queue and eyes that looked right through you and out the other side. Robert said, "What's this about?"

Ebeniah Kendall was a big man. Robert was solidly built, but the sheriff was easily sixty pounds heavier, made weightier by the knowledge of his own power. He said, "There's a law against seditious meetings. I've seen my share of dissenter preachers calling for rebellion, so don't try to play holy and innocent with me. And don't try to tell me this is just neighborly talk, either. This is the kind of thing the governor wants to put an end to. Which is what Colonel Drake and I are here to do."

"This being Colonel Drake, I gather." Robert nodded toward the stranger, who appeared to be examining the room. Plain oak walls and simple plank benches, a few windows, a front door that Kendall had forced open, and a second exit behind the unadorned pulpit. Drake pulled his attention from his perusal and wordlessly inclined his head, either bored or simply content to remain quiet. Out of the corner of his eye Robert saw Saul McBraden move restlessly. *Lord, help.* If Saul got it into his head to knock the sheriff upside the head or some such thing, five and a half feet of musket would blow the pastor of the Ayen Ford Baptists from here to kingdom come. Robert wanted to go to heaven, but not that way.

"Put the gun down, Sheriff," he said evenly, hoping his tone would give Saul the hint to calm down. "I'll give you fair warning that you're on God's property and He's watching you, but beyond that I'm not aiming to run and I'm not aiming to fight you."

Kendall glanced at Drake and started to lower the musket just as Saul McBraden exploded. "But Pastor, they have no right to come on in through here unprovoked and—"

So much for calming Saul down.

"I told you, there's a law," Kendall snapped.

"That doesn't mean the law is right," Saul muttered.

"Or the way you enforce it, either."

Robert slipped in front of Saul before Drake could see the young man's clenched fists. Saul's hair was more blond than red, but every now and then, the red showed in his temper. If Saul got mad enough, and the officials got mad enough, everyone would get riled and they'd all end up in jail. Which they would anyway if Sheriff Kendall and this Colonel Drake fellow found out they'd been meeting to discuss unjust taxes.

"If you're here to break this up, then break it up," Robert said. "There's no need for it to get out of hand."

Geoffrey Sheridan came forward a step. "These are good men, Colonel."

"I'll be the judge of that, Justice." Drake's gaze roved over the small gathering of men, church members and otherwise, before again coming to rest on Robert. But he said nothing more, letting Kendall do the talking.

"Everyone get out," the sheriff said, motioning with his musket.

The men looked at Robert. Robert nodded. One by one the men moved to the front door and filed out. Robert knew, and they knew, that the colony's riot act said anyone who didn't leave a meeting within an hour of the sheriff's order would be guilty of felony. Sometimes a man had to pick his battles. Saul was last to go, looking like he'd just as soon stay and fight it out with the law.

Robert locked eyes with Colonel Drake, each man gauging the other. Drake was all chiseled edges and poise, dark and polished, how Robert had always envisioned an eastern military man to look. Robert was more a continuation of the rough brown wood of the meetinghouse. Oak-brown hair, bronzed skin, buckskin hunting shirt. Not of Drake's world at all.

"I would never have guessed," the colonel said slowly, "that a building as small and plain as this could ever be suspected as the breeding ground of mass rebellion. Or that a man like you should be suspected as the leader of it."

"Life is full of surprises, Colonel."

"Are you admitting—"

"Nothing at all."

A spark of something like humor flickered in Drake's dark eyes. "I see." He held Robert's gaze a moment longer, then wheeled abruptly and motioned for Kendall to follow.

Kendall moved obediently toward the door. "If anything comes of this, preacher," he said, "we'll be back. And we'll be coming for you."

"It'd not be the first time," Robert said quietly.

"And you, Justice." Drake paused at the door. "This is the last time you'll play with fire."

When Robert got home, Susanna's piping seven-year-old voice instantly called from the bedroom. "Is Papa home? Can I get up and say good night, Mama? You said I could if I was awake. I'm awake."

"So I hear," Magdalen Boothe murmured as Robert leaned down to kiss her.

"Let her wait a minute," Robert whispered into Magdalen's hair. Thick dark bronze ringlets, loosely bound back, smelling of lye soap and thyme. Robert's manservant, Gunning, entered the room and hastily edged back out. Gunning could wait, too.

Magdalen gave Robert the minute he'd asked for plus a little more, then pulled away and called back to Susanna. "Come say good night. Then back to bed."

Susanna padded out, her light blond curls wisping out from under her nightcap, her cornflower-blue eyes suspiciously heavy. She stopped a few feet short of Robert and asked, "Why are you holding Cricket?"

Once, while Robert was loading his rifle, Susanna had watched him close the frizzen, the hinged steel that struck sparks over the priming pan. It squeaks, she had said, just like a cricket. The rifle had been named Cricket ever since. Persistent squeak notwithstanding, Cricket was a beautiful gun. Tempered .45 caliber bore, flame-maple stock, brass fittings, scrolled carving that Robert had done himself on long winter nights. The flint was knapped sharp, the trigger as smooth as any he had ever known. He'd take Cricket and a good horse over any other advantage a man could name. But there were times, like tonight, when a good rifle was not the answer.

"You know Papa brings his rifle down to the meetinghouse with him sometimes," Magdalen said smoothly.

"Can I go with you next time, Papa?"

"Depends how late it is and what I'm doing." Robert reached around her and set Cricket in the corner.

"What were you doing this time?" Susanna wanted to know.

"Talking with some men."

"About the vestry tax?"

Robert frowned. "Who told you about that?"

"Benjamin told me," Susanna said.

That explained it. Benjamin Woodbridge, older brother of Susanna's best friend, was twelve and knew everything.

"And I heard you say it to Mama after church last Sunday," Susanna added.

Robert glanced at Magdalen, wondering what else Susanna had overheard in days past. "The vestry tax is a mighty heavy subject for so late at night, Susanna. And a mighty heavy subject for a curly little head like yours."

Susanna would not be deterred. "But what is it?"

"Money we have to chunk in to support the Church of England," Robert said. "Even if we don't agree with the Church of England."

Susanna's forehead puckered. "But that's not right."

"Well, some of us don't think so."

"Rob..."

The soft southern in Magdalen's voice turned his name into a syllable and a half, a quiet warning that it was late, that this was no time to rehearse one of his worst grievances. So he amended his statement in silence, thinking, *A whole slew of us don't think it's right. Baptist, Presbyterian, Quaker, who knows what else, all of us hate it. All except the Anglican clergymen it profits.*

But Susanna was not satisfied. "Does everybody have to pay the vestry tax? Benjamin said so."

"Everybody around these parts has to," Robert said.

"Supposed to, leastways." This from Gunning, who came all the way into the room this time. "Sorry, Master Rob, I didn't mean to walk in on you and the missus while you were—uh—"

"No harm done, Gunning." Robert winked at Magdalen.

"While you were what, Papa?" Susanna piped up.

"Nothing, pumpkin. And neither is the vestry tax. Nothing to bother your head about, that is." Robert didn't mind explaining things to his daughter—but how did one explain a decade and a half of injustice to a seven-year-old who didn't know what "extortion" meant?

"Papa," Susanna said, "what's extortion?"

"Benjamin again?" he asked.

She nodded.

"I figured," he said.

"I don't hear anything that sounds like *good night*," Magdalen hinted.

"Good night, Papa," Susanna said obediently, lifting her face for a kiss. Robert complied and gave her a gentle nudge in the direction of the bedroom.

Gunning said, "How was the meeting?"

"You just heard. Nothing to bother your head about."

Gunning gave him a look. "That might work on Miss Susanna, but not on me, no sir."

"It doesn't work on her, either," Robert said wryly. "John Woodbridge needs to grub up more work for Benjamin to do. Aye, we were meeting about the vestry tax. More than that, though. The scouts say that four days ago Governor Tryon got permission from his council to muster his militia and march our way. We've got a conference of Regulators planned for the twenty-seventh, but in the meantime, we're studying on what to do. We didn't get far before Sheridan came to warn us."

He gave them the short version of the night's events and his encounter with Colonel Drake, passing lightly over the details, not wanting to frighten his wife. Not that Magdalen Davies Boothe was an easy woman to frighten. She had left her life as the privileged daughter of a plantation owner to follow Robert to his mountain circuit, where she had known things far more frightening than officials with overinflated views of themselves.

"Is there anything you can do to—prepare?" Magdalen asked.

"Get a license," Robert said with a humorless smile. "That's all a man like Drake wants—control over what I say and where I say it."

"He thinks he's got more say over it than the Lord does?" Gunning's smile was equally mirthless.

"If he thinks he does, he's wrong," Robert said. "The county has no authority to limit where and when a man may preach the Word. But even Geoffrey Sheridan doesn't seem to understand that, obliging as he's been. I didn't tell him how some of the boys and I are fixing to preach on the street tomorrow. I don't think he'd have taken to that idea, though he'd know better than to think he could change my mind."

"Give him time, love," Magdalen said gently. "The Lord didn't show you everything in a day."

"Geoff's had nine years," Robert said dryly. "But you're right, of course. You always are."

"I try to be." Abruptly the teasing left her voice and she said, "This man Drake who came with the sheriff—did he know who you are? How you've organized the Regulators here and led petitions and all?"

"If he did, he didn't say so," Robert said. "Which is what worries me."

# Two

"Rob. Wake up."

Magdalen was shaking him. Robert opened one eye, grunted. "Mm."

"Wake up. Did you hear that?"

He rolled halfway over. "Hear what?"

"*That.*"

The straw tick crackled as Robert sat up and listened. Someone across the street seemed to be making an unholy racket. He glanced at the kitchen window through the doorway. Dawn was still well on the other side of the horizon.

"Some no-account out celebrating. Though what there is to celebrate these days I don't know." He lay down again and waited for Magdalen to settle beside him. "More likely, maybe, someone making a protest in his own way."

A crash. Like a door rending from its hinges. Across the street but loud enough to be their own front door.

"I don't think that's it, Rob," Magdalen said in a small voice. "Across the street—that's—"

"Sheridan's house. I know." Robert was already on his feet, reaching for the garments that lay over the chair in the corner. "Something's wrong. Stay here and I'll go see."

"Be careful, Rob."

He finished throwing on his clothes. "Don't you worry, love."

Torchlight flared from Geoffrey Sheridan's house as Robert stepped into the street. A pair of horses moved restlessly in front of a splintered void in the front wall. Robert's fingers tightened on Cricket's cool barrel. If whoever was over there tried to cross the street and kick Robert's door in that way, Cricket would do the talking. Robert was a peace-loving man, a Baptist pastor, after all. But when it came to protecting family, Baptist pastors in these parts could shoot.

He moved closer, his steps cautious as he edged past the horses. Voices carried from within the building. Sheriff Kendall's, strident as always. Sheridan's voice, too, and a deeper, quieter one. The words were indistinct, but the tones indicated an argument.

Footsteps neared the doorway and Robert faded into the shadows. Sheriff Kendall appeared, carrying a torch. Behind him came Colonel Charles Drake, the governor's emissary. He was escorting Geoffrey Sheridan. Sheridan's lips were pressed together, his hands clasped in front of him.

Not clasped.

Shackled.

Anger surged through Robert, a notch shy of white rage. Without moving from the shadows he said, "What do you think you're doing, Drake?"

Colonel Drake wheeled. The torchlight accentuated the sharp lines of his face, turned them hard as stone. "Reverend Boothe. I might have known."

"I asked you a question, Colonel."

"What do I think I'm doing, was that it? I might ask you the same thing."

Robert moved forward. "I'm looking out for law and justice, is what I'm doing."

"Don't try, Rob," Sheridan said in a low, weary voice.

Drake's smile showed straight, perfect teeth. "On the contrary. Law and justice say that Sheridan has undermined the governor's authority long enough."

"That's a rank lie."

"You would say so," Drake said with a shrug. "From what I understand, you've been reaping most of the benefits."

"This is wrong, Colonel."

"My word here is law."

"Not to God."

"Listen to me, preacher." The smile was gone. Drake's gaze pinned Robert's. "The only reason I'm not taking you with him is that I'm giving you just enough rope to hang yourself."

Magdalen looked out the window, seeing dim silhouettes in the torchlight across the street, two men, no, three, parting from one lone figure. Dark shapes, but nothing more. What if Rob—

*No, Lord. I'm not going to go there.*

She forced herself to turn from the window. The taper she'd lit and set on the kitchen table flickered as Gunning let himself in the back door. "You all right, Miz Maggie?"

She almost couldn't see him, the way his dark skin blended with the shadows. But his deep voice was comforting. "I'm all right. Rob went to see what all the noise was."

"I figured he would. That's why I come in. He'd have wanted me to."

"I just hope Rob doesn't do anything foolish."

The front door opened behind her. Robert said, "I haven't, though I've surely a mind to."

Magdalen turned. Robert shut the door. His voice and face were calm. Too calm. But when he looked at her the candlelight showed that his eyes, the deep color of warm molasses, were not. Magdalen could tell even in the semi-darkness that her patient, gentle husband was mad enough to spit, as her mama would say, God rest her soul.

"What happened?" she said, as much for Robert's benefit as her own. "I thought I saw the sheriff."

"Aye." He set Cricket in the corner with care but a little more force, she thought, than was strictly necessary. "And Charles Drake."

"But what were they doing at Sheridan's house? In the middle of the night?"

"Arresting him for treason."

"Oh, Rob, no."

"I thought you said he let Sheridan off with just a warning at that meeting of yours," Gunning said.

"'When he speaketh fair, believe him not: for seven abominations are in his heart,'" Robert said bitterly.

"What did you do?" Gunning wanted to know.

"I'd have shot him if my conscience would've let me." He rubbed the back of his neck and looked at Magdalen, dark anger still in his eyes. "We had some peace with Geoff on the court. He kept the rest in line. But now it's up to us."

"And all the other men like you," Magdalen said softly.

She was scared to death of what could happen to him, standing against men like Drake and the governor. But she was proud of him, too. She let her eyes follow the rugged line of his profile, his wide shoulders, his nut-brown hair cut just above the back of his collar. Next to the Lord, she'd never loved anyone like she loved Robert Boothe. He was an easy man to love, as a rule. But she knew for a fact she wouldn't want to stand in his way when once he'd had enough.

# Three

IN THE MORNING ROBERT STILL HAD A SET TO his jaw that told Magdalen he wasn't happy. But he left to preach on the street corner as planned, saying as he left that the town would need it now more than ever. Magdalen took Susanna in tow and went on a mission to deliver a basket of fresh bread to the Thurmond family, a gaggle of motherless boys under the care of their only sister. Their father, Caleb, had nearly lost his leg in a woodcutting accident, and the ensuing infection still threatened his life. Sixteen-year-old Elsie could use all the help she could get.

Elsie's heart-shaped face was grateful as she took Magdalen's basket. "Oh, Mrs. Boothe, thank you so much. For the bread, but just for coming. It's so nice to have womenfolk about now and then. Come in and set a spell, if you don't mind the house. I try so hard to keep it tidy, but—"

Magdalen touched her shoulder. "You do a fine job, Elsie. We'll stay for a bit, if it won't be a trouble."

Susanna tugged Magdalen's arm. "Mama, may I play in the yard with Abner?"

"Yes, you may. Stay out of the road."

Susanna vanished out the door and Magdalen added, "I'll sit down, Elsie, but only if you will. You look tired."

"I'm always tired now, I guess," Elsie said with a wisp of a smile. She led Magdalen into the small house with its simple, handmade furnishings and pungent scents of old ashes, fresh broth, and grave illness. "Saul says when we're wed he'll not let me be tired anymore." She blushed to the edge of her honey-colored hair. "But you know how Saul is. He doesn't do anything but sweet-talk me these days."

Magdalen *tsk*ed playfully. "Is this the Saul McBraden I know?"

"I reckon he doesn't say those things where most folks hear," Elsie said, dropping her eyes.

"No, I reckon not," Magdalen said with a laugh.

"And I don't tell most folks, either," Elsie added shyly. Magdalen was one of few people to whom Elsie opened up. Saul McBraden, on the other hand, said what he thought when he thought it. It must be true that opposites attract.

"Have you planned a time yet?" Magdalen asked, watching Elsie take the kettle off the fire and thinking that the girl seemed so young to be getting married. Still, she was sixteen, the age Magdalen had been at her marriage to Robert, and many girls were married even younger than that.

"Saul had said right after planting." Elsie filled a pair of cups and brought them to the table, not looking at Magdalen. The earthy spice of sassafras rose with the steam. "But then Pa had his accident, and it's all different now. Saul still wants us to marry and then move Pa in with us until he's well, but Pa's not even strong enough for that yet. And until he is, he needs me here."

"How is he today?"

"Not so good. The fever's down, but he's so weak it scares me. And there's no way to know if his leg will heal or not." Elsie sat down and lifted her cup, trying unsuccessfully to hide the tremble of her lips. "The doctor wanted to take his leg, you know. Everybody prayed and the doctor changed his mind. But now I wonder if he waited too long to set the break, seeing as he thought it'd be no use." She sipped slowly, as if gathering strength for her next words.

She set the cup down but played with a nick in the rim. "Pa might not ever get well. Not really *well*. And I'm happy to have him with Saul and me when we get married, but I don't know if Pa would be happy that way."

Magdalen leaned toward her. "You're a brave woman, Elsie, and a good woman, to be willing to take your whole family into your new home."

Elsie shrugged. "We're family. It's what we do." She gave a shy little smile. "I just hope Saul and I get some time to ourselves. We hardly do now, with him only visiting. I hate to think what it'll be when we're all in the same house."

Magdalen smiled. "Trust me, Elsie, when a man takes a wife, he can get downright feisty about having her to himself."

Elsie blushed again. Magdalen had known she would.

Caleb Thurmond called from the bedroom, his voice raspy but still hinting at his former strength. "Elsie, someone's coming in the yard."

"I'll see to it, Pa," Elsie called back, rising. To Magdalen she said, "I'm sorry, I'd best see who's here."

Magdalen turned in her chair and watched as Elsie opened the door. A tall, black-haired man, Robert's age or a little younger, stepped into the opening without invitation and bowed briefly to Elsie as if he owned the place and her with it.

Magdalen frowned. Other women might have swooned over the stranger's dark good looks. But not a woman who was already happily married to the man she loved. And not a woman who saw Sheriff Kendall on the man's heels. *Lord, tell me this isn't what I think it is.*

"Can I help you?" Elsie asked.

"My soul. I didn't expect such a beautiful young woman to answer the door." His smile was a study in masculine perfection. "Caleb Thurmond's place of residence, is it not?"

"Yes, but he's not able to see folks," Elsie said softly.

"I'm afraid he hasn't much choice in this matter, Miss Thurmond. I am Colonel Charles Drake, representative of

His Excellency William Tryon."

    I knew it, Magdalen wanted to say. How she knew, she couldn't have said. But when Drake's smile slipped away, she saw a man who could throw Geoffrey Sheridan in a dungeon somewhere and not have his conscience bother him a whit.

    Drake went on, "I have here a writ of execution for a civil debt in the amount of three pounds, eight shillings and sixpence, payable to Ebeniah Kendall, past due by thirteen days."

    Elsie said with a catch in her voice, "Mr. Sheridan ordered two months' stay of execution to give us time to get the money. We've more than a month left."

    Not to Drake, you don't, Magdalen thought. She got up and went to stand behind Elsie.

    "Sheridan has been removed from his office on charges of treason," Drake said. "Any order given by him is now to be considered unlawful and invalid. Your father must pay the debt immediately or have his goods distrained for public auction."

    "There's no money in the house." Elsie spoke in a low voice. Magdalen knew she was trying not to disturb her father.

    "Then distrainment will begin at once." Drake turned. "Kendall, bring in your men."

    Magdalen could hold her peace no longer. "Colonel Drake, this family barely has a home to call its own. Caleb Thurmond was all but killed by falling timber not three weeks ago, and it's taken all they have to save his life. If you had any kind of human conscience, you'd not dare to sell their goods from under them."

    Drake's eyes raked her up and down before he bowed. "I don't believe I've had the pleasure."

    "I don't see as that matters, Colonel." Ordinarily she didn't mind her petite build, which fit perfectly into Robert's side. But today she wished she was a foot and a half taller, so she could look down at Drake instead of up. And she didn't like the way his gaze played over her. Rob had always told her, half-teasing, that she was too fetching for her own good . . .

Sheriff Kendall said, "Robert Boothe's wife, sir."

"I might have known. Pity, though. She doesn't look like a preacher's wife." Drake paused long enough to flash a taut smile in her direction. "Get out of my way, Mrs. Boothe. And tell your husband the same thing."

"Colonel, you can't—"

"Yes, madam, I can. Go ahead, Kendall."

Sheriff Kendall shouldered between Magdalen and Elsie, four burly men following on his heels. Magdalen squeezed Elsie's arm and turned just as Caleb Thurmond appeared in the bedroom doorway, a blanket around his shoulders and one hand gripping the doorframe. He was not much older than Rob, but the last three weeks had aged him by years.

Elsie turned around and saw him. "Pa! You shouldn't be up. You're not strong enough!"

"Sometimes the strength isn't there till you need it," Caleb said, quietly intense as he had always been.

"At least sit in your chair by the window," Elsie pleaded.

"Get that too," Kendall called over his shoulder to his men. "It'll bring something at least."

"I made that chair for my Jemima before she passed on, God rest her," Caleb said. He took a step forward, dragging his heavily splinted left leg. Pain washed over his face, yet he held his ground. "That's one thing you ain't taking."

"We'll take whatever we want," Kendall snapped.

"Not that," Caleb said.

Kendall shoved him. Caleb fell hard. Elsie screamed. She broke from Magdalen's side and pushed the sheriff away with a force no one would have known the girl had. "Leave him alone!" she flared at Kendall.

Caleb said, "Elsie." Then his eyes drifted shut and he went still.

The three Thurmond boys who weren't working the

fields burst into the room with Susanna tagging behind them. "What'd Elsie scream for?" Edward demanded. He stopped to stare. "What—"
    Susanna's eyes went wide. "Mama—"
    "Susanna, you and Abner go back outside." Magdalen's voice caught. "Now. Edward, Owen—go get Pastor Boothe and Saul. Hurry!"

#  Four

ROBERT BELIEVED IN A SIMPLE GOSPEL THAT could be summed up in the words *repent and believe*. Those were words Christ had used to preach the message of the kingdom. They were the words Robert was preaching now on the street corner just down from the meetinghouse. And they were the words that tended to make folks mad. "The only cure for mankind is Jesus Christ and Him alone. Not baptism or the Eucharist or any doctrine of man. Not any earthly thing between you and God. Only a true repentance and faith in the saving work of Christ on the cross."

Some farmer called, "Some folks say baptism is what puts you in the Church, and if you ain't in the Church you ain't the Lord's a'tall."

"I can't answer for other folks," Robert replied. "All I know is that this is what the Bible says. Faith comes first. Then baptism. Not the other way around. And Christ taught baptism by immersion, to show the picture of His death, burial, and resurrection. It has nothing to do with becoming one of God's children."

Another voice said, "That's blasphemy."

The farmer said, "Shut your mouth."

Robert said, "What any man believes is between him

and God. I can tell you what the Bible says. But what you do with it, that's up to you. The Lord wants folks to follow Him because they choose to, not because any man or church or government forces them to."

Governor Tryon had made it his mission to make North Carolina a stronghold of the Church of England. From what Robert heard, Anglican clergy was nervous about settling in the somewhat hostile villages of the Piedmont Plateau. But Ayen Ford did have an Anglican vestry and its share of lesser church officers, and those were the men who gave Robert trouble. He wouldn't have minded so much if the vestry would come and carry on a fair discussion, but they seemed to like sending their head vestryman to corner Robert the minute he finished preaching. Even now, Jacob Chauncy was watching from across the street. Robert ended his simple presentation of the gospel and braced for the inevitable.

The head vestryman was a sparsely built man just past forty, with an expression of being under habitual pressure. His wheat-brown hair was unpowdered and tied with a simple black ribbon, an unpretentious style well suited to Ayen Ford. Jacob Chauncy was an unpretentious man in other ways, too, one who Robert suspected would prefer to leave doctrinal arguments alone, if only his vestry would let him. He began with his customary hesitation. "I hate to think ill of anyone, Reverend Boothe."

"As do I. Go on."

"Your—" Chauncy seemed to search for the proper word. "Discourse, today."

Discourse, Robert thought. Now it's never been called that before. "Who put you up to this, Chauncy?"

"Put me *up* to it? Reverend—"

"Your vestry again? They're tired of folks asking them questions they can't answer."

"You're causing the parishioners to question what they have been taught, Reverend. To question the authority of the Church."

"The only authority that matters is God's," Robert said.

"Then, after that, those to whom He has given authority. When those authorities overstep their God-given bounds, folks have no obligation to obey an unbiblical command. Your people aren't questioning the Church of England for questioning's sake. They're beginning to compare it with the authority of God. There's a vital difference."

"But the Church *is* the authority of God!"

How Robert hated that philosophy, hated the idea that a man could stand in the place of God. "Strong words, Chauncy. And unscriptural."

Out of the corner of his eye he saw Owen Thurmond, a rail-thin boy of ten, pushing his way through the group of bystanders. Chauncy said, "Were you not claiming to have the authority of God just a few minutes past?"

"I was pointing to the authority of the Scriptures," Robert corrected. "Where I teach anything against the word of God, let God be true and every man a liar. When folks hear my street preaching and come to you with questions, Chauncy, you'd best have answers. Or they'll find them somewhere else."

"Meaning you."

"Meaning me, or a rank heretic, or, heaven forbid, the Bible itself."

"There's no need to be sarcastic." Chauncy glanced around at the clustered onlookers. "This street preaching, as you call it—what are you going to do about it?"

"Nothing until the Lord tells me otherwise. Like the Apostle Paul said, the love of Christ constraineth me."

Owen Thurmond was beckoning now. Robert moved a half-step in that direction. It was time for this discussion, the same discussion as always, to be over.

"Give me a plain answer, Boothe," Chauncy said. "For all I know, you're being sarcastic again, only in biblical terms."

"You already know what I'm saying, Jacob. Christ loved me so much, I have to share it. I have to do what He wants me to do. You can control your parish any way you choose.

You have the governor and the whole Church of England behind you. Do what you can. And I'll go on preaching freedom and the cross and the glorious grace of God."

Chauncy sighed. Robert turned away. Owen barely waited for him to come within earshot before he said in a frightened whisper, "Mrs. Boothe said to come get you, and hurry. There's a passel of men in the house and I think Sheriff Kendall hit Pa."

Chauncy said behind them, "Reverend—"

"Go tell your vestry the truth will hold its own," Robert said and followed Owen at a half-run, leaving Chauncy to give his vestry the same answer Robert always gave.

Saul McBraden and Edward were coming from the other way. Saul said in a low voice, "I'm glad you're coming too, Pastor. I'd be liable to shoot somebody if you weren't. If they've hurt Elsie—"

"If they've hurt Caleb that's bad enough."

"I know. What kind of brute would hit an injured man in front of his daughter?"

"Charles Drake, that's what kind of brute," Robert said, knowing intuitively that this was Drake's doing. "Kendall may have done it, but I doubt he'd have the nerve if Drake wasn't behind him."

Saul's jaw muscles twitched. "I don't care who did it or who was behind it, they can't trample our God-given rights."

"At the moment they can do anything they want to."

"Justice Sheridan won't let them."

"Drake arrested Sheridan for treason last night. He's on his way to New Bern for trial."

Saul said, "No!"

Owen Thurmond said, "Mr. Sheridan gave Pa two more months on the money he owed the sheriff."

Robert looked at the boy. "Your father had a debt to Sheriff Kendall?"

"More'n three pounds," Edward said, answering for his brother. "From when Pa took him to court over high fees and the court made Pa pay all the costs after he lost. We've been trying to pay it, but everything's so tight, and then the accident happened—"

"Lord have mercy," Robert said. "That's what Drake's after or I've not learned anything the last nine years."

Saul said, "Caleb Thurmond doesn't have three pounds to his name in the whole county."

"I know," Robert said. "And I'd dare to wager Drake knew it too."

When they reached the Thurmond house, it was too late. Drake and Kendall were gone, but Robert could tell where they had been. Kendall and his men had quickly and efficiently loaded everything that would bring any decent price at auction. Far more than three pounds, eight shillings and sixpence' worth.

Caleb Thurmond lay on the floor where he had fallen, his head in Elsie's lap. Robert had been the one to find him in the woods, pinned by the tree he had been felling. Caleb was a gentle man with a hidden steel most people never saw. Robert couldn't tell if Caleb was conscious or not. Even if he was, it would be his way to suffer in silence.

Saul said huskily, "They can bide at my place, Pastor. I'll sleep in the barn. I'll bring my wagon over and we can move anything they want to take. If Elsie wants."

"This is home," Elsie said, just above a whisper.

Saul went around to Caleb's other side and got down to meet Elsie's eyes. "But Elsie, think of your pa. You can't stay here with nothing to sit on or sleep on—or eat, either. They took the last of the grain, too, didn't they?"

She nodded dully.

"Let him take care of you, girl," Caleb said hoarsely, not opening his eyes.

"But Pa, are you strong enough?"

"I am if I've got to be," Caleb said.

Saul rose from his crouch. "I'll get my wagon. Don't fret, Elsie, it'll be all right."

Her face said she wanted to believe him. Magdalen's

said the same thing.

The rest of the morning was spent moving the Thurmond family and their remaining worldly goods to Saul's cabin. "I'd meant to carry *you* over the threshold," Saul said regretfully to Elsie. "Not your pa. But someday it'll be your turn."

She tried to smile. But her eyes were worried, looking at her father.

Magdalen was bravely cheerful all morning, save one brief glance at Robert, a look that said, *Can't you do something?*

Just you wait, he wanted to say. To her, but mostly to Charles Drake.

When the moving was over, Robert motioned Saul outside and closed the door. "This is why we're Regulators," he said. "Let's get to work."

# Five

WHILE ROBERT AND HIS REGULATORS DISCUSSED plans and prayed for guidance, Colonel Charles Drake sat awaiting the arrival of Malcolm Harrod, Governor Tryon's most trusted right-hand man. Drake toyed with his wineglass and thought about the day that honor would be his. Not fantasizing. Estimating in cold, hard terms just what it would take to win the governor's highest approval.

Malcolm Harrod was on time to the minute, as Drake had known he would be. Harrod was a few years younger than Drake at approximately thirty, a rail-thin man with narrow features and brown hair in a severe queue. If looks mattered to the governor, Drake would have bested Harrod, no contest. But Harrod had a reputation for shrewdness and tenacity that neither his age nor appearance suggested. He seated himself across from Drake and said, "Well?"

Drake said, "May I offer you a glass of the best Madeira the Carolinas have to offer?"

"I'd be a fool to refuse," Harrod said. "And a worse fool to let such an offer distract me. Are you doing what you vowed to me you would?"

Drake paused in his pouring long enough to retort, "I didn't vow it to you, I vowed it to the governor."

Harrod took the glass. "It might as well be the same thing."

Drake let that one pass. "This town is *abominable*. Packs of rebel farmers, utter disrespect for His Excellency the governor, and women who might as well be ice."

"You are, of course, most put out about the women."

Drake took a sip and gave Harrod the smile that had always won favorites with the ladies of New Bern. "You might have scruples about mingling work and pleasure. I do not."

"I will assume you have been doing at least *some* work, and not spending all your time in pining over your lack of lady friends."

"Of course. The more I accomplish, the sooner I can leave this forsaken place."

Harrod motioned with his glass. "Tell me something I can tell the governor. That, I can't."

"I've begun to establish my allies. The sheriff, for one. Jacob Chauncy, head vestryman, is another. Many of the townsfolk are set against the vestry tax, and he's desperate for help with his vestry's business affairs. He's a man easily pressured, and seems willing enough to support me in return for my aid. Which of course will be the least I can manage."

"Of course," Harrod said. "I would expect nothing less."

His tone might have been sarcastic. It might not have been. Drake chose to assume the latter. He took another sip and went on. "Geoffrey Sheridan is on his way to New Bern for trial. I intend to have him held long enough to—*encourage* him to divulge a little more information. Leaders' names, meeting places, that sort of thing."

Harrod tested his glass and nodded his approval. Whether of the wine or of Drake's plans, it was hard to judge. "And if he won't?"

Drake shrugged. "He'll hang either way. That's already settled. And before he ever knew whose side I was on, he told me of the most influential rebel in this corner of the country. Robert Boothe. Dissenter preacher, refuses to be licensed. He either leads or supports any resistance in this area, and has for several years. Jacob Chauncy came to me this afternoon to complain about Boothe's preaching on street corners."

"The unlicensed ones are the most dangerous," Harrod said. "There's no knowing who they are, what they teach, or who listens to them. Get them licensed and you can control them. There's your next target. Break his spirit. Get him licensed or get him behind bars."

"Getting him licensed won't shut him up," Drake disagreed. "He had the nerve to tell me what I'm doing is wrong."

Harrod gave a short laugh. "Anything a man does for power or money, someone will tell him it's wrong."

"Not me," Drake said darkly. "Some things I'll not stand for."

"Kill him, then," Harrod said. "The governor won't care. What is he but a rebel?"

"I'd be the third most hated man in North Carolina if I tried that," Drake said with a laugh. "Next to Governor Tryon and Edmund Fanning."

"It's an elite group you're aiming for. If people knew all I do and have done for the governor, I'd be on that list as well." Harrod paused. "I didn't mean that, what I said a moment ago. You know that. But I'm in earnest when I say a man like that is dangerous."

"He won't be for long."

Harrod lifted his glass as if making a toast. "See that he isn't."

# Six

IT WAS HARD THE NEXT MORNING FOR ROBERT to put his full attention on the service. He had had a long night of dispatching scouts, some to locate Geoffrey Sheridan and others to find the Thurmonds' commandeered furnishings and learn when the auction would take place. They would meet after church to discuss the reports. Robert was not the only one, he noticed, who had come to church armed. That was normal in Ayen Ford; one could never tell what might happen on the way to or from the Lord's house. But today it seemed darker, grimmer. As if danger was just over the horizon and even God-fearing, peace-loving churchfolk wanted to be prepared.

Caleb and Elsie Thurmond were both absent. Caleb had a fever again, Saul said. Deacon Ashe led in prayer, both for the service and for Caleb's healing. Then the congregation sang the opening hymn and Robert opened his Bible. "Proverbs chapter three verse five: 'Trust in the LORD with all thine heart; and lean not unto thine own understanding.'"

He took a deep breath. He had talked with Magdalen late into the night, knowing if he did not get things off his chest, he would preach angry this morning, and preaching angry was one thing he despised in a pastor. His mind did not belong with Colonel Drake and debts and arrests and Regulator meetings. This was the word of God. These were His people, and Robert's people. This was where his attention belonged.

"Salvation is where trusting starts," he began. "The plan of almighty God makes no sense to our own understanding. Trusting in the Lord means our own way is no longer enough. But trusting in the Lord doesn't stop there. Job had been a righteous man for a long time when he said, 'Though he slay me, yet will I trust in him.' When trials come, do we look to our own strength, or do we trust in Him as Job did?"

He was nearing the end of his sermon when his own question hammered him between the eyes.

Do I trust in Him like that? All the way to the death?

He kept preaching, but the question had caught him aback. Of course he trusted in God. He'd believed that all his life. Son of a preacher, he'd probably learned it in the womb. Would he be risking jail for preaching without a license if he didn't trust God? And yet—to trust in Him like that . . .

Just before noon he closed his Bible and said, "Let's pray." As he bowed his head, movement rustled in the doorway behind him.

There was only one thing that could be.

And Robert wasn't backing down.

"Father," he said, raising his voice above the disruption, "we thank You for Your many blessings. Help us to—"

Then Ethan Hardy yelled, "Look out!" and someone grabbed Robert from behind and dragged him from the pulpit. Charles Drake said, "Boothe, you're under arrest in the name of the Crown."

Sheriff Kendall kicked Cricket out of Robert's reach and jerked Robert's arms behind his back. The sharp clank of iron brought the bitter taste of fear for a brief instant. Then only an odd detachment, the sudden realization that this, what he had risked so long, was happening.

It had happened before. On his preaching circuit, years

ago. Different towns, different officials. Same hatred of the gospel. But never in front of his flock on a Sunday morning.

The first manacle locked around his left wrist, a click echoed in the hush by the cock of a rifle hammer. Robert swiftly scanned the congregation. Saul McBraden was taking aim.

"Saul." Robert spoke in the voice of command he used for tension-laced situations when lives and testimonies were at stake. Like now. "Put the gun down."

The second cuff clattered shut. The look on Saul's face said Robert might as well have slapped him. "But Pastor, they're—"

"Put it down."

Saul obeyed. Reluctantly, but he obeyed.

"I'm God's man on God's property and He'll deal with it," Robert said. "There's a time to fight back. This isn't it."

Saul folded his arms, clenched his teeth, and gave one curt nod. He had heard. He would obey. But he would not be happy about it.

"I'd have come peaceably, Sheriff," Robert said over his shoulder, "had you given me the chance."

"I'm not one to trust a rebel and a dissenter," Kendall said.

"Trusting me has nothing to do with it." Robert had seen this often enough to know that Drake and Kendall were making an example of him, warning his congregation, Stand against us and you'll be next. "You're trying to make a point. To me and every other dissenter in Ayen Ford."

Without warning the riding crop in Drake's hand cut across the side of Robert's face, leaving blood in its wake. "That's our business, preacher. Stay out of it."

Saul exploded, "Drake, you're a coward to hit a man when he can't hit back."

Drake pointed the crop at Saul. "If you know what's good for you, you'll keep your mouth shut."

Susanna whimpered, a soft, frightened sound that made Robert wish he could take back what he'd just told Saul about not fighting back. Hard as it was to force his church to stand by and watch, it was worse to have his daughter see it. He ducked his head to wipe away the blood and said, "Whatever you're charging me with had better be good."

"As long as you've been daring the law, I'd have thought you would know," Drake said. "Preaching without a license and holding an unlawful assembly. Despite repeated warnings. If you can call Sheridan's halfhearted cautions 'warnings.'"

"The One who gave the gospel may give its authority to whom He will, Colonel."

"I've told you once, preacher. I am the only authority here."

"I've told you once, too—not to God."

Those other times this had happened, it had been a matter of a night in jail, orders to move on. He had a hunch it wouldn't be like that, not this time. Drake was out for blood, and would be until Robert yielded and bowed to him. Which, as far as Robert was concerned, was not going to happen. Ever.

"Enough." Drake's voice was a blade. There was no smile today. "Kendall, take him away. The rest of you, disperse or you'll go with him."

John Woodbridge shouted from the back row, "If you want me you can have me."

"Take us all if you can arrest a man for preaching the gospel," Ethan Hardy added belligerently.

"Boys." Robert spoke quietly. His fear was no longer for himself, but for his people. "Don't make it any worse. Go home. The truth will hold its own."

A half-dozen voices said as one, "But Pastor—"

Robert said, "Go."

Susanna whimpered again. Robert looked her way, tried to tell Magdalen with his eyes that he loved them both. Magdalen put her arm around Susanna, her own eyes brimming. Beside them, Gunning sat poised on the edge of the bench, tensed and leaning as if one word from Robert was all it would take to bring him forward. Robert said, "Gunning—"

"I know, Master Rob. I'll take care of 'em."

The sheriff pushed Robert toward the door. Drake said, "By rights we ought to take McBraden, too. Maybe all your rebel followers. But I'll give them what I gave you, preacher. Enough rope to hang themselves. Just as you have."

## 200 Miles West
## The Blue Ridge Mountains

# Seven

MITCHELL BOOTHE LOOKED UP AT THE SKY and said out loud, "Lord, I can't do this anymore."

He was dead tired, had been dead tired for the last eleven years. He'd worn three horses out, and lately he didn't feel far behind. Mitchell had always been long and lanky, but a decade of life in the mountains had stripped him down to raw sinew and bone. Circuit-riding would do that to a man; he'd known that going into it. Most of the time he'd had a partner. Jesus had, after all, sent His apostles out by twos. But Mitchell's last partner had been wounded in a Cherokee attack three months ago and had chosen to go back east to an easier life. Robert was back east now, too. Mitchell didn't blame his older brother for getting married and settling down—that was what God had led Rob to do. But so far, Mitchell still felt called to bring the gospel to the mountain settlements. Called, but tired.

"All I'm asking for," he went on, "is someone to come alongside me and be an extra pair of hands when I need it. Even Moses had Aaron and Hur, holding up his arms during the heat of the battle. These days, Lord, I haven't got anybody. Rob's two hundred miles away. I'm never in one place for more than a month at the outside. It's just You and me—"

His horse whinnied sharply, as if offended at being left out. Mitchell amended, "You and me and Samson. And that's fine. You're enough, just You. But couldn't You send someone to be Your hands and feet to me? I don't care where he comes from. You can drop him out of the sky if'n You want. But I don't know how much longer I can do this."

No one fell out of the twilit heavens in answer to Mitchell's prayer. Not that he had expected such an immediate and dramatic response. The wind moaned in the pines. Samson whinnied again. Mitchell pushed dark hair off his forehead, rubbed tired eyes, and searched the trees for some sign of journey's end. In the gray dusk he caught just a glimpse of the cabin ahead. "Home" was an abstract concept to a circuit-ridin' preacher, but the cabin was about the closest thing Mitchell had. It was there he stopped every so often, lit up the darkened fireplace, and rested for a week or so before again taking to the trails—where there were trails.

He slid stiffly out of the saddle and led Samson to the lean-to stable at one side. Normally Mitchell enjoyed freeing Samson from the heavy saddlebags, rubbing the sturdy stallion down, and provisioning him for the night. But tonight it only made him wearier. He slung the saddlebags over his shoulder and took his rifle in the crook of his arm and the lantern in one hand, leaving the other hand free to open the door. He was on the doorstep when he smelled it. A raw leathery scent mingled with sweat and oily grime. It wasn't coming from him, even if he had been riding hard and working harder for the last week. He paused and swung the lanternlight over the small room. The shadows danced, revealing nothing.

Then he heard heavy breathing in the corner by the empty fireplace. Smelled another smell. *Corn whiskey.*

Mitchell's jaw set. He dropped the saddlebags by the door, lifted the lantern, and strode across the room. The light confirmed his gut feeling. A hulk of a man in buckskins was piled in the corner. Sound asleep. Dead drunk.

There was no telling where he'd come from. He might

as well have been dropped out of the sky.
Mitchell said, "Lord, this is not what I asked You for."

In the morning the man was still there, still sound asleep. Mitchell dressed and shaved and spent some time with God, but still he could not relish the thought of dealing with a drunken stranger. Deciding the job could wait a few more minutes, he went outside for some firewood and some fresh air. Mist rolled away through the trees, reflecting the early sunlight in a soft haze. Mountain mornings had always made Mitchell feel alive, and today was no different, even with an uninvited guest asleep in the cabin. Mitchell gathered an armful of wood, then paused, hearing something move behind him. A soft nicker in his ear made him jump. Have mercy, how did Samson get out?

But it wasn't Samson, it was a sorrel mare with the tired look of having been out all night. Mitchell dropped his wood and coaxed her closer. He had a hunch this unattended horse went with the unattended drunk who was passed out on his cabin floor. And if so, Mitchell did not intend to scare off the man's sole means of transportation.

Once the mare was safely corralled and provisioned, Mitchell picked up his load of firewood and went inside, steeling himself to the task of waking the man and sending him on his way. He stoked the fire first, then bent and gave the man a sound shake. "Wake up, man. It's broad daylight out there."

The man grunted. Shifted. Then groaned and emitted a few choice words that made Mitchell nudge him with the toe of one boot. "Watch your mouth, mister."

Eyes under bushy eyebrows flickered open and focused with an effort. "What's it to you?"

"This is my house, for one, such as it is, and the things you're saying are displeasing to my Lord, for another."

"I didn't mean to cause no offense." The words were a low rumble. The man blinked, seeming to notice his surroundings for the first time. "Your house—why am I—"

"My thoughts exactly," Mitchell said lightly. "I'd like to hear all about it as soon as you haul yourself out of that corner."

The man grimaced as if the thought of moving was too much to take. "Feel like I been clubbed in the head."

"I don't wonder," Mitchell said dryly. "Coffee?"

"I'd be much obliged. Lemme get up here a minute—" He struggled to rise and fell back with another grimace. "Hang it. I forgot about this blamed ankle. Or maybe I didn't know about it. I disremember."

"What's wrong with it?"

"Lamed, I guess. Or broke. All I know's it hurts like—" He caught Mitchell's eyes and finished lamely, "It hurts somethin' fierce."

"Let me take a look."

Mitchell reached for his belt knife and slit open the layers of buckskin in his way. He sheathed the knife and probed for a minute, then said, "Looks like you did it up pretty good, all right. Your boot braced it enough for you to limp or crawl in here, whichever it might have been. Can't tell if it's a fracture or just a bad sprain. Either way, you're not going anywhere for a good while, that's sure." He got to his feet. "Let me see what I've got to fix you up with."

He put more water on to boil, then went to the far corner and rummaged through his meager belongings. He said under his breath, "All right, Lord. If You gave me this to handle, then I allow as You'll help me handle it."

His guest called, "Who you talkin' to over there?"

"God," Mitchell called back.

A long pause. Then, "You *are* right in the head, ain't you?"

"That's anybody's guess," Mitchell said cheerfully. He selected a ragged sheet and began tearing it into strips as he turned around. "Of course, you weren't any too right in the head yourself last night, so I don't reckon you can say much."

They looked at each other for a moment, sizing each other up. A preacher, son of a preacher, lean, clean-shaven, and just turned thirty. A rough-hewn mountain man, bearded and fifteen years farther down the road of a hard mountain life.

The man grunted. "I reckon you reckon right, at that."

"Now grit your teeth and hang on," Mitchell said. "This is going to hurt."

Working as swiftly and carefully as he could, Mitchell washed the badly swollen ankle and bound it firmly. He sat back on his heels. "That's the best I can do. You'll have to stay off it for some time, give it a chance to heal. Where do you stay at?"

"Other side of the ridge. Out Watauga way. Come over here to do some huntin' and got a mite too much of something a mite too strong. I seem to recall falling out of a tree."

"So you crawled in here for shelter."

"I reckon it was somethin' along those lines."

"That your horse I found wandering around outside? Sorrel mare?"

"That'd be Daisy," the man said. He sounded regretful. "Must have got loose from her picket line. I didn't mean she should stay out there all night. She look all right?"

Mitchell softened a little at the man's obvious concern for his horse. "She looked fine to me. I put her up with some provender. I'm just glad she let me."

"She's always been a friendly thing. I 'preciate you lookin' out for her."

"I hate to see a good animal go uncared for," Mitchell said, gathering up his leftover medical supplies. "Well, it looks like you're stuck here a while. I can't get you back over the ridge on my own, and you're not in any shape to ride. You've already given that ankle more than it can handle."

"I hate to be beholden," the man growled.

"All you're doing is saving me the trouble of hauling you over the ridge." Mitchell extended his hand. "My name's Boothe. Mitchell Boothe."

"Hank Jonas." His grip was hard enough to match the mountain-man look of him. "How long you been here?"

"I've had the place about six years. Only live in it every couple months, though. I'm a circuit rider."

Jonas looked slightly askance. "A preacher?"

"Something the matter with that?"

Jonas shook his head, then winced at the movement. "Only wondering why you ain't raked me over the coals yet for bein' drunk."

"What good would that do?" Mitchell helped Jonas to a chair and handed him a hot mug. "You already know you were drunk. You know you've got a busted ankle and a splitting headache on account of it. I don't see as I need to tell you again. Which I more or less just did."

"A man has to have a good time now and again." Jonas sounded halfway between defensive and belligerent.

Mitchell said slowly, "That's your choice, I reckon. If it was me, I'd just as soon find a good time that didn't include falling out of trees."

"You ain't like any preacher I ever laid eyes on."

"Maybe that's a good thing."

"Most of the ones I've met are all hellfire and brimstone."

Mitchell grinned. "I've got a share of that myself, if you get a hankering for it. But I like talking about love and grace a sight better."

Jonas looked skeptical. "I'll wager a fat milch cow God ain't holdin' out much love and grace for the likes of me."

"Then you lose your wager." Mitchell pulled his skillet out of the wood box and dusted it out. "Who knows, maybe you being stuck with me for a month or two is the lovingest thing He's done for you yet."

## Ayen Ford, North Carolina

## Eight

THEY HAD NOT LET MAGDALEN SEE ROBERT AT all Sunday night. But on Monday evening, after a day of trying to calm Susanna's fears as well as her own, Magdalen managed to sway the guard by dint of a winning smile and the timeworn temptation of good food. A wedge of fine cheese, scarcer than good lawmen, and a half-loaf of fresh bread. The guard took her offering with thinly veiled pleasure, his disdain visibly decreased, and told her she could see her husband—just for a minute, of course.

Magdalen was properly grateful and hinted at future gastronomical reward while the guard wielded his massive iron key with an impressiveness just short of conceit. She let him usher her inside, told him to go sit down somewhere and eat, and watched with satisfaction as he nodded to her and went out, leaving her alone with her husband.

Robert barely gave the man time to exit before he pulled Magdalen close, basket and all. "Maggie. You're a sight for sore eyes."

She didn't want him to let go. "So are you."

He stepped back a little. "I'm a sight, at least, I know that much."

A smear of dried blood marked where Drake's riding

crop had struck him. His dark hair begged her fingers to straighten it. There were gray shadows under his eyes. But Magdalen didn't care. He was still the handsomest man in the Carolinas.

She uncovered her basket and began sorting out its contents. "I brought a blanket, and some bread and cheese—less what I gave to the guard." She brought out a jar wrapped in a towel. "Soup, too. You'd better eat that while it's hot. I thought of bringing your Bible, but I know if they found that here—"

Robert nodded. "I've been making do with what's in my head."

Magdalen knew how much that was. Chapters and chapters that he had drilled into his memory on the preaching circuits of the mountains. She glanced around the starkly furnished room. "How are you, Rob, really?"

"All right. Really." He blew on the soup to cool it and took a careful swallow. "You and Susanna—what about you?"

"We're getting by. She's frightened, I think. I've tried to explain, but she's so innocent and trusting, she doesn't understand why anyone would do this."

"Sometimes I don't either." Robert half-smiled. "I still don't know when I'll be released . . ."

He stopped, but Magdalen heard the unfinished thought. *Or if I'll be released.*

"Are the scouts back yet?" he asked.

"They came in this forenoon. I talked with Elsie, and she told me what Saul told her. The scouts rode well into Wake County, but there's no sign of Mr. Sheridan."

"They're moving fast, then. That's not good." Robert finished the soup and looked at the barred window, thoughtful. "Drake's taking no chances, I reckon. He went so far as to admit that if I had a license or was any other brand of preacher, they'd leave me alone. Governor Tryon's willing to tolerate Moravians, Presbyterians—anything but the Baptists. We're nothing like the Anglicans, we'll not let him control what we believe and teach, and we're a threat." Abruptly he broke off, as if realizing Magdalen already knew so much of what he was saying. "Any other news?"

Magdalen took the empty jar and began rearranging her basket. "You have a Regulator conference planned for Wednesday, don't you?"

"Aye. Over yonder in Rocky River. Though nothing's certain anymore."

"I heard bits of things after church yesterday. None of the men want to leave town for the meeting. They're afraid of what Drake might do while they're gone—more of what he's done to the Thurmonds."

"I don't blame them." Robert waited for her to look at him before he went on. "Maggie, I hate to do this to you and Susanna, but I can't back down. I can't give the government authority over what God tells me to do. Before God, I can't."

"I know, Rob. And I wouldn't want you to. Your men want to get you out, of course, but they know that's not what you want."

"Well, I don't aim to be a martyr about it." He lowered his voice. "And I'm committed to the conference; I have to be there. I'll get out somehow, only it won't be by mob attack and it won't be by getting a license."

"Be careful, Rob. There's a guard here all the time now."

His smile was twisted. "Drake again. That muddles things."

"We'll get through this, Rob. We've gotten through everything else." For a moment she remembered the early days of their marriage, a twenty-four-year-old circuit rider sweeping her off her sixteen-year-old southern-belle feet and carrying her off to a new life in the mountains. Then had come the dark, dark days alone, with Robert away on his circuit, the terrifying Cherokee attacks and the early childbirth that had taken their first baby. Robert had moved them to Ayen Ford not long after. Just two years after that first heartbreak, Susanna had smiled her way into their world. After Susanna, Magdalen had lost another child, five months into the pregnancy, and after that, nothing. Magdalen began to accept that perhaps it was better that way, to never carry a new life again rather than repeat the sorrow. And perhaps it was better that there were no more children to witness the growing persecution, to watch for Robert to come home and know that one day he might not.

Robert reached out and clumsily wiped away a tear she had not even noticed. "Maggie, are you sure you're all right?"

Footsteps outside. Now was not the time for tears. She shook her head to clear her eyes and spoke in a hurried whisper. "I'm all right. The guard's coming. Is there aught I can do? To help you, the men—anything?"

Robert pulled Magdalen into a fierce embrace and spoke against her hair, barely loud enough for her to hear. "Keep doing what you're doing. Anything you can. Trust the Lord. Pray. And know that I love you."

When Magdalen got home, Saul McBraden and John Woodbridge were sitting at her kitchen table, talking in low voices with Gunning. They rose at her entrance. Saul said, "We were hoping you'd be back soon."

Gunning said, "I don't know what they want to talk to you about, Miz Maggie, but whatever it is, I tried to talk 'em out of it. As if you need any more worries."

"It's all right, Gunning." She motioned the men to resume their seats. "What can I do for you?"

Woodbridge spoke first. "We're sorry to disturb you, ma'am, what with the pastor in jail and all, but that's why we had to come. We had a meeting just the night before he was taken—"

He paused. Saul said, "It's safe to talk, Mrs. Boothe?"

"No one's here but Susanna and Gunning. Susanna—"

"Playing in the yard," Gunning said. "And I can keep a secret as well as anyone."

"All right, then." Woodbridge forged ahead. "We had a meeting, and he sent out all manner of scouts to get reports on what the sheriff's done with Thurmonds' house plunder. We were supposed to meet again yesterday, only the pastor was taken and that upset things a mite. He wanted to try once more to be peaceable and legal-like and write a petition laying out our grievances. I don't see that it'll do much good, but he wanted to go to that conference on Wednesday knowing he's done everything he can to keep the peace."

"The thing is, Pastor Boothe always wrote that sort of thing for us," Saul said, taking over. "Well, the law won't let us anywhere near him—"

"You should try bread and cheese," Magdalen said.

"What?"

"Never mind. Go on."

Saul obeyed. "We need you to write it in his place."

"Most of us, we don't write so good," Woodbridge explained. "You'll make it worth reading to the Colonial Assembly itself."

"You do so well on Pastor's sermons," Saul added, his eyes a flicker of faint humor in the grimness of the day.

It was a standing joke of the church, her writing Rob's sermons while he only preached them. "The words are all his own, even if I do copy his notes for him sometimes."

"The words will be our own for this, too." Woodbridge was in deep earnest. "We'll tell you what to write. You'll just polish it up and make it sound good on paper."

"And there's no one else who could do this." Magdalen was grateful that her rearing on a wealthy tobacco plantation had allowed for a good education. But there were times when she wished it was not common knowledge.

Saul said, "We ain't gonna sound it all around town to find out."

Gunning said, "I told you I tried to talk 'em out of it."

Magdalen waved at him to stop, much as she wished he had succeeded. Rob's men had far more faith in her ability than she did. But Rob had told her to do what she could. This, she could do. Or at least Saul and John thought

she could.
"Tell me what to say," she said.
"Get paper and an ink pen," Woodbridge said. "And set down."
Their list of grievances was long. Magdalen did nothing at first but take notes. Twice-paid debts, embezzling officials, onerous taxes, court fees set too high and charged too wantonly. And the unjust seizure of property, auctioned to friends of the court for a fraction of its value. Magdalen reminded them of that point, thinking of Elsie.
"And that's the other thing," Saul said. "Elsie. We were meaning to talk to you about that when this was done."
"It won't take long, with the notes. What about Elsie?"
"They've been at my place these last two nights, you know," Saul said. "Which is fine by me. But Caleb's fever broke today and he's got a real hankering for his own home fires. I don't blame him—if I was stove up bad, I'd want my own place too. Then there's Elsie's good name, with us on the same property and not married. I'm in the barn nights, but some folks might not bother about that. And there are fixings from her ma that Elsie wanted for her own place someday, and just things they *need*. Kendall took the last of the grain, too, and it's liable to be slim pickings till harvest."
"Pastor sent us out, night before last, to find out where Thurmonds' goods are being held and when the auction is," Woodbridge explained. "He had something in mind, we think—but he wanted to know more first. We thought maybe you'd have some idea of what he was studying on."
Magdalen thought back to Saturday night and Robert's report of the meeting, parsed into terse sentences edged with determination. "He didn't say, really. Only that he wouldn't take Drake lying down, and that Kendall had got to be shown that he's not above the law just because he *is* the law."
"If he *weren't* the law," Saul said darkly, "I'd find me a good dark night and lay some sense into him."
*A good dark night.* The thought that came to mind was

so bold Magdalen was almost afraid to acknowledge it. But it was the sort of thing she had heard Rob speak of, and somehow she knew it was what he had intended all along.

She said slowly, "When you scouted on Saturday night—what did you find?"

"The goods are in one of the outbuildings behind Kendall's place," Saul said. "And the auction—"

"Tomorrow afternoon," Woodbridge said.

"Then there's one thing I think Rob would have done. But it's an awful risk."

Saul shoved his rust-blond forelock out of his eyes. "*Life* is an awful risk these days, Mrs. Boothe. Don't let that stop you."

"Well, then, can you gather the boys by, say, midnight? Only our church men, not the others." Radical Presbyterians, disowned Quakers, men from all walks of life had been drawn to Robert's leadership. She had no doubt that they were ordinarily a very helpful lot, but tonight so many people would only increase the risk.

Woodbridge looked at Saul, shrugged. "Easy, Mrs. Boothe. Have 'em out long before midnight."

"But not too early, either. When you send the word out, tell them that when you meet you'll take a special offering."

Understanding was dawning in Saul's eyes. "Like when Mrs. O'Neil had to buy her own cow back and we took up enough money for it and then some."

"Exactly."

Saul's quick flash of smile made him look like the nineteen he was, instead of a man old before his time. "I hope to glory you're saying what I think you're saying, ma'am."

"The only thing I'm saying is that once Thurmonds' debt is paid, there is no longer any legal or moral reason to auction their goods. Which means there is no longer any legal or moral reason not to—uh—*repossess* those goods."

"I like it," Woodbridge said. "It's what Pastor would have thought of, I reckon. He'd be right proud of you."

"And I'll finish the petition in the meantime. It won't

take but half an hour."

"Put Pastor's name on it," Saul said. "The law says you're one, doesn't it?"

"So it does." Magdalen smiled. "Now you'd best go. You can come for the petition before you go to Kendall's, and give it to Drake yet tonight, or in the morning if you'd rather. As long as you don't get caught."

Saul put his hat back on at a slightly rakish angle, his eyes alive with the challenge. "They can't catch us all, Mrs. Boothe."

# Nine

THERE WERE FEW THINGS SAUL MCBRADEN liked better than a challenge. Especially when Elsie Thurmond was involved. Mrs. Boothe's plan was exactly what he wished he'd thought of first, or had had the nerve to think of. It was chancy, for sure. But that only made it better.

Saul counted himself privileged to be one of the few Regulators who had been trusted with every detail of Pastor Boothe's messenger system. By ten minutes to twelve, a dozen men were clustered in the Thurmonds' empty kitchen. John Woodbridge had brought the new petition with the signatures he had already garnered, and its completion was the first order of business. After that, the next item on the docket was the collection of the needed funds, which took less than five minutes and tallied up at five pounds, two shillings. More than enough. Saul picked out four pounds' worth in currency and tucked the bills carefully into his coat pocket. The rest he laid on the shelf over the fireplace, where Elsie would be sure to find it when she and her family returned. Which was, of course, contingent on a successful night.

Orders and roles were discussed and settled quickly. Then the fun began. For Saul there was a tang of excitement in the smell of the soot Ethan Hardy passed around. Saul smeared the thick blackness into every crease of his face, checking with John Woodbridge to be sure only his eyes were showing. The men gathered in close for a word of prayer, then jammed their hats down low and went out.

The night was dark, lit only by a pale sliver of moon. Perfect. The wind was fresh, just strong enough that a little movement in the shadows of the sheriff's outbuildings would cause no alarm. The Thurmonds' house was just across a backstreet, less than two hundred yards away. They wouldn't need a wagon, not even for the larger items. It was almost too easy.

Two men moved to the other side of the building to stand guard. Saul tested the door. Bolted shut, with nothing to get a grip on. Saul moved to the shuttered window. Here the catch gave with one good pull, revealing an empty window frame that pleased Saul immensely. No farmer would use glass in a shed window, but then you could never tell with a man of Ebeniah Kendall's means. Saul swung the shutters back, threw a leg over the sill, and landed lightly inside. Woodbridge passed him a shaded lantern and Saul uncovered it enough for the light he needed.

The Thurmonds' possessions weren't many. A few chairs, a table, a bedstead. A chest of drawers. An iron-bound box, a pair of worn books. And a neat stack of plump sacks. Saul's anger flared at the sight of the grain that Elsie so badly needed to feed her family.

"Everything there?" Hardy asked softly from the window.

"Far as I can tell." Saul heaved a shoulder against the door, did it again, until the bolt snapped free on the other side. He swung the door open and the men filed in without waiting for orders. In disciplined silence they hauled the items out one at a time, working like shadows to carry each piece across the backstreet into the Thurmond house. Saul put his hand on the willow rocking chair. "I'll take this with me. Caleb's been pining for it ever since it was taken, and—"

Hoofbeats broke the night. Woodbridge hissed, "Down!" The men flattened themselves in the darkness. Saul extinguished the lantern, eased the door shut, held his breath. Horse and rider passed. Hardy said, low and through his teeth, "Colonel Drake. Coming to visit the sheriff, no doubt, while no one's out there to catch him at it."

"Then we'd best be finished." Saul scanned the room, even though he couldn't see a thing without the lantern. "As I was saying, I'll take the chair. And the money—I'll do that, too. I've already got it."

"It's dangerous alone," Woodbridge objected.

"I don't have a family. Yet. Give me the note."

Woodbridge handed him the scrap of paper. Saul gave him the lantern in exchange. Woodbridge said, "Be careful."

Saul had every intention, and no intention, of being careful. "Right."

His thanks went unspoken, but understood. The Regulators filtered into the night. Saul stood waiting, fingering the note and bills in one pocket and the nail in the other, giving the men time to get out of the immediate vicinity. He knew what he was fixing to do was reckless. And it thrilled him to the bone.

The chair was light enough for Saul to heft easily with one hand. He carried it as far as Sheriff Kendall's front door, a massive oaken affair that spoke of wealth beyond what one would expect from a county sheriff. Saul set the chair down and picked up a rock. He laid the paper currency carefully against the door and set the note on top.

*Caleb Thurmond's debt. Paid in full and then some.*

Saul took the rock in his other hand. Positioned the nail. Raised the rock to strike.

And almost hit Colonel Drake between the eyes.

Drake bellowed, the first time Saul had heard real rage from him. But Saul was not there. He had swept the fallen money up and ducked into the shadows. As he had expected, Drake came after him.

Saul cut away and tripped on the rock he had flung

aside. Drake's hands were like steel. Too strong for a man who looked like a Hillsborough gallant. Saul twisted as far as he could, coiled his legs, and unleashed a kick that doubled Drake over. Saul helped him fall with one more blow, then scrambled to his feet and took one sideways stride that put the willow rocker in his reach just as Kendall rounded the corner. Saul grabbed the chair, swung it with all his might. Kendall took the blow to the chin and chest and faltered. Saul dropped the chair and hit him again, with a pair of left-right jabs this time, and the sheriff went down hard on top of Drake. Saul picked up the bills, ripped Kendall's coat open, and stuffed the money and note into the inner pocket. Then he flipped the chair over his shoulder and ran.

#  Ten

"Everything is back in the house, Mrs. Boothe. Everything." Elsie's hazel eyes glowed. "I know Saul did it, but he won't say how. Only that we needn't fret about the debt anymore. He brought Ma's chair back himself because he knew Pa wanted it. And you should see the towel Saul left for me to wash last night; it's filthy with soot. I want to know what happened, and at the same time I don't. You understand."

"Oh, yes. I understand," Magdalen said with a smile. "I feel that way every time Rob comes back from a meeting."

"Have you heard anything? About his being released?"

Magdalen shook her head. "Nothing. John Woodbridge took a new petition to Charles Drake early this morning. Maybe that will have some effect."

Elsie looked down at the mending she had brought. "Sometimes, Mrs. Boothe, all I want is a little house up in the mountains—far away from all of this. Life would be hard, mayhap, and there would still be trouble, but we'd be free. Freer than here, I think."

Magdalen reached for Elsie's hand. "You're not the only one, Elsie. Rob feels that way more than he'd ever put into words. All you see is the faithful shepherd standing

firm for his flock. But sometimes—"
    She paused. Elsie said, "Sometimes?"
    "There's something in him that longs to feel the wind and live in a place where the wilderness is his best friend and his worst enemy, both at the same time. A hunger for all he left behind with his preaching circuit in the mountains."
    "Why doesn't he go back?"
    "Robert Boothe," Magdalen said, "would never be happy in a place of his own choosing when God's people needed him somewhere else."

As the day wore on and Magdalen heard no news of the petition, she grew increasingly uneasy. She had not expected a full report. But surely John Woodbridge would have come and told her if her work had been well-received.
    She did her best to put her mind on other things, helping the Thurmonds move back into their own home. Caleb's fever had not risen again, which was an answer to prayer, and despite the fatigue that shadowed his features, he looked almost happy. Happy to be in his own home, and happy to know that others cared enough to lend a hand. Magdalen watched him and thought, He's a strong man; maybe he'll pick up faster than anyone thought—but that leg . . .
    Gunning and Saul both pitched in to help, and Magdalen could tell by the secret exultation in Saul's eyes that he had enjoyed the challenge of "repossessing" the Thurmonds' goods. She had known he would. But he didn't mention the petition, either. That only reinforced Magdalen's misgivings.
    When she and Susanna and Gunning got home, a man had just turned from the front door. Magdalen said, "May I help you, Mr. Chauncy?"
    Jacob Chauncy swiftly doffed his hat. "I thought it might be the other way, Mrs. Boothe."
    Robert would have invited him in, she knew. So she did the same. It was hard, knowing the vestry had used Chauncy against her husband. But "if thine enemy hunger, feed him," the Bible said. She had no idea whether or not Jacob

Chauncy was hungry, but she offered him tea, regardless.

Chauncy declined, seeming ill at ease. "Mrs. Boothe, I want to apologize for what happened to your husband. I must confess that I complained to Colonel Drake about his preaching on the street, but I never thought it would result in his arrest."

"I know Robert has often told your vestry to keep folks under its control any way it chose," Magdalen said slowly, "and the truth would hold its own."

"And you think this is our way of controlling the people?" Chauncy had the decency to wince. "I don't know what I expected Colonel Drake to do. But I had no intention of it coming to this."

"Robert will be glad to hear that, Mr. Chauncy."

"If there's aught I can do to be of help—"

"All that comes to mind is that you please refrain from making any further complaints to Mr. Drake."

"I can certainly promise you that."

His expression was so relieved Magdalen thought, What, did you think I was going to ask you to preach in Rob's place? But all she said was, "Thank you."

Chauncy took his hat from the table. "It's only right, Mrs. Boothe."

Her reply was cut off by a rap at the door. Her first thought was, Maybe it's John or Saul, coming to report on the petition. Or maybe Rob has been released . . . "Excuse me a moment, Mr. Chauncy."

The man outside was not a Regulator. Not Robert, either. Charles Drake removed his cocked hat and bowed. "Madam."

She curtsied in kind. "Colonel."

He motioned with his hat. "May I?"

"Any business we have may be conducted here as well as inside, Colonel." Chauncy, she would allow in her house. Drake, she would not. Not with Robert gone.

"Very well, then. I'm sure you're wondering why I'm here."

"And likewise, I'm sure you're eager to tell me."

"It has to do with a certain petition which I received this morning."

"And what has that to do with me?" The back door closed softly and she risked a glance over her shoulder. Chauncy was not there. Either he did not wish Drake to catch him in Robert Boothe's home, or he was simply as loath to see Drake as Magdalen was.

Drake leaned one hand on the doorframe above her head and looked down at her. He was closer than she wanted him to be. Much closer. And utterly indifferent to the fact that anyone on the street could see him. Or that Susanna was behind Magdalen, watching with wide eyes. Or that all Magdalen had to do was call, and Gunning would kick him across the street. "The handwriting, Mrs. Boothe." Drake's voice was a low hint of a laugh. "Distinctly feminine."

Rob had always teased her about her flowery script. His own was much more no-nonsense. "But why should it be mine, Colonel? I am not the only woman in town. As you no doubt have seen."

"So I have." His tone gave the words an innuendo she had not intended. He had the dark-eyed look of a cat playing with a mouse. Knowing his own power, and reveling in it. "I also saw that your husband's name was first on the petition. Despite the fact that said husband is in custody and has not been allowed anywhere near said petition. Nor has said petition been allowed anywhere near him. Unless, of course, your visit to him last evening had ulterior motives."

So he knew she had been to see Rob. Hardly a surprise, considering his alliance with the sheriff. "My only motive was to see the man I love. The one you have wrongly imprisoned."

"Does the man you love know his wife just had a friendly tête-à-tête with the man who reported him?"

The head vestryman had apparently not found the back door fast enough. "Mr. Chauncy came to apologize. Perhaps you could learn from him."

Drake smiled as if he appreciated her nerve. "Perhaps I could, Mrs. Boothe. But I find apologizing to be a waste of time. Therefore, we will confine ourselves to the business at hand. I have observed you actively helping the Thurmonds. You wouldn't happen to know, would you, whom I nearly caught on Sheriff Kendall's property last night after Thurmonds' goods were stolen?"

"No, I wouldn't." Though she would dare to guess it was Saul. "And I doubt 'stolen' is the proper term, unless you are describing your own actions." She probably ought to be more careful with her tongue. But she hadn't gotten to be Robert Boothe's wife by being timid.

Drake looked mildly irritated now. "You really should watch what you say, madam. And how you say it, and to whom."

"Make your point, Colonel Drake."

He removed his hand from the doorframe, stepped slightly away. "I have no point to make, Mrs. Boothe. None whatsoever. I only wanted you to have the pleasure of knowing that *I* know you are every bit the rebel your husband is. And the two shall become one, isn't that it?" He bowed again. Replaced his hat. "Good day, madam."

She waited until he was as far as the corner. Out of earshot. Almost out of sight. Then she slammed the door as hard as she had wanted to while he was standing in its way.

Charles Drake shut his study door and wheeled to face his guest. "I don't think it's unfitting to request an explanation, Chauncy."

"I could say the same to you." Jacob Chauncy sounded faintly hostile. "I never intended for you to arrest Boothe. Just—discourage him a little."

Drake seated himself and motioned Chauncy to do likewise. Chauncy shook his head and Drake shrugged. Let the man think he had a say. He'd find out differently soon enough. "I told you, Jacob. I am able to give your parish all the help it needs. But I have to do it my way. I admit I may have acted too harshly—" might as well start lying now as later "—but I believe this town is in a much better state without Boothe's influence."

"I refuse to be party to—"

Drake hid a sigh. Chauncy obviously suffered from a fairly healthy conscience. "Trust me, Chauncy. You do your part, I do mine, and your parish is healthy and well."

After a long silence, Chauncy relaxed somewhat. "I don't mean to be ungrateful, Colonel. These are somewhat stronger measures than I'm accustomed to."

"Sometimes stronger measures are what it takes." The crux of Drake's philosophy.

Chauncy fidgeted with the carving of the chair he stood beside. "I admit the tax affairs need attention."

"Vestry taxes included, no doubt."

Chauncy nodded slowly. "The vestry's income has been greatly reduced with all the dissenters in the area. That is my main concern. There are other things—" He paused.

"Other things?" This might be interesting after all.

"No one else on the vestry knows this."

"Go on. I'll not mention it."

"Since we currently have no minister for whom to use the tax income, I invested some of that money in my own business. Now that business is struggling as well, and if vestry taxes fail to be collected in a timely fashion—" Chauncy gave a half shrug. "Not good. For me or for the parish."

Beautiful. A head vestryman with an uncomfortable secret and a lot of unused tax money. Drake leaned forward. "Have no fear, Jacob. You'll get all the income you need. That is precisely why I am here." Well, not precisely. But with a slight stretch, it could be considered a reason.

Chauncy looked away, seeming to consider. At last he looked back at Drake. "I'm troubling myself needlessly. Thank you for your patience, Colonel."

"No," Drake said. "Thank *you*."

For what, he did not say.

# Eleven

AYEN FORD'S JAIL WAS BETTER THAN SOME. The terrible state of the roof, a crude affair of boards supplemented with thatch, let the late March rain pool on the floor, but at least it was clean water. And Robert was thankful to not be locked up with a pair of drunks and the meanest-looking murder suspect in the Carolinas, the way he had been back in '59 in a jail near the Yadkin River. That had certainly been a mission field. And he'd never been bored. But Robert preferred incarceration in solitude, if he had to be incarcerated at all.

Still, solitude could have its disadvantages. Robert had awakened in the wee hours of the morning, and sleep refused to come back to him. He lay on his pallet and listened to the pouring rain. Longing for the mountains, where he could ride up to the top of the ridge and stare at the miles of sky and trees and wrestle with God until he had an answer. He knew a jail in the middle of the Carolina Piedmont was just as good a place for wrestling with God. But so far, no answers.

Magdalen had said the scouts had not located Geoffrey Sheridan. All Robert knew was that Sheridan was out there somewhere, far to the east. The best justice the county had ever had. Clearly Drake wanted him gone, and fast. But they couldn't possibly have gotten Sheridan all the way to the capital and tried for treason in only four days.

Unless they hadn't bothered to try him at all.

Which they probably wouldn't for Robert, either.

"I trust You," he said aloud, though he knew God heard his heart. "Job said he trusted in You even if You killed him. I don't know if I trust You like that yet. But I do trust You."

He was drawn from his introspection by a whispered sound at the window. At first he thought he had imagined it. He opened his eyes and listened.

"Pastor."

Robert threw aside the blanket Magdalen had brought him and went to the window. A dim shadow outside was all that showed against the night. "Who's there?"

The man spoke as if his back was to the bars, his gaze scanning the public square for danger signs. "It's me. John Woodbridge."

Rain threatened to drown all sound. Robert moved closer to the bars. "What's the matter?"

"We gave Drake that petition," Woodbridge said. "The one we talked about. He was so polite and bored-like about it, we knew it didn't get to him a whit. Then we find out he's been over at your house badgering your wife for writing it for us—"

Robert had a sudden urge to throttle Drake, and it had nothing to do with his ignoring the petition. But Woodbridge hurried on. "It's plain what we wrote didn't have the least effect on him. Me and the boys have been going on about it all night. Caleb's doing better, and Saul's getting riled. We've decided we need to be at that conference now more'n ever."

None too soon, Robert thought. They'd have to leave at dawn and ride all day to reach the Rocky River meetinghouse by nightfall.

The problem being, Robert was in jail.

"You gonna make it?" Woodbridge asked out of the

side of his mouth.

"Where's the guard?"

"Taking cover from the rain, I'm thinking. I haven't seen him. You want I should get the boys and—"

"No. Not that. It would only make things worse. What time is it now?"

"Just past five o'clock."

"Go to my house and tell Maggie and Gunning to have Wanderer saddled and bridled by five-thirty. Gather the men, the ones who are going, in Ethan Hardy's barn. If I've not come by six, light out without me."

Woodbridge gave the minutest of nods and slipped away.

Robert turned from the window and surveyed the room around him. The building had been an empty farm shed for years, until Ayen Ford had needed a jail. The four fieldstone walls had been given a new door, bars in the window, and a hasty layer of thatch to mend the rotting roof that was now turning the floor into a swamp. Robert shoved the water bucket over a few feet to catch the worst leak and continued to study his options. The door was hinged and bolted on the outside. The window bars were too close together for anything but a small rodent to crawl through, as Robert had witnessed the night before. The walls, old as they might be, were still solid enough to serve their purpose. Robert leaned against the nearest one and bowed his head. *Lord, show me a way out.*

Water splashed on the back of his neck, interrupting his prayer. He tipped his head back and frowned at the dripping ceiling.

The roof. Of course.

He eyed the level of the ceiling and decided he would just have to risk the guard's reappearance. Even should the man suddenly return to his post, Robert doubted he would be looking *up* to watch for an escape.

*Lord, I hope this idea is from You. If it is, I appreciate it. If it's not, just bless that meeting whether I'm there or not.*

In the distance the Anglican church bell sounded the half hour. Robert set the rickety chair directly under the weakest point of the roof and tested the seat carefully before trusting his weight to it. He had to duck to keep from hitting the ceiling. His fingers searched through soaked and decaying wood, found the edge of a plank, tugged at it gingerly. It came off in his hand and he tossed it onto the pile of blankets below him, then clawed a little more. Thatch dropped softly outside, its sound lost in the rain. Robert pulled off one more board and found the edge of the stone wall, got the best grip he could and hauled himself up. The crumbling mortar left him the foothold he needed to balance on the wall for a moment. One quick look to make sure the way was clear, and he dropped lightly on top of the fallen thatch.

Five minutes to get home, five to greet Magdalen and change into fresh clothing, five more to ride to Ethan Hardy's barn. The men were there, ready and waiting and eager to go before morning light caught them. Robert was just as eager to go before anyone discovered that their safely jailed dissenter preacher was no longer safely jailed. He would offer his thanksgiving en route. God was outside time, but the Regulators' supply was limited.

## Twelve

AFTER A LONG DAY'S RIDING, ROBERT KNEW HE should have been much more tired than he was. But somehow the journey had left him exhilarated. Maybe it was the sense of freedom. Or maybe it was the importance of this conference. Or maybe it was just what he had always loved about riding with the wind in his face. Whatever it was, he felt ready to take on the world. Even Governor Tryon.

"Just so we know where we stand," Robert said as he pulled the meetinghouse door shut behind his men, "we're breaking the Johnston Riot Act if any sedition starts happening."

Saul grinned. "*If?*"

"Granted, it's pretty certain," Robert agreed. "So we might as well just say we're breaking it right from the start."

James Hunter of Sandy Creek said, "It's no way to live, being told what you can say and where you can say it."

Murmurs of assent echoed through the gathering. Robert leaned over the map spread out on the table at the front of the meetinghouse, lamplight flickering over the hand-inked lines. He spoke loudly enough to be heard by all fifty or sixty men, yet with a hush befitting the darkened church and the night outside. "As we likely all know,

Governor Tryon received consent to march with his militia in this direction on March eighteenth. Just over a week ago. He took to mustering militia and gathering funds straightway. He'll have a hard time of it the farther west he looks for troops, because a lot of county militiamen out this way tend to side with us. But he'll bribe or conscript where he has to, I've no doubt of that. Our scouts suggest he'll reach Hillsborough sometime in early May. Which gives us five weeks to organize our resistance."

Saul said, "Mayhap I shouldn't say anything—"

"We're all equals here," someone said from the other side of the table.

"Then why can't we take the offensive, go to meet him and his hired militia as soon as they march and chase 'em back to the capital?"

"Fighting should be a last resort," Robert said slowly.

"When does it become a last resort?"

"When we've done everything else we can do."

"What's left?" John Woodbridge sounded bitter. "We've petitioned him time and again. It only gets worse."

"Protest has been so fragmented." This from Francis Dorsett, the Baptist preacher whose church met in the meetinghouse. He and Robert were as close as two men could be when separated by miles of rough terrain. "The closest we've come to a unified front was two and a half years ago when three, four thousand of us camped near Hillsborough. You remember, Rob. You were there."

Robert nodded grimly. "I remember."

"What you're saying," Ethan Hardy said, "is that we need to get ourselves together and stand up to the governor and *make* him back down."

"Not just a scattered camp," Saul said, catching the idea. "A force to be reckoned with."

The tight circle of leaders exchanged glances. James Hunter said, "When, where, and how many?"

"As soon as Tryon reaches Hillsborough and doesn't stop," Robert said. "Then we'll know he's not coming just to establish his presence. We'll pick our own terrain, this side of the Haw River. With as many men as we can get."

Argument and planning went on long into the night. Robert answered questions, asked a few of his own, and waited for the men to talk themselves out. At last, when they had settled all they could settle, Robert led in prayer and they prepared to part ways. Some of the men had heard of Drake's arrival in Ayen Ford. Now they suggested that Robert take a dozen extra supporters back with him.

"We knew you were the right choice when we chose you to help lead this," Hunter said. "You've been proving us right ever since. We want to give you the help your folks need."

Robert was about to object when an idea took shape in his mind. Something he could not do, but these men could do for him. If they chose. And if they dared.

"If you're looking for someone to help," he said, "there's a court justice by the name of Geoffrey Sheridan. Drake arrested him for treason and sent him to New Bern for trial. That was only four or five days ago. It's likely they're still on the way. I sent scouts looking for him, but it's just too far. If anyone's looking for a challenge—"

A Wake County man said, "You thinking rescue? Or what?"

"I'm thinking anything that gets him out of Tryon's clutches," Robert said. "If it happens to be halfway law-abiding, so much the better."

"Lot of folks with him?"

"I'd say no more than half a dozen of the governor's men. But I can't put a number on it for certain. I figure they're somewhere around Johnson County by this time."

The volunteer shrugged. "We can make that, easy. Me and my boys, we can do it if anybody can. Where do you want him after we get him?"

"I got me a brother in Cheraw, just over the South Carolina line," another man put in. "Ain't no way Tryon finds him there."

"Someplace out of reach," Robert said. "Cheraw sounds fine to me. But you're going to have to get right on it. I expect you can figure that for yourselves."

"Soon as we're done here, we'll light a shuck and head for Johnson." The Wake County man glanced around. "Pert-near finished, ain't we?"

James Hunter said, "We're still set on sending some help back to Ayen Ford with you, Boothe."

Robert shook his head. "That's right kind of you, but you boys need your men as much as I need mine."

"It's not all kindness, if I'm getting Hunter's drift," Frank Dorsett said. "A few extra men might go a long way toward vexing this man Drake you've got bothering you."

"See if we can shake the governor by rattling his man?" Robert gave a slow nod. With Geoff in good hands, no reason he shouldn't put a little attention on the home front. "All right, I'll go with that. Any volunteers?"

He got his dozen easily. Staunch men, hard fighters. The type who would have put in to rescue Sheridan, if they'd only lived in the right part of the country and if others hadn't beaten them to it. Robert said, "I ought to warn you, I broke jail to get here. When we get back, there's no knowing how long you'll have me for leadership."

"Any time at all oughta be enough to get us going." This from the leader of the pack, a steel-edged man who looked vaguely familiar.

"And I don't hold with destroying public property or assaulting random officers of the law and court."

"Neither do most of these boys," Dorsett said. "Leastways I hope not."

"They'd best not if they're working with me." This was a point on which Robert wouldn't take argument. "That's what's giving the Regulators a bad name, the firebrands who take matters into their own hands. The governor is starting to make us all out to be banditti. I'll not judge other men for what they do in other circumstances, but my men won't be the ones to prove Tryon right."

"Not such a bad thing, worrying the governor," Robert's new subordinate said.

"Depends on what you mean by that," Robert said, on his guard.

The man shrugged. "Putting him on edge enough for him to listen is what I was thinking of. Granted, putting him on edge is one thing. Mob rule is another."

"Mob rule is the last thing we want on our hands." Robert gave Dorsett a nod. "If you'll vouch for 'em, Frank, that's good enough for me."

"You're a good man, Boothe." James Hunter offered his hand, a lean hard grip. "Until it's time, then. Whenever that may be."

Robert and his men took advantage of the remaining night hours and left for Ayen Ford while they still had darkness to shield their departure from Rocky River. Robert didn't say it, but he was worried about Maggie. He knew Drake wouldn't hesitate to interrogate her if he thought it would help him find Robert.

The leader of Robert's new reinforcements rode beside Robert within easy speaking distance. Robert knew he had seen the man before. Once they were safely out of town and gray light had begun to streak the east, Robert said, "You're the one who told me four years ago to submit to the majority and be a leader in this."

Alexander Perry was a rawboned man with eyes of flint and a profile rugged as the blade of a tomahawk. The dark copper in his hair suggested a trace of rebellious Irish blood. "I'm surprised you remember."

"I'm not liable to forget something that got me into the state of affairs I'm in now," Robert said dryly.

"Glad you submitted to the majority of the body?"

"I'm not answering that question."

Perry's laugh was as dry as Robert's tone. "You just did."

"I still don't understand why they wanted me. So many

others had been there from the beginning. At the time I'd only spent five years in Regulator country."

"You know what they said. You'd done more in your five years than some did in fifteen."

"I still don't think I was the best choice."

"No good man ever does."

"'Whosoever will be chief among you, let him be your servant,'" Robert said slowly.

"There are a mighty lot who think the spittin'-image opposite," Perry said. "Take Governor Tryon, for instance."

"And look what it's gotten him. A passel of angry citizens." Robert paused. "Speaking of which, any plans for what to do when we get where we're going?"

"You're asking me?"

"I don't know what you're good at."

"What do you need me to be good at?"

"That's not what I asked, Perry."

"Call me Alec."

"Alec, then."

"My point is, I can be good at whatever you need done. Not to brag."

"Then I want your opinion."

Alec fit his words to the rhythm of his mount's easy trot. "First off, these are good men you've got coming back with you. I've worked with most of 'em at one time or another. They're angry men right now, but they don't let the anger take over. Get what I'm saying?"

"I can trust them to stay steady."

"Right. And they can take orders. You tell 'em to let property alone, they'll let it alone. But if ever they need to, they'll make their own decisions, blaze their own trails."

"That's good. No telling how long I'll be around to give orders. If I'm not, can you keep 'em together?"

"And your men with 'em, if it came to that."

Robert nodded. "Good. If we're going to make this work, being a unified force, we can't be Hunter's men from Sandy Creek and Few's men from Hillsborough and my men from Ayen Ford. We have to stand on the same ground, all of us."

Alec might have smiled. It was hard to tell in the faint light on the horizon. "You've got your work cut out for you, Captain."

"Captain?"

"Your men call you Pastor, but that won't work for me and mine. Captain's the best I can do."

"Boothe or Robert or even Rob would suit me fine."

Alec jerked his head in a negative. "Captain suits you better."

"Your choice. I've been called worse."

Alec's teeth flashed in a quick grin, there and gone. "Haven't we all."

"Back to plans," Robert said.

"Being as you're asking," Alec said, "I'd like license to do nothing at all the first while but sneak around and look things over. Just turkey-tail out all over town and be watching. And let Drake *know* we're watching. Nothing like being watched to make a man a mite uneasy."

Robert glanced over. "You sound as if you speak from experience."

Something undefined glinted in Alec's eyes. "Let's just say you get experience in a lot of things these days."

Robert knew that was all he was going to get. He said, "As far as I'm concerned, Alec, you can do all the watching you want to."

When the sun was straight overhead, they stopped by a stream to rest and water the horses. Wanderer, Robert's gray gelding, tossed his head as if sharing his owner's high spirits. It was only twelve men, Robert told himself. Not as if he had a full brigade to back him up. But somehow just meeting with other Regulators made him feel as if he was not the only one in the world bearing this particular burden. It was the same feeling he had after a rare meeting with another Baptist pastor. Heartened and emboldened anew.

He turned away from the stream and said, "Here's the plan, boys. We get back to Ayen Ford, we don't go in quietly. We ride in on the main road in broad daylight, and we let Drake see every move we make. It may be risky, but he can't arrest all of us at once, and it's time we showed him what he's up against."

Saul McBraden said, "Now you're talking my language."

Robert smiled. Saul's bravado was sometimes dangerous, but at the right time it became an asset. This was about to be one of those times. "Then all we'll do is keep Drake on edge. Watch him every minute we can, and let him know it. You boys can do that on your own even if they shore up the jail, lock me up again, and throw away the key."

"Out of curiosity," Alec Perry drawled, "what did they lock you up for this time?"

"Preaching without a license. Officially, that is."

"Officially is never the real reason," Alec said.

"Unofficially, they were making a point. I say that because there was no other cause for Drake to make the arrest in front of my church on a Sunday morning."

"I'm not saying I'm much for one set of doctrine over another," Alec said, "but that sticks in my craw. Didn't his mama teach him any reverence a'tall?"

"A man like Drake don't have a mama," Ethan Hardy said. "He just sorta crawls out of a dark hole somewhere and there he is."

"I'm going to enjoy making this gent nervous," Alec said.

One glance at Alec's slitted eyes and Robert believed him.

# Thirteen

Magdalen was not so much puzzled as uneasy over Drake's failure to come with a search party and look for Robert. Charles Drake was not one to sit idly by and let his adversary do as he pleased. Bored with this town as he might be, Drake did have a governor to impress. His present lack of action might be a temporary reprieve, but it was hardly a good sign.

Magdalen began to put things together after several church women came to see her, one after another. First Elsie, then Nell Woodbridge, then Ethan Hardy's wife and Deacon Ashe's maiden sister. All reported that Drake had come to call and had asked if their men were able to have a word with him. He had politely thanked them and left upon being told that the men he wished to see were not at home.

Politely thanking his targets and leaving was not the colonel's normal way. Magdalen suspected he had been doing some quiet reconnaissance of his own. Charles Drake was not stupid. A Regulator leader missing from jail, several of his best men suddenly out of town—it would be obvious to anyone with a tolerable amount of intelligence that something was afoot. Which explained why Drake had not made any search or interrogation concerning Robert himself. Why bother to send a search party to Robert's house when he was clearly away leading some new Regulator venture?

And that meant, of course, that Drake was simply waiting for Robert to come home.

But then, so was Magdalen. With all her heart.

Susanna said, "Mama, I dreamed Papa came home, night before last. I didn't tell you then 'cause I thought maybe it would make you sad. I dreamed he came in the front door where I couldn't see him from my bed, and you asked how he got away and he said it was better you didn't know, and then you said, 'You're soaked to the skin!' just like that."

Magdalen laughed at Susanna's rendition of her dismayed tone. "You didn't dream that, sugar. He did get away and he did come home. And he *was* soaked to the skin. It was raining and he had to leave again right away."

"Where did he go?"

"Like he told me, it's better if you don't know."

"I know what *that* means," Susanna said. "It means he's doing something with the Reg—"

"Shh. That's something we shouldn't talk about right now."

"I wish he could have stayed," Susanna said wistfully.

Magdalen touched Susanna's fine blond curls. "I do too."

"But at least you're still here," Susanna said with a sigh.

"That's my girl. Your papa would be proud of you, being brave that way."

"I don't feel very brave."

"I don't either. But what does Papa say about being brave? Do you remember?"

Susanna nodded. "He says *being* brave isn't always *feeling* brave. Sometimes it's just doing brave things."

"He doesn't always feel brave either, Susanna. But he still does brave things because he knows God is with him."

"Just like God is with us."

"That's right."

It was a low rumble at first. Then a full-out thunder of hooves, pounding down the main road from the south. Susanna's eyes got big. She swallowed hard and said, "I'm going to be brave."

Magdalen looked out the window. Almost two dozen travel-grimed men were riding into town at a full gallop. One rider in a hunting shirt and cocked hat shouted something and split from the group, waving the rest on. He swung easily from the saddle, knotted his reins over a nearby post, and headed for the house. Magdalen had the door open by the time he reached it. He grabbed Magdalen in a bear hug, swept her up, and kicked the door shut. Susanna pranced up and down on the braided rag rug and clapped her hands. "Papa!"

Robert set Magdalen down and held out both arms to Susanna. "How's my pumpkin?"

She answered with her face tight against the rough linsey of his shirt. "I tried to be brave, Papa."

"I knew you would." Robert plucked his hat off and dropped it on Susanna's head. She giggled and pushed it up so she could see.

"Drake been here?" Robert asked. He motioned for Susanna to hang his tricorne on its peg. "I've been worried."

"So have I, but he never came," Magdalen said. "I found out this morning that he checked around town and found your men were gone too. He must have known there was nothing to do but bide his time until you either came back or stayed gone for good."

"He didn't *really* think we'd left town for good."

"If he did, it only shows he doesn't know you like I do."

"I don't think I'd like Drake to know me like you do," Robert said reflectively. "My goose would be cooked."

"You're happy, Rob. You don't usually come back from meetings happy."

"This is different. I've come back with a dozen reinforcements, and we're ready to get Drake good and rattled. That's why we came into town the way we did. We want him to know we're here and watching him."

"Won't he try to arrest you again?"

"Not if he knows what's good for him. I've got a new man out there who'd like nothing better than for Drake to try it, just so there'd be an excuse to knock him to the next county."

"He sounds like a fine gentleman."

"My wife is not being sarcastic, is she?"

"I'm not sure yet."

"You'd like Alec. Tough as old iron, but a good man, I'm thinking. I'm glad he's on my side, let's put it that way."

"Then I am too." Magdalen slipped one arm around Robert's waist and stretched to peck him on the cheek. His five days' growth of stubble was coarse and bristly, but right now she didn't care. He shifted so his back was to Susanna and lowered his head. Evidently a peck on the cheek was not enough.

Gunning chose that moment to barge in the back door. "Miz Maggie, there's a whole passel of sapsuckers out in the street having a regular hog-killin' time and going on like—" He broke off, his expression changing from ire to delight. "Master Rob! You come home!"

"I confess, Gunning, I was one of those sapsuckers a minute ago," Robert said, releasing Magdalen. "They'll not do any real damage. Saul and the others are out there; they'll keep a handle on things."

"Looked to me like Saul was the worst of the lot," Gunning said. "But I allow as it's no matter, seeing you're here. You want I should put Wanderer up?"

"I'd be much obliged if you would." Robert paused. "Gunning, how do you feel about helping me and the boys?"

"Well, sir, that depends on how." Gunning flashed a smile. "Won't do me much good to paint my face all up with soot the way some of you'uns do, now will it?"

"Here's what I'm needing," Robert said. "You get all around town, and no one pays much heed, because—" He broke off, the reason hanging in the air between them.

"Same reason the soot wouldn't do me much good," Gunning said bluntly. "Go on."

"We need you to learn all you can about what Drake is doing, and bring what you learn to us."

"So do what I've been doing, you mean."

"Only more so."

"No trouble, Master Rob. That all?"

"The other thing I need is a place in the stable to put up a couple of the men till they can find better lodging."

"It's your stable."

"Aye, but you take care of it."

"Then you oughta know it's clean enough to live in. Just don't go asking for feather beds."

"No soot and no feather beds," Robert agreed. "You drive a hard bargain, Gunning."

Gunning flashed another smile. "A man has his limits, Master Rob."

"Don't we all," Robert said. "That's what we're aiming to tell Drake."

# Fourteen

Gunning had connections all over town, and by nightfall he was feeding Robert information about every angle of Drake's private life. How many horses he had, and how often they were used. Which one was his favorite. Who wrote him letters, and which ones he would or would not open in front of the hired help. How he personally felt about Ayen Ford and its inhabitants. How much Governor Tryon allowed him for expenses, and how it was spent. And much, much more. Things that Saul or Alec or especially Robert himself could never have learned without a great deal of highly suspicious questions. Robert was not even entirely sure how Gunning found out all he did, except to know that Gunning was friends with the cook and stable boy Drake had hired out of necessity.

"He never pays mind to what they notice," Gunning told Robert. "They're just help he has to have. He never sees they're folks who can think."

"I hope I don't ever act that way to you, Gunning."

"Haven't yet, sir."

Gunning had been raised alongside Magdalen on her father's plantation to the southeast, and Robert's father-in-law had given Gunning to Robert as a wedding gift. Robert had never been comfortable with the thought of Gunning being property. He was more like family. And right now, he was another set of eyes for the Regulators.

Saul McBraden and Alec Perry spread the Regulators out in shifts, making a point of letting Drake see them. Saul reported that Drake was giving Alec the evil eye every time he saw him and would no longer even meet Saul's gaze. Magdalen moved freely among the widows and spinsters of Ayen Ford, being her usual cheerful, encouraging self and quietly reporting any signs of exploitation at the hands of the governor's men. Benjamin Woodbridge, John's twelve-year-old son, eavesdropped shamelessly on Drake and anyone remotely connected with him. Robert, head of the operation, handled all the reports and carefully noted the information that could be useful. Drake had made no attempt at taking him back into custody. Alec loitered outside the Baptist meetinghouse during services, slipping inside often enough to avoid charges of breaking the Sabbath, yet always making sure Drake knew he was armed and on guard.

For two and a half weeks the Ayen Ford Regulators maintained a constant, wearing surveillance. Robert enjoyed the time at home with his family but kept his scouts and couriers busy, relaying news of Governor Tryon's movements in the capital. Tryon had not yet left New Bern, but every evidence showed increased preparation for a march against those he had labeled "insurgents." The reports only served to make Alec and Saul direct their reconnaissance with a vengeance.

One dark mid-April night, Drake had had all he could take. He and Ebeniah Kendall ambushed Alec.

The way Robert heard it, Alec had been caught in the act of intercepting Drake's mail. Drake and Kendall, angered by this rank outsider defying their authority, had attacked him from behind. Alec had been unconscious before he hit the ground.

"They're keeping him at Kendall's house, seeing the jail's still got a bad roof," John Woodbridge reported in their emergency meeting. "From what Benjamin's heard, they're fixing to drag Alec before the court first thing in the morning, make an example of him."

Ethan Hardy said, "But we ain't about to let that happen, now are we, Pastor."

"I know you boys want to rescue him tonight," Robert said slowly.

"You bet we do!" Saul McBraden was emphatic.

"No," Robert said decisively. "Not tonight."

Outrage showed all around. They trusted him, yes, but that did not guarantee agreement. Robert held up a hand. "Not *tonight*, I said. They would expect that. And, beyond rescuing Alec, it wouldn't do much good."

"You saying rescuing Alec's not the most important thing?" Saul demanded.

"The *most* important thing, but not the *only* important thing," Robert corrected. "We've seen more and more evidence of Drake and Kendall using fees and taxes for their own purposes, and of the justices doing nothing to stop them. Don't you think it's time we called them to account for that?"

"It's been time for weeks now," John Woodbridge said. "But I don't see—"

"Where better than the courthouse?" Robert pointed out. "Meet here at eight o'clock sharp tomorrow morning."

If Charles Drake and Ebeniah Kendall had not been so intent on hauling Alec before the court the next morning, they might have noticed the swarm of Regulators congregating on Robert's property. Robert did not particularly care if they did notice. There was no longer any stopping the men under his command.

"Our goal is to rescue Alec," Robert said. "After that, to get a look at the tax records. We'll deal with Drake and the court how we have to deal with them, but this is not the time to take justice into our own hands. We all know what happened in Hillsborough when the Regulators there broke up the court. We're going to break up this court just like they did that one, but we are not going to whip any officials and we are not going to wreck any property and we are not going to give the government any reason to paint us as thugs. Unless they manage to find a reason in the course of things."

"Which I don't put past 'em," Woodbridge interjected.

"I'm not saying the officials in Hillsborough didn't deserve the licking they got," Robert said. "And I'm not saying some of ours don't, either. I *am* saying it's not our place or our plan. We may need to use force to get Alec out of there and to get the tax accounts. But *only* as far as is necessary."

The men nodded their assent and Robert split them into groups, assigning a special few with specific tasks. Disarming Sheriff Kendall. Keeping the court at bay. Guarding the doors. Robert personally would see to Alec's release.

He finished his instructions, motioned the men in tight, and removed his tricorne. "Lord, You know we're not aiming to cause trouble."

Saul muttered, "Not much, leastways."

"All we want is what's right and just. Guide us, Lord. In the name of Christ we ask it." He paused. "And all God's people said—"

"Amen," the men murmured in unison.

Robert put his hat on, tugged it low. "Now remember—level heads. Don't shoot just because someone else is shooting. Even if it's me. All right, let's go break up a court session."

When they had gathered on the courthouse lawn, Robert moved to the head of the group and checked once more to be sure everyone was in position. Then he slammed the door open, shoulder and hip and rifle butt. Kicked it wide and watched a hundred heads swivel to stare.

The look on Drake's face afforded Robert a split second of satisfaction. Just as quickly, the sight of Alec bruised and in chains replaced the satisfaction with a low-burning anger. Robert said quietly, "Go to it, boys."

# Fifteen

Robert would have dared to bet that no storm wave had ever broken on Cape Hatteras with more force than the Regulators surging into the courthouse. Saul vaulted the railing up front and dragged Sheriff Kendall from his seat, holding him over the rail while John Woodbridge wrested away the weapon Kendall was trying to draw. Ethan Hardy and his command cleared the bench in a battlefront heartbeat and stood guard lest the county justices try to restore order. Robert headed for Drake and Alec.

Drake said, "Boothe, this is treason."

"Unshackle Alec and do it now," Robert said.

"Do you know what we caught him doing?" Drake hissed.

"Do you know what we've caught you doing?" Robert's voice was deceptively soft. Magdalen or Gunning or anyone else who knew him well could have warned of the danger signs in his quiet drawl.

"Are you saying I—"

Robert leaned in and said, "Do it."

Drake's hands clenched. He said, "Kendall has the keys."

Robert said, "Saul?"

"Right here." Saul tossed the ring to Robert. Robert caught the keys without moving his gaze from Drake. "While we're freeing Alec here," Robert said, "I want you to find us the tax records. Or we'll find 'em ourselves." Drake said, "That has nothing to do with Perry."

"Nothing, and everything. Study on that a minute." The chief justice, whom Drake had evidently appointed in Geoffrey Sheridan's place, spoke from the corner where Ethan Hardy was guarding the officers of the court. "Mr. Boothe, the colonel has a legal case against Mr. Perry."

"I allow as he does," Robert said. "And as soon as the colonel consents to an unbiased jury of Alec's peers, he's welcome to press charges. Until then, we'll say Alec was well within his bounds as a loyal citizen. Fair enough?"

The chief justice's expression said that to his way of thinking it was not fair enough at all, but he made no argument, only turned away as if he preferred not to watch his courtroom taken from his control.

Dried blood matted in Alec's loose queue bore witness to the attack from behind. A bruise across the side of his face had closed one eye, and it looked to Robert like Alec was favoring his right leg. But the flint was still in his gaze and he still had a fighting set to his jaw. He turned to let Robert reach the cuffs and said, "I was banking on you, Captain."

Robert unlocked the manacles and dropped to a knee to remove the ankle irons. "That was a mighty risky thing you tried, Alec."

"It's all risky, Captain." Alec's smile was slightly crooked. Crooked and devoid of all humor.

Robert stood up, tossed the shackles to Saul, and swung back to face Drake. "You mind what I tell you, Colonel. Get those accounts."

Drake said, "No."

Robert pulled Cricket's hammer back and leveled the rifle. "Saul," he said, his eyes still on Drake, "the records are in the first cabinet to the right, just inside the door of that office yonder. We wanted to do this decently and in order, but it looks like the colonel won't let us."

Saul shoved Sheriff Kendall at John Woodbridge and moved to do Robert's bidding. Drake exploded to his feet, took one step in Saul's direction.

The crack of the rifle shot shattered the taut stillness. Drake whirled just as Cricket's bullet buried itself in the wall six inches from his left shoulder.

"I'd not be moving much if I was you," Robert said quietly.

If he had wanted to hit Drake, he would have hit him. The shot had been only a warning. But it took a beat and a half for the colonel to find his voice and say, "Look, Boothe, I have the governor behind me."

"Aye." Robert slid his ramrod out. "And I have the people behind me."

Drake said, "Do you *know* what he'll do to you for this?"

Robert didn't answer. He uncapped his powder horn, measured a charge and poured it down the rifle barrel, tamped it down and followed it with a patch and ball.

"You'll hang as a traitor," Drake said.

Robert slipped the ramrod back into place and shook a little black powder into Cricket's priming pan. The rest of the Regulators seemed to sense the way Robert was drawing the silence out. He pulled the frizzen down with a cricket-chirp squeak, loud in the tense hush. Abruptly he said, "Is that what you wanted to see him do to Geoffrey Sheridan?"

"One day Sheridan is going to talk," Drake said, his voice hard as Rowan County granite. "And when he does, he'll tell Tryon enough to hang you and your lackeys four times over."

"Once would do the job," Robert said dryly.

He made a process of checking Cricket's flint, giving Drake time to either simmer down or erupt for good and all. And giving himself time to school his features. No way was he going to let Drake know that they had good men getting Sheridan out of danger.

Saul broke the quiet. "Here's the tax book, Pastor."

Robert said, "Sit down, Colonel."

They locked eyes, Robert commanding, Drake challenging. Then Drake's perfect smile flashed out. He bowed slightly to Robert and seated himself, a picture of gracious capitulation.

That, Robert thought, was not good.

But at the moment, he was willing to take it. He handed his rifle to Alec and said, "See he behaves."

"You can gamble on that," Alec said grimly.

Robert said to Drake, "I advise you to sit still. Alec would love any excuse to hit you as hard as you hit him."

"It'd be better if he couldn't see me coming," Alec said without a trace of a smile. "Same as I didn't see him."

Robert took the account book from Saul and moved to the bench. Ethan Hardy kept the justices herded nervously to one side. Robert laid the book on the glossy surface in front of him and leaned on the oiled wood, his position relaxed but ready for motion. He gave Drake one last glance and opened the book.

Drake sat in silence as Robert read aloud the most recent entries. Sheriff Kendall muttered darkly until Saul gave him a look that could have silenced a grizzly bear. But Kendall wasn't the only one muttering. A low rumble swelled across the courtroom as it became clear that the accounts did not fit with what the people had actually paid. Armed with the information Gunning had gathered, the Regulators knew Charles Drake was living far beyond the allowance Governor Tryon had given him for expenses. That extra margin of income was looking more and more as if it tallied with the discrepancy in the accounts.

"A rough estimation," Robert said, "puts the collection of taxes and fees at four hundred pounds over what's counted here as legally handled. That doesn't cover money taken from folks who never reported it to me or my men."

"That explains why you didn't want us lookin' at them records," Ethan Hardy said to Drake. "You and your sheriff friend have been doctoring 'em a little, eh?"

Drake ignored Hardy, looked straight at Robert. "Who do you think you are," he said softly, "talking about me and taxes while you ignore the vestry tax?"

Robert watched Drake's gaze flit sideways to where Jacob Chauncy sat across the room. A signal, Robert guessed, or maybe more of a silent command, for instantly Chauncy cleared his throat. "Yes, Boothe, what about that? Is that the proper obedience to authority of which you spoke to me?"

Magdalen had told Robert about Chauncy's apology and ensuing hasty exit. Robert could not tell just where Chauncy stood. He knew Drake was using Chauncy to pull him off the subject. But he would not let his personal stand be an excuse for justice to be ignored. "You remember, Jacob, I spoke of *obedience to proper authority*, not *proper obedience to authority*. There is a difference. The vestry tax isn't a tax at all; it's a forced tithe. And that is in no one's realm of proper authority."

"That's exactly the trouble with you Baptists!" Chauncy was not only following Drake's lead now. This was the heart of his vestry's disagreement with Robert. "You take plain words and define them to mean whatever you wish. *Tax* no longer means tax. *Church* no longer means the Church. *Baptism* no longer means baptism. How can any church expect to prevail in the face of that?"

"Perhaps," Robert said slowly, "if you were to take a good square look at the Bible and at history, you would find that we have not redefined things at all."

"If you're insinuating that the Church of England—"

"I'm not insinuating anything," Robert interrupted. "I don't have to. As I said before, the truth will hold its own."

Drake cut in brusquely, as if irritated by Robert's mention of truth. "It's no use quibbling over terms, Boothe. This whole town knows you refuse to pay the vestry tax."

"That's just it," Saul said. "*This whole town* knows where we stand. How about you? Does the whole town know where *you* stand? If they don't, they're gonna find out right quick."

Drake started a retort. Alec nudged him sharply, said to Robert, "Go ahead, Captain."

Robert flipped a page in the tax book, thinking of all Gunning had reported. The whole town, indeed. "From the governor's end, you've collected exactly the taxes you ought to be collecting. And maybe we can't prove anything. But this town knows, Drake. You might think we're a town of illiterate farmers. But you can't lie to that many folks for very long. These records support a theory of ours. That theory being, you've been sending the governor his lawful share of the taxes, but you've been filling out your own income with the rest. Using our hard-earned money for—" He paused. "A new saddle for your favorite stallion, Prince. Fine Madeira and squabs on Saturdays. Entertaining out-of-town visitors, presumably from the governor. A brace of fine English pistols."

"Fresh beefsteak and the best port and brandy," John Woodbridge added. "Not that I would know what makes it the best."

"You'd be a better man, Colonel, and a less expensive one, if you'd just lay off the alcohol," Robert interjected.

"New shoebuckles, solid sterling," Saul put in. "A gold necklet, shipped to a lady in New Bern by the name of—"

Drake said sharply, "Hold your tongue."

Saul shrugged, his unconcern calculated to irritate.

"The finest in letter paper," Alec said. When Robert looked his way, he said, "I did have some chance at those letters before I got ambushed. Address Hillsborough, a man named Malcolm Harrod. You might want to have the scouts check into him one of these days, Captain."

Robert nodded. "Need we continue, Colonel?"

Drake's smile this time was a blatant lie. "Your underlings have done their work well."

Robert saw behind the smile enough to know that they had shaken Drake, rattled him to the core of his confidence. "I told you you can't lie to all of us for any length of time, Drake."

Drake gestured around at the courtroom. "And now what?"

"The case against Alexander Perry is officially dismissed," Robert said. "The court will proceed to the next lawful item on the docket." He glanced at the covey of justices still crowded in the corner. The new chief justice nodded tensely. Probably, Robert thought, he didn't dare do anything else under Ethan Hardy's watchful eye.

"As for you," Robert said, clapping the tax book shut and addressing Drake cheerfully, "we'll give you what you said you'd give me. Just enough rope to hang yourself. I think you're getting close."

## 200 Miles West
## The Blue Ridge Mountains

# Sixteen

A TINY MOUNTAIN CABIN MILES FROM ANY OTHER civilization is not the best place for two bachelors, both set in their ways, to be stuck together for weeks at a time. Mitchell Boothe was finding this out for himself.

The first time he realized he and Hank Jonas might get on each other's nerves was when he came in from feeding the horses and found the cabin not at all as he had left it. "Hank," he said, "what did you do to this place?"

"Straightened it up a little," Hank replied. "You may be a preacher, but you surely have got a disorderly streak."

"It wasn't disorderly. I knew where everything was when I needed it."

"Well, I didn't," Hank said, as if that settled it.

Mitchell said, "It's my house."

"I'm living here too, for the time being," Hank retorted. "Who learned you to keep the skillet in the wood box?"

"It's handy when I'm working right there."

"It's even handier hung up like it oughta be," Hank said.

Mitchell pulled the skillet off the wall and dropped it back in the wood box. "That's where I keep the fire tongs."

"Now it makes more sense to put the tongs in the wood

box and the skillet on the peg," Hank said.

Mitchell hung the tongs on the wall and turned around. "Look, Hank, I don't mean to be peckish about it, but you're the one who's stove up, so doesn't it make sense for me to keep things the way I like 'em so I can run the place?"

Hank shrugged. "Have it your way."

Considering how Hank liked to criticize Mitchell's housekeeping, Mitchell didn't think Hank was any too organized himself. His saddlebags were stuffed to bursting. Hank insisted nothing found good venison like a Cherokee arrow, but Mitchell could not conceive of how Hank had fit an entire Cherokee bow and quiver in his bedroll. The bedroll itself had not been rolled since Hank's arrival. Of course, Mitchell rarely folded his own blankets first thing in the morning or put things away as he finished with them, but that was different. It was his house, not Hank's. And when Mitchell was in one of his tidying moods, he put everything in its proper place, whether it was his or not. The result being, Hank repeatedly shouted that he couldn't find his coffee mug when he had just put it down.

Not that Hank repeatedly saying anything was unusual in and of itself. He had evidently been holed up in his mountain shack too long and was desperate for another human to talk to. So he talked. And talked. He only stopped when he fell asleep, and then he snored. Mitchell was used to doing his Bible study in all kinds of places, from horseback on a rocky trail to a dirt-floored hovel surrounded by squalling children. But somehow Hank Jonas' snore was the most distracting thing yet. Their saving grace was Mitchell's ability to swing in and out of a bad temper with relative speed. Once Hank dropped a subject, Mitchell would too, and then all would be peaceful until the next petty irritation cropped up—usually after Mitchell tripped over one of Hank's saddlebags.

One evening Mitchell at last went outside and had a long talk with God. "Lord, I generally come here to be alone for a while. I don't know what You're trying to do with me and Hank, but I hope it's something good. Maybe I'm just getting old and set in my ways. Whatever it is, I'm liable to need an extra dose of grace this next while."

Hank had started getting impatient after the first few days of sitting around, but by the third week he was worse than stir-crazy. Mitchell had begun to learn that when Hank Jonas was stir-crazy, he would do anything and everything he possibly could for himself, whether or not it was good for his ankle.

Which was why Mitchell was not sure if he was relieved or dismayed when Hank announced his new plan for passing the time. Hank began by saying, "Tell me if you think I'm too stupid for this, and I'll shut up. But I'm about to go mad."

Mitchell wanted to say, Too late. But he didn't, only set down his Bible and said, "Yes?"

"I want you to learn me to read."

"Say that again."

"What, do I have to learn you to hear first?"

"I *heard* you," Mitchell said. "It caught me off guard, is all. I've never taught anyone to read before."

"I've never learned before either. Excepting little bits. I can write my name and make out the alphabet and I know most of the sounds."

"What do you want to work with?"

"What've you got?"

"The Bible and *Pilgrim's Progress*."

Hank grimaced. "If them's my only options."

"I highly recommend the Bible," Mitchell said.

Hank gave him a look. "'Course you would. You're a preacher."

Mitchell let a grin sneak out. "You don't have to say it like it's a disease."

"I'll go with the Bible," Hank said. "But don't go trying to convert me."

They started in the Gospel of John. After the first few

chapters, Hank began to show an interest in what they were reading. By the time they reached the Resurrection, he was beginning to ask questions. Why did Jesus put up with His disciples, who never understood anything? Who was the "other disciple, whom Jesus loved"? Why didn't Jesus strike down all the Roman soldiers at the cross, if He was God?

They finished John and went on to Acts. Hank's questions started getting deeper. By the end of Romans, he could read almost as well as Mitchell, but he never suggested stopping the daily dose of Bible reading. Mitchell gave him every answer he could, but finally he had to say, "Hank, I don't know the answer to everything. My father preached for forty years, and he didn't know the answer to everything. Should we keep trying? Of course. A lot of strange ideas are getting mixed in with the old doctrine these days because men commence to preaching before they get good and grounded in the truth. But we'll never understand all the mysteries of God.

"And yet there are plenty of things we *can* understand. Even a child can know that Jesus is God, and that He died and rose again to pay for our sins. That's what we'll have to answer to God for. That part is plain as God could make it."

Hank was uncharacteristically quiet for a long moment. When he at last spoke, his voice was low and husky. "I'm thinking on it, preacher. I don't know yet just what I'm thinking, but I surely am thinking on it."

AYEN FORD,
NORTH CAROLINA

# Seventeen

FOR ALMOST ONE WHOLE BLESSED WEEK, Charles Drake left Robert and the Regulators to themselves. Robert preached uninterrupted on Sunday. He baptized Benjamin Woodbridge in the Haw River without interference. He enjoyed time alone with Magdalen and let Susanna help him clean Cricket. Saul spent his evenings with Elsie and her family, monitoring Caleb's slow recovery instead of spying on Drake. Alec came and went like the lone wolf he was, his bruises slowly healing and his eyes hard as tempered steel. Robert wondered about Alec sometimes—where he had come from, what had driven him to become a Regulator, why he wouldn't talk about it. Not that it mattered. It was a rare Regulator who didn't have some history he'd rather not discuss.

There was no word of Geoffrey Sheridan yet, but the scouts soon had a report on Malcolm Harrod, Drake's correspondent. One of Governor Tryon's right-hand men, even more so than Edmund Fanning, the governor's man whose very name every Regulator hated. Unlike the money-hungry, arrogant, womanizing Colonel Fanning, Malcolm Harrod was content to stay behind the scenes and focus every waking moment on destroying the governor's enemies.

Robert duly noted his scouts' report but refused to let it dampen the pleasure of being home with his family. If matters came to a head, as the Regulators had discussed in Rocky River, he would be gone soon enough.

Several days after Alec's trial, Robert was carrying in the firewood Gunning was splitting when Magdalen said suddenly, "Colonel Drake is coming down the street."

Robert threw his load in the wood box and brushed chips off the front of his waistcoat. "The sheriff with him?"

Magdalen leaned to one side, angling for a better view from the window. "No, he's alone this time."

"Why don't you go make sure Susanna and Gunning stay out in the yard a mite longer."

Magdalen moved to obey and Robert went to answer Drake's knock, not taking time to bother with his coat or roll his sleeves down. If Drake wanted to interrupt his home life, let him take Robert as he was. Robert glanced at Cricket in the corner but decided against taking the rifle to the door with him. It would only give Drake one more reason to think Robert wanted trouble. Robert opened the door a scarce halfway and said, "Afternoon, Colonel."

Drake shouldered his way inside and shut the door carefully behind him. "Good afternoon, Boothe."

Robert moved to block Drake's advance. "I don't recall inviting you inside."

"I don't recall asking," Drake said.

Robert glanced again at Cricket. Drake was between him and the rifle now. He handed Robert a sheet of paper with the royal seal. "This proclamation lists a number of rebel leaders. James Hunter—I believe you know him. William Butler. John Gappen. Samuel Deviney. Matthew Hamilton. James Few. Rednap Howell. Peter Craven. And you."

Robert flicked an eye down the page, feigning an interest in words he did not really see. "Why me?" he asked, his drawl softening to the danger point. Drake's first warning.

Drake shifted his posture, blending the impossible grace of a Wilmington charmer with the catlike alertness of a longtime military man. "A group of men waylaid the guards who had charge of Geoffrey Sheridan. Distracted, threatened, bribed—the stories differ, but the outcome is the same. Sheridan has disappeared. As I'm sure is no surprise to you."

"I've been here in Ayen Ford all this time, Colonel."

"Clever, but it's all too plain who told those men where to find Sheridan. It's your misfortune that the timing coincided with His Excellency's decision to issue this proclamation. Had the rescue been just a bit later, you might have avoided being included."

He snapped the paper from Robert's grasp and tucked it inside his coat. The rich broadcloth shifted and Robert saw the beautifully carved flintlock pistol in the sash holding Drake's ceremonial sword. Drake leaned in and said, "Every man on that list has been pronounced an outlaw by His Excellency Governor Tryon. You know what that means."

Robert knew. Anyone, lawman or layman, could shoot an outlaw on sight. And be thanked by the governor for doing it.

Robert said in a low voice, "Get out of my house."

"An outlaw has no protection under the law," Drake said. "Not even property rights."

Robert moved forward. "This is the last time I'm telling you."

Drake said, "This is the last time you're telling anyone anything."

Robert saw Drake's hand go to the pistol and was on him before Drake finished his draw. Robert's grip on the gun wrist was enough to make Drake wince. Robert forced the arm back and slammed Drake into the wall.

The pistol hit Maggie's kitchen rug two yards away, the thick layer of rag braid breaking the impact. Robert felt Drake brace against the wall to throw him off and danced back a step just as Drake drove forward. The thrust put the colonel off balance. Robert hammered the hinge of Drake's jaw with all the leverage he could get. Which wasn't much.

Drake fell heavily, down but not out. He rolled away, lunged for the pistol. Robert spun and kicked the gun away. Reaching for it might have been wiser, but there was no time. Drake cursed and came to his feet as the pistol skidded under the kitchen table. There was a look in Drake's eyes that Robert didn't want to think about. He led Drake backward toward the table, staying just out of range, saw Drake reach for his sword hilt and timed his move to the last risky instant.

The blade flashed and Robert dropped and rolled. Swiped at the pistol. Came up on the other side of the table with the pistol in his hand and a prayer that he would not have to kill a man in his own home. Drake's sword thrust carried him against the table and Robert flipped the pistol and slammed the butt into Drake's elbow. The rapier dropped with a clang. Robert flipped the pistol again, cocked it and had it level with Drake's heart when the colonel swung to face him.

"Get out," Robert said, breathing hard. "And don't ever come back."

When Drake was gone Robert leaned on the table, his heart hammering in his throat. It was not real yet, that Drake had come to kill him. Robert wanted to pray, but he could not form the words, any words but *Oh God.*

He felt Magdalen slip her arm around his waist. He said huskily, "Where's Susanna?"

"Out back picking up wood chips and chattering away at Gunning." Magdalen's voice caught. "She doesn't know anything even happened."

"I didn't know you came back in." His words sounded inane to his own ears. He should have had something deep and comforting to say. But there were no words.

"I only came back as far as the doorway. I saw—not everything—but enough."

"I never thought he would—" Robert took a ragged breath. "Not in my own house in front of my wife."

"You did what any good man would have done. And

did it better than most, I think."

He looked down at the pistol still in his hand, feeling cold sweat break out all over. "He's only going to try again, Maggie. If he doesn't, someone else will. I have enemies everywhere on the court."

"Would you be safe if you went to your brother in the mountains?"

"Most likely, but I can't—"

Magdalen turned him gently to face her. "Rob, go if you need to. Come back when it's safe. I'd rather have you gone for a while than watch you get killed right in front of me."

*Run,* his mind screamed at him. The thought made him sick to his stomach. He couldn't leave now, not with Maggie and Susanna here. But Drake wouldn't give him warning next time. And Drake wouldn't care if Susanna was watching or if Magdalen or Gunning were harmed in the process. If Robert's family would be safer with him gone . . .

He laid the pistol on the table and wrapped both arms around Magdalen. She leaned into him and he whispered into her hair. "All right. I'll go."

## 200 MILES WEST
## THE BLUE RIDGE MOUNTAINS

# Eighteen

MITCHELL'S CABIN WAS FAR UP ON THE RIDGE, lost amid towering trees that had just begun to show a misty green. Robert dismounted wearily in front of the squat log structure, his love for mountain country growing to an ache somewhere inside. It had taken a seeming eternity to reach the cabin, an eternity of riding and praying and second-guessing himself. But here in the Blue Ridge it all seemed far away. Which maybe was a good thing, for now.

He turned away from the call of spring in the mountains and hallooed the house, declaring his presence before approaching further. A few beats later a bearded man opened the cabin door, appearing to lean on it for support. "Howdy, stranger. Can I help you?"

Robert hesitated. "Do you know of a Mitchell Boothe anywhere near here?"

Then Mitchell was past the bearded man and was grabbing Robert's hand and pounding his back and pulling him inside. "Rob, what're you doing clear out here?"

"Long story," Robert replied. He stepped back and looked at his younger brother. Tall and lean as always, even leaner maybe, with sharper angles to his face and not an ounce of spare weight anywhere, but with the same rebellious lock of dark hair falling on his forehead and the same sparkle in his eyes. "You look good, Mitch."

"You don't," Mitchell said bluntly. "You look terrible. Like all the Carolinas are after you."

Robert half-smiled. "Close enough. I need someplace to stay a while. But if you already have company—"

"Which reminds me." Mitchell motioned to the bearded man, who was favoring one foot. "This is Hank Jonas. Lives on the other side of the ridge, busted his ankle and couldn't make it back. Hank, my brother, Robert. He's a preacher out Haw River way. Was a preacher, at least. I'll show you where to put your horse up, Rob, and we can catch up a little."

Robert followed Mitchell back outside. Mitchell paused to greet Wanderer. "Hello, boy. Nice animal, Rob."

"Named him Wanderer. Seems fitting just now." Robert ran a hand through the gray's mane. "I still am a preacher, Mitch. Just on the run for the time being."

"What are you on the run from? The law?"

"If you can call it that."

"Now you've got me curious."

Robert gave him the abridged version. Mitchell showed a rare flash of wrath. "He came after you in your own house?"

"And in front of Maggie."

"What a rat. How did you stop him?"

"I don't even remember."

"You used to tie me up in knots. Hit me right here under the jaw once, and I thought I'd been shot. You said it was accidental."

Robert had to smile as he hefted his saddlebags. "You sound like you didn't believe me."

"That's because I didn't."

With Wanderer stabled beside Mitchell's horse, the brothers began the walk back toward the cabin. "It seems so long ago," Robert said.

"And yet not."

"Exactly."

There was a pause. Then Mitchell said, "What do you aim to do?"

"Bide a while, if you don't mind harboring a fugitive."

"You can't be worse than Hank Jonas."

"What, he's worn out his welcome?"

"Welcome, nothing," Mitchell said. "I'm starting to think I'd be lonesome without him. But have mercy, he's stubborn!"

"Sounds like you've met your match."

"Spoken like an older brother," Mitchell said. "You can stay as long as you want to. Now come on, Hank's fixing possum stew for supper."

After supper, Hank Jonas dozed off and Robert and Mitchell sat by the fire late into the night, talking about everything and nothing. Charles Drake and Geoffrey Sheridan. Hank's ankle. Jacob Chauncy and his Anglican vestry. Mitchell's preaching circuit. Robert's congregation. And the things Robert had hoped his younger brother wouldn't notice.

"You sound like you miss the mountains, Rob."

Robert stared into the leaping flames, seeing good memories and bad all mingled together. "I shouldn't."

"But you do."

Robert leaned back. "As soon as I got here, I felt like I was home. Not here particularly. Just—like you said—the mountains. The trees and the air and the clouds so close you can near about touch them. But my people are still in Ayen Ford, facing Charles Drake, and—" He stopped.

"And this can never be home as long as they need you there." Mitchell said it with a compassion Robert had not expected.

Robert nodded. No other answer was needed.

Mitchell said, "So bring your people with you."

"Mitch, that's ridiculous."

"Moses did it."

"God told him to."

"Who's to say God won't tell you to?"

"Lately I don't know what God's been telling me."

"I felt that way when Hank Jonas first took up residence." Mitchell cast a furtive glance over his shoulder at Hank's snoring form. "I had just asked God for someone to come alongside me and help me in the work. My last partner took a Cherokee arrow and went back east. They'd surrounded our camp and we thought they were gone, but they weren't."

"Some things never change."

"That's right, you know all about the Cherokee."

"More than I care to remember." Robert got up and went to stand by the fireplace. A lot of folks knew about the Cherokee attack on the settlement Robert had once called home, but Robert still didn't like to talk about it.

Mitchell went on, "Hank showed up right after I prayed that prayer, and—well, I didn't appreciate God's sense of humor at the time. But it's been working out. We're learning to get along. And he's close, Rob. So close to making a choice to repent and believe the gospel. I'd love for it to happen while you're here."

"As would I," Robert said. "I could do with some encouragement."

"Is it only Drake and the governor, or something else?"

Robert leaned on the fireboard and kneaded the back of his neck, feeling muscles knot. After a long moment he said, "It's nothing I can't handle."

Mitchell looked skeptical. Robert braced for an argument he wasn't sure he could win. But Mitchell let it go. "Well, take a deep breath. You're safe here. Don't try to solve all the world's problems here and now. Just take things one day at a time."

"I don't have time for only one day at a time."

"That's the only way they come," Mitchell said. "Let God give you a little grace, all right? He loves doing that more than we give Him credit for. Now, deep breath."

Robert obeyed. Wood smoke and buckskin and traces

of possum stew.

"That's better," Mitchell said. "You're welcome here as long as you care to stay. I've done said that once, but I think you need to hear it again."

"Maggie said she'd send word when it's safe to go back. That's all I know."

"Fine. You can preach at my meeting on Sunday, then."

"Mitch, I—"

"I don't know what your excuse is, and I don't care. I'm about half sick of hearing my own preaching."

"You're the same ornery little brother you've always been."

"And you're the same hardheaded older brother you've always been. Glory, but I've missed you."

Mitchell would not take no for an answer. After less than two days of resting from his journey, Robert was opening his Bible in front of a motley assembly of mountain folk and praying he'd have something worthwhile to tell them. The words on the worn pages were familiar and slipped off his tongue with ease. But he felt as if he was fighting for anything meaningful to say in support of the verses he read.

There was a phrase among backcountry preachers, a phrase Robert himself had often used: "preaching with liberty." It described a message that even the preacher knew had the hand of God upon it, a message that glorified God and exhorted its hearers with nothing in its way.

Today Robert was preaching with no liberty at all.

It was not that he was tired, although he was. It was not that he was preaching to strangers, although he was. It was simply that he knew God's hand was not on this message. In desperation he used as much Scripture as he could, knowing that the word of God was always powerful. The people seemed to be listening intently. But Robert met Mitchell's eyes and knew that Mitchell knew. God might be working, but today it was in spite of Robert instead of through him.

That was a horrible feeling to have.

Robert cut the sermon short and asked for testimonies from the people. He sat down next to Mitchell and leaned forward, elbows on his knees, staring at nothing, listening to the praises of the people around him. Things he had heard so many times from so many people.

"God is always faithful."

"I'd be nothing without Jesus."

"He saved me when it weren't nothin' I could do for myself."

"I surely am glad the Lord understands."

All of that is true, Robert thought. I know that. *Lord Jesus, what's wrong with me?*

He leaned over and whispered to Mitchell, "You preach next time."

"You don't have to tell me anything you don't want to," Mitchell mouthed back.

"I'll tell you as soon as I figure it out myself," Robert said, hearing sarcasm tinge his tone but not caring enough to stop it.

Mitchell gave him a funny look, but all of a sudden they had a distraction. Because Hank Jonas was standing up.

"For a long time, I didn't think me and God had much to talk about," he said. "Then I busted my ankle and got stuck with Mitchell Boothe. God didn't make nobody more stubborn than Mitchell Boothe, unless it's me."

Mitchell bellowed an amen that brought a laugh all across the gathering. Hank grinned. "I ain't gripin', folks, 'cause his stubbornness is what finally got through my head about what the Good Book really says. And that's what opened up these eyes of mine. I don't care if you're a drunk like me or a preacher like him or just an ordinary character— if there are any of those in the world—there ain't no feeling like knowing you're forgiven and on good terms with God. As of this morning, I found that out for myself. Which, according to the preacher, is the only way to find out."

Robert watched Mitchell clear several benches and give

Hank a bear hug. He heard himself giving Hank an amen. But under the joy of Hank's salvation, a swirl of questions pulled at Robert's spirit.

*God, how can a man like Jonas bring You more glory today than I did? A preacher. Son of a preacher. Working to do the right thing as hard as I know how . . .*

*Lord, I admit it. Something's wrong here.*

## Ayen Ford, North Carolina

## Nineteen

In the year-long days following Robert's departure, Magdalen tried to hold onto some sense of a life that was calm and balanced and under control. But life was not like that. Robert *was* her calm and balance and control. He was a rock, her rock. And he was gone. Not for a few days this time. This time, for no one knew how long.

Gunning was a shadow, slipping in and out, overseeing all the little things Robert had always had charge of. He let Susanna spend more time with him than ever before, trying to keep her mind off her father. As if anything could do that. Virgil Ashe, a respected deacon in the church, took charge of the preaching in Robert's absence. Of Robert's men, Magdalen told only Saul McBraden and Alec Perry about Robert's reason for fleeing, trusting them to spread the word as needed. Alec seemed to step naturally into a place of leadership. He was not the spiritual adviser Robert had been to his men, but he kept the men unified, a difficult task with their longtime leader suddenly gone. It was Alec who knocked on Magdalen's door after church on Sunday, with Saul tight behind him. Gunning let them in while Magdalen sent Susanna out to play in the yard, quietly as befitted the Lord's day. That was the first thing Alec said—"I don't want your daughter to hear this."

Alec still unsettled Magdalen a little. His dry humor, his intense fighting spirit, the hardness in his eyes—it all seemed to stem from some root she could not identify. But when he showed concern for Susanna, Magdalen glimpsed a softness that put her more at ease with him.

Alec wasted no more time in formalities. "The Woodbridge boy's been scouting around again."

"Benjamin."

Alec nodded. "Stubborn as all get out and thinks he knows everything, but he manages to make himself useful."

"His father caught me directly after church and told me what Benjamin heard," Saul said. "Mrs. Boothe, Colonel Drake's coming late tonight to either find Pastor or find out where he is. It's been long enough since Pastor left, I allow as Drake knows he's gone. But he's set on finding out his whereabouts one way or another. I half expect he's coming strictly to bully you. Alec and I want to tell the boys, get 'em together and have 'em waiting when Drake gets here. It's not such business as we'd like to do on the Lord's day, but I reckon He understands."

"We're not fixing to do anything more to Drake than make it plain he's not welcome here," Alec said. "What that'll take, I'm not sure just yet. If you say no, McBraden and I will still stay here in your front room and make sure you and your daughter are safe."

"We have Gunning, Mr. Perry."

Alec said bluntly, "Drake would shoot him without a thought."

"Not if I let daylight into him first," Gunning said.

"The court would hang you in a heartbeat," Alec said. "Self-defense or not. I don't like it, but there it is."

"They'd hang you just as fast, and it's got nothing to do with the color of your skin," Gunning said. "Drake hates you worse than he does me, being as he almost caught you once and you got away. Don't go keeping me out of this."

"Do whatever you think is best," Magdalen said quietly.

"Do you want Susanna and me to leave for the night?"

"That's as you see fit," Alec said.

"Elsie'd be glad to take you in," Saul put in.

"Elsie doesn't need more folks to look after," Magdalen said dryly. "If it's up to me, Mr. Perry, I don't want to risk involving anyone else in this. I'd not put it past Drake to target anyone who sheltered us. Besides, he would notice we were gone and suspect something."

"You're a brave woman, Mrs. Boothe," Saul said.

"No, I'm not. I'm scared to death."

"Nothing to be scared of," Alec said. "We'll look out for you, don't worry about that. But you might send your daughter elsewhere. Some things she just doesn't need to know."

"Why would you be so careful to protect a family you hardly know?" Magdalen asked.

"Pastor would want us to," Saul said quickly. "And you've done so much for—"

"Not you, Saul. Mr. Perry."

He was looking past her to the back door. She turned, saw Susanna hesitating, waiting for permission to come back inside. Magdalen glanced at Alec, uncertain if their business was finished, if he was going to answer her question.

For a brief instant some nameless emotion cracked the hardness of Alec's eyes. "Any family is worth protecting, ma'am." He turned away. "Let's go, McBraden."

Susanna came in, question marks in her big blue eyes. "Mama, isn't it Papa's job to protect our family? That's what he told me once."

"Yes." Magdalen nodded. "Yes, it is. But he's not here right now, so his men are taking his place for a little while."

Susanna just looked at her. Looked at her and said, "Papa's not coming back. Is he."

Magdalen blinked, the sting of tears burning behind her eyes. "Someday he is. Just not right away."

"It's because of those people who don't like the Regulators, isn't it? Mr. Drake and Mr. Kendall. They don't like Papa, either. That's why you told me to stay outside when Mr. Drake came."

"That's right," Magdalen said softly. "Papa has to stay out of town right now because it's very, very dangerous for him here."

Susanna said in a very soft voice, "Is Papa going to die?"

"I don't know, Susanna. Not if the Regulators can help it." She cleared her throat, suddenly very angry at Charles Drake. No seven-year-old should have to know her father was an outlaw. "But even if he does, he believes in Jesus, so we know he'll be in heaven."

"With your babies? I don't mean me. The other ones."

Susanna had been two when Magdalen lost her last child. Magdalen had not told Susanna about it until Susanna asked one day why she didn't have a brother like her best friend did. Susanna had not understood much of Magdalen's answer. But she did apparently remember the promise that both of her siblings were in heaven. "Yes, Susanna. With them. And if we believe in Jesus, too, we'll see them all in heaven someday."

"But I can't *see* Jesus!" Susanna objected.

"He's still real," Magdalen said gently. "Just like Papa is still real even though you can't see him right now, either."

Susanna's eyes brimmed. "I just want Papa to come back."

"Oh, Susanna." Magdalen gathered her daughter close, feeling the slender shoulders quiver. "I know you do."

Susanna sobbed against her. "Why can't God make him come back and stay safe?"

Magdalen cradled Susanna and thought, Oh, Rob, come home.

But not until it's safe . . .

Just as dusk fell, Magdalen took Susanna to the Woodbridge house for the night. Six-year-old Elizabeth Woodbridge was Susanna's best friend, and by all appearances, Susanna was simply spending the night with a playmate. But Magdalen knew Susanna understood far more than had been explained to her.

John Woodbridge had already left when Magdalen arrived with Susanna. John's wife, Nell, told Magdalen in an undertone that Alec Perry was gathering the men across town, issuing orders so they would be ready to take their positions the instant they reached the Boothe house.

"John's talking more and more about fighting," Nell said softly. "It scares me, Maggie, and yet I'm at peace. God has us in the palm of His hand. If He wants to take John that way—" She paused.

"I'm not at peace about Rob yet," Magdalen admitted. "I don't seem to be at peace about anything these days. Rob is the one I'd talk this over with. Now he's not here . . ."

She trailed off. "I should go."

Nell reached for Magdalen's hand. "Let's pray first."

That, Magdalen decided, was a very good idea.

Nell gave her hand a squeeze at the *amen* and said, "Are you sure you don't want to stay here, too?"

Magdalen shook her head. "I left lights burning, and Mr. Perry expects me to be there. They don't want Colonel Drake to think anything is out of the ordinary."

"Then you're right, you'd best be going." Nell gave her a quick hug. "Don't you fret about Susanna, now."

Dusk had already fallen when Magdalen stepped outside. She was across the street before she heard voices a little farther up the road. The sound was pitched low and tight, but she distinctly heard Charles Drake say, "We aren't looking to kill Boothe this time. I want him alive. The only way Tryon will take any note is if I drag that rebel in front of him and let His Excellency see for himself what I've rid him of."

Sheriff Kendall said, "What'd you say the governor thinks of everyone calling themselves Baptist?"

"Enemies to society and scandal to common sense." Drake's tone said it was a direct quote. "And why not? They won't pay the vestry tax, they ignore the law against dissenter marriages, and they have no respect for the authority of the Church."

"They say the Church isn't a true church at all," another man interjected.

"My point exactly." Drake broke off. "What the—"

Magdalen missed the rest of what he said, because she suddenly saw what Drake must be seeing. Alec Perry and Saul McBraden, shoulder to shoulder against the front door. Leaning on either doorpost, their posture a blend of relaxed and alert. Like a pair of panthers waiting for the prey.

I shouldn't have stopped to listen, she thought. Yet at least I know now what Drake wants and why.

But Drake would see her if she tried to go back to Woodbridges'. Maybe she could slip around through the back door before he noticed her.

She edged off the road into the shadows, then picked up her skirt and petticoat and made a dash for it. Fleetingly she glimpsed a Regulator stationed at every window, every door, even at the foot of the chimney. Gunning was posted at the back door. He saw her coming and gestured for her to hurry.

A rectangle of lamplight spilled out as Gunning held the door open. Sheriff Kendall gave a shout. Magdalen caught her breath and ducked past Gunning. Then Colonel Drake was there, shoving Gunning back and forcing his way inside. Magdalen did not have time to run or scream or even think before Drake grabbed her arm. "Where is your husband?"

Magdalen looked into his shadow-dark eyes and knew that she was very, very scared. Knew also that she was not going to let him know it. "Let go of my arm."

His fingers tightened enough to bruise as the front door crashed open and Robert's men poured inside. Drake screamed at her, "Tell me!"

"She's not telling you anything!" Gunning ripped Drake away from Magdalen, sending him into the wall. Saul McBraden slammed the back door in the faces of Drake's men and slid the bar into place with a thud just a degree quieter than the one Drake had made, hitting solid oak planking.

"Get this straight," Alec growled. "You leave here, you make your men leave, and you don't ever bother this lady again. Hear me?"

Drake hissed a threat that Magdalen wished she had not heard. She did not know for certain that it was directed at her. But she knew that if it was, Rob would have sent Drake out on a shutter for saying a thing like that to her.

Evidently the Ayen Ford Regulators were men after Robert's own heart. Saul growled low in his throat. Gunning shoved Drake against the wall again, harder this time. Alec spoke over his shoulder. "Mrs. Boothe, would you kindly step out of the room? We'd just as soon not whip a man in front of you."

Magdalen took a step toward the bedroom. Alec jerked Drake away from the wall and slammed him over the kitchen table. "Last chance, Colonel. Did you hear me or didn't you?"

Drake had gone the color of both murderously angry and afraid for his life. He forced each word out as if it hurt. "I heard you."

Alec let Drake up halfway and motioned with his head for Magdalen to remain. "Apologize to the lady."

Whatever Drake muttered might have been an apology. It might not have been. But the bare appearance of acquiescence was enough for Alec. "I'll tell you what you want to know, Drake. Boothe isn't here. Not in this house, not in this town. He's far away where you'd never be able to get him, even if you knew where he was. Mountains. And trees where a man can get lost and never be found. Ever. And that's all you need to know."

Saul said, "Now tell us you're going to leave Mrs. Boothe alone."

Drake's normally flawless black hair straggled out of its ribbon and down the side of his face. A blurred trail of perspiration showed faintly on one temple. He could not make himself say the words. But he made a motion with his head that could be construed as a nod.

Alec let him off the table all the way this time. "We're watching you, Drake. And we've got more men than you have. You'd be wise to remember that."

"As far as I'm concerned, you're all outlawed as of now," Drake ground out.

"Then as far as we're concerned, you're outlawed as of now, too," Alec said. "Liable to be shot on sight. It's no way to talk in front of a lady, but come to think of it, you're in sight now. And just look at all the guns the boys brought."

Drake said, "I'll *go*."

"Good," Alec said. "Then we might as well let you. Tonight, leastways. Watch your back, Colonel. You're making more enemies by the minute."

# Twenty

CHARLES DRAKE SPENT THE NIGHT LICKING HIS wounds and planning his next move. It was common knowledge that Governor Tryon had left New Bern and would reach Hillsborough in another week. It was time for Drake to head for Hillsborough, enjoy a few days of respite, and wait for Tryon to show up with reinforcements.

Drake rose earlier than was his wont, crossed town with a wary eye peeled for Alec Perry, and issued orders to Sheriff Kendall. Keep a low profile, wait for reinforcements, let the rebels seal their own fate. If Drake was not in Ayen Ford, looking out for royal interests, someone else ought to be, and Ebeniah Kendall had already been established as Drake's ally.

Kendall, however, would not be much help in monitoring the religious pulse of the community. But Drake had a plan for that, too.

Jacob Chauncy was not without reservation where Charles Drake was concerned. Drake seemed a little too severe in his judgments, and too hasty in making them. But Drake represented all the financial help the parish would ever need, and Chauncy could not deny the sad state of the tax affairs. So he welcomed Drake with a cordial smile and a chair and a glass of his oldest port. "How may I be of service, Colonel?"

Drake leaned back and crossed one knee over the other. "I leave this afternoon for Hillsborough, but my work here is not finished. Sheriff Kendall has agreed to watch for any legal trouble in my absence. But he is not a reliable source, shall we say, in the area of ecclesiastical affairs."

"The sheriff is not a particularly religious man, Colonel."

Drake gave a low chuckle at that. "No, he is not. Precisely my point. How has the parish been faring?"

"Little has changed."

"What, not even with Robert Boothe on the run?"

"His church seems to carry on very well without him. That is, I've seen no signs of weakening."

Drake looked thoughtful. Chauncy said, "You seem to take an inordinate interest in Boothe."

"I have reason to." Drake uncrossed his legs, sat forward in his chair. "You didn't know, did you, that His Excellency declared Boothe an outlaw not quite two weeks ago."

"An outlaw? No, I didn't." Chauncy could not imagine the essentially easygoing dissenter preacher warranting the governor's special notice. "What's he done?"

"Led rebel meetings. Ignored the restrictions placed on dissenters. Broken jail. Refused to pay taxes. You saw yourself how he broke up Alexander Perry's trial."

There was a long pause. Chauncy stared past Drake to the bookshelves lining the far wall. The picture Drake painted of Robert Boothe fit well with what Chauncy knew of the man, and yet it did not. "Why are we talking about this, Colonel?"

"Getting to the point. I like that. I'll tell you why, Jacob. In all your disagreements with Boothe, you must know something of his beliefs."

"That is true."

"Tell me what you know. All of it."

"But what has that to do with—"

"A man who thinks he can choose beliefs of his own making is but a step away from thinking he can choose laws of his own making. That is what I have a duty to prevent."

"Well . . ." Chauncy had to think; he had made a practice of shutting out the unsettling statements Boothe often made. "He believes the Bible to be the sole authority for faith and practice, that tradition should be dictated by it rather than the Bible being interpreted by tradition. He believes men can have personal dealings with the Son of God without the intervention of the Church. The very word *church* to him indicates a local meeting of worshippers, believers as he would say, and he calls their sacraments *ordinances*. Entrance to this body is secured by baptism, which he says is to be done only by immersion, and only after a conversion experience."

"Conversion experience."

"Yes." Chauncy tried to hide how uncomfortable this conversation made him. "'Believing and accepting Christ's finished work' is how he once phrased it."

. Drake's expression said that told him all he really cared to know, which was nothing. "What else?"

"He says the state should have no authority in the realm of the Church. That the Body of Christ is under no lordship but Christ's, and therefore is not subject to the state in any way." *The people are, but the church is not*, Boothe had finished. But Chauncy did not think Drake would understand that any better than he had.

"Not in any way?" Drake repeated.

"I believe that's what he said."

"That's sheer anarchy."

"It does lean that direction."

"Go on."

"That's all."

"That's not enough, Chauncy. I need to know how I can use this to predict his next move. Where he is now. When he'll return, *if* he'll return. And what he'll do if he does."

Chauncy felt his usual good nature slipping. "I have nothing more to tell you."

"Then find more." Drake came to his feet. "Get in close to them. You know enough of their beliefs to feign an interest. Pretend to be a convert if you must. But it is *imperative* that I have a reliable source of information on Boothe's teachings and movements *within his church.*"

Chauncy shoved his chair back and rose to face Drake. "I may disagree with Boothe, but I respect him. I could not live under a pretense like that."

Drake's voice went hard. "We all live under one pretense or another. And you'll live under any pretense I tell you to."

Chauncy felt the study walls closing around him. This was not about his parish at all. This was about what Drake wanted, and nothing else. What was it Boothe always said? "The truth will hold its own, Colonel."

Drake stepped back. "You want to talk about truth, Jacob? I have some truth your vestry would be very interested in hearing. About a head vestryman who invests parish funds in his own dying business."

"You have no right to break confidence!"

Drake did not answer, his expression untouched by Chauncy's flare of anger. Chauncy met his eyes and thought, Right or no right, he can break any confidence he chooses. And he will.

The silence stretched taut. Drake shifted and said very softly, "Well, Jacob?"

The anger was gone, a cold weight in its place. Chauncy did not want to do this thing, to be Drake's tool.

But he would still have his position and his business and his reputation. And Robert Boothe would never bother him again . . .

Slowly he moved his head. Not a nod, only a slight inclination. Drake smiled.

"As I thought," he said. "Be ready when I return."

## 200 Miles West
## the Blue Ridge Mountains

#  Twenty-One

Robert finished tethering Wanderer and tried not to grimace openly. For being an experienced rider, he felt more jarred than he had in a long time. "Tell me again why we picked the long and rocky path instead of the not-so-long and not-so-rocky."

Mitchell glanced over Samson's back. "You're getting soft, Rob, living in that comfortable little flatland town of yours."

Robert gave him a look. "I can still whip you any day of the week."

Mitchell just laughed, a contagious sound that had lost none of its youthfulness. "You're getting nigh on to cocky, too. No, we came this way on account of how the other way takes us over Bram Fisher's land. He swore he'd take a horsewhip to me if I set foot on his property again. I don't care about the threat, but I reckon, if he feels that way, I'll not get any closer to reaching him by outright trespassing."

"I've offered to go settle his hash, but the preacher won't hear of it." This from Hank Jonas. "I allow as he knows best, but it does rankle me some."

"Out here folks don't go to the trouble of locking you up if they don't cotton to you," Mitchell said. "They just tell you straight out how they feel, and if you don't listen quick enough, they'll hit you with something. You catch on quick."

"I remember those days," Robert said. "In some ways it's easier. You know what you're up against."

"There's something to be said for that," Mitchell agreed.

"Ain't that the truth," Hank said. "It strikes me as downright mean to outlaw a man and not tell him till it's 'most too late."

"Let's not go over all that again." Robert glanced at the barn that would serve as a meetinghouse a few minutes hence. "Mitch, isn't it about time to start?"

"Only if you're sure you don't want to preach."

Robert waited for Hank to drift off before he answered. "I told you. I'm sure."

"Well, I didn't know if you'd gotten something straightened out since then."

"There's nothing to straighten out, and if there was, I doubt you'd be the one I'd tell."

That brought Mitchell up short. Robert instantly regretted both his tone and choice of words. "I'm sorry, Mitch, I didn't mean that. I'm just tired of working it over."

"It's all right," Mitchell said quietly. "I'm sorry I brought it up again."

Hank was well out of earshot now, mingling with folks as they streamed through the barn doors. Robert said, "Sunday at that meeting, I wondered how God could use a man like Hank Jonas more than a man who's been preaching for fifteen years."

Mitchell rummaged in a saddlebag, pulled out his Bible, didn't look at Robert. "That's pride talking, Rob. I don't know how many times I've had thoughts along those lines, and the Lord's had to hit me upside the head."

"I know. I knew it wasn't right as soon as I thought it. But all my life I've—"

Mitchell swung around and looked at him pointedly, intently. "God doesn't care about 'all your life,' Rob. He cares about right now." He must have caught something in

Robert's expression, for he added, "I know, I know, I'm the little brother and I'm not supposed to tell you off like this. Well, maybe you need to hear it. A preacher can't rest on his laurels and expect things to go on as they've always gone."

"Tell me why I've weathered tough circuits and angry officials and heaven knows what else, and now this time it's all wrong." Robert didn't mean it to sound challenging, truly he didn't. At least he didn't think he did. But it came out that way, and come to think of it, that was how he felt.

Mitchell said shortly, "Maybe you got your eyes off the prize. Now if you'll excuse me, I have a meeting to preach."

Robert thought as he found a seat that Mitchell had preached enough already. It stung more than he wanted to admit, having his younger brother call him out that way. Mitchell was the spontaneous one, the one who took life as it came and made friends with what it brought. Robert was supposed to be the one with the deep theological insights.

But he could not get away from what Mitchell had said. *Maybe you got your eyes off the prize.* He was aware of Mitchell pleading, exhorting, calling sinners to repentance. But Robert was not listening.

*Maybe you got your eyes off the prize.*

Off the prize. Off the Lord and onto himself. Robert shifted, feeling as if everyone in the room could hear the argument in his heart. *Lord, I tried to trust You. I do trust You. But Drake was going to kill me.*

Out of nowhere a verse he had learned long ago flashed across his mind. *In the LORD put I my trust—*

Well, he did. Didn't he?

*—How say ye to my soul, Flee as a bird to your mountain?*

The Lord had just hit Robert Boothe upside the head.

As a rule, when Mitchell preached, he forgot anything and everything else, focused strictly on the message he was bringing, hardly even saw the individual faces in front of him. But today it was different. Every so often his eyes strayed to his older brother, sitting on an upended log near the back of the cavernous room.

Rob was not listening to a word Mitchell said. Mitchell could tell that clear across the barn. Robert sat with his elbows on his knees, staring blankly ahead. At least his stare looked blank to Mitchell. Knowing Rob, however, he was probably mulling something over. If it was possible to think too much, Mitchell thought, Rob would be the one to do it. Good thing there weren't any meetings coming up straightway. Mayhap Rob could get the rest he needed, enough to not woolgather during the preaching.

Having settled that in his mind, Mitchell began to hit his full revival-preacher stride. Time slipped away when he was "preaching with liberty," and he could not have told anyone how long the meeting lasted. He stopped when his voice went hoarse and he had said all God wanted him to say. He did not scream or rant to get people under conviction. His voice was too tired for that. He simply said what he always said.

"If you need to deal with God, do it now. 'Behold, now is the day of salvation.'"

He saw Robert get up, make a beeline for the front, and go down on one knee at the edge of the rough wood platform. *Lord, he wasn't even listening to me preach!*

*No, but he was listening to Me.*

Mitchell had the sudden realization that Robert's business with God was no concern of his at all. But when he had finished making the rounds of the people at the front, offering prayer, a clearer explanation, or a verse to help a troubled soul, he heard a low voice say, "Mitch."

He turned. Robert was at the far end, still on one knee. Mitchell went over and sat down on the edge of the platform, seeing a new peace in Robert's eyes that had been missing before. "You don't have to tell me anything, Rob."

"I was a boor out there earlier, and I'm sorry."

"I reckon I deserved it," Mitchell said. "Butting in and giving advice where I had no right."

Robert gave his deep, easy chuckle, something he had not done nearly enough since showing up on Mitchell's doorstep. "Strange, isn't it, that I should still chafe at taking advice from my little brother. Even when he's right. And you were, Mitch. I'd got my eyes off the prize. So busy being scared of what man could do to me, I ran for the hills and forgot to look to the Lord." Robert's voice went husky. "Somewhere along the way I got my eyes off Him and on myself..."

"He's a lot better to look at than we are."

Robert nodded. "I know that now. And I'll admit, I didn't hear a thing you said all meeting. But I heard what I needed to hear, I guess. And—there's something else."

He got to his feet and waited for Mitchell to do likewise. "God doesn't want me here, Mitch."

"But Rob—"

"Was I wrong to come?" Robert shook his head. "I don't know. But I'd be wrong to stay. Mitch, I'm going home."

# Twenty-Two

MITCHELL WAS ADAMANT THAT IF ROBERT WAS going to go home and get himself killed, he wasn't doing it alone. With almost a doubting-Thomas, "let us also go, that we may die with him" determination, he insisted that he had no more meetings scheduled, had no obligations, had no reason at all to not go with Robert to Ayen Ford and live dangerously. When Hank Jonas heard, he staunchly declared that his ankle was fully recovered and he had always wanted to see Haw River country.

Robert tried to reason with them, told them it was safer for him to go alone, pointed out the attention bound to be drawn by all three of them riding into Ayen Ford at once. He might as well have saved his breath. "We'll ride into town one at a time then," Mitchell said. "Stop arguing. We're going."

They were up just before dawn the next morning. Mitchell and Hank battened down the hatches and made a lot of very strong coffee. Hank dragged an overstuffed pair of saddlebags to the door, piled them with Mitchell's, and tossed his bedroll on top. Robert looked at the wooden object sticking out of the bedroll and said, "What is *that*?"

"Cherokee bow," Hank said. "And quiver. Nothing—"

"Finds good venison like a Cherokee arrow," Mitchell finished for him. "Just make sure the end of that thing doesn't stab anyone."

Cherokee arrows made Robert think of things he'd rather not dwell on, so he fastened his last saddlebag and went out to saddle the horses and say goodbye to the mountains. Only a few short days and the air was back in his blood. But better to face Drake in the flatlands with the Lord than hide in the mountains without Him.

By the time the sun cleared the horizon, they were ready to go. Hank said, "We oughta pray."

"Always," Robert said. "Go ahead."

Hank doffed his hat and cleared his throat. "Lord, uh, Pastor Boothe is fixin' to go home, as I'm sure You know, and we'd surely like to know what'll happen when we get there. But seeing as that ain't possible, I'd just like to ask You to look out for us all. Which I reckon You do anyway, only we need it a little extra right now. And kindly don't let us do nothin' stupid. Amen."

Robert said, "I couldn't have said it better."

Mitchell looked at him, said, "Ready?"

Robert swung a leg over Wanderer's saddle. "Ready as we're ever going to be."

He knew Mitchell had not meant, were they *all* ready, had only meant, was Robert ready. But it was too much trouble to explain how he felt. Like he was going home and leaving home, both at the same time.

Three days later, they camped near Abbott's Creek, a rough forty miles from Ayen Ford. It was a strongly Baptist region and as good a place as any to spend the night. Mitchell busily set about building a roaring fire. Hank hobbled a little as they picketed the horses, but the man did not complain. Instead he stared off to the east and said, "There's another campfire over yonder."

"You don't reckon it's someone coming for Rob." Mitchell was on his feet, moving closer to the others.

"They'd be a bigger group if they was after somebody," Hank said.

"Think we should wander over there?" Mitchell asked, glancing at Robert.

"Whether or not you do, I'm going," Robert said. "Might be news from home."

"Out here?" Mitchell asked doubtfully.

"You knew about the Regulators, away out on the ridge," Robert pointed out. "Word does get around sooner or later."

"Save yourself the trouble," Hank said. "Someone's coming this way."

A deep halloo cut the night air. Robert moved forward, recognizing the voice at once. "Gunning?"

A hesitation, then, "Master Rob?"

The burly figure stepping into the firelight erased all doubt. "Gunning, what on earth are you doing here?"

"Looking for you," Gunning said simply. "Didn't think it'd be near so easy as this. Looks like you picked up some company."

"This here's Hank Jonas, and you've met my brother, of course. Mitch, you remember my man Gunning."

Mitchell's smile flashed out. "I surely do. It's been a coon's age since I've seen him. A pleasure to see you again, Gunning. Hardly thought it'd be all the way out here."

"Now that I know it's you, I've got something in my saddlebag," Gunning said. "Give me just a minute here."

He stepped away and Mitchell said in an undertone, "Rob, I thought you'd said you were going to give him his freedom. A long time ago now."

"Mitch, I'll not trust the protection of my family to just anyone."

"Must be handy having a watchdog to order around," Mitchell said, low enough for Hank not to hear.

Robert ignored the sting in Mitchell's sarcasm as Gunning stepped back into the ring of light. "Miz Maggie, she sent me," he explained. "She'd have come herself if she could have and if I'd let her. She said—"

"She and Susanna—they're all right?"

"Oh, yes, sir. Missing you considerable, though."

"But Drake's not bothered them?"

"Once. But he's not doing it again, Alec laid that out to him flat and cold."

"Gunning, tell me what happened."

"Drake and his men come to the house wanting to know where you were. Saul and Alec and the boys and me told him where to get off, and Alec got him over the table and made him promise not to come back. I wish you'd been there to see it."

"I wish I'd just been there," Robert said grimly.

Mitchell said, "You've still not told us why you were looking for Rob."

"I've been trying," Gunning said patiently. "And when you'uns are finished, I will."

"I'm finished," Robert said humbly. "Go ahead."

Gunning held out something sewn into an oilcloth covering. "A couple of your scouts come to Miz Maggie with a letter for you. From Geoffrey Sheridan."

Robert took the packet and reached for his belt knife. Mitchell said, "This Geoffrey Sheridan, he's the justice you told me about? The one Drake arrested and your Wake County friends rescued?"

"That's the one. And you know as much as I do right now. He was headed for South Carolina. I wonder how he got this to Maggie."

"Well, like I said, a couple of your scouts brought it in," Gunning said. "I reckon they got it from one of the scouts farther south, who got it from one of the Wake County boys, who got it from—you get it."

"Something like." Robert slit the oilcloth, drew out the letter, and broke the seal, an unadorned blob of candle tallow. The page held two paragraphs in Geoff's methodical script.

*1 May, 1771*

Rob,

 Thanks to you and your friends from Wake, I have seen neither New Bern nor any of its prison cells. However, I came close enough to the city, and had contact enough with my guards, to learn of Tryon's preparations. He leaves New Bern very soon (possibly as I write this) with his militia, more of which will be gathered on his way west. Some are reluctant to fight, but they are not to be taken lightly. Tryon has sworn to end this if it means killing every man of you. I did not tell my guards anything, but Tryon already knows enough to see you hang—particularly after this latest episode, I should expect.

 I am in a small settlement just over the border into South Carolina, which settlement good sense dictates I ought not name. I admit to feeling guilty about my relative safety when I think of the danger you and your men are facing. Be on your guard.

       Yours, and forever in your debt,
           G. S.

 Robert checked the date at the top of the page. A week and a half ago. Long enough for a letter to reach him all the way from Cheraw—and long enough for a lot of other things to happen.

 "What have the scouts heard about Tryon lately?" he asked abruptly.

 "Not near enough," Gunning said. "Only that he's coming, and there's no sign that he's stopping."

 "He's not," Robert said. "Sheridan says so. Are the boys doing anything to prepare?"

 "Land, yes, Master Rob. Sure thing. Alec, he's been sort of directing things. There's talk of big goings-on over Alamance way, a unified front, the boys are saying."

 Alamance. Twenty miles northwest of Ayen Ford, give or take a little. "Aye, I know about that. I helped James

Hunter plan it, though I didn't realize they'd decided it was time. Just another meeting, we hope, but a mighty big one, and mighty important."

"Saul and Alec aim on getting over there right directly," Gunning said. "Only I heard 'em planning something else—"

Mitchell was quick to catch Gunning's inflection. "What kind of something else?"

"The kind of *something else* I should know about?" Robert asked. Knowing Saul and Alec, it probably was.

"I don't know all the details, just overheard bits of things," Gunning said. "But it seems there's a wagon train a little way from Dixon's Mill. Chock full of supplies Tryon's been ordering his men to seize, you know the word—"

"Requisition," Robert said.

"That's it. And Saul and Alec, from what I gather, aim to ride out and capture it, or some such thing."

"Just the two of them?" Saul and Alec could be daring to the point of recklessness, but that was sheer madness. "They'll need more help than that."

Mitchell was frowning. "Rob, I thought you said you didn't hold with—"

Robert held up the letter. "After what Geoff says in here, I hold with nigh on to anything. When were they doing it, Gunning?"

"Near as I could tell, tomorrow night."

"Then we'd best keep riding," Robert said. "Hank, your ankle all right?"

"Never been better," Hank said cheerfully. "I'll see to them horses right quick. You'd better rustle up a bite to eat."

"Don't ever spy for the other side, Gunning," Robert said. "It would be over for us for sure."

# Twenty-Three

DIXON'S MILL BELONGED TO A QUAKER WHO reportedly sympathized with the Regulators. The property was on the border of Sandy Creek territory, where the Regulation had been born. A little to the southwest was the meetinghouse where Robert had signed the Regulator pledge four years ago. He knew this country, had preached in many of the settlements and baptized in many of the creeks.

The wagon train was easy to find, even at sunset. Robert broke from the rest long enough to complete a quick scouting mission. Two wagons. Two guards, both bored-looking militiamen. Robert directed his group a quarter mile down the only road from Ayen Ford, and then they waited.

Robert had never before countenanced the destruction or seizure of property. It was a mite strange to think of starting now. But Sheridan's words made him certain of his stand.

*Tryon has sworn to end this if it means killing every man of you.*

Common sense and biblical self-defense thoroughly justified the removal of Tryon's means of conquest. Any and all they could get their hands on.

But surely Saul and Alec didn't have capture in mind. Two men, an entire supply train—that didn't add up.

Robert looked over at Mitchell. "You thinking what I'm thinking?"

"What?"

"They don't want to capture that wagon train."

Robert could not tell what Mitchell was thinking, whether he approved of being there at all, or if perhaps he had gone over to the camp of Baptists that advocated near pacifism. It had been so long, Robert reminded himself, so much could have changed . . .

Mitchell stared down the road, shifted with Samson's movement, his profile all sharp angles against the setting sun. In his softest mountain drawl he said matter-of-factly, "It's been a long time since I got to blow something up."

No, things had not changed a bit.

Gunning stiffened in the saddle and hissed, "Someone's coming."

Hoofbeats echoed along the road. Robert rode forward, motioning the others to follow. "McBraden!"

The hoofbeats stopped. Saul's voice barked, "Who goes there?" The bravado was plain in his voice, the voice of a very young man who was scared and trying not to show it.

In the rose-gray light Robert could see Saul checking his rifle. "Don't shoot, Saul, it's your pastor."

Saul said in disbelief, "Pastor Boothe? What are you doing here?"

"Long story. Evening, Alec."

Alec didn't answer. His eyes moved sharply to Mitchell and Hank. "My brother, Mitchell Boothe," Robert said quickly. "And a friend, Hank Jonas. Your wagon train's got two wagons and a guard for each wagon. I'd say you'll need to get the guards out of the way before you go to blasting."

Saul demanded, "How do you know what we're here for?"

"The same way we got the goods on Drake, back in April. Thanks to Gunning here."

"We didn't intend to tell you," Saul admitted. "We figured—"

"What, that I'd not let you?"

"Something along those lines."

"A week ago, you might have been right. But Geoffrey Sheridan wrote to say that Tryon is bent on stamping us out. That justifies a lot in my book. Just one question. If the others are at Alamance, and you boys and Gunning are here, who's keeping Drake away from my wife and daughter?"

Alec made a strangled sound, like a snort of disgust. But it might have had to do with the dust of the road. Saul said, "Drake lit out a few days before we did. We must've scared him good. The scouts say he's headed to Hillsborough, won't be back for several days. And even if he is, there are still men left in town."

Hank said, "So what's the plan?"

"We don't rightly know yet," Saul said, almost apologetically. "The scouts couldn't tell us much about it. We reckoned we'd ride up and look it over from a distance, then figure out the best way to make 'er blow."

"Making her blow will be the easy part."

Mitchell had not said a word up until now, and that was not what Robert had expected him to start with. He lifted one eyebrow at his brother and repeated, "It will."

"Sure thing. A wagon train like this, headed for Governor Tryon, will have plenty of powder to do the job. Split the kegs open and pour the powder into a pile, then lay out a powder train, stand back, give it one good blast with a rifle and there she goes."

Robert said, "I don't want to know how you know that."

Mitchell just shrugged, a smile playing at the corners of his mouth. Robert thought, *He's enjoying this too much.*

"Sounds like it would work," Hank said. "What do you think?"

"Just give us time to take the guards out," Robert said, jamming his hat down over his eyes. "We'll truss 'em up and haul 'em out of range. Wait for my signal."

Alec spoke for the first time. "That's a heap of trouble for a couple of sorry militiamen."

"They have families too," Robert said sharply.

"They leave their families for this, they deserve what they get." Alec's voice was harsh. There was no dry humor in his eyes tonight.

Robert said quietly, "You don't mean that."

"Don't try to tell me what I mean. I know what I'm talking about better than you ever could."

There was a double edge to that, Robert could tell. But now was not the time. "I'll not have blood on my hands if I can help it, Perry. McBraden, you come with me."

They left their horses tethered in the nearest copse of trees and took the rope Saul and Alec had brought. The two guards were stationed on either side of the wagons, walking back and forth, back and forth, as if just trying to stay awake. Robert had a clear view of them both as he and Saul slipped toward the foremost end of the supply train. He waited until both guards were facing away from him, then motioned to Saul, crossed the open space at a run, crouched and slid under the lead wagon. The guards' footsteps beat an unsynchronized rhythm on either side. Robert held up a hand. *Wait.*

The guards passed, turned, passed back the other way. Robert chopped the air in Saul's direction, a silent signal, slipped from under the wagon, and took the guard down from behind. A quick hard blow and a muffled sound in the night, echoed by Saul's assault on the other side of the wagon, and it was over. Robert wove the rope securely around the guard's wrists, checked the knots, and dragged the man as far as a stand of trees within sight of their own hiding place. Saul met him with the other guard. Robert headed back to the supply train and leaped atop a wagon. In the dim light he could just make out the shapes of blankets and foodstuffs and kegs of gunpowder. He put two fingers in his mouth and whistled a single shrill note.

Mitchell was first to reach the wagons. "Hank and Gunning are staying with the horses," he said. "Hank says this way he feels like he's helping, but not enough to get strung up for it. Besides, his ankle's bothering him again. And Gunning says he doesn't trust Hank by himself. What he meant by that, I don't know and I don't think I want to. What do you want me to do?"

"Unload everything you can lay hands on," Robert said. "Alec, you give Saul a hand."

When everything was on the ground, Robert joined Mitchell in breaking open keg after keg of gunpowder and pouring out the contents. Saul and Alec added their own share until at last Robert said, "Looks like that's all."

"Now rip up the blankets and we'll use those for the powder train," Mitchell said.

They tore the blankets into strips and laid the pieces end to end, while Saul and Alec followed behind to pour gunpowder over their handiwork. When they were finished, they had a long trail from the pile of powder and broken kegs almost to the thicket where Hank and Gunning still held the horses. Mitchell motioned Alec to dump a small heap of powder on the very end of the line, then straightened up and called over his shoulder, "How's it look?"

"Ready for blastin'," Hank called back.

They retreated to the thicket and Robert looked at Saul and Alec. "Ready?"

Saul's grin was wide in his sweat-streaked face. "More than ready, Pastor. You do the honors."

"You and Alec ought to do it. It was your idea."

"Just do it and have it done," Alec said.

Robert took his rifle from Gunning. "All right, then."

He knelt and sighted in on the end of the powder train, pulled the hammer back, squeezed the trigger. The earsplitting crack and first explosion were amplified by the stillness, but that was nothing to the thunder that erupted three, four, five beats later. The ground bucked and the night lit up as two wagons' worth of gunpowder went sky-high.

The impact slammed through Robert's chest, shoving his heart up into his throat. For a minute he thought his ears were ringing. But no, it was Mitchell shouting one long drawn-out victory yell. On his other side, Saul let out a whoop and hollered, "Sweet Caroli-na!"

Robert wondered if Tryon had heard the explosion clear over Hillsborough way. He sort of hoped so, had a sudden desire to shout in that direction, We're not going to lie down and play dead, Your Excellency.

But he was a minister of the gospel. Ministers of the gospel didn't holler things like that at the governor . . .

He glanced at Mitchell and said it. Not shouting, but not quietly, either. Mitchell amened him, revival-meeting style.

"Now that's the beat of anything I've seen in all my born days," Hank said. "We been any closer, one of them barrel staves would've took us out."

"I heard one fly past," Gunning said. "I'm trying not to think about it."

Alec cut in. "We'd best ride before someone comes to check this out. Unless you feel a noble urge to go untie the guards, Boothe."

The sarcasm was palpable. Alec must be good and mad about something to cut the celebration short and call his captain *Boothe* in that tone of voice. Robert said, "Mount up, boys. We'll follow in a minute."

Mitchell and Saul gave him a strange look, but they mounted up. Gunning and Hank followed. Alec started to do likewise, but Robert moved between him and his horse. "Alec, if you're upset about my taking over your operation, I'm sorry, but it's hardly—"

"It's not that." Alec looked out at the billowing smoke. "Not even close."

Robert waited. Abruptly Alec swung to face him, his eyes filled with a low hard rage. "You should be ashamed," he ground out, "leaving your family to fend for themselves that way. You're a lot of things, Boothe, but I never figured you for a coward."

Robert had never seen Alec angry. Not like this. He wanted to say, I blow up a wagon train at the risk of my neck and now I'm a coward? But Alec was only voicing what Robert had already wrestled over. Robert spoke slowly. "That's why I'm going back."

"Now's a fine time," Alec said harshly. "After Drake's had two weeks to—"

Robert started to say, "But he didn't, because you were there."

Alec talked right over him, not even hearing. "He could have torn your house apart, torn your family apart, *anything*, and you would have come home to—"

Robert caught a glimpse through Alec's anger and knew what this was about. "To what you came home to."

Alec turned swiftly away, his breath suddenly coming hard. "I came home to nothing. Nothing but ashes and—"

He stopped. Robert said nothing, having no words to speak, feeling every shard of Alec's pain. After a moment Alec said, "I swore the Anson County oath, to pay no more taxes and to rescue anyone who got arrested for not paying theirs. Didn't think much of it at the time. Then the governor's men took to watching me. I left, just for a few days, I said. I couldn't stand being spied on all the time. When I came back, they'd burned the house to the ground. No one would tell me anything."

Alec did not elaborate further, and Robert did not ask him to. Nor did Alec explain how he'd pulled up stakes and gone looking for a fight. Robert could fill that part in on his own. "I was wrong, Alec. It's true."

"I don't object to a man leaving for a cause," Alec said. "Running from a threat—that's what I did. So I reckon I'm hardly one to talk. Only I know what it can cost. And I'd hate to see it happen..."

To you, Robert knew Alec wanted to say but would not. Just as Robert would not tell Alec that it had already happened, years ago, long before anything Alec had a right to know. But the memory of the Cherokee attack in the Blue Ridge was still fresh enough for Robert to understand Alec's strange blend of anger and concern, to appreciate the concern and acknowledge that he deserved the anger.

"We'd best go," Alec said quietly.

They both mounted up in silence, but it was no longer a threatening silence. There was no time for personal grudges or lengthy self-condemnation. A lot of Regulators were waiting for them at Alamance.

But first, home.

## Ayen Ford, North Carolina

# Twenty-Four

Magdalen was so glad to see Robert again, she didn't even care that he'd brought his brother and a rough-edged mountain man home with him. "I can't believe Gunning found you so fast," she said. "I thought it would take at least a week."

Robert spoke over Susanna, still tight against him. "We sort of found each other. I'd made up my mind to come home earlier, after one of Mitchell's meetings."

Mitchell said, "Can you believe my preaching is that bad?"

"His preaching was that good," Robert corrected. "We ran across Gunning on our way, and Saul and Alec the next night. I'm sorry I ever left, Maggie. You needed me here."

She had. Oh, she had. But she would not tell him so, lest she stand in the way of the work he had to do. She put her finger over his lips. "You're here now. Not for long, I know, because there's talk of Alamance all over town. But you're here for today. That's enough."

"I hear this rat Drake heard we were coming and ran for the hills," Mitchell said. "A shame, that. I'd rather like to meet him."

"I'd wager a fat milch cow that ain't all you'd like to do

with him." This from the mountain man whom Robert had introduced as Hank Jonas.

"Rumor has it he's going to meet the governor in Hillsborough," Magdalen said.

"Saul mentioned something about that," Robert said. "What else has rumor had it?"

"The boys could tell you more than I could," Magdalen said. "Tryon's subordinate, Hugh Waddell, was forced to retreat, over in Rowan County. About two thousand Regulators gathered there and made enough noise to scare him off. From what I hear, Waddell's men didn't want to fight."

"Hugh Waddell." Robert shook his head. "I remember when he led a demand on behalf of merchant ships that were seized for ignoring the Stamp Act, back in '66. It's a sad irony how many easterners who hated the Stamp Act don't realize we're only fighting the same thing in a different form. Or if they do, they ignore it."

"They're the east and we're the west," Mitchell said. "Nothing changes."

"How's the church?" Robert asked.

"Caleb's fever hasn't returned, and he's gotten a lot of his strength back," Magdalen said. "The only worry now is his leg. He still can't put much weight on it, and it's been over two months. Elsie's tired, but she's holding up. Jacob Chauncy seems to be around a good deal. I've seen him talking with Deacon Ashe, and he showed up at a prayer meeting once."

Robert frowned. "Any trouble?"

"No. He's just—there."

"I don't like that at all," Robert said. "I'll have to talk to him. Someday. When I have time. Any other news?"

There was plenty of news, but Magdalen assumed Robert did not want to hear about Widow O'Neil's rheumatism or who the wheelwright was courting or what the Anglican vestry had quarreled about last Sunday. "The week after you left, nine young men from two Rowan County Presbyterian churches disguised themselves as Indians and blew up Waddell's powder wagons down in Mecklenburg."

Robert looked at Gunning and Mitchell. "So that's where Saul and Alec got the idea."

Magdalen did not want to know what Robert meant by that; it was apt to be dangerous and possibly illegal and certainly something she'd wish she hadn't heard... "What idea?"

Rob's wink was a wonderful thing to see. "I'll tell you later. If you're sure you want to know."

"About this Alamance thing," Mitchell said. "Where do I come in? I'm happy to help, sure. But I'm wondering if I'd be of more use here, staying with your church. Gunning can look after Maggie and Susanna; I know that. But with all the men *out* of town, the more y'all have *in* town, the better."

"It's your choice," Robert said.

"Then I'll stay here. I don't know enough of what you're meeting about to do much good. Hank, how's your ankle?"

"Not so good," Hank said with a grimace. "I'd better stay here and make sure you don't go off into heresy or nothin' while your brother's gone."

Robert looked at Magdalen. "You're sure you can handle these two without me?"

"I don't think anyone can handle Mitchell. But I'm sure we'll be fine."

"Good. I expect I'll leave in the morning with Saul and Alec, then... I hate to go, Maggie."

Out of the corner of her eye Magdalen saw Gunning shooing Mitchell, Hank, and Susanna out the door. Bless that man. She needed time with her husband.

"I don't mind your having to go, Rob," she said. Robert put his arms around her and she nestled against him. "Well, I do mind, especially since you just got home. But I understand. You promised to help with things like this, and I know it's important. Only I'm worried about Susanna. She's been asking a lot of questions."

"Hardly a surprise."

"No, different this time. Like why God doesn't fix it all and make it go away."

Robert said, "I'll talk to her, love. But I can't say I always understand that either."

Robert found Susanna playing with Gunning's pile of wood chips. It required a good imagination to see the wood chips as Susanna saw them—fine dishes and all manner of good things to eat. Robert sat down on an upended log and said, "Your mama says you've been asking questions about God."

Susanna looked up. "Mama explained some things. But I don't understand why God made folks that are so ugly to each other. Like Mr. Drake is to you."

"That's not God's fault, pumpkin. It's ours."

Susanna squinched up her face. "Ours?"

"Remember the story Mama and I tell you about Adam and Eve in the garden?"

Susanna nodded. "Everything was perfect until they ate from the one tree God told them not to eat from."

"Did God make them do that?"

She shook her head. "No-o."

"Then it wasn't God's fault that something bad happened."

"But He could have *made* them not eat the fruit."

"What if I made you love me, whether you wanted to or not?"

"But Papa! I *do* love you!"

"I know, pumpkin. But if I made you love me, would that be real love? Or just a have-to kind of love?"

"Have-to, I guess."

"God didn't want Adam and Eve to love Him with a have-to kind of love. He wanted them to choose to love and obey Him. If you let someone choose, they might choose the wrong thing, right?"

Slowly Susanna nodded. "Sometimes you tell them what the right thing to choose is, and they don't choose it anyway because they think they know better."

"That's right. And that still happens today, just like it did in the garden. God wants us to love Him and do good.

That's why He made us. But He wants us to *choose* to do it. He wants Mr. Drake to love Him. But Mr. Drake thinks he knows better, and he's made the wrong choice."

"But does everybody have to choose? Even me?"

"Everybody. Even you." He thought, Shame on you, Boothe, your daughter needs to know these things, and where have you been? Fleeing as a bird to your mountain, that's where.

"Mama says folks who don't believe in Jesus don't go to heaven. Is believing the same as choosing?"

"Well, the Bible says in one place, 'Choose you this day whom ye will serve,' and in another place it says, 'Believe on the Lord Jesus Christ, and thou shalt be saved.' So God uses both words."

Susanna bit her lip. "I don't think I've done that yet. But I want to. I'm scared to not go to heaven. And I know I don't love God very much, because sometimes I'm bad—" She was crying now. "And I don't want to stop being bad, but I do want to stop."

"Jesus will help you want to stop, Susanna. He'll forgive you for all of that. It's like a gift He wants to give you. All you have to do is take it."

Susanna nestled up tight against Robert and he put his arm around her. "Just tell Him what you told me, Susanna. He'll understand."

Susanna sniffled. "Jesus, I want You to forgive me and take away all the bad things I do . . ."

As Robert held his daughter close and listened to her simple prayer, he knew that this was exactly where he was supposed to be.

For today.

Tomorrow, Alamance.

MAY 15, 1771
ALAMANCE,
NORTH CAROLINA

# Twenty-Five

GREAT ALAMANCE CREEK WAS A LITTLE RIVER that snaked eastward into the Haw River. The Regulator camp was not hard to find. It was large and sprawling and easily matched the rumors of two to three thousand men. An almost casual air pervaded parts of the camp, as if this was just another excuse to gather and talk and laugh, to wrestle and run footraces and boast of marksmanship. Others seemed more somber. Robert thought of Geoffrey Sheridan's warning and thought, No, this is not just another meeting. This will settle our future.

James Hunter of Sandy Creek greeted Robert with the same single-minded intensity he had shown at the Rocky River meetinghouse. Hunter was definitely one of the somber ones. "Looks like the time has come," he said. "I never thought—"

He paused. Robert said, "We thought, but we hoped we were wrong."

Hunter nodded. "We still do. Most of the men here don't really believe Tryon is camped just over yonder for the sole purpose of crushing us."

Robert glanced around. "They still hope it was just a mistake, that Tryon does want to listen to our grievances."

"I admit I hope so, too," Hunter said.

"I think we all do." Robert had seen the camp of government militia, twelve hundred men maybe, just a few miles away. He had felt the strange mix of fear and anger and disbelief. Surely Tryon would not really march on them. But he had thought that about Drake, that Drake surely would not come after him in his own house. And look what had happened there.

"We'll know soon enough," Hunter said. "We just sent one more petition over to Tryon, asking him to straighten all this out, if it was a mistake. 'The lives of His Majesty's subjects are not toys,' we said. If he doesn't listen to that, we're in for a rough time of it."

Tryon said he would respond at noon on the sixteenth. But by ten-thirty the next morning, an hour and a half early, his militia had marched within a hundred yards of the Regulators, drums beating and flags flying. Alec Perry and Saul McBraden prowled the Regulators' front lines, aiming the occasional taunt and eyeing the governor's troops as if they were prey that could just as easily turn predator. Voices on both sides started to rise, threats, challenges, defiance. The gap closed to fifty yards, then twenty-five. Robert began to feel a tightening in his gut, a silent, throbbing prayer of *Dear God, no . . .*

The Regulator leaders held a quick conference and chose three men to attempt negotiations. One was David Caldwell, a conservative Presbyterian who had been James Hunter's pastor until their politics conflicted. Caldwell was here, not because he was a Regulator, but because he was a voice of reason who might provide some slim chance of averting bloodshed. The other two messengers were Regulators from the rank and file, one named Matear and the other named Thompson. Robert did not know Matear at all, and he knew Thompson only by reputation—a good-natured but vocal farmer who had sworn that no government man was going to take his land away.

Caldwell, who had gone on horseback, was the first to return. His sober expression left no doubt as to the word he brought. "Those of you who aren't too far committed should desist and quietly return to your homes. Those of you who have laid yourselves liable should submit without resistance. I and others promise to obtain for you the best possible terms—"

"Submit without resistance!" Saul snorted. "Not on your life."

"The governor will grant you nothing," Caldwell said.

"We're not looking for him to grant us anything," Robert objected. "Only to listen. Is that so much to ask?"

Caldwell shook his head. "You're unprepared for war. You have no cannon, you have no military training, you have no commanding officers to lead you in battle. You have no ammunition. You'll be defeated. You can't—"

A gravelly Scotch brogue shouted from somewhere down the line. "Dr. Caldwell, get out of the way or Tryon's army'll kill you in three minutes!"

"Tell us what Tryon said," Robert ordered. "Not what you think of our chances."

"He still wants an exchange of prisoners. Seven Regulators for his two officers who were captured last night."

James Hunter looked at Robert. Robert said, "I'm in favor of that. Keeping those two here any longer is only going to breed trouble. They'd be more of a bloody mess now if we hadn't intervened last night, and there's no promise some of our firebrands won't try to finish the whipping they started."

Hunter nodded. "I agree. But surely that's not all."

Caldwell cleared his throat. "Tryon also commands you to lay down your arms, turn over your outlawed leaders for trial, and swear to obey all the law. Do that and he will not attack."

Alec Perry made a sound of angry disgust. "That's not negotiation, that's demand for surrender."

"Tryon can jump in the creek right yonder if he thinks

he'll get *my* rifle," Saul added.

"Where are Thompson and Matear?" Robert cut in. "They should be back by now."

Hunter looked past him. "They're still in Tryon's lines. That's the governor yonder, front and center."

William Tryon was a stout man with an extreme military bearing and a self-importance that Robert could see even across the distance between the two camps. Robert said, "What's keeping them so long?"

Hunter said, "It can't be good . . ."

Alec muttered, "This waiting is hard on a man."

"It's better than the alternative," Robert said.

Alec grunted. "Maybe a good fight's just what we need."

"Half our camp doesn't even think it'll come to that."

"They will soon, I'm thinking," Alec said.

Robert glanced out at Tryon and the two messengers again. The one on the left, that was Thompson, he looked like he was saying something Tryon was not liking . . .

The governor moved with such unexpected swiftness that Robert almost did not see him rip the musket from the hands of a nearby militiaman. Hunter said, "What is he—"

Then the shot cracked. A single heart-stopping explosion. Tryon's answer to their final petition.

Saul screamed a raw, soul-deep rage that said what words could not. Robert's own anger was so strong and blinding it scared him. This time he said the silent prayer out loud. "Dear God, no."

Bobby Thompson was dead. Shot by his own governor.

Whatever Tryon was trying to accomplish by shooting Thompson, all he had done was make the people under his rule hate him all the more. They were too angry now to disperse, even with the hour's warning Tryon had given them. A few men mounted up and slipped away, but only a few. Robert did not blame most of them; some were pacifists who would gather and talk and petition but had a real conviction against armed resistance. That was their lookout.

Robert didn't want to fight, either. Caldwell was right—they were not prepared. They had not come looking for a fight, at least Robert hadn't. But this one, he was sticking out to the bitter finish.

He looked at James Hunter. "You're the one to take command, Hunter, to hold this all together."

Hunter shook his head, his eyes trained on Tryon's army, his expression grim. "We're all free men. Everyone must command himself."

"'The race is not to the swift,'" Robert said slowly, "'nor the battle to the strong...'"

Hunter glanced at him. "There's truth there, you know."

Robert stared at the governor's lines, close enough now for Tryon's advance guard to engage the frontmost Regulators. "But not a promise."

Then it began. A sudden thunder of government cannon, a scattered volley of Regulator fire, an answering volley of militia fire, now a stronger barrage from the Regulators. At first Tryon's cannon was misaimed and the Regulators fought from the cover of rocks and bushes and forest, and Robert thought maybe there was hope, though how this could ever come out right was beyond him. But then the cannon became more accurate, the militia more confident. A Regulator fell, then another, that one was John Woodbridge, *oh God, not Woodbridge,* but there would be time to weep after the battle, they could not stop now, ammunition was running low . . .

In two hours it was over. A decade of Regulator work, of careful organization, of everyday folk standing up for their homes and their livings and their consciences. All of it, over. Robert watched the blaze of the nearby trees that Tryon had set afire to drive the Regulators from their cover. The smoke drifted, there and gone, and Robert thought, Like that.

Over.

# PART II

## Refuge
May 19 – October 5, 1771

"I will lift up mine eyes unto the hills,
from whence cometh mine help."
Psalm 121:1

## Three Days Later
### May 19, 1771
### Ayen Ford,
### North Carolina

## Twenty-Six

"You actually decided to move to the mountains if Alamance went awry?" Mitchell couldn't remember his brother ever even hinting at such a plan.

"It's not like that, Mitch. We didn't decide anything, and it didn't have anything to do with Alamance."

"What I heard at that prayer meeting just now sure didn't make it sound that way."

Robert pulled the meetinghouse door shut and fell into step beside Mitchell. "We've discussed for years what we would do if things never got better, or if the governor ever mustered the militia against us and Ayen Ford was no longer safe for men with families. And yes, moving farther west did come up in the discussion. Yes, we did lay plans for what to do in that case. But we never made any official decision. And we had no idea the Alamance meeting would escalate the way it did, or that Tryon would start a march of terror the way he has, or that we would be right in range of his return trip the way we are. Which is why, right now, no one knows what the next step should be."

"But the plans are in place if you chose to move."

Robert said shortly, "Yes. If."

Mitchell moved a step closer to Robert so Gunning

could move up beside them. Hank Jonas, bringing up the rear with a slight limp, said, "Well, it ain't as if you've got much time."

"I think it's a good idea," Mitchell said. "All around my place is free country. Your whole church would be safe—"

Robert did not look at him. "You're going back to what you said about bringing my people to the mountains with me. Like Moses, you said."

"I was thinking more along the lines of 'When they persecute you in this city, flee ye into another.'"

Robert said slowly, "God wanted me here and I left when I should have stayed..."

"You without your people and you *with* your people are two different things, Rob."

"I know."

"Do you?"

They slowed as they neared the house. Robert said, "It's not as easy as it sounds, Mitch."

"'With God all things are possible.'"

"'Thou shalt not tempt the Lord thy God.'" Robert was fighting fire with fire.

Behind them Hank Jonas said, "You boys even argue like preachers."

Mitchell held the door open and said, "'Behold, the LORD's hand is not shortened, that it cannot save.'"

Robert said, "The Lord expects us to be sensible."

"Now that's stretching it," Gunning said. "I don't recall seeing that 'un any place a' *tall* in the Good Book, no sir."

Mitchell shut the door and shrugged out of his coat. "If what the Lord has called us to do thus far is anywhere near sensible, I'm missing something."

Robert held up the hand that was not holding Cricket. "I admit, that was unscriptural. But Mitch, I—"

Magdalen appeared from the bedroom, her finger over her lips. "Susanna's asleep. How was the meeting?"

"No answers," Robert said. "Other than the ones Mitch thinks he has."

Mitchell wheeled. "You don't have any alternative, Rob. You've said that yourself."

"But to ask everyone to just up and leave." Robert's voice began to carry a stubborn edge. "What about Caleb Thurmond? Elsie wouldn't go without him, and Saul wouldn't go without Elsie. Caleb may be stronger than he was two months ago, but don't try to tell me he would make a trip like that. And Woodbridges—so soon after losing John. I will not ask them to leave everything for no one knows what."

"Better they stay here and face everyone knows what, is that it?" Mitchell turned away and hung up his coat. Have *mercy*, Rob could be bullheaded sometimes. "More of what's happened to you and John Woodbridge and Bobby Thompson and Geoffrey Sheridan and—"

"At least Geoff's safe now, more or less." Robert paused, then went on, his voice suddenly quieter. "And so is John, I reckon. Safer than he's ever been before."

"I hope you're not saying you want to stay put just to see how fast you can get to heaven," Mitchell said grimly.

"I'm not saying *anything*." Robert rubbed his face tiredly. "I've not thought of anything worth saying yet."

"You been fightin' a war," Hank said shortly.

Magdalen slipped in close beside Robert, one hand moving to gently rub his back. "Give yourself a night to just rest, Rob. Anyone would need that, after what you've had to see."

"If I only knew what to do." Robert reached over his shoulder and took Magdalen's hand. "Moving everybody is a decision I'm not ready to make."

"*You're* not moving them," Gunning pointed out. "It's got to be their decision. You can tell folks what you think is best but you can't make 'em do it. Especially not this lot of folks. Guess Tryon learned that his own way."

"We would have to be so sure," Robert said wearily.

"Well, if there's one thing I've learned," Mitchell said, "and I'm sure you have too, it's that when God wants you to do something, you'll be sure." He put a hand on Robert's other shoulder, feeling tightly knotted muscle. For the first time he realized his brother was unutterably weary. Right now Rob didn't need someone telling him how to fix things. He just needed some quiet assurance. "You may think it's insane and it may scare you to death. But you will *know*."

It took Jacob Chauncy three passes up and down the street before he worked up the nerve to cross over and approach the Baptist meetinghouse. Charles Drake would be back soon, and Chauncy suspected Drake would not be pleased with the trivial information Chauncy could give him. Chauncy had slipped into a prayer meeting two weeks ago, but he had been met with a blend of friendliness and suspicion that disconcerted him more than the knowledge was worth. He hadn't tried again since; mostly he had gleaned what he could as an outsider looking in. Drake thought it was all so simple. You already know what these people believe; you become one of them and find out more.

But Chauncy knew what *he* would think if Robert Boothe suddenly started seeking entry into the vestry's business meetings. Imposter, Chauncy would call him. Liar.

Which was exactly what he was calling himself. But Drake had been emphatic. Find out what Boothe's next move will be. You don't dare get close enough? Start daring.

Chauncy had mounted the first step before he was fully aware of the broad-shouldered, tautly muscled man standing in the shadow just to one side of the door, rifle stock resting on the ground in front of him and both hands clasped lightly around the barrel. "Evening, vestryman."

Chauncy stopped mid-step, knowing he had seen this man before. In a courtroom, that was where. Standing trial. So why did Chauncy feel like *he* was the one on trial? "You're Alexander Perry. Alec, Boothe calls you. The one charged with—what was it?"

"That depends on who you talk to." Perry's voice was a lazy drawl, but his eyes were hard and alert, openly taking

Chauncy's measure. "Drake called it 'gross violation of governmental privacy.' Me, I call it fair play. You looking for someone?"

"I'd—like to speak to Reverend Boothe."

"He's busy."

Alec's laconic tone left no room for argument. Chauncy said, "Are you a member of his—" He paused.

"Church," Alec supplied.

"I was going to say congregation."

"His congregation is a church if there ever was one," Alec said. "And no, I'm not anything. Not anything but one halfway decent man looking out for a much better one."

"You're standing guard."

Alec shrugged, letting Chauncy draw his own conclusions. Chauncy motioned to the door behind Alec and tried again. "I was wondering why Boothe's—*church* is meeting. On a Tuesday night."

Alec lifted the rifle and cradled it in his arms. "Mr. Chauncy, you're the head of the vestry, am I right?"

"You are."

"And your vestry, do you ever disagree?"

"Of course." Chauncy had no desire to tell this man just how often that was.

"And what happens then?"

"We vote. The majority carries the day. That's business."

Alec's tight flicker of smile did not reach the gunmetal gray of his eyes. "And that's why, Chauncy, you'd never understand why those folks are meeting tonight. Even if I told you."

Robert had been pleased but a little puzzled when Alec chose to stay after the rest of his group had gone home. But then, if what Alec had said was true, he did not really have a home to go to. His verbal fencing match with Jacob Chauncy carried clearly from outside, and Robert figured Alec could hold his own against anyone, including a spy for the other side. Which Robert suspected Chauncy of being.

You never knew who you could trust these days, and regardless of the many discussions they had had in the past, Robert did not trust Jacob Chauncy.

The voices faded and Robert put his mind back on the meeting. Mitchell had just finished the opening prayer Robert had asked him to offer, and they were waiting for Robert to say something.

"Whatever we do next," he said, "we'll do together. There are no unimportant members in the body of Christ. We'll make a decision only when prayer has brought us to a place of unity."

He was not going to mention the possibility, *im*possibility was more like it, of moving the whole church west. Let the other men speak first; then maybe he would bring it up. Maybe.

Caleb Thurmond cleared his throat. Robert looked his way. "It's good to see you here, Caleb."

"I'd get up, but I'm thinking that's not a good plan," Caleb said with a grimace. His leg had been bad enough Sunday he'd had to leave church early. Robert had not expected him at the meeting tonight, but Caleb had the grimly determined look of a man willing to bear what he had to bear for a bigger cause. He shifted his weight a little and said, "Elsie and I got to talking with Saul last night . . . You remember those days when we talked about pulling up stakes and starting over someplace wide open and free?"

There was a moment of utter silence. Robert looked sharply at Mitchell, thinking, Did someone tell Thurmonds what we talked about? Mitchell shook his head; it hadn't been him.

"I remember," Robert said slowly.

Deacon Ashe spoke from across the room. "There's a verse I read in Genesis this morning, where God tells Abraham 'Get thee out of thy country, unto a land that I will show thee.' Now I'm not claiming God said that to anyone but Abraham. I'm not claiming He's saying it to us. But it got me to studying."

Ethan Hardy said, "The same idea crossed my mind last night. But I woke up thinking I'd not say anything about it, because it's not the sort of thing a man takes serious-like. Even if we did sort of make plans for it, back in the day."

"It'd not be easy," Robert said after a pause. "Not easy at all."

Caleb said, "We weren't thinking it'd be easy, Pastor."

Robert looked at him. "Whose idea was this, Caleb, yours? Or Elsie's? Or Saul's, for that matter."

"It was all of ours," Caleb said. "That's the way families work, ain't it?"

"Look, Caleb, I don't think any of you realize how hard it would be."

Caleb leaned forward, his eyes intense. "I know how hard it would be, Pastor. I've done my share of traveling. I fought the wind and the rain and the land and I carved out a home, *here*, when there wasn't much here but me and the girl I married. And I know what it's like to want that home to be safe. I know what it's like to want a place where you can worship God and work with your own hands. And I'm willing to fight all North Carolina to do it again."

"Are you willing to fight the Cherokee?" Robert said sharply.

"All North Carolina, I said," Caleb said steadily. "If the Cherokee are in North Carolina, that means them too."

No one said anything for a long moment. Robert thought, How do you argue with passion like that?

The silence stretched another beat. Then Caleb said, "I know. It's crazy. But it's my heart."

Mitchell said, "I don't think it's crazy at all."

This whole thing is crazy, Robert thought. Either crazy or the hand of God. Or both.

But Mitchell was not finished. "Matter of fact, me and Rob had the same thought."

Hardy said, "Why didn't you say nothin' right off?"

"I was waiting for confirmation," Robert said. The room suddenly seemed charged with an unseen spark. He glanced from Saul to Caleb, from Deacon Ashe to Ethan Hardy, and said, "It looks like I got it."

Robert did not know how to tell Magdalen about the discussion. So it was just as well that Mitchell walked in the door and said, "Tell Rob to tell me I'm brilliant, Maggie."

"Rob, tell Mitch he's brilliant," Magdalen said, "and what are you talking about?"

Robert shot Mitchell a look known only to older siblings. "Caleb and Saul and Deacon Ashe and Ethan Hardy all think we should move to the mountains."

"Did I mention that I think so, too?" Mitchell put in.

Magdalen looked straight at Robert. "What do *you* think, Rob?"

He took a deep breath. "I think," he said slowly, "that if I had wanted a clear answer, it couldn't get much clearer than having Caleb Thurmond bring up the idea of his own accord. The one man I thought would never be able to make it and wouldn't want to try. We'll have another couple of meetings, one for the men and one for everyone, before we make any decision. I told the men it won't be easy. They don't seem to care."

"Nothing worth having comes easy," Magdalen said.

He had not expected that. He would have thought she'd be the last one to agree with his men, because it meant going back to what they had left behind. The mountain country, free, open, wild. And heartbreaking.

But the fact was, she *had* agreed. Now he was mightnigh the only one who hadn't. He wanted to do this, *ached* to do it, to go back to the mountains. That was what scared him—that the decision might be based in his will and not God's. Alamance had shaken him, shaken him down deep. But he could not deny the Lord's leading. And even in his fear, he could not deny his own heart's certainty.

*It's time.*

# Twenty-Seven

SUSANNA KNELT IN THE BACKYARD NEXT TO Gunning's woodpile, being careful to keep her dress smoothed down like Mama said ladies did. She pushed a little pile of dirt together and patted some blades of grass over it. That was a mountain. She would build a house on the mountain out of Gunning's wood chips. Gunning made beautiful wood chips for building houses.

Feet tramped noisily through the yard and she looked up. Benjamin Woodbridge had come in. "Is your pa in the house, Susie?"

"Don't call me Susie." She felt sorry for Benjamin because his papa had just died, but he was an awful tease sometimes. He *knew* she didn't like to be called Susie. She had told him before.

Benjamin did not apologize, which wasn't very nice, but at least he didn't call her Susie again just to annoy her. "Just tell me if he's here. His brother wants to know what needs packing at the church."

"He's talking to Mama. In the kitchen."

Benjamin banged through the back door and Susanna went back to her house on the mountain. They were all going to go live in the mountains, Mama and Papa had said so. Mama said mountains had lots of trees. Maybe leaves would do, stuck straight up on their stems . . .

"What are you building, little lady?"

Susanna looked up again. A man was standing by the fence watching her. Susanna knew who he was; his name was Mr. Chauncy and he talked with Papa a lot, in big words like *atonement* and *sanctification*. She stood up and tucked her dirty hands behind her. "It's a house on a mountain. Sir," she added, remembering her manners.

"That is exactly what it looks like," Mr. Chauncy said, bending over for a better look. Susanna would not have thought a grown-up man would be interested in dirt and wood chips.

"Not *exactly*," she said, because it was important to be honest. "But it's hard to make it just right."

"Well, you do your best." Mr. Chauncy straightened up. "But why aren't you helping your mother? Isn't she busy? Everyone seems busy lately."

"Yes, sir, she's busy. But she doesn't need me right now; she's talking to Papa."

"Oh, I see." Mr. Chauncy paused. "What is your papa doing these days?"

"A lot of things," Susanna said. "Mostly right now he's telling his men what to do. My papa is good at that. He's good at everything. That's why all the men like him. Only not everybody likes him. Mr. Drake doesn't like him. Do you know Mr. Drake?"

Mr. Chauncy's neck got kind of red around his fancy neck ruffle, the same color Saul's neck got when he was talking about Elsie. Mr. Chauncy said, "Yes. That is—yes, I do."

Mr. Chauncy must not like Mr. Drake either. "Well, Papa says folks like Mr. Drake are mean because they want to be, not because God makes them that way. But Papa says Mr. Drake won't bother us very long."

Mr. Chauncy looked uncomfortable. Perhaps his neck ruffle was too tight. "What else does your papa say?"

"Oh, that everyone needs to work together, and that

sometimes God uses people to do His work for Him. Sometimes Papa uses words I don't understand, like—" What was it that Papa had said was every man's right but not an option this time? "Words like *self-defense*. And *cooperation*. And he says—"

The door banged. "Susanna!"

Susanna turned around. Papa and Benjamin were both frowning, but Papa was frowning at Mr. Chauncy and Benjamin was frowning at her.

"You can't just go around telling everybody everything," Benjamin hissed.

"I wasn't telling everybody everything," Susanna shot back. "Only Mr. Chauncy, and only what he asked."

"You still ought to've known better," Benjamin said, as if that settled it.

Papa was over by the fence, talking to Mr. Chauncy. "Far as I can see, Chauncy, there's only one reason for you to look nervous talking to a child, and that's a guilty conscience. I know what you're after, and you're welcome to come to our Sunday meetings or our prayer meetings anytime and learn all you care to learn." He was using his quiet-angry voice now. "But *stay away from my daughter!*"

"See?" Benjamin whispered. "That's why you shouldn't tell folks things. You're too little to know what they're after."

"I am *not* little," Susanna said. "And I don't believe *you* know what Mr. Chauncy's after, either, even if Papa does."

Benjamin scowled fiercely at her. She made a face at him, remembering too late that ladies did not make faces at boys. But she felt triumphant because Benjamin had not answered her. He might be almost a man grown, now that he was twelve, but he did *not* know *everything*.

When Charles Drake rode into town on Saturday afternoon, Chauncy had his report ready, complete with a verbatim account of his conversation with Susanna Boothe. When Chauncy had finished, Drake said, "You look upset."

"Of course I'm upset. Have you any idea how it feels to

use a seven-year-old girl as a source against her own father?"

"What ought to upset you," Drake said, "is the information you now have. You do realize we have another possible insurrection on our hands."

"The girl said nothing about an insurrection."

"Chauncy, you're being naïve. The references to self-defense, cooperation, and Boothe's telling his men what to do, all combined, hint at that very possibility. Not to mention Boothe's claim that I'll not bother them much longer."

"I imagine you take exception to that."

"You imagine right." Drake shifted his position, and Chauncy became disturbingly aware of the sword hilt on Drake's left side. "It is a happy coincidence that I have help coming tonight, and an even happier coincidence that extra funds made it possible."

"Extra funds?" Chauncy stared at him, seeing pieces fall together. He had not been able to reconcile the vestry's accounts in weeks. "Dare I think—"

"Do us all a favor and leave the thinking to me." Drake rose. "Get Ebeniah Kendall for me. I will *crush* those rebels. And I'll do it better than Governor Tryon did."

# Twenty-Eight

ALEC PERRY HAD MADE A BUSINESS OF AVOIDING organized religion. Or any religion at all, for that matter, besides a vague belief in a higher power and a general sense of good and evil. His first memory of anything connected with religion was being eight years old and watching his Irish Catholic mother argue with his British Anglican father. That was thirty years ago now, and the bitter hypocrisy still disgusted him. His next brush with religion had been the Quakers down the road, whom he had regarded with neighborly indifference until an Indian attack came and the men refused to fight back. Alec had been so sickened that it was years before he could speak to a Quaker without seeing the senseless capture of the families next door. What man who loved God and had any decency could stand by and let the Cherokee take his children?

After he'd set out to seek his fortune, Alec had run into men and women who believed everything from the most orthodox of Anglican doctrine to the most mongrelized of free thinking. A few had been genuine. Many had been frauds. And most had tried to convert him. Alec had learned to see it coming and steer clear. The only man who had ever dented the armor was an Anson County preacher who still haunted him and whom he would just as soon forget.

So he was not sure just why he had asked to stay with Robert Boothe's church on its exodus west, instead of moving on to the next challenge. He told himself it was because there were a lot of gullible sheep in that church who needed someone to look out for them.

But he knew, if he'd said that out loud, he would have laughed at himself. Because there were men in that church he wouldn't like to square off with. Boothe himself was head of the list. Not explosive, not aggressive, not even particularly outspoken, but a man who would hold his own against all comers. He had not hesitated to explain his version of church authority to Alec, but it hadn't been an argument waiting to happen. Matter-of-fact, almost, as if Alec could take it or leave it but Boothe would not change. Maybe that was it, Alec thought. Robert Boothe was a man he could respect, if not agree with. There was something very real about Boothe and his people. Alec aimed to get close enough to find out if they were as real as they looked.

And no, he thought grimly as he packed his bags, it didn't hurt that there might be a good fight waiting in the offing.

Saturday night. The time to departure could almost be counted in hours now. Come Monday dawn, sixty-nine Baptists and one self-proclaimed skeptic would be on their way out of Ayen Ford. The church had prayed for three days solid before making the decision to leave. Just where they were going, they still did not know. Mitchell had ideas, but they were long on theory and short on details. Mitchell could be that way sometimes.

Still, Mitchell had been right in one thing: If the idea was of God, Robert would *know*. And Robert knew.

He had been a little surprised when Alec actually asked if he could join the exodus, instead of simply telling Robert he was coming. Robert had done his best to explain that the church of the Lord Jesus Christ was a living thing before

God, and Alec, as an unbeliever, could not be a true member of Christ's body. Whether or not Alec understood that, he had seemed to grasp the authority structure. Robert had assigned him to advance scouting detail with Mitchell and Hank. An interesting combination, Magdalen had said. Aye, Robert had agreed, but it would keep them out of trouble.

He stepped into a bedroom that had been stripped down to bare last-minute necessities and a few larger items that would have to be left behind. The whole house had a hollow, forlorn look to it. Other houses around town looked the same way. All that could be packed had been packed. Tomorrow was the Lord's day. And after that—

"I don't know if I'll sleep much this next night or two," Magdalen said with a small laugh.

"We'll be awake together, then." Robert glanced through the bedroom doorway. Mitchell and Alec were both rolled in blankets on the kitchen floor, neither one showing any signs of life. Hank and Gunning had already bedded down in the stable, within earshot of any trouble with the team or the wagon that stood just outside the back door. Robert eased the bedroom door shut. "I doubt I'll sleep either. Unlike—" he jerked his head toward the kitchen "—certain other folks."

He sat down on his side of the bed. "Caleb Thurmond's splint was due to come off tonight. I probably ought to have gone over there."

Magdalen pulled the last few pins from her hair and dropped them into the small wooden box Robert had carved for her during a long winter in the mountains. "You'll see him tomorrow at church."

Robert did not bother to mention how his mind would be on other things by tomorrow. Which would come much too soon, and not soon enough.

"I'm sorry you've got so much on your mind, Rob."

"Aren't *you* worried, Maggie? I mean, when you think what we're fixing to do."

"Not if I'm with you," she said.

He was framing a response when a distant, cautious knock interrupted him. A grunt came from the kitchen, followed by the soft sound of a falling blanket, and then Alec said through the bedroom door, "You want us to get that?"

"I'm coming." Robert took the candle Magdalen held out and opened the door.

As dead as Alec had looked a few minutes ago, he did not look now as if he had even begun to drift off. His hair, muted from copper to brown in the dim light, was still in its loose queue and the only changes in his clothing were his missing waistcoat and open collar. Mitchell, on the other hand, was on his feet but most definitely not awake. Dark hair splayed in all directions, his shirt was half in and half out, and he tried unsuccessfully to smother a yawn. Robert immediately wrote him off as possible help should the man at the door be someone like—Charles Drake.

But then, Drake would not have bothered to knock. Robert edged the door open and was instantly on his guard. "It's past ten o'clock, Chauncy."

"I know. Just let me in." Jacob Chauncy darted a glance over his shoulder as if expecting an army to descend upon him. Robert pulled the door open a little farther and the vestryman slipped inside. Alec reached for his rifle. Robert moved between Alec and Chauncy as Mitchell, looking suddenly more alert, moved between Chauncy and the door.

Robert said, "This had best be important."

"Drake is back, and he's dead set on believing you're starting another insurrection." Chauncy sounded halfway between unnerved and outright angry. "He's only waiting for his reinforcements. He won't listen to reason and it's my fault. I'll not keep quiet any longer—"

Robert cut him off. "When?"

Chauncy looked away. "I don't know. Perhaps during your service tomorrow. But his men arrive in an hour. Maybe two."

Alec exploded. "You think your telling us now makes any difference?"

Robert said sharply, "Perry!"

Alec subsided. Chauncy glanced over his shoulder again. "If he finds out I told you—"

"Then you'd better go right quick," Robert said. "And Jacob, whatever he's got on you, remember—the truth will hold its own. And the truth will make you free."

He thought he heard Chauncy say, "Too late." But then the door was shut and the man was gone.

Mitchell, fully awake now, said, "Rob, an hour's hardly enough time to—"

"It'll have to be," Robert said grimly. "Alec, get Hank and ride out to Hardy's barn. Mitch, follow them out and give the word to every family between here and there, and then meet up with Hank and Alec at the barn. Send Gunning in here and we'll warn the rest. Thirty minutes to finish loading, thirty to hitch up and get out of town. Pray God holds Drake's men off that long. Go!"

# Twenty-Nine

THE WAGONS GATHERED AT ETHAN HARDY'S barn with very little left of the time Chauncy had estimated. The advance scouts were there. So was Robert's family, Gunning included. Woodbridges, Ashes, Hardys . . .

Robert finished the check, came up short, said sharply to Mitchell, "Where are Saul and the Thurmonds?"

"They should be here; Gunning warned them." Mitchell paused. "Didn't he?"

"I thought you had," Gunning said. "They were along your path to—"

"But I took the back way, and I thought—"

"Never mind," Robert cut in. "Mitch, you and Hank and Alec ride out. Lead west a quarter mile to the fork. Take the north side onto the side trail, not the main road where Drake's men will come in. Keep everybody on that side road and wait for us there. Gunning, take our wagon. You hear me, Mitch? North side of the fork."

Alec was the one who said, "North side, Captain."

"Mitch, you lead in prayer," Robert said. "Then get out of town."

Mitchell nodded and Robert wheeled Wanderer around and took the main road at a near gallop. A light was still glowing in Thurmonds' window when Robert reached the house. He swung out of the saddle and rapped sharply at the door. A shadow moved against the light of the window and Saul opened the door a few inches. Robert shouldered inside and shut the door. "I hope you don't mind my asking why you're in Elsie's kitchen at eleven o'clock at night, Saul."

"It's Caleb's leg," Saul said in a low voice. "That doctor is an *idiot*. He didn't set the bone fast enough nor straight enough, and it's healed sort of crooked-like. He made Caleb walk on it and Caleb like to passed out from the pain. Doc says he can't do anything for him without breaking it again. Caleb can't sleep, so of course Elsie can't sleep, so I stayed to talk things over—"

"Let me see him."

Saul led the way to the bedroom. Elsie stood to one side, looking worn to a thread. Caleb was propped up on a pillow, his face locked in a determined grimace of pain. Before Robert could say anything, Caleb pushed himself upright and said, "If you're here at this time of night, it can't be good."

"It's not." Caleb's businesslike approach erased whatever sympathy Robert might have voiced. There was no time for sympathy. "Drake's got reinforcements coming any minute and we've got to be gone by morning."

Elsie said, "By *morning*?"

"If you have anything left to pack, pack it." Robert looked back at Caleb. "If you're sure you want to go."

"I'm going," Caleb said through his teeth.

Robert had expected no less. "Elsie, have the boys help you load. Saul, help me get Caleb out there, and then bring over anything from your place that needs to go. And all of you—pray."

Elsie set her lips firmly and packed. Robert and Saul settled Caleb in the bed of the wagon, on a straw tick braced on all sides by assorted household goods. Saul tucked a few of his own belongings in the cracks, then came around the other side to help Robert pull the canvas cover tight over the wagon bows. Robert said, low, "Can I count on you to take charge of Thurmonds while Caleb's down?"

Saul said, "Long as Elsie lets me."

"Any reason why she shouldn't?"

Saul's voice dropped. "When we found out about Caleb's leg, I said we should have wed before now, and I wanted us to get married after church tomorrow, so's I could have the right before God and ever'body to take care of her and Caleb. But Elsie said, not with Caleb like he is, that's where her heart is right now. Then I said I thought he should get it broke again and get it over with, and—I shouldn't have said that."

"I reckon not," Robert said, giving the canvas a final tug. "But I want her and Caleb and the boys safe as much as you do. So help them whether Elsie lets you or not."

Saul nodded, a quick, abrupt motion. "I love her, Pastor. I'm not ashamed to say so. I just don't do so good at showing it sometimes."

"Well, now's your chance to prove it. Go tell her it's time to go."

Saul went to the door and leaned in. "Elsie, you ready?"

"I think so." Elsie came to the door, holding a basket in one hand and guiding a sleepy younger brother with the other. "Are all the other boys out there? I don't see Owen."

"Over here," Saul said, pointing.

Elsie pulled her shawl closer and squared her shoulders. "I'm ready."

Saul gave her a hand up into the wagon. Robert lifted six-year-old Abner in after her. "I'll ride out ahead of you, Saul. Follow me close, but not too close. If there's trouble coming, I'll warn you in time for you to drop back."

Saul gave a tense nod and Robert mounted up, settled his rifle across his pommel, and rode out to the edge of the street. The way was clear, and his quick signal brought a low "Giddap" from Saul.

Robert kept a watchful eye on Drake's rented house as they passed it. Lamplight burned low in a few windows, but the house remained quiet. A steady creak behind Robert indicated that Saul was following according to instructions. At the edge of town, near Ethan Hardy's barn, Robert caught a new sound over the creaking of the wagon.

Horses. A lot of them. Coming straight into town.

Robert halted Wanderer and motioned Saul to stop alongside. "That'll be Drake's men," Robert said grimly. "Now they won't know me from Adam, but anyone's bound to ask questions about a wagon packed like this at nigh on to midnight. Pull around behind Hardy's barn there, out of sight. I'll handle Drake's men. Once they're well past, head out of town. Don't wait for me. Take the north fork a quarter mile out and you'll find the rest of our folk."

Saul said, "Yessir, but—"

"No time," Robert said. "Go."

The team plodded on and the wagon creaked its way out of sight behind Hardy's barn. At least it *had* been Hardy's barn. Robert reckoned it was free for the taking now.

He pulled his tricorne down over his eyes, a motion that, back in his circuit-riding days, would have meant he was headed into Indian country, riding with the wind in his face, relishing the danger. Tonight the rush came back with a strength he had not felt in so long it half scared him.

He took the main road out of town at an easy trot. Hoofbeats drummed louder until Robert could make out the riders. Twenty, twenty-five men maybe. Hard to tell in the dark, but that would work both ways. Robert hailed them as if he'd been waiting for them. One man answered him and Robert rode closer. "You boys here for the colonel?"

"Yes, if that's Colonel Drake you're meaning."

"You're in the right place. I'll show you the way."

The leader came up alongside Robert and the rest fell in behind. Robert led them down the main road to the corner by the meetinghouse. The man said, "You're one of his men?"

"We met the very day he arrived as emissary of His Excellency," Robert said. He was thinking of that first meeting

Drake had helped Sheriff Kendall break up. But these men did not need to know that. Just as they did not need to know that most of this route they were taking was highly unnecessary. Robert paused on the next corner and pointed to his own freshly abandoned dwelling, buying time any way he could. "That frame house there belongs to Robert Boothe. Drake's sure to tell you about him. Worst rebel dissenter in these parts." At least Drake thought so. And he was probably right. "The livery stable is on down around this way."

He led the way around another corner and past Deacon Ashe's general store. He stopped again in front of a large, squat building. "You've got how many horses?"

"Twenty-four," the leader said, glancing around. "How long will this take? I don't like to keep the colonel waiting."

"There's no cause to fret," Robert said cheerfully. "It's just a matter of waking the liveryman, is all."

A lusty pounding at the door, however, failed to bring forth the liveryman. Robert saw no need to mention that the livery owner was a good friend of his and was currently waiting on the north fork in a wagon packed with his family and all his worldly goods. Mentally Robert calculated the passage of time, thinking that Saul must surely have gotten that wagon out of town by now. Robert would have preferred to direct Drake's men down another side street with vague instructions about taking a right to the second house on the left, but these men were treating him like a bona fide escort. If Robert was going to keep up that perception, he would have to lead them right to the door.

He turned away from the livery stable and gave an apologetic shrug. "I'll take you to the colonel. He'll be more than able to direct you regarding your horses. And as you say, it's best not to keep him waiting."

Robert took the party around the corner onto the main road, past Thurmonds' darkened dwelling, past the sheriff's house, up to the quarters Drake was renting. Dim light still showed in several windows and Robert thought he saw Sheriff Kendall's horse tethered near the back. He said,

"This is the place. He's expecting you; go on in."

The leader dismounted and Robert edged Wanderer to the side, not wanting to appear too eager to slip away. It was hard to act as if he had all night when sixty-nine people were waiting for him on the north fork. Make that sixty-one—Saul and the Thurmonds were likely still en route.

The leader knocked instead of walking straight in as Robert had said. Robert edged a little farther away. Drake himself opened the door and Robert realized too late that his move toward retreat had placed him in the lamp glow spilling from the doorway. Directly in the light, a clear figure on horseback, a little apart from the rest of the men. Three reasons for Drake to see him, recognize him, and order him shot.

Drake's eyes flashed over and met Robert's own. Robert gently lifted his hat. Then he spun Wanderer about, set his spurs, and headed for the north fork, leaving a trail too winding to follow, riding with the wind in his face.

#  Thirty

"Kendall, if you're joking, I'll have you reprimanded by the governor himself."

The sheriff shook his head emphatically. "No joke, sir. They're gone. All of them. Hitched up their wagons and left."

It was bad enough to have his sworn enemy politely tip his hat and ride off into the night, but Drake had not bothered to look for him simply because Boothe would get what he deserved soon enough, when Drake surrounded his meetinghouse on Sunday morning and demanded surrender. Now here it was Sunday morning and Kendall was saying neither Boothe nor any of his people were anywhere to be seen. "Why didn't you stop them?"

Kendall looked slightly exasperated. "How could I have stopped them when I didn't know? Sir, I think they've been planning to run like this ever since Alamance."

"That's insane," Drake said. "No one tries to move seventy people on a week's notice. Get the men in order. We're giving chase."

His force was not large, as far as the numbers. But they were all well-armed and primed with fearsome tales of Regulator cruelty, carefully crafted and spread by Drake and others like him. Their brief experience with Robert

Boothe the night before had convinced them of the Regulators' capacity for trickery. Not to mention, these men had been paid far too well for them to be unreliable now. Drake smiled thinly at the remembrance of Jacob Chauncy's outrage when the vestryman had learned how his vestry funds had been used. Chauncy had been absurdly easy to deceive.

Ebeniah Kendall reported that the wagon train had moved due west. The men were ready. Drake rode to the head of the column and began to issue orders.

"As soon as we come within range, spread out and surround them. If anyone runs or resists, fire without compunction. Kendall and I will—"

"Drake, what do you think you're doing?"

At the new voice Drake wheeled his horse around sharply. He would personally *crush* anyone who dared speak to him that way—

Malcolm Harrod. Second in command to the governor himself. The one man Drake did not want to see right now, and the one man he could do nothing to punish.

And if Malcolm Harrod had come all the way from Hillsborough, something was very wrong.

Harrod rode up beside Drake. "You have no authority for an act such as this. Tell your men to disperse."

"You're mad," Drake hissed at him. "I'm on the verge of ending this once and for all."

Harrod's gaze was ice. "Correction. You're on the verge of a court-martial. Cease and desist, and have your men do the same. That's an order."

Drake lost the staredown and gave the command. The band began to dissolve. Drake said, "Harrod, what *is* this?"

Harrod gave him what passed for a smile. "Trust me, you really don't want me to answer that in the midst of a public street. We'll go to your quarters and discuss it there."

Drake fully understood his lack of choice in the matter. Understood it and hated it. He buried his smoldering rage as best he could and led Harrod to his rented dwelling. Once in his study, Drake did not bother to offer Harrod a chair, nor to take one himself. "Harrod, what *possibly* brings you all the way from Hillsborough, now, today?"

"The fear of something just such as this," Harrod said laconically.

"Such as what?"

Harrod waved at the window. "Making a fool of yourself, launching a militant strike without orders. It's fortunate I arrived when I did. His Excellency heard of the reinforcements you were gathering and found intervention advisable."

"The rebels are within my reach," Drake snapped. "All of them. I would have been the toast of Governor Tryon and all his supporters, had you not interfered."

"Let me tell you something, Colonel." Harrod was unmoved by Drake's ire. "You think you are here solely to win the governor's favor and advance your career. You are not. You are here because someone was needed here, and because His Excellency is heartily sick of having you in his sight."

"How dare you—"

"Spare me, Colonel. I daresay he doesn't care who you seize or what havoc you wreak, as long as he is not bothered with you. But this, what you are attempting without his approval, this could begin another war—after he has just ended the last one. He could not care less about the rebels themselves, women and children notwithstanding. But His Excellency is a military man who expects his men to operate under his orders. You are not under orders for military action. After this you'll be fortunate to have any orders at all."

Drake ground out, "It would have been over before you ever came, had they not had warning."

"Then find the man who warned them, and vent your wrath on him," Harrod said. "Send him to languish in a Hillsborough prison. Then at least the governor could put him to good use, telling what he knows. But you'll not become a political favorite by courting disaster. Or in any other way, for that matter. You've been a fly in His Excellency's ointment long enough."

Jacob Chauncy was on edge that night with a nameless fear. He could not have explained exactly why he had warned Robert Boothe. He was only sure he could not have lived with himself otherwise. And after the way Drake had confiscated the vestry funds to pay his men, Chauncy was too angry to care what Drake told the other vestrymen. Besides, Chauncy had told himself, Drake would never know who had sounded the warning. If only he could make himself believe that . . .

Which was why Chauncy was still awake at midnight, sitting up in his study and trying to distract himself with a book, when the front door splintered in.

Chauncy came to his feet, panic rising in his throat. Deliberately he forced it down and laid his book on the desk. He had taken the risk. There was nothing he could do now but pay the price.

He blew out the candle and stepped into the front room. Sheriff Kendall's torch flung a harsh glare on the walls. In the half-shadow Colonel Drake's eyes were darker than ever.

"What do you want, Colonel?" Chauncy asked quietly, taking some small consolation in the careful steadiness of his voice.

"Do you *know* what you've cost me?" Rage hardened every line of Drake's chiseled features. "And do you know what it's going to cost *you*?"

"It's already cost all the funds our parish had!" Chauncy shot back. "What more can you do? I don't care what you tell my vestry." He really did not. Not anymore.

Drake gave a short laugh. "You fool, do you still think that's the only price you'll pay? Where I come from, we don't report traitors to their vestries."

"I've done nothing traitorous."

"Other than warn Boothe and his people of my plans."

So Drake knew. Cold fingers of fear closed around Chauncy's heart. "What if I did? Is that treason?"

"It's close enough." Drake closed in another step. "Did

you really think you would get by with it? *No one* gets by with *anything.*"

Chauncy did not know where he found the nerve to say, "Will you?"

Drake's sword hand reached, flashed, a backhanded blow with the flat of the blade. Chauncy stumbled to his knees.

"You deserve worse than that," Drake said, sheathing the sword. "Had you not turned coward, it would be Robert Boothe I'd have on his knees." He reached for the manacles Kendall held out. "As it is, I'll settle for you."

SOMEWHERE WEST
OF AYEN FORD

# Thirty-One

ELSIE THURMOND CAME AROUND THE FRONT OF the wagon and tilted her head. "Saul, what are you doing?"

"Driving your wagon," he said, resisting the urge to say, What does it look like?

"You've driven our wagon for the last two days."

"I know."

She waited for him to go on, but he didn't. Then she let out an exasperated breath and said, "Saul, I know how to drive a wagon."

He said again, "I know."

"And so do the boys."

"I know." He couldn't help a grin.

She paused again, doubtless waiting for him to get off the wagon seat. Saul didn't budge. She said, a bit pointedly, "You ought to have your own wagon to handle."

"I don't have enough to warrant my own wagon. You know that." Saul refused to let himself think how much fun it was to see Elsie feisty. Better to focus on the orders Pastor Boothe had given him. Saul had been exempted from any duty that might take him outside camp, just so he could stay and watch over Elsie. And her family, too, of course.

Her voice turned plaintive. "There are so many other

things you're needed for, Saul. I want to do my part."

"Pastor's orders," Saul said. "You'll have to talk to him. Besides, you're already doing your part. Just being here. You know, with me. And the boys. And everything."

How she could smile at that clumsy string of words was a mystery, but she did. He hoped she wasn't only amused by his awkwardness.

"You're sure you don't mind," she said, as if she was still afraid of keeping him from more important things.

"I don't mind."

"You're sure?"

"I'm sure." Elsie couldn't have stopped him anyway; he had to follow orders, but he liked to be her hero.

Despite heavy rain that turned lowlands to swamps and roads to mud, the wagons forded Deep River after only four days of travel. They were out of Sandy Creek country now, and much as Robert had enjoyed the friendships he'd made there, Sandy Creek would not be safe for a long time. All along the way were signs of looting and burning. Robert kept the men on the alert, knowing Tryon's army was somewhere on the road ahead of them, blazing a trail of destruction and reprisal. Rumor had it that Baptist communities were hit the hardest. Back in Ayen Ford, Drake's men were no doubt wreaking havoc of their own. There was no going back. But going forward was risky too.

On Sunday, a few miles from the Forks at Abbott's Creek, they camped for the day and held services as normally as possible. After supper, Robert called a meeting of his advance scouts. He did not want to ford Abbott's Creek until he knew what was on the other side.

Alec had made himself unofficial leader of the scouting detail, but from what Robert heard, Mitchell was the one who kept Alec and Hank from doing each other bodily harm. Hank had a way of speaking his mind. Alec had a way of not liking what Hank said.

"It'll take us 'most all day tomorrow to find out what's

over there," Mitchell said. "You can camp here tomorrow, or go as far as you feel safe. That's your choice. We'll meet up with you tomorrow night."

"Pervided we don't get ourselves captured by Indians or stragglers or nothin'," Hank interjected.

"I'm about half ready for you to get captured by Indians or stragglers or somethin'," Alec said out of the side of his mouth. "Not that they'd keep you long. Even Indians don't like to go deaf."

"Although they might find some interesting loot in your saddlebags," Mitchell said. "When's the last time you cleaned those out?"

"I don't," Hank said. "Not 'lessen I have to. The last time I did, I forgot to put something back and then I needed it and didn't have it. Let's see . . . that was sometime before I fell out of the tree."

"Fell out of the *tree*?" Alec repeated.

"That's all I had to say," Robert interrupted. "You boys had better turn in. Long day ahead of you tomorrow."

At the crack of dawn, Alec dragged Mitchell out of his blankets and together they dragged Hank out of his. Jerked venison and leftover cornbread did service as a quick breakfast, and then they headed out. They were across Abbott's Creek by midmorning.

"Don't take this wrong," Hank said. "But it's starting to feel mighty pointless. Ridin' out. Ridin' back. Ridin' out. Ridin' back. Not making much progress, you know?"

"You got a better way?" Mitchell asked.

"See, that's why I told you not to take it wrong," Hank complained. "I knowed you was gonna say that. 'Course I ain't got a better way. Just commenting, is all."

"You'd be a better scout if you'd quit your commenting and keep your eyes peeled for Indians," Alec said shortly.

"Obviously," Hank said, "you don't know nothin' about scouting. If there was Indians this far east, we'd have heard about it."

"If there are Indians this far east, they've already heard us coming," Alec deadpanned.

"So I like to talk," Hank retorted. "So there ain't no law against it."

"The Johnston Riot Act," Alec said. "You're a seditious meeting in and of yourself."

"All right, I'll shut up," Hank growled.

"I've heard the wind blow before," Alec said.

"What, you don't think I can?"

"You haven't yet!"

"Both of you, quiet," Mitchell said sharply. "Someone's coming."

Alec and Hank instantly went serious. Hank squinted into the distance and said, "He don't look like a militiaman. His horse is plumb wore down to whitleather. The governor's men would have better horses."

The rider drew closer and Mitchell said, "What he looks like is information."

Whoever or whatever the rider was, he saw them coming and made a break for it. But while his horse was not literally worn down to salted hide, the animal was not in its prime either. Catching up to the man was easy. Calming him down took a little more work.

"This horse is all I've got." The man was on the verge of panic. "I don't have much money, but you can have it all if you won't take my horse. Haven't you stragglers taken enough already?"

"Easy," Mitchell soothed. "We don't want your horse and we don't want your money and we're not stragglers. No cause to be skittish."

"With all that's happening around here, a man's got a right to be skittish," the man retorted.

"What's been happening?" Mitchell asked, as if he didn't know. Which to some extent was true. That was why they were here.

The man looked at him askance. "You can't be from around these parts if you're asking a question like that."

"We ain't," Hank said. Not using any more words than necessary, for once.

"All we've heard is, Tryon's on the warpath," Alec said, following Mitchell's lead. "He's been here? Already?"

"He's been at Jersey Settlement the last couple of days," the man said. "Ruined Ben Merrill's place. You know Ben Merrill?"

Mitchell knew Ben Merrill. A good Baptist and an outspoken Regulator. "Not well, but yes."

"They took him prisoner and seized his farm. Tryon's up Reedy Creek way now, heading farther north, I reckon. Or northwest, mayhap. His men are all over, raiding and burning and what have you. Nowhere this side of Abbott's Creek is safe. I'm on my way out right now if I can make it, and never been more thankful that I don't have a family."

Alec said in a strangely tight voice, "North or northwest, you say?"

"It's hard to know," the settler replied. "I've heard rumors of Bethabara next. But I've heard too many rumors to put much stock in any of 'em."

"How long is he in one place at a time?" Mitchell asked.

"No more'n a day or two, thank heaven. Only long enough to take what's worth taking. Then he's gone, off wreaking havoc somewhere else."

"Well, thank you kindly," Mitchell said. "And Godspeed to you in getting out of the country."

"If you're wise, you'll do the same," the man advised.

"We're working on that," Mitchell said with a wry grin. Us and sixty-seven others.

When the man was gone Mitchell said, "Heading north. Raiding and burning. And Merrill's—I knew Ben Merrill; he was a good man. It rankles me, thinking of Tryon just taking over his farm."

"A whole slew of things rankle me these days," Hank said. "Only I don't know what to do about 'em."

Alec stared at the horizon, seeming more disturbed than the circumstances dictated. After a long moment he said, "We go back and we tell your brother—what?"

Mitchell got the feeling that Alec already had the answer and was only asking to see if Mitchell measured up. "If it was me, I'd not ford Abbott's Creek at all yet."

"Neither would I," Alec said laconically. He seemed disengaged somehow, as if his mind was already on to the next challenge. A challenge he was not sharing with Mitchell. "We'd best head back now. No point in going any farther."

Robert listened to the scouts' report and called a meeting. He spread his rudimentary map out on the wagon seat and let Mitchell point out the spot where the scouts had met the settler. Mitchell recounted the exchange and Robert penciled a tiny X farther south, near the Forks at Abbott's Creek.

"That's about where Ben Merrill's place is, right there," he said. "Reedy Creek is up here. There's a small settlement nearby, with ties to the Moravians at Salem and Bethabara. I've preached at Reedy Creek once or twice, so I know the area, but I can't say for sure what the politics are like there. The Moravians in Bethabara favor the governor, on account of how he's granted them special privileges. They're legally recognized as a parish, so they don't have to pay vestry taxes, and they've all obtained the right to vote even though nary a one meets the landholding terms. They don't want to risk losing those privileges by opposing the governor."

Alec made a disgusted sound that expressed his opinion better than words. Robert added quickly, "To be fair, with those privileges they've had and the tight communities they're in, I don't know that the Moravians ever experienced the trouble we did with taxes and property and all. Maybe if they had they would understand us better. But as it is, their opinion of us isn't very high. Rightly so, maybe. Some of the Regulators around there are pretty belligerent."

"The kind you say give the rest of us a bad name," Saul McBraden put in.

"Exactly," Robert said. He eyed the map on the wagon seat. "We could be far more certain of the way if our map were more complete."

"What it needs is Tryon's movements, past, present, and future, outlined in red," Mitchell said.

"That would help," Robert agreed ruefully. He looked up at the men gathered around. "I think it's pretty clear that crossing Abbott's Creek right now would be foolhardy. Turning to the south takes us away from Tryon, but it also adds weeks of travel. It means going down and around by way of Salisbury, or at least Trading Ford, before turning back in the direction we're actually trying to go."

Saul was first to respond. "Caleb, you think you could handle a trip that long?"

Caleb shifted his weight and winced. "Well, I'd sure try. But I can't promise much more than trying."

"To say nothing of the young'uns some folks have," Deacon Ashe added.

"You've got to admit, we don't have enough provisions for a trip like that," Caleb added. A valid concern. His boys could go through foodstuffs like nobody's business. "Nor cash nor barter to *get* enough provisions."

"We'll have a slew of river crossings, too, going south and then doubling back," Mitchell pointed out, leaning over the map. "And it's been wet enough already, the wagons won't hold up forever."

Alec said, "There's no promise against the governor having men down Salisbury way, either."

More and more voices joined the discussion. At last Robert held up a hand for silence. "What I'm hearing is that y'all don't want to go south."

Hank said, "You think?"

"Turning north takes us around the head of Abbott's Creek," Robert said, tracing a line on the map as he spoke. "The danger there is in how close we might come to Tryon's army again. Now I'd like to think he'll be gone by the time we get near the Moravian settlements—"

"That settler said Tryon never stays in one place more than a day or two," Mitchell reminded. "If that's so, he'll be long gone by the time we get there. Especially if he's on his way to Bethabara already, as the rumors say."

Saul spoke again. "To my mind, it's easier to go up and curve down a little to Brother Mitchell's cabin—slowing down if we have to, to avoid Tryon—than to go all the way around through Salisbury."

"Neither way is a straight shot," Alec said. "But I'd say the northerly way is a straighter shot than the other. Once you get to Shallow Ford, you should be back to plan."

Robert was probably the only one who noticed, but he could not help thinking that Alec always referred to the group as "you." Never as "we." It was a subtle reminder that Alec was not one of the family, even in his own mind. Robert said, "Does anyone have any objections to turning north?"

When no one spoke, Deacon Ashe said, "You haven't said yet what you think, Pastor."

"If it were just me, I'd go north," Robert said. "But it's not just me, it's—"

"It's all of us," Hardy said. "And if I'm hearing what I think I'm hearing, all of us want to go north."

Robert flipped the map shut. "North it is."

They camped that night where they were, the nearby river filling the night with a steady rushing that made Robert think of the Haw River near Ayen Ford. As he settled onto the straw tick beside Magdalen, he wondered fleetingly if there would be a river to make that soothing sound beside their new home. Wherever that might be.

Magdalen nestled against him with a sigh. "I'm tired, Rob. I don't remember being this tired last time we moved."

"I pray sometimes," Robert said slowly, "that somehow God would show us there's still new life and joy in the midst of all the death and sorrow."

"Maybe after we're somewhere safe, that will come."

"Somewhere safe." The words resonated somewhere inside him, a chord that was all too familiar. "That's just it.

It's getting harder and harder."

"We could go straight north all the way to Virginia." He slid one hand behind his head and massaged the tight spot in his neck. Virginia was just as dangerous for him as North Carolina was. "Would you be happy in Virginia?"

"If I was with you and you were happy in Virginia."

"Mitch wouldn't be, I know that much. He's a son of Carolina, through and through."

"I didn't marry Mitch, love."

Whereupon Robert decided to stop talking, seeing as he'd just thought of something else he wanted to do with his lips.

Saul's urgent voice outside was an unwelcome interruption. "Pastor? Is Mrs. Boothe there? Caleb's ailing, and Elsie needs help."

Magdalen was already out of Robert's arms and sitting up. "I'll be right there, Saul. What's the matter?"

"He's got a fever and cold shakes and he can't keep anything down." Saul sounded genuinely anxious. "Elsie's about worried herself sick, too."

"I'm coming." Magdalen laced her long-sleeved block-printed bodice over her gown, tied a hasty bowknot, groped for her shoes, and slid out of the wagon. Robert threw on the nearest garments handy and stepped over the still-sleeping Susanna. With Caleb sick, Robert thought, Tryon and his militia would probably be back in Hillsborough before the Ayen Ford Baptists were anywhere near the Moravian settlements.

Saul had a lantern lit and motioned with it toward Thurmonds' wagon. Robert said, "Go on. I'll find Alec and check the camp. We're more vulnerable during a crisis."

Saul swung his lantern in a vague arc that indicated the other side of camp. "He usually beds down over yonder, other side of the big fire. I sleep on one side and he sleeps on the other. He might be up yet, keeping the fire stoked." To Magdalen, "This way, Mrs. Boothe. Watch your step."

Robert cut across the circle of wagons, to the far side of

the bonfire the men built each night to ward off wild animals. He would not have been surprised to find Alec still awake. Mitchell had mentioned, just in passing, that Alec seemed to have something on his mind. Robert knew how hard it was to settle in for the night with something on your mind. He'd tried often enough himself.

But Alec was not there. His belongings were not there. On a hunch, Robert went looking for Alec's chestnut gelding. The horse was not there, either.

Alec was gone for good. Or at least long enough to count as the same thing.

# Thirty-Two

THE MORNING LIGHT DID NOT LIE. ALEC HAD left with all his worldly goods and enough supplies to last to the next settlement. Saul was surprised, but Mitchell wasn't.

"He was studying on something from the moment we talked to that settler," Mitchell said. "I know he wouldn't take on Tryon's army singlehanded. He's got more sense than that. But something got him to thinking."

"I don't know if you knew," Robert said thoughtfully, "but Alec started out as an Anson County Regulator. He's here—*was* here—because the governor's men burned his house to the ground. He didn't give particulars, and I didn't ask him to. But from all the things he *didn't* say, or started to but stopped, I'd say it's a fair guess that he had a family and something happened to them in the fire."

Mitchell said, "You think maybe that settler got to him? Talking about the looting and burning and all, and how he was glad he didn't have a family? Maybe Alec went looking for someone he could help. Someone who *did* have a family. Because he understood."

Robert shook his head. "I don't know what I think. But Alec's his own man, and he'd not thank any of us for butting into his business. And we need to get moving. Alec can overtake us. He knew which way we were going."

Saul was reluctant to go on without Alec, but he made no argument and went to help Elsie hitch up. Robert watched him and saw a young man aching to take action. What kind of action probably didn't matter. Much as he loved Elsie, it could not be easy for Saul to stop being a Regulator.

The wagon train made more headway than Robert expected. Which was good, because that night Elsie's two youngest brothers came down with whatever their father had. Not long after, Caleb suffered a backset and Magdalen began to look exhausted. Nell Woodbridge would have helped, but her daughter was complaining of feeling poorly. Robert resigned himself to the impossibility of travel for the next few days. He had that feeling again of being vulnerable, the sickness in camp undermining the usual watchfulness. He went to tell Saul to stay alert, only to have Elsie smile wearily at him and say that Saul had left camp an hour ago.

Robert wanted to say, He *what*? But exploding at Elsie would not help matters. He shut down on his vexation and asked in carefully measured tones why Saul had left and when he would be back.

All Elsie could tell him was that Saul had felt he was in the way of the women caring for the sick folk, and he had thought maybe he'd find some trace of Alec. Elsie did not think Saul would be gone long. He had told her not to worry.

But by nightfall Saul was not back. Neither was Alec, and Robert had the fleeting thought that perhaps the entire adult male population of the camp was going to melt gradually into the countryside until he was the only one left.

He finished his check of camp and came back to the wagon to find Magdalen violently ill. Robert stopped thinking about Saul and Alec, held Maggie's hand, and prayed.

"I'm sorry, Rob," Magdalen whispered. "I know you want to be moving again."

"It's all right, Maggie." He paused, then had to admit, "Our provisions are getting low. That's the trouble. It's a good sixty miles at least to Mitchell's cabin, and maybe more to real safety. If there is such a thing in this world."

Magdalen squeezed his hand. "The trying of your faith worketh patience, Rob."

"You'd think, after all that's happened, we'd have all the patience we need."

Magdalen smiled faintly, her eyes drifting closed. "I guess that's where the faith comes in."

A few more days, and Magdalen insisted she could handle the movement of the wagon. When they made camp Saturday evening, Robert investigated the food supply. It would last them to the settlement at Shallow Ford, or close enough. Bethabara was much closer, but the Moravians there had made no secret of their support for the governor. The fatal flaw in Robert's calculations was the chance of more delays. He'd tighten his belt and go without if he had to, and he didn't doubt some of his men would, too, but a lot of folks didn't have much strength as it was.

He shouldered his rifle and went out to a rise that rolled down and away to the head of Abbott's Creek. It was a good place to pray. For healing in the camp, for the food to stretch, for Alec and Saul, for the blunt things Robert was afraid he'd say when they came back. *If* they came back. Not that Saul would deliberately walk away. And Robert did not believe in the least that Alec had gone to take the oath of allegiance, as some folks suggested. It was natural that an unbeliever should not see eye to eye with the people of God, but that didn't mean Alec's politics were suspect. Which was why Robert was worried. If Tryon's army was as close as the scouts had warned, a lot of things could happen to a Regulator who wandered too far.

He tried to pray, but found he was staring at the horizon, jaw clenched, feeling himself harden inside. It was just like the night Geoffrey Sheridan was taken, like the day the governor crushed the Regulators at Alamance. Once more, Robert was the only man standing guard for his people.

Robert did not know how long he had been there when

Mitchell's voice said behind him, "Care if I join you?"

"You can do anything you like other than leaving camp without telling me." Robert paused. "Or taking sick or using up our food stores."

"Kind of everything all at once, isn't it."

"We should have been at Shallow Ford by now, according to plan. I don't even know if there is a plan anymore."

"You ever think about just waiting to see what God does?"

"Actually, I do," Robert said. "And it scares me to death."

Mitchell laughed. Robert knew his brother didn't have an organized bone in his body, and was happy that way. Robert also knew what would happen if seventy people tried to outmaneuver the governor without a plan. The disorder would be something like the inside of Hank Jonas' saddlebags. It was too close to reality for Robert to see any humor.

Mitchell went serious and said, "What happened to keeping your eyes on the Lord?"

"Alamance happened," Robert said flatly.

"What does that have to do with it?"

"I trusted Him at Alamance, Mitch. And I watched good men die. I watched the whole thing fall to pieces because we didn't know what we were doing. Now this—it's the same thing. We don't know what we're doing."

"You really think what you know—or what Saul or Alec or anyone else knows, for that matter—is a substitute for trusting the God who knows everything?"

"'Though he slay me, yet will I trust in him,'" Robert said quietly. "I don't, Mitch. God help me, I don't trust Him like that. I thought I did. But I can't stand to watch this end the way Alamance ended."

"Rob, not everything ends like Alamance did. That's not the only thing you've ever trusted Him for."

"No. It's not." Robert swung to face Mitchell. "There's the time I trusted Him to protect my family through a Cherokee raid because I was too busy scouting and preaching to protect them myself. And that was the day that—"

"That Indians came and burned everyone out because folks didn't have gumption enough to be prepared," Mitchell said shortly. "It's not God's fault. And it's not yours, either. You can't save the world, Rob."

"Mitch, it's not like that." Robert was suddenly angry at his brother. "It didn't have anything to do with saving the world. They burned our cabin. Maggie lost the baby. And I wasn't even there. I trusted God, Mitch. I trusted Him, and do you know—" Robert had to stop and breathe, trying not to remember. "What that's like?"

Mitchell looked away. "No," he said quietly. "I don't."

"Well, I do," Robert said, tasting the bitterness in the words.

There was a long pause. Robert said softly, "I reckon now you know why I don't talk about it."

"I don't have the answers, Rob."

"No. I know. No one does except Him. And I'm trying to believe that. I do believe it. It's just that—"

"Trusting is hard."

"Yes. It is."

"That's why there's grace, Rob."

Robert took a deep breath. "Thanks, Mitch."

"I don't know what for, but you're welcome."

There was another brief stretch of silence, more comfortable this time. Then Robert suddenly became conscious of a shift in the subdued cacophony of camp, several hundred yards behind him. The noise had dropped to near silence, broken only by the abrasive sound of an argument in the making. A group of mounted men was clustered near the wagon that held the remaining provisions. Several of the men of the church were nearby, appearing to protest.

*Lord, I need some of that grace to trust You right now, because this doesn't look good . . .*

One of the mounted men reached down and ripped back the canvas that covered the supplies, and Robert knew they had trouble.

Deacon Ashe broke off his remonstrance as Robert approached. The leader of the band made a show of glancing at his saddle holsters. Robert ignored the veiled threat. "What's this about?"

"His Excellency sent us out for supplies," the man said. He had the look of an officer, though Robert could not have said which militia unit he represented. "As well as horses, which we'll see about as soon as we've finished here."

A requisition party, then. Robert said, "Our families need these provisions more than Governor Tryon does."

"Our orders are to take supplies wherever we find them," the officer said. "Resistance won't be taken lightly."

"Neither will the theft of our goods." Robert moved a step sideways and slipped one foot up on the wagon tongue. Ready for action. "Our families come first. Now why don't you ride on before there's trouble."

The officer did not reply, at least not verbally. His answer was to reach down again, pull the canvas away, and slip from the saddle into the wagon bed. Robert stayed where he was, letting the man count sacks and barrels and think he was having his way. Saul would have acted already. Alec, too. But neither Saul nor Alec was here, and Robert was waiting for his moment to come.

It came when the officer ripped open a sack to assess its contents, and Hank Jonas leaned over and slapped the riderless horse. The beast took off as if it had been whipped. The officer bellowed at his men to stop his horse and the attention of the entire party swung away.

Robert let them get a good twenty yards after the horse, then sprang into the wagon, knocked the officer backward over a pile of flour sacks, and heaved him over the side. The man landed hard, but not too hard to yell. A musket came up, then another. Robert shouted at his men to get down, took a knee behind a barrel, heard the shots crack in unison and felt the cask rock with the impact. Molasses pooled around the base of the barrel. Robert leveled Cricket over the side of the wagon, moved just enough to get a good sighting, cocked and fired. Then Mitchell was over the side of the wagon and down behind another cask, shoving his rifle at Robert and reaching to load Cricket almost before Robert had let go.

Down under the wagon, another rifle shot cracked. Someone was firing prone, which meant it was someone on Robert's side. Mitchell's rifle was not Cricket, but it was a good gun and it put the frontmost militiaman out of the fight. Hank shouted a warning just as the officer came over the side. Robert had to give him credit for guts, even as he mentally called the man a fool and brought Mitchell's rifle up in a solid blow that caught the officer's jaw and sent him sprawling on the floor of the wagon. Mitchell yelled something in Robert's ear, whipped out his belt knife, slashed at a rope that bound a bale of provisions, yanked the cord free, and lashed the officer's hands. Cricket was freshly loaded and Robert drew a bead and got off one more shot before lead stung through his left sleeve. He ripped off his coat, then reached for his hunting pouch and motioned for Mitchell to keep his own rifle.

Mitchell yelled something else and Robert looked down to see the officer coming out of his daze. The man pushed himself up to a sitting position and said, "You won't get away with this. When Tryon gets here, he'll string the lot of you up like the traitors you are."

Robert didn't have time to waste on the man's threats, or on the throb in his arm. The motion of reloading Cricket made it worse, but he'd fought hurt before. The officer evidently mistook Robert's silence for indifference, for his voice edged up a notch as he said, "You don't care now, maybe, but you will when the army leaves Bethabara tomorrow and runs right over you on the way to Hillsborough."

"Leaving when?" Robert said sharply, pausing in the midst of ramming a charge home. Bethabara to Hillsborough, and their own camp at the head of Abbott's Creek—the man wasn't lying. They were right in Tryon's line of march.

"If you think I'm going to tell you—" the man began.

"Then I'm dead-on right," Robert said. Another musket ball split wood somewhere behind Robert and an answering shot exploded from Hank's position down below. "By the time Tryon gets here it will be too late for you and your men anyway," Robert added, finishing his tamping. A horse screamed and a man echoed the cry. Robert glanced over his shoulder just in time to see a militiaman make a hard landing in a wild azalea bush. "Like I said."

Mitchell sighted along his rifle, thumbed the hammer back, and pulled the trigger. The officer winced at the closeness of the explosion. "Six o'clock in the morning."

"Good." Robert primed the rifle, snapped the frizzen down, and said, "Now I'm a God-fearing man and I don't like bloodshed. You shout out there for your men to throw down their arms, and no harm will come to you. You can go back to Tryon and you can go back to your family and you'll never have to see us again. I'm not going to spell out the alternative. Lie there a minute and make up your mind."

The man only needed half a minute. Robert took aim just as somebody's musket ball splintered the wagon bed, and the officer yelled at Robert to stop, he would tell his men to lay down their arms. Mitchell helped him get to his knees and Robert listened to him shout the order. Those of the band who could still handle a weapon lowered their muskets, hesitating, and Robert shouted for his own men to hold their fire. From what he could see, four or five of Tryon's delegation appeared to be wounded, and some had been thrown from their horses or had dismounted to take cover, but no lives had been lost. The officer shouted again, more urgently this time, and Robert watched a dozen weapons hit the ground.

"Tell them to dismount," Robert said, and the officer obeyed. Robert ignored the sticky feel of blood on his arm and issued quick orders. Deacon Ashe gathered up the muskets and rifles. Ethan Hardy, Gunning, and Hank took charge of the horses. Others confiscated the soldiers' boots, turning a deaf ear to the loud complaints. Robert ordered the militiamen to head out, knowing that without guns, horses, or boots there was no chance of a sneak attack. The officer had the good sense not to argue. Mitchell took his riding boots and untied his hands, dumped him out of the wagon and sent him after his men. They would make it back to Tryon's camp, but not for a good long time. And by then Robert intended to be out of range.

Mitchell said, "If he's right about Tryon leaving Bethabara at the crack of day, we'd best light out."

"I'd hoped he'd be long gone before we ever got this close," Robert said. "Now I just hope he stays put long enough for us to get around him. Six in the morning—that's maybe ten hours from now." He glanced over to where Hank was laying claim to a pair of confiscated boots. "You and Hank ride out and scout ahead for a way. I'll spread the word and see if we can't be hitched up by the time you get back."

"You'd best get that arm taken care of before you do anything else."

"I have to check on Maggie and Susanna first. They'll be worried."

"You go in there with blood all over you like that, they won't just be worried, they'll be scared to death," Mitchell said. "Look at yourself."

Robert risked a glance. As he had thought, it was only a flesh wound, but Mitchell was right. He was a mess. What wasn't stained red was smeared white and brown from flour and molasses that had spilled during the fight. He let Mitchell tie a piece of flour sack around his arm. Then he took Cricket in his other hand and headed for the other side of camp.

Magdalen was still fighting her illness, but had claimed to be feeling better at supper. Even so, she paled a little when Robert climbed into the wagon. "Rob, your arm—"

"I'm all right, Maggie. Just grazed, is all." He glanced around sharply. "Where's Susanna?"

"I'm over here, Papa." The quilts and straw tick moved and Susanna came into view. "I was—trying to be brave.

But I wasn't very. All those guns going off. So I hid under Mama's quilt."

"Well, right about the same time, I was hiding behind a barrel," Robert said. "But it's all right now. My arm's just bleeding a little, but your mama's going to fix it right up as good as new."

"I heard Mitchell call for Hank," Magdalen said. "Are they scouting again? This late at night?"

"We just found out we're in Tryon's line of march." Robert heard the weariness in his own voice but couldn't quite reconcile it with the rush of danger still pounding through his body. "They're checking for the safest way out."

Magdalen eyed Susanna and did not ask for details. Robert appreciated that. He didn't have many details to give.

Susanna came out of her refuge and watched curiously as Magdalen ripped Robert's sleeve away and washed and bandaged his arm. "Does it hurt, Papa?"

"Not much," he said evasively.

"Why are you all white?"

He assumed she meant the foodstuffs coating his clothes, although it might have been a reference to his complexion as well. He did feel a little wrung out, come to think of it. "It's flour. From the supply wagon."

"No questions right now," Magdalen said. "Sit quietly and watch, or play with your doll. But no questions."

Susanna said, "Yes, Mama," and lapsed into silence.

Magdalen worked while she talked. "No one was really standing guard. All of a sudden they were here, and there was no time to get you. I saw them ride up, but then they went down behind the supply wagon and I couldn't see anything else."

"It's just as well," Robert said. "It wasn't pretty."

"Was anyone else hurt?"

"A few of their men got winged. Hank's limping a little; he did something to his ankle, diving under the wagon for cover. He got off some right decent shots from under there."

Magdalen tied the bandage neatly and tucked the ends

under. "Susanna, get me one of Papa's shirts."

Susanna moved to obey and Magdalen said, "What did they want? They didn't look like stragglers."

"Tryon's taking supplies anywhere he can get them," Robert said. "Even where there's none to spare." He grimaced, picturing the chaos of spilled provisions in the supply wagon. He'd bled on most of it himself. "We'll have to get more victuals, Maggie, and soon. Most of what we had is ruined now. We can't make it more than a few days on what's left. There's hunting—but someone's liable to hear the shots, and that someone won't be on our side. Especially after all the shots they heard today. After Tryon has moved on, maybe . . ."

Susanna handed him the shirt and Magdalen shooed her out of the wagon before helping Robert off with one and on with the other. She said quietly, "The only place close enough is Bethabara."

"I know." Robert reached to clasp Magdalen's hand as she adjusted his sleeve over the bandage. "But not tonight. First we've got to pray. Pray and get out of Tryon's way. Or supplies won't do us any good at all."

## Somewhere Northwest of Abbott's Creek

# Thirty-Three

It was a strange thing, Mitchell thought as he and Hank rode out beyond Abbott's Creek. Alec was not there to needle Hank for talking, and yet Hank was quieter than he'd been in the last two and a half months. Mitchell glanced over, said, "Something on your mind?"

Hank must have been thinking along the same lines, for he said, "Alec. Wondering where he went, and just thinking that he's stubborn. Like me. I'm trying to think what it'll take to make him give in."

"Give in to what?"

Hank gave him a sideways look. "You know. The only thing that matters."

"It's harder for folks who are used to doing things for themselves."

"If'n you think it would help, I could get him drunk and let him fall out of a tree, same as I did."

"I admire your enthusiasm," Mitchell said carefully. "But your methods are a little questionable. If you're trying to help Alec, you might want to start by keeping your mouth shut when he wants you to."

Hank sighed. "Not knowin' what to say makes me jumpy-like. So I say whatever I think of, just to be talking."

"This may shock you, Hank, but some folks actually like silence."

"I reckon it takes all kinds," Hank said. "You hungry?"

"Hank, we don't have *time* to be hungry right now."

"I've got some venison jerk in my saddlebag. That don't take long." Hank cranked around in his saddle and Mitchell heard him rummaging. "Must've fell down in the bottom. Under all this other—what is that?"

"How would I know?" Mitchell said. "Watch where you're going, Hank."

The saddlebag flapped shut and Hank straightened up. "Old clayware bottle, that's what it was. I plumb forgot it was in there. Must've had it right before I fell out of that tree and you took me in. I didn't do no riding for a good month after that. Told you I don't ever clean my saddlebags out."

Mitchell shook his head. He'd thought he was the absent-minded one. "Hank, we really need to pay attention right now."

"I am," Hank said. "Now, what was we talkin' about?"

"Peace and quiet," Mitchell said.

"That's right. And folks who like it that way. Your brother's like that, wouldn't you say?"

"I'd say sometimes he just needs to go out and listen to the wind and let the quiet sort of clear his head."

"What do *you* do to clear your head?"

"Nothing particular."

Hank grunted. "Well, that explains some things."

Mitchell had walked into that one. "Won't argue with you there."

"Arguing ain't my style," Hank said. "I says it like I sees it, and if you don't like it, it ain't my fault."

"Maybe that's part of the trouble with Alec. Give him room to have his own opinion, even if you think he's wrong."

"What if I don't just think it?"

"I give up," Mitchell said.

"I get what you're saying," Hank said hastily. "I just ain't good at thinkin' things over in silence."

"You might want to start trying," Mitchell said, "because if I'm not mistaken, that's a camp up ahead. Where a camp ought not to be."

Hank lowered his voice. "How close we gonna go?"

"Close enough to find out who they are and what they're doing here." Mitchell paused. "Was that a sentry?"

"I didn't hear it," Hank said, but he didn't sound convinced.

Mitchell gently reined Samson in, unsure if the moonlight was a blessing or a curse. It depended on who could see whom first. He listened for a moment, hearing only the wind in the grass and the heavy breathing of the horses. Then the challenge came again, but not aimed at them.

Grass rustled louder, several yards ahead and to the right. Mitchell edged forward until he saw the shadow of a man on horseback. A familiar voice said, "It's only me. I'm hardly the type you need a sentry for."

Hank hissed, "That's—"

Mitchell cut him off with a swift hand motion. The last thing Saul McBraden needed was someone blurting out his name in front of what Mitchell suspected was a detachment of government militia. A man couldn't tell in the dark just how large the camp was; Mitchell and Hank had almost ridden into it themselves. Saul was not necessarily a fool for mistaking these campfires for the church's. He would, however, be a fool if he said too much more.

Suspicion laced the sentry's voice as he said, "Dismount so I can see you."

Saul slipped off his horse and Mitchell did likewise, ready to move forward if Saul should need help. Hank dismounted softly behind him and Mitchell prayed neither of them would do anything foolish.

Saul was in the patch of moonlight now, his face in profile to Mitchell. The sentry came forward into the light and alarm registered on Saul's face.

"What's your business here?" the sentry demanded.

Saul put on a grin that was pure bluff, and not very

good bluff, either. "Looks like I made a mistake."

He made a move toward his horse, but the sentry blocked him. "Not so fast. You look a mighty lot like a Regulator to me. Matter of fact, I think I saw you at Alamance. Front lines. Right before you all commenced running." Militia. Definitely militia. Not friendly, either.

"We didn't *all* run," Saul said defiantly. "Some of us are just waiting for next time."

Mitchell winced. Saul, please. Shut up.

The militiaman laughed at that. "For you, there won't be a next time. General Waddell's going to be right interested in talking with you."

Mitchell recognized the name at once. Hugh Waddell, subordinate only to Tryon himself. But what was he doing west of Bethabara? Mitchell shifted his position just a hair, straining to hear. The sentry was still talking.

"For all I know, you could be an outlaw," he said. "James Hunter, maybe. Or Robert Boothe. Or even one of the rascals what blew up the general's powder down in Mecklenburg."

It had not been Waddell's powder that Saul had helped blow up at Dixon's Mill, but Waddell wouldn't care whose powder it had been. Saul said through his teeth, "I don't know what you're talking about and neither do you."

Mitchell heard Hank scrabbling quietly in a saddlebag behind him, but he had no time to wonder what Hank was doing, because the sentry had his pistol out. "Shut your mouth, rebel. Save it for the general."

The pistol jerked, motioning Saul forward. Mitchell waited another tense beat, gambling on the fact that the pistol was not cocked. Hopefully the man thought Saul was too potentially valuable to shoot.

Saul didn't budge, and the sentry reached for him. Saul's voice came out a growl. "Keep your hands off me."

The sentry's gun arm flashed back. Hank grunted softly and something arced through the air, glinting a streak of moonlight. The object struck the sentry in the shoulder just as he brought the pistol down. Saul ducked, not fast enough, and took the barrel just below the temple. He went to one knee, dazed by the weakened blow that otherwise would have laid him senseless. The sentry flashed a glance around and started to bring the weapon back again, but this time Mitchell was on him. He ripped the pistol away, tossed it to Hank, and drove his free hand into the point between neck and jaw. The sentry's eyes went wide and his face contracted. Mitchell knew what the man was feeling because Robert had once done it to him, wrestling in the clearing behind their boyhood home. Accidental, Rob had said. But there was nothing accidental in it tonight.

Hank was dragging Saul out of the way. Mitchell hit the same spot one more time, watched the muscles spasm, knew the man was faltering for a strong breath and heartbeat. Mitchell gripped the man's lapel, swung him around, and had him flat before Saul was back on his feet.

"You're with General Waddell," Mitchell said. A statement, not a question. "What's he doing here and where's he going next?"

The sentry was gasping for breath, trying to recover from Mitchell's attack on several vital nerves. But he was not ready to give in. "That's none of your business."

"You want to meet your Maker out here under the stars, that ain't our business either," Hank drawled.

The sentry writhed under the weight of Mitchell's knee. "You'd be a fool. You fire one shot and the whole camp will be in arms."

Mitchell twisted enough to show his sheathed belt knife. "No one said it had to be a shot," he said cheerfully, quick to follow Hank's bluff. At least he hoped it was a bluff. Mitchell had a healthy and biblical aversion to bloodshed. "Now, what I want to know."

"Tryon sent us out to teach a lesson to any rebels who haven't come to their senses." The sentry sounded sullen. "We're going to the head of the Catawba from here."

Mitchell sat back on his heels, referencing his mental

map of western North Carolina. The head of the Catawba River was at least twenty miles south of his cabin in the Blue Ridge. Far enough to be safe. He hoped. "And after that?"

"Farther southwest. Maybe as far as Tryon County. That's all I know."

Mitchell glanced at Hank and Saul. The sentry dived for the pistol.

Hank hit him. Just once, but hard. Turned him over, lifted one eyelid, and said, "He'll come around by morning. With a nasty headache, but it won't be no worse than if he'd been drinkin' all night."

Something glinted dully in the grass near the sentry. It was the object Hank had thrown when the sentry threatened Saul. Mitchell said, "Hank, what'd you chunk at him?"

"That bottle that was in my saddlebag," Hank said. "First thing I laid hands on, and I needed a way to get rid of it anyhow."

Mitchell picked up the glazed stoneware bottle and pulled the cork. The smell made his eyes water. "If this is what you drank before you crawled into my cabin, I don't wonder you fell out of a tree."

"Whatever that is, just the smell of it is enough to bring me around," Saul said, shaking his head and wincing at the movement. He did not ask why Mitchell and Hank were there. Mitchell figured Saul had sense enough not to ask questions at a time like this, a guess that was confirmed when Saul added, "We'd better get out of here."

"Just a minute." Mitchell eyed the unconscious sentry. "A nasty headache, right? Like he's been drinking all night?"

"What are you thinkin' on?" Hank asked suspiciously.

"Only that I have no compunctions about getting one of the governor's men in trouble." Mitchell held his breath and splashed the pungent liquid over the sentry's shirtfront. He dropped the open bottle and the pistol beside the man and stepped away. "There. Drinking on his watch, and certainly not to be trusted in anything he says. Now, let's ride. We've got a church to move."

# Thirty-Four

BY THE TIME MITCHELL AND HANK HAD BEEN gone for an hour, the camp had been alerted. Families met for prayer, then began to put out cookfires and pack up. Magdalen's illness flared again before Robert had finished spreading the word. He wished he could leave the camp where it was and let everyone get rested. But there was nothing he could do. Tryon was coming and there was no way to stop him. *We can rest when we're dead*, Robert thought grimly. *Which will be soon if we don't get moving.*

Susanna was sitting on the step across the back of the wagon. The bustle in camp was enough to keep anyone awake, and with Magdalen ill, she was getting away with it. As Robert passed, she said, "Papa?"

He turned around. "What is it, pumpkin?"

"Why is Mama still sick? Everyone else is getting better. Even Betty Woodbridge, and she took sick the same time Mama did, almost."

"I don't know the answer to that. I wish I did." He glanced back into the wagon, thinking, *I've never known her to be sick like this except when—*

*Lord, what am I thinking? It's been five years. Maggie's liable to slap me if I even suggest it.*

That one was going to take some contemplation. And there was no time for contemplation tonight. He eyed the darkening sky and figured they had seven hours before Tryon's army left Bethabara. "Listen, Susanna, I need you to be very brave tonight and help your mama and Gunning get the wagon ready like we do when we're fixing to move again. Understand?"

"But Papa, it's dark out! We don't move when it's dark."

"Tonight we do. I'll explain later. Just do as I say."

"Yes, Papa."

"That's my girl." He gently tugged her braid and headed out to get things moving. As soon as everything was in order for a quick departure, he took his rifle and went out to check the perimeter of camp. Once or twice around, and then he'd come back and hitch up.

But he never made the first circle. Halfway around camp, near the grazing area where the horses were picketed, the rustle of grass broke the quiet. Robert paused and listened. Nothing at first. Then the distinct sound of footsteps.

Robert cocked the rifle, took one quick stride, and met a rock-solid shoulder. His bandaged arm stung and he caught himself just short of clenching down on the handiest thing, which would have been the trigger. The lean shadow grunted hard and said something that was not exactly swearing but not something Robert would say in front of his church, either. Followed that with, "Easy with the rifle."

"Alec?"

"Captain?"

"Perry, where have you *been*?"

Alec moved just enough for Robert to see him dimly by the light of the bonfire. Unshaven and beyond dirty, but unmistakably Alec. "Fine welcome, that."

"You leave without telling anyone, you ought to be grateful for any welcome at all."

Alec shoved a hand through russet-brown hair made red by the firelight. "You know how close you are to Bethabara?"

"Aye. I also know that Tryon's army leaves at the crack

of day to head back for Hillsborough. Which gives us maybe seven or eight hours to get out of their way."

"Which way are you going?"

"I'm not sure as you have a right to know that, Perry. You come back just to find out what our next move is?"

Alec spoke in a voice that was suddenly tight. "I came back because I finished what I went to do. And because I figured you needed me."

"We did," Robert said. "We do. But we have to be able to depend on you. When you're part of a group—"

"I'm a drifter, Captain." Alec's low laugh had no mirth in it. "Not part of any group since Anson County. You said it yourself, I'm not one of you. That's why you've got men like your brother and Saul McBraden and—"

"Have you seen Saul?"

"Should I have?"

"He left Wednesday. To look for you."

"I swear, Captain, I never meant for him to do that. And if I'd seen him, which I didn't, I'd have told him so."

Robert believed him. Alec might hide a dozen things from him at once, but Robert would bank on anything Alec actually verbalized. "Never mind. Nothing now makes any difference, so long as we're out of Tryon's way in time. But north and west is all I can tell you of where we're going."

"I only asked on account of how Tryon sent General Waddell out west today with a good share of the army," Alec said. "And if you're going anywhere that direction, you'd best watch out for them."

"How far west?" Robert asked sharply.

"Like I said, they only left Bethabara today. They can't be far from there."

"Mitchell and Hank are out there now," Robert said.

"Give me a minute to get shed of my things and saddle up again, and I'll join up with 'em," Alec said.

Robert said, "No."

Alec's right eyebrow twitched ever so slightly. "*No?*"

"Not until you've proven we can count on you." And

that, Robert thought, was exactly what he was going to tell Saul McBraden, too, next time he saw him.

Something flared in Alec's eyes at Robert's tone. But he clamped down on any protest he might have made. After a long minute he said, "I allow as I ought to apologize for leaving like I did. But you'd not apologize if you were in my place. And you'd not expect me to if you understood."

"Someday you're going to get tired of handling everything yourself."

Alec said, "Haven't yet."

Robert heard the words, but what he saw was a man very close to the exact opposite. He didn't have time to reply before Mitchell called his name. "Sounds like our scouts are back."

He headed in the direction of Mitchell's voice, aware that Alec was close behind him. "What'd you find, Mitch?"

"Saul McBraden, for one thing," Mitchell said, just as Robert realized there were two men with his brother instead of one. Half of Saul's face was in shadow, but the half Robert could see looked dirty and tired and typically unabashed.

Robert opened his mouth to speak, but Saul beat him to it. "You found Alec."

"Actually, Alec found us," Robert corrected.

"I tried that," Saul said with a wry half-smile. "Didn't work so well. Is Elsie all right?"

"Elsie is worried *sick*," Robert said. "Her family's ailing and so is my wife and we're closer to danger than we've been yet. Your orders were to stay here and look out for Thurmonds. You had no business leaving that way."

Saul's expression was strained, as if he wanted to react but knew better. "I didn't intend on being gone so long, Pastor. But I went farther than I realized, and by the time I managed to dodge the army and get back, you'd moved on."

"I'm not talking about how long you were gone," Robert said. "I'm talking about your leaving at all. When Elsie and Caleb needed you."

"They had Mrs. Boothe and Mrs. Woodbridge, and

Caleb was doing better and I thought—" Saul trailed off.

"They *had* Maggie and Mrs. Woodbridge," Robert agreed. "But they needed *you*."

Saul rubbed the shadowed side of his face and flinched. At what, Robert couldn't tell. The young man gave a slow nod. "I reckon you're right."

"He's more than right," Alec said. "He's talking the dead-on truth. You don't leave your family if there's a chance in this world that they need you." He paused, then added more quietly, "Your family, or any of the folks who are banking on you."

Saul let the silence stretch for a beat. The Thurmonds were not really his family, not yet at least. But they were the closest thing he had. Saul said quietly, "I'll go talk to Elsie."

"Help her hitch up while you do," Robert said.

Saul turned away and Robert saw for the first time that Saul's left temple bore a bruise the size of Orange County. Orange County *before* it had been split into three smaller counties. "What happened to your head?"

Saul turned back and gave a weak grin. "It's what I get for running into Waddell's army and opening my big mouth when I should have been doing what I promised to do."

He walked off and Robert looked at Mitchell. Mitchell said, "It, uh, has to do with why I smell like I should be walking crooked."

Robert's eyebrows went up and Alec made a strangely muffled noise. "Long story," Mitchell said hastily.

"Don't worry," Hank said. "It wasn't his whiskey; it was mine."

Alec made another strangled sound. Robert said, "I don't want to know what you're talking about. Not tonight. Just tell me if we can make it past Waddell's detachment."

Mitchell snorted. "It would have helped if we'd known Waddell was out there, going into it. As it was, we had to get what news we could out of a very reluctant sentry. Same sentry Saul tangled with. See, I told you it was a long story."

"Get to the point," Robert said, trying not to snap.

"We know where they are now, so we can steer around 'em," Mitchell said. "And come to think of it, even if you did stray too close, no one would know who you were. Excepting General Waddell, being as you rode scout for him once."

Alec looked sharply at Robert. Robert said, "It was a long time ago. It's not important now."

"What's important is getting you'uns on your way," Mitchell said. "Ready to go?"

Mitchell probably didn't really need an answer, but Robert gave him the only one he had. "We've got to be."

In another half hour they were moving. Robert sent his scouts out ahead in a three-pronged guard detail, Hank and Mitchell on two points, Alec on the third because he was Robert's only option. Every other man had a wagon to handle. Robert himself left the reins to Gunning and rode beside the wagon, rifle across his pommel. Watching for trouble, attention divided between earth and sky, relying on the stars for both time and direction. One hour . . . two . . . three . . . north . . . now northwest . . .

Sometime in the hour before dawn, the sound of wood splitting in two cracked like an explosion against the rustle and creak of moving wagons. Robert jerked around in the saddle. Thurmonds' wagon lurched and another crack echoed the first. Elsie screamed and Saul yelled at the team. By the time Robert got there the wagon lay sharply canted to one side, the front left wheel in two pieces and the rear wheel cracked straight across from the sudden shift of weight. The front axle had hit the ground and snapped on impact.

"Get the team unhitched before they spook and drag this any farther," Robert called. Saul moved to obey, helping Elsie down behind him. Robert gingerly tested his weight on the wagon seat. The wagon shifted under him and the other rear wheel groaned. Not good. He slid to the ground, careful not to make any sudden movements. "Gunning."

Gunning appeared out of the dark. "Yessir."

"See what you can find to brace that back corner before

I go in. I don't want to flip the whole thing over."

Gunning nodded and vanished. Owen Thurmond called from within, "You want we should get out, Pastor?"

"No!" Robert said. "Don't move. Don't move at *all*. Understand?"

"Yessir." Owen sounded scared. "I think something happened to Pa."

*Oh, Lord. We don't have time for this.* "Just sit tight, Owen. We'll get him out in a minute."

Magdalen said behind him, "Can I help somehow?"

"I don't know yet. Maybe once I see what needs doing."

A fluttering drumbeat stirred in the distance, a far-off rustling, as if the night was rousing. Magdalen said softly, "What's that?"

"Roll call in Bethabara." Robert watched Gunning go behind the wagon, his arms loaded with crates and firewood and other things Robert did not really see. They had an hour, maybe two, to get this done and get moving again.

Gunning came from around the wagon. "She won't flip on you now, leastways."

"All right. Go find the scouts and tell 'em to come in close and keep a sharp lookout. Tryon's liable to be on the move right directly, and I don't want to be caught unawares."

Gunning left and Robert clambered carefully over the wagon seat. "One of you boys got a lantern?"

Fumbling sounds in the dark said that someone had one and was trying to light it. Elsie slid in behind Robert and reached across for the lantern. A moment later the flame glowed, casting dim light through the wagon. Caleb lay on his back, a chest of drawers pinning one leg. His bad leg.

Elsie shut her lips tight and did not say anything. Which was good, because Robert did not think he could handle an injured man and a hysterical young woman, both at the same time. He took the lantern, leaned down, and said, "Caleb. You all right?"

Caleb was not all right. He was not even fully conscious, which in a way maybe made it easier. Saul said from the wagon seat, "Done with the team. Is there anything I can—oh, Lord, have mercy."

"Don't say *anything*," Robert said, flashing a warning glance in Elsie's direction. "I'm going to have the boys ease that bureau off and Elsie and I will get Caleb out from under. You stay right where you are and be ready to help move him on out." He glanced around for the youngest boy and saw him hunched in the corner, staring at his father. Definitely in need of something to do. "Abner, take those blankets there and lay them on the ground outside, over by my wagon. You know where my wagon is? Good. You do that. Everybody ready? All right, easy now."

Between all of them they got Caleb out without overturning the wagon. The angle of Caleb's bad leg made Robert's stomach turn. It was ugly. And it was broken again, Robert had no doubt of that. His wounded arm burned as he helped Saul carry Caleb over to the blankets Abner had laid out. Magdalen followed them and Robert said, "You might not want to look, Maggie, with how you've been feeling."

"I'm feeling fine right now," she said. "And Susanna nodded off a long time ago; don't worry about her. What do you want me to do?"

"Get the box of medical supplies from under the seat. Saul, cut down one of the bows from Thurmonds' wagon and trim the two straightest lengths from it and bring them here. Then you and the boys unload the wagon and fit as much of the load as you can wherever anyone has a spare corner. There's no way to get that wagon repaired away out here, not with the kind of time we have. I'm going to do what I can for Caleb's leg and we're all going to pray Tryon doesn't leave Bethabara early."

Saul, Gunning, and the Thurmond boys vanished to do as ordered. Magdalen brought Robert the box of supplies and a second lantern. Robert asked for rags and she disappeared into the wagon again, coming back with a badly torn apron and the shirt he had ruined in the fight with the requisition party. Several yards away, a wagon bow came down with a faint swish and thud. Caleb opened his eyes and winced, and Robert prayed he could do this job quick and right. Being a circuit rider had given him experience in a lot of things he'd just as soon not have had to do, such as setting broken bones with nothing but his God-given sense and fire-breathing moonshine for the pain. Just like tonight. Saul came back with two straight lengths of wood, and Robert gave Caleb a stiff shot of the strongest stuff in the medical chest and set to work.

The break was at a weak point in the bone, the same place it had been broken before. If the bone had knit properly three months ago, Robert doubted the falling bureau would have caused more damage than a nasty bruise. He gave Elsie and Magdalen careful instructions, forcing himself to ignore the gray on the horizon. Time was short. There was nothing he could do about it now.

He told Elsie, "Don't watch," and pulled the leg straight. Caleb gave a sharp groan and passed out. Robert guided the fractured bone into place, working by feel and by sound. The soft grate of the broken ends meeting was a chilling sound but a good sign. At least it was a clean break. Robert said, "Tear up the rags, Maggie."

Just as Magdalen finished ripping up his old shirt, four horses galloped into the sprawling line of wagons. Gunning could not possibly have had time to ride out and find all three scouts, which meant they had already been on their way in. Mitchell was the first to dismount. He glanced at Caleb but didn't comment. Instead he said, breathing hard, "We're not a half mile from Bethabara, Rob. And Tryon's men are packing up. It's a matter of half an hour before they get here. What do you want to do?"

What Robert wanted to do was saddle up and go. Get out of Tryon's way, get out of Moravian country, get out of range of any threat ever again. But that was not happening. Not with a wagon wreck and a broken leg to deal with. "Tell everyone to hunker down, stay quiet, and pray."

Alec swung down beside Mitchell, looking outraged. "Are you an *idiot*?" he burst out. "Tryon's men, half an hour out, and you're just going to sit here?"

"And pray," Robert said.

"As if that makes any difference," Alec said harshly.

Magdalen turned on him. "You should be ashamed, Alec Perry. Prayer is the most powerful weapon we have because it opens the way for a mighty God to show His strength on our behalf. You want to laugh at prayer, go ahead. But don't do it in front of folks who have seen God answer."

Alec opened his mouth. Shut it. Said in a huskier voice, "Beg pardon, ma'am." To Robert, low, "Just let me get some men together, why don't you, and—"

"And what?" Robert said sharply. "Take on the whole army? This is where authority comes in, Perry. We've talked about that, and I don't have time to go over it again. You don't have to pray if you don't want to. I don't reckon it'd do much good if you did. But you had best get out there with Mitch and tell all God's people to start storming heaven."

For a minute Alec just looked at him. Then he touched his forehead in salute and led his horse away. Mitchell followed him. Robert said, "We'll pray while we work. Put the splints where I can reach them."

He reached for one of the lanterns and saw Alec come back and take a position near the far end of the wagon, his rifle in his arms. Robert started to speak, then changed his mind. Let Alec stand there with a rifle if it made him feel better. Robert couldn't expect him to understand that praying was as much an act of defense as standing guard. Even more so, maybe.

Magdalen and Elsie helped lay the strips of wood on either side of the break and pad the slats with pieces of Robert's ruined shirt. The women held the splint in place while Robert bound it firmly with strips of Maggie's old apron. In the uneasy quiet, the sound of approaching hooves rumbled like distant thunder. Robert tied the final knot, then stood up, reached for Magdalen's hand, and said, "Pray. Now."

Elsie said in a small voice, "Should I stay here or go look for Saul?"

Robert glanced at the wreck of Thurmonds' wagon. "Saul's just over yonder. There's nothing more you can do to help your father; that shot of whiskey I gave him will keep the pain down a while yet. You might as well see if there's anything you can help Saul unload. I'd just as soon have you with him anyway."

Elsie gave a tight little nod and slipped away. Robert looked out at the night and saw the danger coming, a mass of steadily moving shadows. He pulled Maggie against his side, his chest constricting with something he did not want to admit was fear. The army was not swinging around them. It was coming, coming straight on. And there was nothing Robert could do to stop it. Nothing he could do but pray, *Thy will be done.*

Caleb moaned. Something stirred in the wagon behind them. Magdalen slipped out of Robert's hold. A sleepy little-girl voice called plaintively, "Mama? Where are you?"

Magdalen flew like a mother bird to its young. She swept Susanna off the wagon step and safely out of sight. Robert watched them vanish into the wagon together, turned back to the advancing shadows, forced himself to breathe. The men were close enough now, Robert distinctly saw the officer whom he had thrown out of the supply wagon. No doubt Tryon had reoutfitted the requisition party with confiscated rebel property. The officer was leading a unit of militia now. He and his men could not have failed to hear or see Susanna. Robert only prayed God would protect her and Maggie if he himself was captured. Or worse.

Trusting is hard, Mitchell had said. But that's why there's grace.

"Can't get home soon enough for me. Though I wish I had more to show for it." The words of a nearby militiaman carried clear on the warm June breeze. Caleb moaned again.

"Almost makes you want to seize the first rebel you meet, just so you'd feel you'd done something," another man agreed. "Something more than just looting and burning, I mean. That's not the sort of thing a man can brag about."

The requisition officer spoke. "Wouldn't it be a royal pleasure to capture some rebel like that scoundrel with the supply wagon, and then find out he was an outlaw? Then you'd have a reward to boot."

Robert caught movement off to one side. Alec had moved into the shadow of the wagon and was bringing his rifle up. Robert lunged to stop him. "Alec. No."

"They're not going to take anyone or anything without being called to reckon for it!" Alec said in a furious whisper.

Robert heard the hammer click and reached for Alec's wrist. Alec resisted. Robert tightened his grip, swung Alec sideways, pinned him against the wagon. "You don't want to answer for the one foolish move that puts all our lives in the balance. And I don't want to answer for letting you."

There was no way they had not been seen. But if no shots were fired, maybe the men would take only Robert and let the others go. Alec looked at him, breathing hard. Robert held his gaze. He knew Alec could kill him. And maybe had a right. If Tryon couldn't tell him what to do, why should Robert? But this wasn't about Alec; it was about the women and children who would get hurt if Alec started taking potshots at the army.

Alec said under his breath, "They're still coming, Captain."

Robert turned halfway and watched the oncoming sweep of men. Closer now. So close Robert could see the mottled swelling on the requisition officer's jaw, evidence of where Robert had struck him during the fight for the supply wagon. Alec's rifle moved again at the edge of his vision and Robert held out a warning hand. Alec went tense, then slowly lowered the rifle. And then Robert stopped trusting what he saw.

Because he saw the officer ride on, straight ahead, not

looking at him, not looking at anyone, not even turning his head. Riding straight through the gap between Boothes' wagon and Thurmonds' wreck. Leading his men straight through behind him. Melting into the rest of the army and never looking back.

Robert watched, and knew Alec watched, until the shadows faded into the night.

AYEN FORD,
NORTH CAROLINA

# Thirty-Five

CHARLES DRAKE WAS SICK AND TIRED OF AYEN Ford. Sick of the rural lifestyle. Sick of the lack of respect from those left in town. Sick even of the raiding and destruction. He was especially sick of Malcolm Harrod.

Harrod made as if he was there to reinforce Drake's position, a silent background figure who kept the remaining townsfolk aware of governmental authority. But that was all a façade. A lie. Harrod knew it; Drake knew it. Harrod was not there to reinforce him. He was there to police him.

Twenty miles away, Hillsborough beckoned, wealthy and cultured and the utter opposite of all that made this town and this assignment abominable. But wealth and culture were not enough anymore. Drake knew that in the circles of quiet society gossip, it would not matter that he had arrested Geoffrey Sheridan for treason and given Jacob Chauncy his just dues and come *so close* to crushing a dangerous outlaw dissenter and his rebel followers. "Almost" was not good enough. Not good enough for the Hillsborough elite, not good enough for the governor. Drake refused to go back to a reminder of just how far he had fallen short. And he refused to go on trying to run Robert Boothe to earth unless there was hope of recognition from the governor. Which there was not. Malcolm Harrod seemed to take a quietly sarcastic pleasure in the way his presence reminded Drake of that.

So Charles Drake was trapped. Trapped between the bitter mockery of political oblivion and a complete lack of interest in any other life. He should have been a farmer, he reflected bitterly. A shopkeeper. Something that would never have let him taste the power that was slipping away from him.

Two weeks he had spent like that after Boothe and his pack of rebels were gone. Waiting for an incentive to go out and take action. Waiting for some action to go out and take. Then one long and tedious Sunday morning in the middle of June, Harrod let himself into Drake's study and said, "Your rebel has a price on his head."

"He is not *my* rebel," Drake said between his teeth.

"Shall I assume that means you're also uninterested in the bounty?"

Drake put down his pen and took a long, slow breath. Perhaps if he did not directly meet Harrod's eyes, he could get through this conversation without going mad. Or doing murder. "How much?"

"One hundred pounds, one thousand acres. To be obtained upon the capture or death of James Hunter, William Butler, Rednap Howell, Herman Husband, or Robert Boothe. His Excellency announces it from Bethabara today."

"From Bethabara?" Sixty miles, easily. "And you already know?"

"I do have special privileges, Colonel."

Envy burned deep at the thought of such access to the governor, access that would allow prior knowledge of his plans. "You are telling me this why?"

"I expected an offer such as this to be no less than what you've hungered for. A challenge to meet, with an attractive reward attached."

Drake said slowly, "If the reward is so attractive, why are you not pursuing it?"

Harrod said, "I have other business to attend to."

"And you want me out of your way, is that it?" Drake could feel the bitterness welling up into a current as dangerous as the undertow of the Haw River. "If I do this, you're free to stop watching me and attend to whatever business you wish. Because I'll be somewhere out in the wilderness, miles away from annoying you or Governor Tryon or anyone else of real importance. Whether or not I am successful."

"An apt assessment, Colonel." Harrod's expression was nothing short of a smirk. "I do not suggest, however, that you place an undue emphasis on the idea of success."

"You don't think I'm capable." Drake was back to talking through his teeth, low and tight, his gaze carefully aimed at a point just beside Harrod's head.

"I have no doubt that you are capable," Harrod corrected. "Only that you are capable *enough*."

At the moment, Drake felt capable of shoving Harrod straight through the study wall with nothing but rage and his bare hands. More so when Harrod gave a minute shrug and added, "It's your choice, of course."

*His choice.* Just another lie to add to the list. Drake met Harrod's gaze squarely, set his jaw, and decided. He would go. He would prove Harrod wrong. He would make Robert Boothe pay for making him out a fool. If power still evaded his grasp, a thousand acres of property and a hundred pounds of government silver would help to dull the pain.

## West of Bethabara, North Carolina

##  Thirty-Six

The wagon train made camp three miles west of Bethabara and stayed there for the Lord's day. After Sunday service Saul McBraden crossed camp with his Bible in his hand, still thinking about Tryon's army marching right through without a backward glance. Saul was ashamed of how he hadn't prayed all that much until he had no other choice. Pastor Boothe had preached today about the horses and chariots of fire that had surrounded Elisha in the second Book of Kings. Soldiers had come to seize the prophet and God had blinded their eyes. Just like last night. Saul only wished he could have seen the Lord's host like Elisha had.

Saul had seen how Pastor had had to stop Alec from blowing everything. Alec had admitted this morning that he'd gone off half-cocked. He'd admitted that something had happened that he couldn't explain. But he was sure there had to be some explanation. Saul knew the only explanation was God. But he could feel for Alec—he'd gone off half-cocked himself, more than once.

Which was why he had something to tell Caleb Thurmond, if Caleb was awake. Saul was so deep in thought that he was all the way across camp before he remembered that Thurmonds' wagon was no longer there. He doubled back toward Deacon Ashe's wagon, where Caleb was supposed to be resting. Saul was almost glad to see Elsie on the other side of camp, talking with Mrs. Boothe. Elsie had been quiet ever since Saul's return. Quiet enough to make things a little awkward. Saul wasn't sure why. Wasn't a girl supposed to greet her betrothed with shouts of joy or something? Not that he would know.

He jumped when Caleb called his name. Saul wheeled and saw that Caleb was sitting up.

"You're awake," Saul said, somewhat needlessly. "How's the leg?"

"Bearable," Caleb said. "Saul, I want to talk with you."

"Yessir?"

"Come set down."

Saul clambered into the wagon and sat down on a crate of something, probably dishes. "Before you say anything, sir, I want to get something off my chest. Your wagon likely would've been fine if I'd stayed and looked after things like I ought to have done, and I'm sorry about that."

"Got my leg reset just like the doctor ordered," Caleb said with a slight grimace. "The Lord knew what He was about, I reckon. But I want to know, is the wagon all you aim to be sorry about?"

"Sir?"

"Tell me, McBraden, what is my daughter to you? Is she a challenge for you to pursue? A cause for you to champion? A damsel in distress for you to rescue?"

"I—I don't know what you mean."

"What I mean is, you fight for her when there's a battle to be fought. That's a good thing. But when there's no battle to fight, or there *is* a battle but you can't handle it, you leave and go looking for a fight somewhere else."

So *that* was what Caleb was after. "You mean going after Alec like I did."

"Well, that's the most recent one," Caleb agreed. "And maybe the biggest one. But it's been happening in little ways for a long time. 'Way back to when you went off and blew up a wagon train while Elsie was trying to take care of me and was so plumb give out, she like to made herself sick. There wasn't much heroism for you in staying home and helping to care for a man with a bad leg. Then there's the time when the doctor took my splint off and you told Elsie I should have it reset and get it over with. Not that you weren't right, mayhap. But that's not what you were thinking about, was it? You were thinking about how you could fix the problem, even though I reckon you knew Elsie didn't need that just then."

"I've tried to make up for that, looking out for her this whole time," Saul defended. "Until the last few days, at least."

"That's just it," Caleb said. "You've looked out for her because you were trying to make up for something. Saul, you care about a woman, you've got to look out for her whether it does anything for you or not. Otherwise, sooner or later, you'll figure you've paid your dues, and then you'll go and do something stupid. Like leaving her with a family of sick folk while you go worrying over a grown man with his own life to live."

Saul wanted to be angry at the things Caleb was saying. The problem was, he couldn't tell if his anger was at Caleb or at himself. "I'm an uncaring dolt, is what you're saying."

Caleb's sigh said Saul wasn't getting it, which annoyed Saul just a trace. "Just keep one thing in mind, McBraden. My daughter's a treasure. You treat her that way, or I'm telling you what, this broken leg ain't half of what I'll do to you."

# Thirty-Seven

ROBERT WENT INTO BETHABARA TWO DAYS LATER with only Gunning to watch his back. Since the wagon train was still camped, Maggie and Susanna would be safe enough while Robert and Gunning were gone. A settler with his black manservant was a common enough sight in these parts, one that Robert hoped would not arouse suspicion.

He knew where the Moravian store was because he had ridden through Bethabara once or twice in his circuit-riding days. The settlement, neatly laid out in precise rectangles around wide streets and tidy gardens, looked none the worse for the army's encampment. The roads were rutted and the grass in the great meadow had been clipped short by hundreds of horses, but that was all. Robert contrasted it with the destruction he'd seen in Sandy Creek and tried not to get angry. Funny what a difference loyalty to the governor could make.

Gunning stopped the team at a hitching rail outside the store and Robert said, "Stay here with the wagon." He jumped down and walked inside, feeling every eye in Bethabara boring through his back.

The store was dim inside and warm from the June humidity. It smelled of tin and cloth and spices and gunpowder. A big hearty man with soft wrinkles around his eyes stood behind the counter, marking in a ledger. He looked up and said, "With what may I help you, *mein Herr*?"

"My family needs victuals." Robert willed himself to relax. *Thou preparest a table before me in the presence of mine enemies . . .*

Not in the *absence* of his enemies. Right in front of them. He added, "Flour, molasses, salt pork. Cornmeal. Salt. Coffee if you have it."

"But of course we have coffee. The flour and cornmeal, these you will find at the mill with Brother Kapp. The rest here we have. You want very much of all this?"

His accent was deep, guttural, very German. Robert gave him the amounts, bracing for an interrogation. But the storekeeper did not question the quantity. "And this, you pay how? I do not think I see you before; I do not think you have the credit here."

"Cash," Robert said, hoping no one would find that unusual. "How much?"

The price was high. Robert had expected that. He voiced a cursory complaint, dickered a little, put the money down and went out to get Gunning. The storekeeper followed him out and pointed down the road. "The mill, you will find there by the river," he said. "And I will pray you do not meet any of these Regulators when you leave town. We heard that some of them stopped wagons the Brethren were driving, and searched for weapons. God was merciful and no one was hurt. They are, I think, all frightened away now."

Robert declined to comment on this bit of news. He thanked the man and loaded their purchases. Then Gunning clucked to the team and they moved toward the mill.

Brother Kapp, the miller, showed mild surprise when Robert explained how much flour and meal he wanted. "But this is so much, you have many children, *ja*?"

"The families nearby need provisions as well," Robert said. You could not get any more "nearby" than traveling together in a wagon train.

Brother Kapp squinted appraisingly for so long that Robert began to feel uneasy. But at last Brother Kapp said, "I think only, do I have so much here to spare? But I think *ja*, there is enough. You have brought a wagon?"

Robert gestured over his shoulder. "Right yonder."

"*Gut*," Brother Kapp said. "We will load this, then."

Gunning came in and began carrying sacks, and Robert followed the miller back inside to settle the bill. Robert usually bartered for most of what his family needed. But the Ayen Ford Baptists were very limited in what they could carry. Even pelts to trade would have taken too much space. So it had to be cash. Robert glanced over what they had left and prayed the journey ended soon.

Something thumped dully outside, followed by a pair of restless snorts from the team. Sounded like Gunning had knocked a sack off the wagon. Robert finished his transaction and went outside. The sack lay in the dirt, spilling cornmeal from a split seam, but Gunning was nowhere to be seen.

Robert frowned and scanned the street. He saw the black stallion tethered on the other side just as he heard noise from around the corner of the mill.

". . . reward for him, dead or alive, and I'll not be kept from it by any obstinate son of Ham who won't tell me where to find him!"

Robert knew that voice. He rounded the corner and saw Gunning pinned against the side of the mill. His eyes flashed to Robert's. When Charles Drake glanced over his shoulder, Robert was ready for him.

The first thing on Drake's face was surprise. Robert did not see what came after that because he had already ripped Drake away from Gunning and into a pile of old barrels. Drake staggered to keep his balance and one of the casks tumbled and splashed into the river. Robert had to get in close to be heard over the rumble of the millwheel. "You want to talk to me, Colonel, you talk to me. Don't ambush folks in alleys.

And don't use the Bible as a source of name-calling."

"The name I'd call you is a fool," Drake said, struggling with Robert's grip. "Do you know the price on your head? A hundred pounds, a thousand acres, for you, James Hunter, William Butler, Herman Husband, or Rednap Howell. If walking straight into loyalist territory doesn't make you a fool, I don't know what does."

Robert wondered briefly where the other outlaws were. Herman Husband had likely run, as he had from Alamance. But James Hunter of Sandy Creek was a rebel straight through to his radical Presbyterian core, and Robert wouldn't have been surprised if Hunter was still in North Carolina somewhere. Just like Robert. "Before you call me a fool, Colonel, don't forget that the Bible says the fool hath said in his heart, There is no God. According to that, you figure out which of us is a fool."

"Can't you speak to a man without ramming a text down his throat?" Drake said through his teeth.

"I'm a preacher, Colonel. What would you expect?"

"Take your hands off me," Drake said, "or I swear I'll raise such a stir the whole town will—"

"No, you won't." Robert pulled him away from the barrels and up against the wall where Gunning had been a minute before. He dropped his voice to a gentle drawl. "From what I hear, I'm worth a hundred pounds and a thousand acres to you. Knowing you, you don't want to share the reward. Or the glory. Especially not with a lot of psalm-singing Moravians."

"If you think you'll leave this place a free man—" Drake grabbed Robert's arm. Right over the flesh wound Robert had gotten a week ago. Robert winced before he could stop himself. Drake tightened his grip and shoved Robert away. "You're wrong, preacher."

Gunning yanked Drake away from Robert and within a yard of the riverbank. The chance was too good to miss. Gunning let go just before Robert hit Drake with his whole right side. Straight into the river.

It wasn't a baptism because that included coming back out of the water. And Robert wasn't giving Drake any help on that front. He pulled Gunning around the corner and tossed the fallen sack into the wagon. "Reckon it'll take him about three minutes to get out and back in the saddle. Let's see how far we can make it in three minutes."

# Thirty-Eight

MAGDALEN IGNORED HER WEARINESS LONG enough to welcome Robert and Gunning back into camp and make sure they had something to eat. Robert sat beside her and recounted the day's events while he ate. Magdalen was so glad he was back safely, she didn't have the heart to tell him that the smell of the food still made her feel ill. Knowing Charles Drake was less than a day's journey away if he got on their trail didn't help her feel any better.

"Let me check your arm," she said, to give herself something else to think about.

He winced when she pushed his sleeve up. "It's not bad, really. Only hurts when there's pressure on it."

She peeled the bandage away and was pleased to see that the wound was healing cleanly. "Another week and I don't think you'll need a bandage at all."

"Good. I thought maybe I'd overdone it today, but I didn't have much choice." He paused. "Maggie, I ought to tell you—Drake says there's a price on my head."

"The governor put a bounty on you? He thinks you're that dangerous?"

Robert nodded. "Along with four others. James Hunter's one of 'em. A hundred pounds and a thousand acres."

She'd grown up with wealth and she was used to sums like that. But a hundred pounds was a year's wages for most working men. And a thousand acres—that would be a prize worth pursuing. "Does it frighten you, Rob?"

"Somehow it doesn't seem to matter. I've lived with danger for so long, what difference does it make that someone's put a price to it?"

She watched him, seeing more than just a lack of fear. "You're feeling that thrill of the challenge again."

Robert set his plate aside. "I was feeling it back in Ayen Ford already. But it gets stronger the closer we get to the mountains, seems like."

"The mountains always did bring out the best in you."

"And the worst."

She knew what he meant. "You still blame yourself, don't you. For not being there when the Cherokee came."

His silence was answer enough. She said gently, "You didn't do a thing wrong, Rob."

Robert looked at her, his eyes suddenly deep brown weariness. "Sometimes I don't know which is worse. The blame I lay on myself, or the fear that it will happen again."

"But we're not going all the way to Cherokee country again. Are we? I thought—"

"There's a lot more danger in the world than just the Cherokee." He sighed. "With Drake so close, and us not having a set destination—I've got a lot on my mind, Maggie."

"I know. So do I."

He must have heard something in her voice, for he glanced over and said, "Are you feeling all right?"

She was suddenly very tired. "I think I'd best lie down a while, if you don't mind."

Robert lifted her gently to her feet and helped her into the wagon. "Do you need me to fetch you anything? I don't know where Susanna went, but—"

"She's with Betty Woodbridge. I told her they could play a while." Magdalen saw the concern on her husband's face and no longer had the strength to deny her heart's certainty. "Rob, I—I think I know what's wrong with me."

"Do you?" His smile was gentle, and she knew that he knew. Or at least suspected.

"I think I'm with child."

His eyes softened to an indefinable tenderness and she stopped even trying to fight the tears. "I'm scared, Rob. So scared. I want this baby. I've wanted all of them. And I'm trying to trust, but—"

"Trusting is hard."

The deepness of his voice gave her an inexplicable calm. He was here with her this time, being her strength, her rock. "It is. So hard."

"So we'll do it together." His hands moved to cover hers. "Trust and pray."

Magdalen drifted off with unusual rapidity, another sign Robert remembered from her other pregnancies. He gently pulled the blankets straight and slipped out of the wagon. He still blamed himself for the way Maggie's first confinement had ended. His fear was a force almost as strong as love, because he loved her too much to watch her heart break again. But there was nothing he could do except be sure he was there when she needed him.

It was late, but he called a meeting, laid out the maps, and asked for counsel. He did not mention the new life Magdalen was carrying. For now, it was enough to simply say that they had traveled too long without a goal.

Mitchell said, "I thought we were aiming for my cabin."

"We are," Robert said. "As of now. But only as a means to an end. Unless you think you can fit all of us in there."

"Are there any nearby settlements?" Deacon Ashe asked. "Somewhere to stay, either permanently or while we establish our own settlement?"

"The next settlement beyond my place is a full day's journey at least, and that's with a good horse," Mitchell said. "It's not what you'd call a settlement, at that. Only a few cabins chunked together with a place to trade. And it's mighty close to Bram Fisher's land. Baptists don't set well with Fisher. Any farther than that, you're in Cherokee country, and I don't think—"

"No," Robert said sharply. "We're not going into Cherokee country."

Mitchell opened his mouth, then caught Robert's look and shut it again. He shrugged. "Just as well."

"What about this side of your place?" Saul asked. "Right on the side of the ridge, mayhap. Any likely places there?"

Robert answered for his brother. "There are settlements, sure. But they're wide open for anyone looking. I want our families someplace safer than that. Any man with eyes in his head could find any village between here and the ridge."

"Any village but one."

At Alec's voice Robert glanced up. "You know something I don't?"

"Maybe it's none of my affair." Alec pushed off the side of the wagon he'd been leaning against and came over to the map. "But there's a village right here. Sunrising. My brother lives there, is how I know."

Saul shouldered in for a look. "But that's no more sheltered than any other place. Just as wide open as what Pastor said."

"But it's not." Alec drew a line across the paper with a callused fingertip. "There's another ridge across here. They call it the Brushy Mountains. The Yadkin Valley lies down in here, between the Brushy and the Blue Ridge. The village is across the valley and halfway up the east side of the Blue Ridge. Tucked down in a hollow, forest all around. You'd hardly see it if you weren't looking for it. Good people, and no friends of Tryon. Half of 'em settled there when all the land agents back east were cheating folks. That's why my brother's there."

"I didn't know you had a brother," Robert said.

Alec shrugged. "You didn't know about Sunrising, either."

"Mitch and Hank and I know the way as far as the foothills," Robert said. "We'll have to leave the wagons there, more'n likely. The teams would never make it. Anything else we should know?"

Alec paused, hesitated. "No. Not now."

"You're sure."

"Aye. I'm sure."

Robert was not sure. Not sure at all. Alec had that look of hiding something again. But Robert was sure on one count. Alec might not be leader of this undertaking, but if Sunrising was their safest bet, Sunrising it would be.

Susanna was very tired of this adventure. It was not an adventure anymore; it was just long and bumpy and full of mud. Mud was all right when you could step in it and watch it squish, but it was not the same to have it get on everything and then dry out in the wind and blow all over inside the wagon. Mama said they would be shaking dust out of things until kingdom come but they must not complain because Papa was trying so hard to find a new home for them. So Susanna did not complain.

She did think a lot. Especially at night when everyone thought she was asleep but she wasn't really and just lay there listening to Gunning tie the canvas shut for the night while he hummed songs he said his mama had taught him. Susanna thought that must be a very long time ago. She liked the songs Gunning sang in his nice deep voice. They had a sort of comfortable sound. It was good for thinking.

But tonight, Gunning stopped humming in the middle of a song and told Papa they ought to be at Shallow Ford by Sunday. Susanna didn't know where Shallow Ford was, but she knew what a ford looked like and what *shallow* meant. That made her start thinking again. She knew people were supposed to get baptized after Jesus saved them, although she didn't understand quite exactly why. She had thought she would ask Papa to baptize her when they got to their new home. But that seemed like a long, long time now. The trip might go on forever and ever.

So in the morning she asked Papa if he would baptize her when they got to Shallow Ford. Then Papa put his coffee down and talked with her for a long time about what baptism was. It was like a picture, he said, that showed what something else was like. Susanna understood that; it was like the house on a mountain that she had made with Gunning's wood chips. It was not really a house on a mountain, but it showed what one was sort of like.

"When I put you down under the water, it's a picture of how Jesus died and was buried," Papa explained. "Then when I bring you back up, it's a picture of the way He came back to life. It shows that you believe He did those things, and that you've done them with Him spiritually."

"Oh." Susanna didn't quite know what the "spiritually" part meant, but Papa said she didn't have to understand it all at once.

"Being baptized tells everyone that you want to follow the Lord," Papa said, and Susanna understood that. Then Papa prayed with her about it and said he would be very happy to baptize her once they got to Shallow Ford—if it worked out. He didn't explain what that meant. There were a lot of things that the grownups did not talk about in front of Susanna. She assumed this was simply another one of those things.

On Sunday Papa looked worried and would not say why. Susanna thought it might have something to do with the way Mr. Perry left right away to go scouting, and then a man came on a horse and gave Papa a letter. Papa looked at the letter and frowned, and when Mr. Perry came back Papa looked at him and frowned again. But Papa did not say anything, because it was time for Sunday meeting. They had the service right on the riverbank, and then Papa took her down into the cold, cold water and asked in front of everybody if she had trusted Jesus to save her. Susanna shivered and said, "Yes," and she thought everyone could hear her teeth chatter.

Papa covered her face with his hand and told her to hold on tight to his arm, and then he said, "Susanna Boothe, on your profession of faith in Christ, I baptize you in the name of the Father, the Son, and the Holy Ghost, buried in the likeness of His death—"

She squinched her eyes up tight as the water splashed up and over, Papa's arm holding her steady, down and back up. His hand came away and she gasped from the cold. Papa said quickly, "Raised in the likeness of His resurrection."

Somebody said, "Hallelujah," and Papa prayed, but fast, because she was shivering again. Then he helped her up the bank and Mama wrapped her in a blanket. The sunshine felt good, but not as good as her heart. If only Papa didn't look so worried.

## Shallow Ford, North Carolina

# Thirty-Nine

"Two dozen men." Robert shook his head and glanced past Alec, already envisioning Charles Drake on the eastern horizon. "He must have brought them out from Ayen Ford with him."

"They're a ways off yet, so there's no danger straightway," Alec said. "Just thought you'd like to know."

"I had hoped we'd get some good fellowship here." Robert motioned over his shoulder at the Shallow Ford Baptist meetinghouse. "Joseph Murphy was pastor here. He's in hiding now, and most of his people aren't far behind."

"You're not safe yet, that's sure," Alec said.

Robert felt suddenly cold, and not only from the baptism he had just finished. He folded his arms over the front of his Sunday coat, feeling the crackle of the letter the rider had brought a few hours ago, and he wondered if they would ever really be safe. Especially with Alec in the picture.

"Alec," he said quietly, "I think it's fair to say there are a lot of things you haven't been telling me."

Alec's expression went guarded. "If we're being fair, there are a lot of things you haven't been telling me, either."

"I've never lied about anything."

"And you're saying I have?"

Robert pulled the letter out of his coat, making no move to hand it to Alec. "A rider came in today while you were scouting. He came from the west and left a letter for you."

Alec reached for the folded paper. Robert pulled it away. "And he added that your *wife* said it was urgent."

Alec moved so fast Robert had no time to sidestep before Alec ripped the letter out of his hand. "What my wife says is no concern of yours."

"I'm not saying it is. What's a concern of mine is how you happen to have a wife when, so far as I knew, you lost your family in a fire. And how she happens to know where to find you. Not to mention what else that rider said to me. *Seems like everything's been urgent ever since his work for the governor back in Anson.*"

"That is *none* of his business. Nor yours, either."

"Actually, it is."

"Give me one good reason why."

"Because," Robert said, moving in a step, "Charles Drake is less than a day's journey away, and we've staked everything we've got on what you've said about some village called Sunrising. If that's not a good reason for you to level with me, I don't know what is."

Alec looked him in the eye. Robert held the stare until Alec gave. "I'll admit, I let you think my family was dead. I've let a lot of folks think it, because that fire happened just as I said it did. I'm a wanted man as much as you are, and the only way I can be certain sure my wife and children are safe is to let folks think they're gone. Until the threat is over and we can all be safe together."

"They're in Sunrising with your brother. Aren't they."

"That night that I left camp alone, I went to see them," Alec admitted. "We'd heard Tryon might be going that way and I had to know they were safe. My Sarah found out then that I was traveling with you, headed west."

"Is she the only one who knows?"

"She and my brother, most likely; he'd be the one to write for her. And that rider she sent out, though Sarah would know not to tell him everything. Sounds like he knows enough of his own," he added bitterly.

"Which brings us back to what you did for the governor in Anson County."

"Does it matter?" Alec said shortly.

Robert had a distinct feeling that Alec was not angry so much as scared. Scared of the truth. "Something tells me you're afraid to drag that part of your past out in the open."

Alec said, "No more than you are."

"I'm not afraid of anything."

"No?" Challenge laced the word. "Then let's hear what you did for General Waddell and what you have against Cherokee country and why you're so all-fired jumpy about getting to Sunrising even though you told me God protected us from Tryon's army."

Robert looked away. "Whatever you did, you're afraid of doing it again."

Alec said hoarsely, "How do you know that?"

"Because if there's anything I'm afraid of, it's that."

"I worked as a strong-arm for the governor's men in Anson County." Alec stared at the horizon. "I lived for the power, watching loudmouthed rebels give in when push came to shove. My wife saw the change in me first. I was angry, and proud of it. I said, I can ease off any time, I'm only giving 'em the taking down they need. Then someone swore out a warrant on a preacher."

Some corner of Robert's memory yielded up a flash of remembrance. His best friend on the floor of the barn where he'd been preaching, Alec standing over him, men gathered all around. Another of the governor's men had taken Robert down before he'd had a chance to see Alec's face. But he knew beyond a doubt that it was Alec who had held the warrant for Robert's longtime partner. "Josh Remington. Old man Harper's barn."

Alec went rigid. "You were there?"

"Josh was my best friend, and the best partner I ever had. You didn't see me; one of your men had already dragged me outside by the time you finished with Josh. We had run a lot of circuits together. By that time, he was mostly working in Anson, but I was there with him that day."

"Then you know he didn't give me a lick of fight, even when I came after him." Alec's voice was low. "I don't know what stopped me. It had to have been that preacher's God. I backed away and went out and tried to breathe. I'd almost killed a preacher, a man who'd never done me any harm. I still don't know, did he—"

"He recovered. Took him a while, but he was back on the circuit, last I knew."

"I quit that night," Alec said. "When I got my eyes off my own conceit, I started to see what some of those men had been fighting for. The next year I joined up with the Regulators. But now—" He stopped.

"You're angry again."

"I can't tell you how it felt, watching Drake knuckle under when I came after him at your house, that night he came when you had left town. It was the feeling that I could do anything, that I held the power of life and death. Tell you the truth, it scared me. Because it felt—good."

"I was a circuit rider, but I was also a scout for Hugh Waddell." Telling the story for the second time in two weeks did not make it any easier. "He was a good man once, maybe still is. Only somewhere along the way he took up with the wrong ideas. I loved what I did, enough that when I heard rumors of a Cherokee attack, I didn't pay much mind. I had meetings to preach, messages to run, danger to face."

Alec said quietly, "And then."

"The Cherokee work in small bands," Robert said. "Only a few men, sometimes. You fight back and they run, and then they come back from a different angle. Again. And again. And again. Maggie was in our cabin in the settlement and she'd heard me talk about the way they attack. So when the other settlers pushed the Cherokee back, she knew it was only a matter of time. Gunning was out felling a tree and she went out to warn him. They came back just as the cabin went up in flames. Maggie was in a family way . . ."

When Robert was finished Alec let the silence hang for a long minute. Then he said, "So when I hauled you over the coals for running off to your brother and leaving your family behind, I wasn't telling you a thing you didn't know."

"No," Robert agreed. "But I needed to hear it. You may be scared of turning into what you used to be, but I lie awake nights thinking what could happen if I fail my family again."

Alec said without preamble, "A baptism like today, you do it often?"

"When I'm asked and I believe it's the Lord's will. Why?"

Alec said quietly, "You recollect how you told me that someday I'd get tired of handling everything myself?"

"I remember." And it was ironic, Robert thought, how he himself felt like he'd hit the same point.

"I'm getting there," Alec said. "And I thought maybe—"

He paused. Robert said, "It doesn't start with baptism, Alec. It's got to start with giving up your trust in yourself and putting your trust in the Lord."

Alec looked at him for so long Robert began to brace himself. Then Alec said, "You really believe that, why don't you give up your trust in yourself and start trusting the Lord to look out for your family?"

"It's not that simple, Perry."

Alec's smile was twisted. "Thought you'd say that."

Robert wanted to say, You don't even believe any of this, so what business do you have calling me out on it? But he could not muster the anger to support the thought.

"I'm only saying it because I'm looking for something I can bank on," Alec said, low. "And if the man who teaches it doesn't believe it, what good can it be?"

"Alec, that's not—"

But Alec was already turning away. "Forget it. I'd best see what Sarah says is so urgent."

Robert watched him go, walking away from truth. Because of Robert. *Oh God, what have I done?*

Sarah Perry's message was urgent enough that within five minutes Alec was back to tell Robert they needed to pack up *now* and *go*. Hugh Waddell's detachment was just southwest of the Brushy Mountains, and rumor said they were turning northeast within a week. If the wagon train didn't get to the gap before Waddell came within range of the foothills, Robert and his people risked being followed straight through the gap, across the river, and into the village.

"If Waddell once turns back this way, he won't be out of the area for a good long time," Alec said. "You go in now or you don't go in at all."

Robert deliberated, mentally counting days and miles. "We'll have to lighten the load at the gap. We can't make any kind of headway if we don't."

"Double up the teams?" Alec said.

"We knew it'd come to that, sooner or later." Robert motioned sharply for Mitchell to join them. "Mitch, how long you figure it'll take to make it from here to Hunting River Gap?"

"With what we've got?" Mitchell glanced around. "Three, four days."

"Call it three and we'll push hard," Robert said. "Spread the word; we're shifting the load."

The side of Alec's mouth pulled in a grim half-smile. "Looks like you'll have to do some trusting on this one, Captain. Like it or not."

## HILLSBOROUGH, NORTH CAROLINA

## Forty

JACOB CHAUNCY HAD NEVER CONSIDERED himself a nervous man. But something about sitting alone in a Hillsborough jail cell made fear rise up every time footsteps echoed in the hall. Chauncy had spent hours arguing out in his mind why he had done nothing contrary to law. And at the end of every mental argument, he had to admit that nothing he said would ever hold against a man like Charles Drake.

The footsteps tonight stopped at his own door. He willed himself to rise and stand by the far window as if fear had no hold on him at all. The door swung open and two men entered. One was the warden. Chauncy submitted wearily as the officer chained his wrist to a ring in the wall. What did they honestly think he would do, spring on the warden and smother him with the rotting mattress?

Chauncy had seen the other man in Ayen Ford, talking with Drake shortly before Chauncy's arrest. Tall, narrow, his hair the color of dead leaves, he moved with a lean intensity that suggested his authority over the warden, over the prison, over Jacob Chauncy himself.

"My name is Malcolm Harrod." His voice would have been as featureless as the rest of him, save for a faintly caustic edge. "It may or may not interest you to know that I am personal representative of His Excellency's concerns."

Chauncy said flatly, "And what has that to do with me?"

"I'm well aware that Colonel Drake arrested you for little more than spite," Harrod said. "There is, of course, some small chance of a treason charge. But I feel that you would be better dealt with in other ways. I have a proposition to make to you."

He paused. Chauncy said, "Go on."

"There is a message that must be carried to Drake as soon as possible," Harrod said. "I propose your release in exchange for your service as courier."

Another encounter with the colonel? "No."

"It's that—" Harrod motioned around. "Or this. And later—who knows what may become of you?"

He had a point. Chauncy said, "Where is Drake now?"

"In the vicinity of Bethabara. Perhaps a bit farther west."

"What business could he possibly have there?" The questions might annoy Harrod, but Chauncy wanted to know what he was agreeing to before he agreed to it.

"He is attempting to locate a dangerous outlaw." Harrod's expression became a slightly sardonic smile. "Robert Boothe. You may have heard of him?"

Chauncy clenched his fingers, unmindful of the shackle's bite. All the way to Bethabara—eighty miles or more. At such a distance he could surely foil Harrod and Drake both. Discard the message, make his own way, perhaps even warn Boothe again if he could find the nerve . . .

Harrod added quietly, "We know where the colonel is and what he is doing because we have eyes everywhere." The smirk was firmly in place, a warning now. "You understand? Everywhere."

His threat was implicit. Chauncy did not care. Any chance at all was more than he had now. "I'll do it."

Harrod gave a brief nod. "Excellent. Warden, unshackle him."

The chain fell away and Chauncy said, "There is one

more question I should wish to ask."

"I do not guarantee an answer."

"Why should you choose me?"

Harrod looked as if he had expected the question, and as if the answer amused him in some satirical way. "This message confers upon Colonel Drake more authority than I should have chosen to give him. Your—shall we say—*reappearance* will be a fitting reminder that my authority still exceeds his."

Chauncy looked at him bitterly, thinking, Nothing but a pawn. Again. Well, it's better than the alternative.

## Somewhere West of the Yadkin River

# Forty-One

Two days out from Shallow Ford, the scouts rode in and reported. Hunting River Gap was six miles ahead. Drake was two miles behind. And closing in.

Half of the wagons had been abandoned at daybreak, split for firewood or left to the weather. Possessions had been sorted, wept over, discarded. Remaining belongings had found places in the wagons that were left. Horses had been harnessed into double teams, preparing for the rising terrain ahead. There was no time now for Robert to do anything but act and pray he did the right thing. They had to put some distance between their families and Drake.

"Deacon Ashe, you'll take the lead and head due west," Robert directed. "Mitch, Alec, Hank, I'll need you . . . You too, Gunning." He paused, gaze landing on Saul McBraden. He wasn't about to order Saul to help; after all, Robert had just about ordered him to stay with Elsie.

But Saul caught the hesitation. He looked at Caleb, then at Elsie. Caleb said, "You've got to do something with yourself, McBraden, or you'll drive yourself and the rest of us daft. And I reckon I just don't care anymore."

Saul said slowly, "Elsie, I—"

"Just go, Saul," she said, and looked away.

Robert let Saul join the group, deciding there wasn't time to hold court on Caleb and Elsie's reactions. "Caleb, I'll need one of your boys to look after my share of the load."

Caleb said, "Abe, that's you."

"The men I've named will stay with me," Robert said. "Make sure you have plenty of powder and shot, boys."

He could see them checking powder horns and hunting pouches. They couldn't afford any extra time, but Robert remembered how it had felt to be within range of Tryon's army and realize he had not prayed like he should. He also remembered how it had felt to have Alec drag his lack of faith out in the open. Neither feeling was one he wanted to relive. "Gather 'round, we're going to pray."

They clustered in. Robert removed his hat. "Lord, fight against them that fight against us. Stand up for our help. Keep us safe, make the way clear. In Christ's name, amen."

He had no time for more, though there was more he could have said. But what he had said, he had meant with all his heart. "Everyone head out. Deacon, lead the way. Gunning, go on up to the top of that rise there." He pulled a firebrand from a dying cookfire and blew until it flared. "Take this and wave it the moment you see Drake's men. Then fall in with the rest of us. We'll picket our horses in that thicket over yonder and spread out just this side of the rise."

Hank said, "Gunning can take my rifle. I've got my bow and quiver. Can shoot just as straight with that, if I do say so myself."

"Perfect," Robert said, and silently blessed Hank for his mare's nest of belongings.

The remaining wagons rumbled out, followed by able-bodied folk who walked to further lighten the load. Mitchell said, "Rob, do us all a favor and tell us what we're doing."

There were a dozen ways Robert could have described it. But he settled his hat lower and picked the one that Mitchell would understand. And the one that required the most honesty. "We're going Cherokee."

The trees to either side of the trail were thick, dense, perfect. Robert rested Cricket across a low pine branch and sighted carefully as Drake rode into range. Click of the hammer, squeeze of the trigger, an artistic miss that split the feather in Drake's cockade. Drake reined in hard and jerked out one pistol, firing at an unseen foe. Mitchell unleashed a Cherokee war cry so authentic it made Robert's scalp prickle. Then Mitchell's rifle cracked and a branch came down on the hindmost pair of riders. An arrow hissed between the riders, not two feet from either man. One fought pine needles out of his face and yelled at Drake. "I didn't sign up for Indians!"

"Hold your ground," Drake shouted, drawing his sword and motioning a wide arc. "Don't knot together; it makes a better target for—"

A rifle ball sang off the blade with a metallic ring. Alec began reloading. Saul covered the softly percussive sound with a shot that nearly unhorsed a rider twice, once when the man ducked and once when his horse reared. Gunning chased Saul's shot with one of his own. A man on the near side lurched in the saddle and clutched his arm. Contrary to orders, Drake's men began to knot together.

Drake bellowed, "Return fire!"

But Robert and his men were no longer there. They had each fired, once around the circle, that was all. They melted into the fading light, three hundred yards up the trail. Even from there they could hear Drake giving orders and expressing his contempt and triumph at how quickly the enemy had fled. In minutes his men were again so close that Robert could see the nervous tension on their faces.

"Drake'll laugh out of the other side of his mouth yet," Alec muttered beside Robert. He pulled the trigger. This time the attack was a smooth rhythm, one man cocking as another man fired, firing as another reloaded, reloading as another primed his next charge. Hank's next arrow nipped the man who rode just behind Drake. Robert, last to fire, reloaded swiftly and they moved on out, another few hundred yards.

Third time around, Drake had had enough and gave chase. Which was exactly what Robert had been hoping for all along.

His war cry was louder and longer than Mitchell's, a note of defiance impossible to ignore. Robert did not even try to be quiet as he plunged down the heavily wooded slope, luring Drake back the opposite way. Mitchell faded into the trees at his right, Hank and Alec to his left, Gunning and Saul just ahead. Robert did not know whether Drake still thought they were Cherokee or not, or if he ever had. What mattered was slowing him down. And scaring the wits out of his men wasn't a bad idea, either.

Down an incline and deep into trees well away from the path, Robert's movements went silent and he took refuge behind the massive trunk of a fallen red oak. Quiet rustles all around indicated that his men had followed his example. Drake came into view, still on their trail, and Robert prayed his men would obey orders and not try to take Drake down. He's still representative of the governor, Robert had said. Until it comes down to his life or ours, shoot as close as you like but aim to miss. Putting a bullet—or an arrow—in the governor's emissary would only cause more trouble.

Another round of shots, more rustling, another war cry, and they led Drake deeper into thick forest that blocked even the slanting rays of the western sun. Robert knew this country. Drake did not. Robert led him on, staying just out of sight, while on either side the five marksmen hid behind trees and bushes and fired one at a time, another militiaman wounded, the hat knocked from Drake's head, every shot calculated to keep the colonel and his men off balance. When Gunning's last shot died into a far-off echo, Robert pivoted, took a knee behind a stump, and fired low across the front hooves of Drake's stallion. The horse snorted and reared. Drake shouted and pulled at the reins. Hank's bowstring twanged from off to the right and the arrow passed just in front of Drake, skimming the horse's withers. The animal reared again, higher this time, came down hard and threw Drake from the saddle. Mitchell's final shot sent the horse bolting for the hills. Drake wouldn't be chasing anyone for a good while.

Robert and his party of five slipped stealthily back to the trail and on to where their horses were picketed, far up the path and out of sight. Robert could not fight the weary smile that pulled the corner of his mouth as he mounted up. Drake's men were far, far behind, their fear-heated argument lost to the distance. The wagons were somewhere up ahead, nearing the foothills for sure. *Five of you shall chase a hundred,* the Bible said, somewhere in the Books of Moses. God had been faithful once again. And it could not be much farther now.

# Ayen Ford, North Carolina

## Forty-Two

WHEN JACOB CHAUNCY REACHED AYEN FORD, he hardly recognized the place. Or perhaps he didn't want to recognize it. Destruction was everywhere, from the Baptist meetinghouse to his own home, a bitter reminder of the price of defiance. Robert Boothe had been wise to get out.

Ebeniah Kendall's house was still standing, damaged only by the cursory vandalism of a few Regulator sympathizers. Malcolm Harrod had appointed the sheriff as personal escort for Chauncy's travels, which irked Chauncy more than he would admit. Kendall alone could just as easily have been Harrod's courier. But no, Harrod had a point to make, and he wanted to use Chauncy to make it.

Kendall told the stable boy to have a fresh horse waiting through the night in case of urgent orders from Harrod. Then he ushered Chauncy into a bedroom furnished with such opulence that Chauncy understood for the first time what had made the Regulators so angry. Not the wealth of another man, but their own hard-earned money lining a greedy official's pockets. The luxurious surroundings would have made Chauncy feel like a guest instead of a prisoner, had the circumstances been different. Then Kendall went out and turned the key in the lock and even that faint illusion was gone. Just like everything else, Chauncy thought bitterly. His vestry, his business, his good name. Everything but Robert Boothe's nagging words. *The truth will hold its own. And the truth will make you free.*

"I told the truth," Chauncy said to the velvet drapes. "And look what's come of it."

When Kendall started to snore on the other side of the wall, Chauncy took out the oilskin packet that held Harrod's message to Drake. The candle on the bureau flickered as Chauncy held the paper close to the light. The message said much what he had expected. When this reached Drake, the colonel would have full authority, military and civil, for the purpose of apprehending Robert Boothe and any other outlaw in western North Carolina.

Chauncy stared at the precisely inked words until they blended together in the shadows. He stood like that, thinking, until the candle burned low and the clock in the other room struck midnight. More time had passed than he had realized. He swept his cloak off the foot of the bed and threw it on, held the letter in the flame of the taper and watched the paper flare and shrivel into blackness. He folded the heavy velvet drape against the windowpane and drove the back of a chair against it. The glass fell in a curtain of shards. Chauncy pulled his cloak around him and climbed through.

He had traveled from Hillsborough to Ayen Ford on a borrowed horse. The animal was at the livery stables now. But Kendall's was not. It was ready to ride, just as the sheriff had directed. Chauncy untied the knotted reins with fingers that were surprisingly steady. When Sheriff Kendall got the door open and shouted his name, Jacob Chauncy was already on the road to South Carolina.

When morning came, Chauncy spent an hour in a roadside tavern, sleeping harder than he'd ever slept in his life. He awoke confronted by a version of himself that he did not recognize.

He, Jacob Chauncy, had stolen another man's horse and was running for his life, flouting the authority he had always prided himself on obeying.

Head vestryman, most respectable man in Ayen Ford, he had not known he had it in him. But if he thought hard enough, he could see the signs of his own self-interest all the way back through his first opposition to Robert Boothe. And now this. Liar, thief, just like Drake. Chauncy knew in his heart that he would have killed Kendall if the sheriff had tried to stop him.

*For all have sinned, and come short of the glory of God.*

For the first time in his life, Jacob Chauncy believed it.

He went out and found a northbound traveler and persuaded him to deliver the horse to the livery stables in Ayen Ford. Then he hitched a ride south with a farmer. He, Jacob Chauncy, begging a ride in a farm wagon. The farmer talked all the way through Anson County. About his crops. About the Regulators. About his move west. About how he hadn't stepped foot in an Anglican church since a preacher by the name of Josh Remington had told him to repent and believe the gospel. The man talked a lot more after that, but Chauncy didn't hear a word. Robert Boothe had said that, too. Repent and believe. Chauncy had never thought he had much to repent of.

But this time he knew better.

By the time the South Carolina border came in sight, Truth held His own in the life of Jacob Chauncy. And Truth had made him free.

When Malcolm Harrod heard Kendall's report, he quietly and decisively terminated the sheriff's career, wrote another copy of the message, and packed his saddlebags. His passage was already paid on the ship that would take Governor Tryon to New York. But first, Harrod intended to settle this matter himself. Clearly no one else was capable. Kendall, his status wrecked by his own failure, was proof of that. Harrod considered it time well spent to ride west through the decimated Regulator settlements and remind himself of the power of the British Crown. The power *he* represented. The power that unfortunately Charles Drake would represent, too—*after* the governor's orders reached him. Not before.

Drake was bored with his two dozen Hillsborough recruits. It had taken a deplorable amount of time to find his horse, and his men had complained enough for a regiment. More than that, Drake needed more men if he was going to withstand any more Cherokee attacks. Never mind that he hadn't heard from the governor in weeks. General Waddell was within riding distance. Waddell had plenty of men. And there was no need for him to know about Drake's lack of fresh orders. There was no need for him to know anything except that what Charles Drake wanted, Charles Drake would have.

## Somewhere West of the Yadkin River

# Forty-Three

THE AYEN FORD BAPTISTS CROSSED HUNTING River Gap late Wednesday, leaving Drake and his men somewhere on the east side. Next came the ford over the curving arm of the western Yadkin River. From here to Sunrising was a straight shot. Robert dared to slow the rate of travel just a trace, for Maggie's sake. He had cushioned the wagon bed as much as he could and she said she couldn't feel the bumps at all, but her game little smile showed she was as worried as he was.

Robert called an early halt Thursday night, knowing the river and the Brushy Mountains were now between them and Drake. When the remaining wagons had circled and pine-bough shelters had been thrown up around a roaring fire, Magdalen smiled her relief and promptly fell asleep. If there had been any doubt that she was with child, her remarkable propensity for sleep would have been enough to cause suspicion. But tonight, Robert couldn't blame her. He picketed the team, made sure Susanna was fed, and helped her into the wagon beside Maggie. Then he rolled himself in a blanket beside the wagon and did not wake until early the next morning, when he jolted awake as surely as if he had been struck.

He lay still, wondering what had awakened him, until he heard the thud and crackle of fresh wood on the bonfire nearby. Alec was up already. Robert stared at the hazy dark overhead, some deep sense of unease rankling in his mind. Something he could not define, but could not shake.

This was going to be a hard day. He knew it. And he'd dare to bet Alec knew it too.

He sat up and found he was still fully dressed, which meant he had been exhausted the night before. Still was, come to think of it. He reached for his belt knife and the pistol that had been his spoils of war in his first fight with Drake and shoved both weapons into his belt. Today was a day to be prepared. He tossed aside the blanket, got to his feet and crossed to the fireside. "Alec."

Alec glanced up. "Couldn't sleep."

"Today's the day. Isn't it."

"Just the way I felt." Alec looked over his shoulder, back toward the river and the gap. "I'm thinking I'll scout a ways behind us, just to make sure . . ."

"Give me five minutes to wake Maggie and I'll come with you."

"There's no need. I can fetch your brother."

"No. This time I need to see for myself."

Alec looked as if he would object. Then he nodded and said, "Just as you say, Captain."

Magdalen was slow waking up. Her voice was sleepy as she asked, "How far will you go?"

"I don't know. And I don't know when we'll be back, either. If we meet Drake—"

The sleep slipped from her eyes, replaced by the time-worn fear of countless days and nights. "I understand."

"Do you?" he said gently.

She nodded. "'The good shepherd giveth his life for the sheep.' We've spoken of it before."

"I'm not leaving you alone this time, Maggie. Not if I can help it."

"And if you can't—" She smiled wearily. "We'll cross

that bridge when we come to it."

It took longer than five minutes for Robert to say all he wanted to say, and for the prayer they prayed together. Alec had the horses saddled before Robert dropped from the back of the wagon. It was a matter of moments to wake Mitchell and give him his orders: look out for Magdalen and Susanna and start moving if Robert and Alec didn't return by noon. Then Robert mounted up, and Alec mounted up, and they rode out to meet the sunrise.

They made a full circle a mile east of Hunting River Gap, moving south and circling back toward the north. The sun was halfway to its zenith when they again reached the gap, where mountain slopes rose to either side and the Yadkin River Valley dropped away in front of them. The elevation and the view left Robert a little short of breath. But that was nothing to what he felt when he saw what lay between them and the valley.

Smoke. A dozen cookfires, maybe more. That was might-nigh a hundred men. Not a quarter mile off.

That camp hadn't been there when Robert and Alec first came through. Whoever it was was on the move.

"Drake or Waddell," Alec said quietly, as if fearing his voice would carry the distance. "Not that it matters. They can't have missed the wagons we left back of the gap. The ford is the first place they'll go. They go through there, they'll follow us straight into Sunrising."

*Us.* A few weeks before, Alec would have said, They'll follow *you*. The change was a subtle signal that the storm was just over the horizon and it was no time for anyone to stand aloof. Robert caught the layers of worry in Alec's words and said, "It doesn't endanger only us. Does it."

Alec shook his head. "Most of the folks there are just like you and me. On the run from something. Or hiding someone who's on the run from something. Half the town would be arrested if the governor's men found their way in and took to investigating. Arrested or burned out or . . ."

He stopped. Robert thought of Alec's family somewhere in that village, a woman who loved Alec as much as Robert loved Maggie. There was no point in running any farther; the governor's men were simply too close to outrun. But there was nothing to do but try.

Robert said, "If they've stopped to eat this early, they're planning on some action, soon and hard."

Alec looked at him and said simply, "What's the plan?"

"Split up," Robert decided. "You go around them to the right and I'll go to the left. That way at least one of us makes it. And whichever one of us does will tell folks to hitch up and go and not stop for *anything*. Waddell's farther south. It's got to be Drake. With reinforcements."

"Reinforcements or no," Alec said grimly, "you know who he's coming for. Us."

"No," Robert said quietly. The west wind was in his face, smelling of smoke and danger and the knowledge of what lay ahead. "He's coming for me."

# Forty-Four

SAUL MCBRADEN WAS ABOUT TO GO DAFT. HE was still living on the thrill of attacking Drake's men Cherokee style. But he was also responsible for the safety of Elsie's family. And Elsie did not seem to appreciate that. Right around midmorning she got him up against a wagon and told him she'd been talking with Mrs. Boothe a lot lately, and she'd come to realize a thing or two. Saul would never stop being a Regulator. And that was all right. He would never stop loving a challenge. That was all right, too. Elsie was learning that she had been designed to help Saul, not the other way around. She didn't even mention his venture to find Alec. But what she *did* say hit him harder than an argument ever could have.

"I love you as you are, Saul," she said. "And I'll love you whether you're a hero or not. You don't have to prove anything to me. Ever."

He wasn't trying to prove anything, was he? Only a little, maybe. "I just want everybody to know that I can take care of you, Elsie."

Her smile seemed sad somehow. "Maybe running Colonel Drake off isn't the only way to take care of me."

Then she went to pull her youngest brother out of the

river and Saul went to have a man-to-man talk with Pastor Boothe.

Only, Pastor Boothe wasn't anywhere to be found. Saul gave up looking for him and went to ask Mrs. Boothe, which he hated to do because he knew she hadn't been feeling well. But all Mrs. Boothe could tell him was that Pastor had gone out, early, to scout with Alec.

Saul thanked her and started for Thurmonds' side of camp, his hat still in his hand. He was halfway there when Alec rode out of the trees. Saul paused, figuring he'd better not tell Mrs. Boothe just yet. She'd want to know if Pastor was with Alec, and Saul would rather not tell her he wasn't.

Alec bore the scratches and grime of a hard ride through straight wilderness. His gelding was lathered and heaving. Saul didn't have a chance to speak before Alec swiped the sweat out of his eyes and started giving orders.

"Drake's not a quarter mile off. Captain wants us to light out and he'll catch up with us." He pointed at Mitchell. "Go ahead and take the lead, seeing as you know the way."

Mitchell nodded and moved swiftly to help Gunning break camp. Two of Elsie's brothers were hitching up. Saul figured he had time to ask, "Alec, where's Pastor?"

Alec had begun to strip down his gelding. "I told you. He'll catch up."

"Why didn't he come in with you?"

"We split ways so at least one of us would get here," Alec said. "I took the norther way, through those woods. He went the other way. Trail or forest, I don't know which."

"But if Drake sees him—"

"I reckon he's thought of that." Alec went around the gelding's other side. "He gave his orders, and what he does now is his lookout. Not mine." He glanced up briefly. "And not yours, either."

Saul worried the brim of his hat, thinking. He could tell from Alec's matter-of-fact tone that Alec was covering his own unease. A lot of things could happen to keep Pastor Boothe from reaching camp. One of those things was a man named Charles Drake, and Saul hated to think how that could end without anyone to lend Pastor a hand.

But Pastor had already hammered it to him once that a man didn't leave his responsibilities just because he thought he had a better idea. Caleb had hammered it to him, too. So had Saul's own conscience. It was time to stop making excuses and show Elsie his love the hard way. Saying he loved her was easy. Proving it was another matter. Saul glanced down and realized he'd crushed the brim of his hat.

"All right, Lord," he muttered under his breath. "Looks like I know what I ought to do. I'll look out for Elsie. You look out for Pastor. And I'll try to leave it at that."

Alec glanced up again. "You talking to me?"

"Not unless you're the Almighty and can settle the trouble I'm studying on," Saul said.

Alec gave him his twisted half-smile. "Maybe once I'd have thought I could. Now I'm not so sure."

"There are a lot of things I'm not so sure of anymore," Saul said. Such as, how he could think he knew everything, only to find that the simplest decisions were the hardest. He tugged his hat back into shape and went to help Elsie pack up. Maybe after that he'd have a few minutes to go out on a hillside and pray the way Pastor liked to do. Glory knew they could use it.

It was a long time before Robert felt safe in moving ahead of Drake's band of men. Alec had made a run for it while Robert watched Drake's next move, but now the same trees that kept Robert out of Drake's view made it hard to judge just where Drake was. Robert wanted to give Wanderer the reins and let him run. But he didn't want to tangle with Drake's rear guard, and he didn't want to cut ahead so soon that Drake would see him and follow him. Robert could feel the strain of patience slowly develop into a knot between his shoulders as he held Wanderer to a slow jog trot and prayed Alec had made it to camp in time to sound the alarm.

When Drake hit the ford of the West Yadkin, Robert

saw his chance. The crossing would take some time with as many men as Drake had. Robert cut downstream on the other side of a canebrake and was across in seconds. He still had rough terrain to fight. And Drake was not far behind. But Robert had a slim chance of outstripping him, and any chance at all was something.

Just where the elevation started to rise again, a horse bolted out in front of him. Robert reined in hard. So did the other rider. An ax was lashed to his saddle and the cockade in his hat suggested he was militia. Robert chose to fall back on a previously used line of defense.

"Have you seen the colonel?" he demanded, the haste in his voice no act at all. "He was near here, I could have sworn. I've got a message for him." What that message was, Robert wasn't saying. But it was along the lines of, *You go through me to get to my people.*

"I'm looking for him myself," the man answered. "He sent a couple of us out to block the trail up ahead of those rebels he's after. It's done and I'm heading back to report."

That explained the ax. Quickest way to block a trail out here was to cut down a tree and leave it. It was a fair guess that the wagons were still too far up the trail for anyone to hear the tree come down.

"I knew he was after them, but I still haven't heard what he aims to do when he catches them," Robert said. His voice was even, steady, betraying no sign of the tension he felt. *Plead our cause, O LORD . . .*

"If his plan works, he'll surround 'em and demand surrender," the man said. "He wants Robert Boothe, and he'll get him one way or another, even if he has to take some hostages to do it. I imagine the rebels won't be so brave if Drake's got their women and children in hand."

Maggie and Susanna. And the baby. *Oh, dear God. Fight against them that fight against us.*

"Me and my mate, we saw one of their men out on a hill a ways off and followed him back," the man went on. "Scotsman, looked like he was talking to himself, didn't even see us. We're on their trail now. Soon as we catch up to the colonel, that is."

Scotsman. Going by looks, that would be Alec or Saul. Alec would have the good sense to stay in camp. Saul, on the other hand—but out on a *hill*. What would *any* of the men be doing out on a hill at a time like this?

The rider added, "Hold, that's my mate now."

Another horse crashed out of the brush, another rider with a woodsman's ax and the same cockade as the first. He said to his partner, "Colonel Drake passed us already. We'll have to double back to meet up with him." He jerked his head toward Robert. "What's all this?"

"He's looking for the colonel. I've seen him before—I'm thinking he was in that first lot of men the colonel brought with him from what's it called, Ayen Ford, isn't that right?"

The other man looked at Robert, narrowed his eyes, brought his horse in so close Robert saw the recognition dawn and the warning form on his lips.

Robert and Magdalen had talked about the day when it might come down to the good shepherd giving his life for the sheep. But Robert didn't aim to do it any sooner than he had to. And he didn't aim to have things out with anyone but the colonel himself.

He did not draw his pistol so much as whip it in one seamless arc from his belt to the man's temple. The blow jarred all the way through Robert's shoulder and down to the saddle. The man dropped from his mount like one dead. The other rider fumbled for his saddle holsters, saw Robert flip the hammer back, and took to the woods.

Robert let the hammer gently down and jammed the pistol back in his belt, took one hard breath and wheeled Wanderer west. Drake's man would wake up where he'd landed. But by then Robert meant to be protecting his wife and daughter and unborn child. He rarely used his spurs with any force. But this time he made an exception. Wanderer laid his ears back and ran.

# Forty-Five

Magdalen watched Mitchell shift and look out over the wagon seat where Gunning was handling the reins. She wished her brother-in-law would stop moving. Where Rob would have been calm, cool, and collected, Mitchell was as restless as a tree squirrel. Magdalen already felt guilty for having a place in the wagon when so many others were on foot. "We're all right, Mitch, really. Go ride with the other men."

He did not pull his attention from the landscape outside. "I promised Rob I'd look out for you and Susanna."

"Looking out for us doesn't require pacing back and forth like you're doing. Gunning has the wagon well in hand, and I'm really all right."

"Of course you are." He still didn't look at her. "It's not as if your husband is somewhere out there with a rabid bounty hunter on the loose."

Magdalen bit her lip. "It's hard enough already, Mitch."

"Sorry," he said huskily, turning. "I allow as I'm feeling it too. The waiting. And wondering what it was he felt this morning when he went out with Alec. Least I can do is stay close. You've got enough to worry about."

True enough. The wagon jolted over a rock and her

hands went instinctively to her abdomen.

Mitchell's eyes followed her motion and he frowned. "You all right?"

She tried to smile. "Other than what we just talked about, yes."

"I don't mean that way." His frown deepened and she could see him thinking, no doubt remembering her lingering illness. "Maggie, are you—"

She tilted her head toward Susanna. Mitchell broke off. Magdalen nodded, answering his unfinished question. If Rob had told his brother to look out for her, Mitchell had a right to know.

"Does Rob know?" he demanded.

"For almost two weeks."

Mitchell whistled through his teeth. "No wonder he's in a hurry to get you to Sunrising."

"How much farther is it?"

"Might have to leave another wagon or two, but we'll be there by tonight if we try."

Magdalen shifted her weight, sensing a change in the wagon's movement. "Then why are we stopping now?"

"I don't know. Gunning, what—"

"Tree down up ahead," Gunning said. "I'm circling to the side of this clearing so there's room to work, and then I'm stopping till the way's clear. I don't aim to wreck us now, not with Drake a quarter mile back."

"Strong wind last night," Mitchell said. "I'll take a look. Hank's a mean hand at cutting trees, if it comes to that." He dropped from the back of the wagon and headed for the downed basswood. Alec and Hank joined him. Magdalen watched them from under the canvas cover that Gunning had rolled up and lashed out of the way to let in the breeze. Susanna leaned against Magdalen's arm, not saying anything. Susanna was quiet today. Most everyone was, sharing whatever unnamed tension Rob had felt just before dawn.

Mitchell came back a few minutes later and climbed into the wagon bed, stepping gingerly over the goods piled in every spare corner. "Looks like it was cut," he said. "They're going to try to get it out of the way, and hope some settler doesn't get irritated when he finds his tree chopped up for him." His tone was facetious, as if he was trying to make light of a situation that deeply disturbed him. "Might as well give Rob a chance to catch up. He should've been here by now..."

Mitchell trailed off and Magdalen saw the uneasiness in his face. "There's an ax under the seat," she said, deciding he needed something to do. "We'll be fine while you work."

"They don't need another hand," Mitchell said. "Too many woodsmen spoil the cutting, and all that. There'll be work to do once it's down to manageable size. Come here, niece of mine, and help me put a new flint in my rifle."

Susanna stared pensively at the long gun. "I helped Papa do that with Cricket once, back at home."

"Well, you can help me with mine here. Not to your new home yet, but close enough, I'd say." Mitchell unscrewed the hammer pin, tested the flint, unscrewed a little more.

Susanna shook her head. "It won't be home until Papa's there too."

To his credit, Mitchell didn't try to answer that. Just laid the rifle down and held out his arms. Susanna buried her face in his shoulder and Magdalen thought, Maybe he's more like Rob than I thought.

She turned away, watching the buzz of activity around the fallen tree. Caleb Thurmond had dragged himself over to a dead log near the stump and sat there as if his very presence would somehow move the tree. Hank was mindlessly twirling a hatchet with one hand, not noticing the way men were edging away from him. Alec and Saul were discussing why the tree had fallen in the first place. Gunning maneuvered around the upper end of the trunk, branches snapping in his wake, and reminded Alec and Saul that they didn't have time to argue it out. Magdalen smiled in spite of herself. She'd seen this state of affairs before, when it seemed there was no order at all and yet somehow the job was done in record time.

Then she saw the horses. Pounding in from the east. Breaking branches, crashing through brush, too many for the trail. They cut between the wagons and the knot of men by the massive trunk. Magdalen started to say Mitchell's name. But she never got that far. Charles Drake was brandishing a torch from the head of the line.

The world went still. Women and children huddled around the wagons, taking shelter where they could. The men stopped moving. Even the wind seemed to sigh and die out. Every word Drake said was as clear as if he spoke directly to her.

"Five minutes," Drake said, his voice cool, impersonal, measured. As if he had reached the point where he did not need to waste time with threats. "Surrender in the King's name, or if not, those wagons go up in flames."

Magdalen squeezed her eyes shut for one brief moment, hoping it would all be gone when she opened them again. But it was not. Oh, Rob, Rob, where are you?

Susanna made a small, frightened sound and clung to her uncle. Mitchell pried her away from him, reached for the rifle, fumbled in his hunting pouch for a new flint. Magdalen watched the dance and flicker of the lone torch, directly in front of her. The other militiamen carried unlit pine branches that would snatch the flame and spread it at the moment of Drake's order. The canvas was dry from the wind. And the wagons were old wood by now.

"Mitch," she said softly. "He's right in front of me. I can reach the water barrel—do you think I should—"

"Anything to buy time," he said, almost too low to be heard, and jammed the flint into the hammer.

Magdalen said under her breath, "'What time I am afraid, I will trust in thee,'" and reached for the bucket.

The water splayed out in a wide arc. For a moment time stopped, freezing the look on Drake's face. Then the torch hissed out and she jerked the rolled-up canvas free and yanked it down over the opening.

Mitchell paid her a single nod of approval over the approaching sound of angry footsteps. He pushed the rifle at her, leaned over and grabbed the empty bucket that was still in her hand. "Susanna, sit down on that blanket over yonder and don't move. Maggie, get behind me."

"But Mitch—"

"Now!"

Men leaped into the wagon, men who didn't know that she was Robert Boothe's wife and was, as Drake had once said, every bit the rebel her husband was. The bucket in Mitchell's hands was evidence enough. They seized Mitchell, knocked the bucket away, pinned his arms behind him, and Magdalen realized in a sickening moment that not only was he going to let them, he had meant for it to happen.

Because Mitchell was Rob's brother, and he would not let anyone come after a woman if he could take the punishment instead.

Susanna started to cry and Magdalen heard herself say, "Wait, no, he didn't—"

Mitchell looked over his shoulder and said the most self-sacrificing thing she'd ever heard him say. "Maggie. Shut up."

Drake's men dragged him out, and the ache inside turned to a cold throbbing that spread all through her. Gunning was still on the other side of the clearing, in the cluster of men that Drake was now giving a second warning. She sank down beside Susanna and let her daughter lean into her. Mitchell was gone and Magdalen had no one to lean on anymore. She only prayed that Robert would come in time to stop all this. And that if he was in time to stop it, he would be able to.

The men hadn't even seen Drake coming. Alec blamed himself for that. No wagon to handle, no family on hand—he should have been the one most on his guard. But no, he'd had to let himself be distracted by an argument about a fallen tree. He'd had a bad feeling about that tree, sure. It had seemed mighty suspicious that it should be this particular tree on this particular stretch of trail. It looked even more suspicious now that it was clearly to Drake's advantage. But it hadn't been worth arguing over. Cut it up, get it out of the way, argue later. That would have been common sense.

Now Drake's hundred militiamen formed a tight cordon between twenty-five good men and their families. Few of the men had their rifles at hand, and firing on Drake's men wasn't even an option. No matter how good a man's aim was, only a fool would even try to shoot at moving targets positioned in front of women and children. Drake had obviously thought of that. He wasn't likely to give up for one bucket of water. And he wasn't going to stand for any resistance. Mitchell Boothe was on the ground in irons to prove it. The man was lucky he'd not been shot. Yet.

Saul had gone motionless. He said in a slightly stricken voice, "Elsie's over there."

"I know," Alec said, his sharp tone calculated to bring Saul up short. "And so is every other man's woman. And children. What we're going to do about it is what we've got to think about. Surrendering won't fix anything; they'd still be unprotected."

"Surrendering ain't in our blood," Hank Jonas said, as if he'd been a Regulator from the day they signed the oath.

"Miz Maggie and Susanna are over yonder without anyone a'tall, now that Mitch is down," Gunning said. "So if we're not going to surrender, we'd best figure out right quick what we *are* going to do."

Alec scanned the scene, watching for an opening. "If we could just get a man across behind them," he muttered. "Coming in where they don't expect it. Get Drake down, and I don't think the rest of 'em would last long."

"If only it wasn't for this leg of mine," Caleb said in frustration.

"I'll go," Saul said eagerly. "For Elsie, I'd—"

"For Elsie, you're going to stay put," Alec said sharply.

"You won't do her any good dead. No, if anyone goes it'll be me."

"But you've got family too," Saul argued. "If you—"

"They're probably safer with me out of the way." He didn't add that on his last visit, his youngest child hadn't even remembered him.

Gunning said quietly, "Master Rob wouldn't want you to do it unless you knew where you were going if you didn't make it."

"Gunning, we don't have *time*," Alec said. He shut out their concern, building a wall, hardening himself with the same anger that had carried him through Alamance, through his arrest in Ayen Ford, through his work for the governor. He was going to buck the odds, stop him who dared, and it was no one's business but his own. Maybe in some way it would atone for what he'd done to that preacher he'd beat up in Anson. If there was such a thing as atonement.

The men had the sense to keep talking, giving him noise under which to slip away. There was not much cover in the clearing. He skirted the edge, watching for the first angle that would let him take Drake down without endangering any innocent bystanders. Ten feet. Twenty. Thirty. His rifle was slung low in both hands, loaded, primed, slick against the sweat on his palms.

Forty feet. Fifty. The only cover here was underbrush, stubby pines, fallen branches. Alec moved to go prone and someone shouted a warning. He swung to identify the threat, heard another shout, saw Drake turn away from Mitchell and draw his pistol.

Alec had his rifle to his shoulder and his finger to the trigger before he saw the preacher's wife and daughter framed in the opening of the wagon just behind his target. One inch wrong on his aim and it wouldn't be Drake; it would be one of them. His thumb still snapped the hammer back, an automatic movement, and then he knew he could not make himself pull the trigger.

The pistol shot exploded before he had time to drop.

Fire ripped through his left shoulder, a blazing pain he had not known existed. Warm blood spilled through his hunting shirt as he went down, the brushwood rising up around him, blocking out Drake and the wagons and everything but hard ground and gray sky.

There was no help now in the anger. Or the cynicism. Or his own stupid pride in his own stupid strength.

All that was left was Robert Boothe's God and the knowledge that he could not handle this anymore.

# Forty-Six

ROBERT HIT THE EDGE OF THE CLEARING JUST as Charles Drake said, "One minute."

Robert couldn't see everything, but he could see enough. Drake's men were ranged out in front of the wagons, easily a hundred strong, five men to every one of the former Regulators who stood on the far side of the clearing, tense, watchful, waiting. Mitchell was not among them. Neither was Alec. Something in the brush caught Robert's gaze, something buckskin and homespun and dark crimson. Alec was down. *Lord Jesus, have mercy.*

Drake shouted impatiently at his men, something about a fire and why was it taking so long. Robert put the pieces together faster than it took to comprehend the words. If Drake intended to set fire to the wagons, Robert had very little time to do anything. No one would pull the trigger on Drake because it meant risking the women and children.

Robert had had plenty of opportunities to feel like a failure. But never like this.

Husband. Father. Pastor. Christian.

His wife was with child and in danger. Again.

His daughter was seeing things no innocent seven-year-old should have to see.

His church was losing its chance at a new life and new home.

And Alec was on the ground, still breathing, maybe, but facing an eternity without Christ because Robert had lived a mockery of his claim to trust God.

Robert was trusting God this time because there were no other options. And right now, trusting God meant failing as a Regulator, too, and doing the hardest thing he'd ever done.

Drake had not seen him; he was sure of that. He cut in close to his own wagon and slid his rifle gently under the canvas and over the side, wanting his family to have all the defense he could give them. The canvas was pulled up from within and Magdalen said on a caught breath, "Oh, Rob."

He said softly, "It's time."

She nodded. "I know."

Drake was still giving orders when Robert rounded the head of the wagon train and reined Wanderer in for a brief instant. "Colonel!"

Drake swung around in the saddle. Without a word Robert wheeled Wanderer into the woods. Behind him came shouts and crashing brush and hoofbeats that punctuated his silent prayer. *Dear God. Help me. I can't do this.*

But he had to.

Drake shouted to his men, an order to stay by the wagons and let him handle this. Which meant Robert's men would be occupied for the time being. Robert didn't want to drag them in any deeper. He could not ride up to Drake and turn himself in; Drake would think he had an ulterior motive. But neither could Robert let his family and church keep sharing his danger.

Drake's black broke through the brush ten yards away, two other riders coming behind. The metallic chink of wrought-iron chain against the silver trimmings of Drake's saddle said that Drake had come prepared. The foliage was dense here, the terrain rough enough that Robert could slow down and look natural in doing it. Even though everything in him screamed at him to run.

He was done running. For good.

They caught him just where the forest opened for a brief space. Three of them, closing in, cutting off escape. Drake's pistol whipped back and forward and down, too fast for Robert to duck. Whether he fell or was dragged, he didn't know. He came down hard in the soft dirt and dimly heard Wanderer whinny and snort as strange hands took his bridle. Then a stab of pain in Robert's side jerked the world back into harsh focus. Someone had kicked him. He gritted his teeth and rolled halfway over, braced against the pain and Drake's words overhead.

"Robert Boothe, you are under arrest for treason in the name of the Crown."

Robert got to his knees, his temples thundering in time to the slight sway of the world around him. The pistol was cocked now. Drake did not make any threats. He did not need to. He flicked the silver barrel a fraction of an inch and said, "Amherst."

"Sir."

"Search this man and put him in irons."

Amherst was a squarish man with the features of a bulldog. When he moved closer, Robert recognized him as the militia leader Robert had led astray in Ayen Ford. Today he did not look fooled. He hauled Robert to his feet, shoved him against a tree and ripped his hunting jacket open. Robert breathed hard against the throb in his side and concentrated on the still small voice. The fact that he even heard it was a miracle of God.

*Except a corn of wheat fall into the ground and die, it abideth alone.*

Amherst stripped Robert's belt knife and handed it to Drake.

*But if it die, it bringeth forth much fruit.*

Robert's pistol next. The butt was splintered where he had struck the rider in the woods. It would have been so easy to do the same to the man who was searching him . . .

*Greater love hath no man than this, that a man lay down his life for his friends.*

Drake passed the irons to Amherst, then held his pistol steady and watched, impassive, as Amherst shackled Robert's wrists. Robert locked his gaze on Drake's, giving himself a focus so he would neither succumb to the lingering unsteadiness nor do something to Amherst that he would be forced to regret. Amherst slapped ankle irons into place and Robert said, "Answer me one thing, Colonel. What has any Baptist ever done to you to make you hate the whole lot?"

"How can I countenance any faction that so openly flouts the authority of both church and state?" Drake said. His tone was light enough to border on mockery.

"You don't care a lick for the church and you know it." Robert spread his feet as far as the chain would allow. A stance not of defiance, but of bracing for the consequences of what he was about to say. "All you want is power. Power and control. And we want freedom. On every front. It's every man's birthright, the freedom to make his own choices before God. Freedom for *you* to accept God or reject Him. His truth, His forgiveness, His righteousness. Your choice, because He created you free. Just like every other person ever born."

"I've made my choice." Drake ripped the words out. "And that choice is no affair of yours or His."

"Which is why any threat of freedom," Robert said, measuring the words, "scares you to *death*."

Drake's openhanded blow admitted the truth. Robert had never known anyone angrier than a man without an answer.

Drake's men had clearly been ordered to look the other way. Both stared off at nothing as Robert fought to stay on his feet and Drake said, "The flat of a sword next time, Boothe."

Robert didn't answer because he didn't trust himself to

speak. He had a new grasp of Christ's choice to suffer when He could have spoken the command that would have brought justice. Or simply made it happen without a word.

Christ had chosen to take it. It was an impossible example to follow.

*My grace is sufficient for thee.*

*You promised, Lord,* Robert thought grimly. *I'm holding You to it.*

Drake spoke for the first time to the man holding the horses. "Go and dismiss the men from their posts. I doubt the rebels will give us any more trouble. The men are free to return to General Waddell."

The man mounted and rode off. Drake stood holding his black and waiting until the horses of a hundred militiamen rumbled away in the distance. Robert released a breath he had not known he was holding. In one thing, at least, he had not failed. There was a bitter irony in knowing that the only Regulator work he had succeeded in was getting himself arrested.

The hoofbeats faded and Drake said, "Just enough rope, Boothe. I warned you."

# Forty-Seven

BY THE TIME THE LAST FEW MILITIAMEN WERE gone and Gunning had gotten Mitchell free and on his feet, Saul and Hank had stopped the worst of Alec's bleeding. Mitchell had been roughed up enough to miss a lot of details, but he had heard the shot that had taken Alec down. There was no missing that. He brushed off as much dirt as he could and helped move Alec to Ethan Hardy's wagon.

The ball had gone through the left shoulder. Over and down a little, and it would have been Alec's heart. As it was, the ball had missed the bone and gone clean through. Alec stirred and grimaced at the pressure Saul put on the wound. After moving him brought no further response, Saul poured a slug of whiskey down Alec's throat because it was the only thing left to do.

Alec choked and winced and opened his eyes halfway. He focused unsteadily on Mitchell and slurred, "Captain make it?"

Mitchell looked at Gunning. Gunning looked away. Saul stabbed the cork back into the bottle and didn't look at either of them.

At last Gunning said softly, "Drake's gone. Leave it at that."

Mitchell heard it in his voice; Rob was gone too. Alec's eyes closed again almost at once. But for a brief moment the steel glint had come back. So they all knew now. Drake had Rob, and it was too late.

Mitchell sat back on his heels, looked up at Gunning, said, "How's Maggie?"

"All right." Gunning spoke in the same flat tone as before. "Quiet. Like she's scared what'll happen if she lets herself talk about it."

Mitchell knew the feeling. There were angles to this that he didn't dare think about until he'd had time to hash them out with God. "I'll go talk to her. Try to keep Alec still."

Alec said, without opening his eyes, "I can hear you, you know. It's not as if this confounded bandage is wrapped 'round my ears."

If that was any indication, Alec would be just fine. Mitchell slid gingerly out of the wagon, feeling every bruise Drake's men had given him. Saul slid down behind him and fell into step alongside. "I prayed," he said fiercely. "Like Pastor does, you know? Went out alone and told God everything. And then this. It wasn't supposed to end this way."

"I know." That was one of the things Mitchell wanted to discuss with the Almighty. When he had time. Then something Saul had said caught his attention. "Went out alone? When?"

"Right after Alec came in. There was a hill over yonder from where we were camped—"

Saul broke off. His voice went grim. "They saw me. Drake's men. Didn't they."

Mitchell didn't answer. Saul said, "You go out and pray and that's what puts Drake on your trail? It's just—wrong somehow."

"Rob would tell you to do the right thing for the sake of the right thing. Never mind the consequences. Me, I don't know what to tell you."

"Caleb said that about the right thing, too." Saul stared at the fallen log where Caleb still sat, Elsie now beside him.

"Not the same way, but that when you care for someone, you look out for them whether it does anything for you or not. That's what I was trying to do. Guess maybe it goes for praying, too. You do it whether it works out or not."

"I wouldn't know about the caring for someone part." Mitchell had never met the right woman and doubted he ever would. "But the rest of it, I'd say you're right on."

"I'm going to see if Elsie needs help." Saul kicked a rock. "Makes you mad, some things. And nothing you can do about it."

He turned away. Mitchell checked on Magdalen, bracing for the breaking of the dam. But Susanna was the only one with tears. Whether or not she understood everything did not matter. She clung to her uncle as if afraid he would leave, too. He didn't have the heart to tell her how his bruises complained at her fierce grip. Magdalen looked out at the trees and rested one hand on her stomach and said softly, "What is it that Job said, Mitch? 'The thing which I greatly feared is come upon me.'"

He loosened Susanna's arms ever so slightly. "But you're all right? I mean—"

"Yes. I'm all right. *We're* all right. All of us. As far as I know, that is." She paused. "How much farther to Sunrising?"

"Two miles. Maybe less."

"I don't want to camp here. Not after—everything." She glanced out the opening again. "I can still smell smoke."

"We'll move as soon as we can. With Alec hurt—"

"I know. Never mind. It's no matter, really, compared to all the rest." The deep sorrow in her gaze made her tired smile a lie. "I've told Elsie so many things about trusting. Trusting the Lord when there is no one else."

"I'm not leaving you, Maggie."

She did not even seem to hear him, just smiled wearily again and said, "It is so very different to do it yourself."

Alec was tougher than half-cooked gamecock, as Magdalen's father would have said, and he was not quiet about wanting to keep going. So they kept going. Everyone walked now, but for the smallest children and the injured. And Magdalen. She wondered if anyone would think she had special privilege only because she was Robert's wife. But no one seemed to notice. The wagons rumbled and creaked and lurched into Sunrising about the time Susanna cried herself to sleep in Magdalen's lap.

Mitchell halted the caravan and handed Magdalen down before a stout log building. Two buildings, actually, with a dogtrot that ran between them like a tunnel, open on both ends. Magdalen could see all the way through the passage, past the doors that opened off either side, to the wooded riverbank behind the property. A shed-roof porch ran the length of both buildings. Over its wide steps was a slightly crooked sign with a white bird, a cluster of green leaves, and the words DOVE & OLIVE. A spry, silver-headed little woman bustled out, introduced herself as Kate McGuiness, and welcomed everyone with a lively Scotch brogue.

"So this is Sunrising," Magdalen said.

Cabins sat in squat groupings along rudimentary roads, here and there a place of business. Trees towered all around, maple, hickory, poplar, white pine. Giant oaks and basswoods gave the impression of a timeless forest that did not even notice the civilization that had imposed upon it.

It wasn't like Ayen Ford at all. But Magdalen was sure it would feel like home. Someday. If only Rob could have been there, too.

"Do be coming in before the townsfolk swarm on you," Kate McGuiness said. Up close her blue eyes sparkled with life. Magdalen liked her already. "It's naught so very grand, dearie, but it's a bit of a spot for resting weary bones, it is. Now what did I tell you, here comes our good Mr. Pembrook now. He used to be a judge or some such thing, and he's not gotten over it yet. He's a might testy, but don't let him be scaring you."

The gentleman in question was large and solid and wore his authority, however bygone, like an amiable autocrat. He inspected the gathering and demanded, "Might any of you be loyalist?"

Mitchell swung Susanna down beside Magdalen and moved in close to them both, making his protection obvious. "Not a chance, and that's the very reason this lady needs some peace and quiet."

"There's no harm in being sure," Pembrook rumbled. He nodded to Magdalen. "Though I beg pardon if I've disturbed you, madam."

"It's all right," Magdalen said wearily. "Who's that coming across the street?"

"That'll be the Perrys," Kate said brightly. "Coming to see their Alec, no doubt."

Magdalen was not sure what she had expected Alec's family to look like, but she certainly hadn't imagined the beautiful raven-haired woman who carried a small child on one hip and led a gaggle of older children behind her. "I'm Sarah Perry," the woman said shyly. "Is Alec—did he come with you?"

Alec was not steady on his feet yet, but that wasn't going to stop him. Mitchell helped him maneuver out of the wagon. Sarah Perry's eyes widened at the sling that immobilized Alec's shoulder. Mitchell murmured a low explanation, aimed away from the children's ears. Alec's wife handed off the toddler to the oldest girl, a young woman a little younger than Elsie, and led Alec gently toward the cabin across the street, her arm around his waist. He whispered something that made her smile in the dusk. Magdalen couldn't watch anymore.

Kate said, "There will be time for meeting folks later. You and your wee lass come right along."

Mitchell nodded to Magdalen. Simon Pembrook stood courteously aside. Kate led the way up the porch steps, and Susanna whispered loudly, "Mama, why does she call me a wee lass?"

"It's the Scotch way of saying *little girl*," Magdalen whispered back.

"But I'm not little. Am I?"

"No, sugar. You've been just as brave as any young lady could be."

Susanna sighed and yawned. "She can call me a wee lass anyway if she wants. I like her."

Kate turned around. "I'd not be calling you a wee lass if I was knowing your name, now, would I?"

Susanna said with grown-up dignity, "I'm Susanna. And this is my mama." Her formal tone faltered as she added, "My papa isn't here."

Magdalen elaborated for her. "I'm Magdalen Boothe. My husband—" She paused, also at a loss. How did one explain to a complete stranger?

Deep understanding muted the sparkle in Kate's eyes. "It is so very hard to lose the one we love, is it not?"

"Yes," Magdalen said softly, afraid that saying the words any louder would break her control. "Yes, it is."

Kate pulled her into an embrace as strong as it was unexpected. The warmth of it was Magdalen's undoing, warmth as deep as the peace that passed all understanding. She wept on Kate's shoulder and knew that she was home.

# Forty-Eight

MITCHELL AWOKE FROM A RESTLESS NIGHT stiff, sore, and dead certain that this wasn't over.

And somehow he was the one to make sure of that.

He untangled himself gingerly from the blankets he'd spread in the wagon bed and started piling them aside, hoping Maggie and Susanna had had a good night in the inn. Widow McGuiness was just what Maggie needed. Of course, it wouldn't hurt for Maggie to have her husband back, either, and that was where things got thorny.

"Lord," Mitchell said, tossing the last blanket onto the pile, "this feeling I've got had better be from You, or else I need You to stop me before I do something knuckleheaded. You know better'n anyone that I don't want my brother in the clutches of a man like Drake. But what I want isn't enough to risk more trouble over. So if You're the one who wants me to do something, I'd appreciate it if You'd make it real clear, real soon."

He belted his hunting shirt and dropped off the back of the wagon, suddenly wondering how Alec was this morning. Couldn't hurt to find out. Maybe it would be just as well to leave Maggie be for a while yet anyway.

The Perry family's cabin was chinked neatly in every

crack and bore a tight thatch roof that spoke of regular maintenance. Mitchell guessed Alec's brother took care of that in Alec's absence. The man who answered Mitchell's knock was a lean giant of a man with fire-red hair and Alec's exact facial angles.

"One of the new folks, right?" he said. He was younger than Alec and spoke with an easy drawl. "I'm Bryan Perry."

"Mitchell Boothe. Just wanted to know how Alec is."

"Come on in." Bryan motioned him forward. Mitchell had the vague impression of far too little space for the number of children in the room. With the ease of habit, Bryan paid no heed to the toddler he nearly tripped over as he introduced his wife.

"We live in the cabin next door, as a rule," he explained. "Only with Alec like he is, we stayed to give Sarah a hand."

"She's in there with him now, but she won't care if you want to see him," Bryan's flaxen-haired wife said. She held a mug toward Mitchell and offered, "Coffee?"

Mitchell accepted the cup and followed Bryan into a small bedroom at one side. Alec was propped up in bed with his own steaming mug. "Morning, Boothe."

"Well, your eyes are open and you're drinking coffee, so I'd say that's a good sign," Mitchell said.

Alec lifted his mug with his good arm. "It's not as strong as the stuff McBraden dumped down me yesterday, but I'd just as soon not get used to being a drinking man." He motioned with the mug toward his brother. "You've met Bryan, I see. And my Sarah, too, haven't you?"

"Last night." Mitchell nodded to Alec's wife, liking the gentle possessive Alec used. It was a side of him Mitchell hadn't seen before. "I'm sorry to disturb you, ma'am."

"No trouble. You men talk all you wish, only don't tire him too much." She smiled at Alec and slipped out. Mitchell took her chair and shoved it a little farther away from the bed, not comfortable with being *that* close to Alec.

"I'm already tired," Alec said. "Don't see how talking will make any difference."

"I mean it when I say you look more alive than you did yesterday," Mitchell said.

Alec leaned back. "Still feel like I've been rode hard and put up wet. But more alive than I've ever been before."

His brother said, "I don't see how you can say that."

"It has to do with a preacher I beat up in Anson County seven years ago, and how I heard him telling folks to repent and believe the gospel," Alec said. "And then that's what I tried to do, lying flat on my back out there in the scrub with nothing else to think about."

Mitchell said quietly, "If you tried, He heard you."

"That's what I'm banking on," Alec said.

"I still don't see it," Bryan said.

Mitchell opened his mouth. Alec said, "I've told him, Boothe. Sometimes it just takes us Perrys a little extra time. Thickheaded, you know." He winked at his brother. "You heard anything about the captain?"

Mitchell shook his head. "No. But it hasn't stopped me from thinking."

"You reckon we could do it?" Alec said.

"Do what?"

"You know what. Get him out of harm's way and keep him there."

"I don't see how. And there's no *we* about it; that shoulder's not up to a rescue."

"I forget. Or wish I could." Alec sipped his coffee, watching Mitchell over the rim. He lowered the cup and said, "Don't you lie to me, Boothe, you've got some idea of how to do it."

Alec was right. Mitchell did. Rob would have called it daft and discarded it right out of hand. But Mitchell had a niggling feeling that it might actually work. And he had no idea where it had come from, except from the One he'd asked for guidance.

He sighed and tipped his chair back against the wall, looking at Bryan. "Anyone here in town speak Cherokee?"

After the last few days, Saul had decided something. The right thing could also be the hard thing, especially when it didn't turn out like you thought it would. But sometimes that was what had the most caring in it. So when he told Elsie about Brother Mitchell's plan, he had already decided that he was not going to help, no sir, he was going to stay put and look after Elsie and prove that he cared, even if it killed him.

And then Elsie said, "If they need you, Saul—go."

"Elsie, I've done the wrong thing too many times. I'm not doing it again."

She studied his face. "What do you mean by *the wrong thing*?"

"You know. Leaving, all those times I should have stayed to take care of you."

"But it's not about that. Not anymore." There was a soft peace in her smile. "God will take care of me. I know that now. And you weren't made for me; I was made for you. Made to help you go do what God made you to do."

"But all those other times—"

"God was teaching me, Saul. Just like He was teaching you. Maybe I didn't need you to stay—I just needed to know that you would if I needed you to. And I couldn't know, or tell you, if you left without giving me the chance."

Saul began to feel stubborn. For all the right reasons, he hoped. "I don't want to go, Elsie. I want to be here for you."

"The Lord is here for me. That's enough."

"Elsie—"

"Saul. Please."

He looked away. He'd had his mind made up . . .

"Does God want you to do it?" she said softly.

"Caleb said to treat you like a treasure," he said slowly. "And I'm going to. Because you are one."

"Pa has always treated me that way," Elsie said. "And he treated Ma that way, too. Not because he was always home, but because we knew he'd always listen. And that whatever he had or did was ours to have or do with him. If

God wants you to help Brother Mitchell—and I think you know the answer to that—all I ask is that you let me share it with you."

Saul had a sudden vision of what it would be like to go conquer the world with the knowledge that a good woman was behind him and with him in everything he did. He had been trying to conquer the world alone, trying to prove his own strength, instead of sharing his strength, his challenges and triumphs, with the one God had made to be a help meet for him. Someone perfectly suited to him. It was not good for man to be alone.

Sweet Carolina, he'd been a royal bonehead. "Elsie, I'm an idiot."

"Not an idiot. Just learning. Like me." She tilted her head and smiled that smile that set his heart to racing. "If this is being an idiot, I like you better that way. Now go conquer the world and hurry back to tell me about it."

## Shallow Ford, North Carolina

##  Forty-Nine

When Charles Drake crossed Shallow Ford with his prisoner, Malcolm Harrod was waiting for him on the other side.

Drake's fingers clenched on the reins. "Harrod, what under heaven are you doing here?"

Harrod nodded at Robert Boothe. The man was still in chains and bore the dirt and bruises of two days' hard travel, yet his face held a quiet strength that Drake did not like at all. Harrod said, "I assume this is either Robert Boothe or another rebel like him."

"Answer the question," Drake said. "What do you want?"

Harrod indicated a small house on the outer edge of the settlement. "Let's discuss it out of the mud, shall we?"

"There is nothing wrong with right here."

Harrod said with a note of steel, "This way, Colonel."

The two-room cabin had probably belonged to a rebel family before the conflict at Alamance. It was abandoned now, one of many. Drake found a grim satisfaction in using it for the governor's business. His two subordinates stayed with the horses while Drake shut the prisoner in the smaller room and faced Harrod across a heavy puncheon table.

"My original intent," Harrod said, "was to notify you of an increase in authority for the purpose of Boothe's capture. My messenger, Jacob Chauncy, unfortunately absconded."

Chauncy's name rankled. Harrod knew how to dampen the gratification of fresh power with one simple sentence. Drake said, "And now?"

"Now my intent is to find out how you carried off this arrest without that increase in authority."

"I am still backed by the governor," Drake reminded. "General Waddell was pleased to loan me eighty of his best men. Combined with my own men, it was more than enough to engage Boothe's men while the capture was made."

"Do you mean to say," Harrod said, "that you acted as if you already had the authority for military action when in fact your orders had not reached you?"

A seedling of unease began to break ground. Drake stamped it down with anger. "What difference does it make?"

"You acted beyond your present authority, and would have continued to do so, had I not intervened. Furthermore, you removed eighty of His Excellency's troops from their rightful posts so as to effect a militant operation against a pack of worthless backcountry *Baptists*." Harrod's voice grew harder with each word. "With absolutely *no* orders to do so."

Drake held his ground with what some would call the strength of desperation. "This is absurd, Harrod. I can give the governor the man he wants."

"Yes. If you have time." Harrod seemed faintly amused. "The governor sails in a week's time for his new post in New York. Unfortunately, Colonel, I very much doubt that you will accompany him."

Robert leaned against the wall and listened to the heated voices on the other side, using the argument as a distraction from the bone-weariness of two grueling days. This man Harrod must be the same Malcolm Harrod who had corresponded with Drake back in Ayen Ford. Robert gathered that Harrod was in some way Drake's superior and that Drake did not like it one bit. The displeasure was clear in Drake's voice as he said, "Are you saying it does not even matter that I captured Boothe at all?"

"Certainly it matters," Harrod said. "The governor did, after all, order it, and he is quite serious about the matter. He hanged six other rebel prisoners the day I left Hillsborough. I only mean that your success is not likely to compensate for your breach of authority. Yes, Boothe will go to the gallows. And yes, you will be there to see it, with a thousand acres and a hundred pounds besides."

Drake said, "It's not enough."

"It will have to be."

Something in Harrod's tone drove it home. The only reasonable ending to this was a hangman's noose somewhere back east, far from the mountains and the bracing wind. Six other good men had already met the same fate. Robert had promised Magdalen he would be there when her time came. He could not keep that promise. It was hard enough to trust God with the unknown. It was just as hard, if not harder, to trust Him when the future was spelled out as plainly as a name on a wanted list.

*Though he slay me, yet will I trust in him.*

There was more to that verse. *But I will maintain mine own ways before him.*

Like Job, Robert had maintained his own ways, had trusted in his own reason and righteousness, even while he claimed to trust in the Lord. And like Job, his own reason and righteousness were not enough.

"Oh God, forgive me."

*Our God is able to deliver us,* the three Hebrew children had said. *But if not,* they had finished, they still would not bow to the king's idol.

"If You save me, Lord, I trust in You."

*But if not . . .*

"If You kill me, I trust in You."

Here was where it got hard. Tension burned behind his eyes as he said, "If You protect Magdalen and our child, I trust in You. And if You don't, I still trust in You."

The words hurt worse than his bruised side. He took a deep breath, hearing his words to Mitchell come back to taunt him. *It's nothing I can't handle.*

He could not handle any of this. He was helpless. But God was not.

*Trust ye in the LORD for ever: for in the LORD JEHOVAH is everlasting strength.*

And then he heard the war cry.

Long, shrill, hauntingly familiar.

Drake said, "What *is* that?"

Harrod said, "I would assume the Cherokee, Colonel."

A shot exploded outside and glanced off a wall. One of Drake's men screamed. The war cry came again, closer this time. Robert jerked his head up, listening closely to the drawn-out chant that followed. Words stirred in his memory, words he had learned on his frontier circuit, working with General Waddell on the Indian front and Josh Remington on the soul-saving front.

*Be strong and of a good courage.*

Mitchell's signature blend of drawled vowels and careful Cherokee enunciation was unmistakable. Robert pushed himself off the wall, mentally repeating the end of the verse. *For the LORD thy God is with thee whithersoever thou goest.*

The door slammed open. Drake looked as if he had aged and hardened just in the time between war cries. "Boothe. You know this country. Do you speak *any* Cherokee?"

Robert eyed the rifle slot that allowed him a thin glimpse of the woods outside. Slowly he said, "Aye, some."

"It's no use, Colonel," Harrod said from behind Drake. "They're savages, man. Shoot him and we'll get out while we can."

"Do you take me for a fool?" Drake's voice edged upward. "Here, without witnesses? I could never prove it was I who killed him and not you. I'll not surrender my reward just for—"

"Your reward or your life, Colonel. I know a war cry when I hear it."

Drake ignored Harrod, grabbed Robert's arm, and shoved him out into the other room. "Find out what they want."

Robert fumbled with the latch of the front door, the motion made clumsy by the irons on his wrists. He stepped outside and glanced around. The horses were tethered nearby, pulling nervously at their restraints. Wanderer pawed the ground and snorted. Drake's man Amherst was down and moaning. The rifle ball had caught him on the ricochet. The other man wasn't anywhere to be seen. And neither was anyone who looked like a Regulator.

But Robert knew they were out there.

He cupped his cuffed hands to his mouth and hoped he got the right words for what he wanted to say: *"What do you want?"*

*"We want you!"* Mitchell's Cherokee was half drawl, half shout. Robert prayed Drake wouldn't notice the drawl.

*"They won't believe that."*

*"Tell them, and we'll make them believe it."*

Robert turned and said, "They say they want me."

"You lie," Drake said, but with a noticeable lack of conviction. "Why would they want you and no one else?"

Robert slipped back into Cherokee and called to Mitchell, *"I told you."*

Another spine-tingling war whoop split the air, this time with a touch of Saul's flat Piedmont twang. Robert's mind briefly registered the fact that Saul was supposed to be with Elsie, just before an arrow hissed out of the trees and buried itself in the dirt between Drake's feet. That would be Hank. Mitchell yelled, *"Tell him again."*

Robert translated very loosely with, "They aren't fooling, Colonel."

"But as he says," Harrod objected, "what would the Cherokee want with you?" Suspicion tainted his tone.

The next war cry was even closer. Mitchell began a low droning chant that a second, unfamiliar voice took up. The throbbing sound would have given Robert chills if he hadn't known what it was. A bead of perspiration slid down Drake's temple and he moved for the brace of pistols in his belt. One was the pistol Robert had carried for several weeks, its grip still splintered from the confrontation in the woods two days ago. Robert said swiftly, "Don't. The Cherokee have started wars for less."

"I don't understand this." The words were taut. "A band like this attacked me not two weeks ago. They didn't want anything but trouble. Now you tell me the savages want a man they've never met?"

Harrod said suddenly, "Where was this other attack?"

Drake said, "Near Hunting River Gap."

"We've had no reports of Indians there for months. Or here, either, for that matter."

"They were there," Drake said on a bitter laugh.

"Were they?" Harrod said mildly.

"Harrod, what are you trying to say? That I don't know my own mind?"

"No. Only that Robert Boothe here speaks Cherokee, you know."

Drake stared at him. "And you think—"

Robert locked his hands together and swung for Harrod's jaw, so hard that the chain of the manacles slashed across both wrists with bruising force. When bone met bone, Robert felt the impact clear to the ground. Harrod crumpled on top of Amherst.

Drake watched him fall, seeming rooted by sudden comprehension. "These Cherokee—they're not Cherokee at all."

Robert had just knocked a man out to keep that question from getting answered. "Either way you're outnumbered."

"You'll not get by with this!"

Robert shifted his weight back, massaging his bruised knuckles. "Easy, Colonel, or you'll be next."

Drake moved like a snake. The ankle irons kept Robert from the full stride he needed to hold his ground. Drake grabbed Robert's hunting shirt and slammed him against the cabin. "I won't be stopped, Boothe. By anyone. You or your men or even your God. Tell them to disperse or I swear I'll put a bullet through you right here and now."

Another arrow twanged into the chinking, missing Drake by inches. Robert heard Hank say something the Holy Spirit was probably trying to break him of. If the Regulators' cover hadn't been blown before, it was now, but the rush of danger had pushed Robert past any trace of fear. "I can tell them to go, Colonel, but it doesn't mean they'll listen. And I can tell you right now, God doesn't take orders from anyone. There's no wisdom nor understanding nor counsel against Him, the Bible says."

Drake jerked his right pistol out and up. When the hammer went back Robert dropped his shoulder and hit hard. Out of nowhere Gunning dived in front of him. The pistol roared in Robert's ear the second before he and Drake both hit the ground. Gunning was pinned between them and Robert heard a groan that might have been his or might have been Gunning's. Feet ran up and Mitchell dragged Gunning out of the way. "We're here, Rob, it's all right."

But that pistol wasn't the only one. It had a twin, a silver-barreled beauty with a splintered walnut grip. And Drake was going for it.

Not aiming for Robert this time. Aiming for Mitchell, the man who had made Drake out a fool.

Robert went for the gun with both manacled hands. Drake brought his full strength to bear, forcing the pistol up. Robert rolled sideways and braced against the ground, jerked the pistol hard and got his finger through the trigger guard. Drake threw him off and got to one knee, still grappling for control. The moment his fingers slipped from the pistol, his sword hand flashed for his hilt. The blade sang from the scabbard as Robert struggled to get a thumb on the hammer. Drake whipped the blade back, going for

Robert or Mitchell or Gunning, Robert didn't know which, and for one chilling heartbeat Robert was back on Maggie's kitchen rug with the swordflash overhead and Drake's pistol just within reach.

Only this time, Robert already had the pistol. And this time there was no stopping halfway.

The hammer click and the explosion sounded as one. The sword dropped an instant before Drake did.

It was over. Drake was dead. Robert knew it. But still he gripped the splintered stock until Mitchell pried his hands away and said, "There is no wisdom nor understanding nor counsel against the LORD."

# Fifty

Harrod was still unconscious after Mitchell had found the keys and unlocked Robert's irons. Alec's brother, a redheaded giant, found an old blanket to throw over Drake's body. The men tore off a strip of cloth and bound up Amherst's shallow scalp wound. Then they mounted up and rode. They were halfway to Hunting River Gap before Robert saw the blood on Gunning's leg.

Drake's wild shot had not missed after all. When Robert played out the scene in his mind, he knew the pistol ball would have killed him point-blank if Gunning hadn't taken it instead. Right leg, a flesh wound just above the knee. How Gunning had managed to hide it, Robert didn't know. He and Mitchell performed impromptu surgery on the side of the trail, while Gunning gritted his teeth and Hank turned green and Robert felt a nagging guilt over the way he'd taken Gunning for granted. It made him glad he'd been able to act on Gunning's behalf, although Drake's death would not have been Robert's choice of an ending. God had never meant men to kill each other. But sometimes saving someone else's life came first.

Mitchell said, "What do you think, Rob? Do we keep going or not?"

"We've got to, if Gunning can stand it," Robert said. "Harrod and the governor have a boat to catch, from the sound of it, but that's no promise Harrod won't come after us first."

"The quicker we get back, the better I'll feel," Gunning said.

Robert had some pain of his own, but he had a feeling he'd feel better, too, the minute he saw Maggie and Susanna. He helped Gunning find the most comfortable position in the saddle, then took Wanderer's reins from Saul. Saul said, "You really think they'll come after you for this, Pastor? It was self-defense. Or at least saving a life."

"The law doesn't always see things the way we do, Saul. It hasn't for a long time now." Robert put a foot in the stirrup and swung himself up. "I'm already an outlaw, and they already want to hang me. I don't see as this changes things much."

"I forget." Saul mounted and fell in beside Robert. "That this doesn't mean you're safe, I mean. You're still an outlaw."

"But thanks to you boys, I'm a live outlaw. I'll take that over being a dead outlaw any day."

When Robert dismounted in front of the Dove & Olive the next day, the first person to meet him was John Woodbridge's twelve-year-old son, Benjamin. Ever since John's death at Alamance, things had been hard for the Woodbridge family. But there was no trace of worry on Benjamin's face. "Pastor! You're back! Want me to take your horse?"

Robert handed him the reins. "Doing stable duty, are you?"

"Mrs. McGuiness here at the inn, she heard what happened to Pa, and she up and took us on," Benjamin explained. "Ma and Betty are going to help with cooking and washing, and I'm to help with the horses. We'll get room and board free. It's good for Ma, only I wish I could have gone with all the men yesterday instead of mucking stalls."

"Your time will come, Benjamin," Robert said wearily.

"I hope to God it's not too soon."

"That's Kate McGuiness coming now," Mitchell said. "She can tell you where to find Maggie. We'll get Gunning settled and tell Alec how things came off. He'll be suffering to know, seeing as he talked Bryan into helping."

Kate McGuiness came directly to Robert, as if by some motherly homing instinct. "And you'll be Robert Boothe, now, won't you? You look like just the sort of good strong lad to be lovin' a sweet lass like that Maggie darlin'. She and the wee one are right along inside."

Robert didn't feel much like a good strong lad after the events of the last few days, but he'd not deny that he loved Maggie. So he was annoyed when Saul McBraden trailed through the dogtrot and into the west room behind him.

"Saul," Robert said pointedly, "I'm about to greet my wife after four horribly long days, and I'd just as soon do it without your watching me."

"I'm just looking for Elsie," Saul said, not seeming to notice Robert's tone.

"Well, go look somewhere else," Robert said.

Saul didn't get a chance to answer because Magdalen appeared just then, and Robert wouldn't have heard him anyway, but he did have the good sense to fade out of the room. Robert talked with Magdalen for a long, long time, about a lot of different things, not the least of which was Gunning. Robert was surprised when he went looking for writing materials and found Saul still waiting on the porch.

"I thought you were looking for Elsie," Robert said.

"I was. I'm waiting for her to finish helping Mrs. McGuiness so we can talk."

"What, you've got to patch things up again because you left without telling her?"

"We patched things up before I left. That's *why* I left." Saul's smile appeared slightly distracted. "We decided *together*. I was a fool, Pastor. But she didn't mind. I guess when I know I'm a fool, I maybe quit acting like I know everything."

There was a lot Robert could have said to that. But he said only, "Here's the thing to remember. When you think you're right, don't forget what it feels like to be wrong. And you'll be less liable to do something you'll regret later."

Saul said, "You say that like you know."

"Trust me," Robert said with a short laugh. "I do."

Then he left Saul to his woolgathering and went in search of paper and pen.

Finding the words he wanted was hard. It meant acknowledging things that were ugly by the light of truth. Robert would never have said out loud that Gunning was part of his excuse for not trusting the Lord, or that his lack of faith was why he hadn't done this a long time ago. But it was true. As long as Gunning obeyed orders, Robert could assure himself all was well on the home front. Gunning was convenient. More convenient than Robert leaving his work to protect his family himself or trusting God to do it when he honestly could not. Robert did not write any of that on the paper in front of him. But it was the force that shaped the words.

Robert signed his name and laid the pen down. "Lord," he said, "there was nothing I could do yesterday to control what happened. There was nothing I could do to change Drake's decisions. He made his choices; I made mine. And You know I haven't always made the right ones. But right now I'm trying."

He blotted the ink and folded the paper and crossed the street to Alec's cabin. He was a little taken aback to find a regular convention of Regulators crammed into the small room. Alec said, "You're not supposed to be here, Captain."

"Maybe he can think of something," Mitchell said. "Rob, we want to know if—"

"In a minute," Robert interrupted. "I need someone to witness this for me."

Mitchell read the paper, grinned at Robert, and signed. He passed it to Alec, who glanced over the words and scrawled his own name. Robert said, "I'll be at the inn."

He crossed the street again and headed for the room where Gunning was supposed to be resting but probably wasn't. He found Gunning sitting up and whittling away at what looked like a doll's head for Susanna. He looked up at Robert's entrance. "I'll be on my feet again in no time, Master Rob. You wait and see."

"There's no hurry, Gunning." Robert walked over and watched the movement of Gunning's big hands, laboring over something so small. The love Robert saw in the work brought the guilt of knowing he should have done this a long, long time ago. Eleven years ago, in fact, when he'd first been convicted about it. But he'd worried what Magdalen's father would think. And then that excuse had been lost under a lot of others. Saul wasn't the only one who'd been an idiot.

"What's this?" Gunning said, setting his carving aside and taking the paper Robert held out.

"I don't know if it will hold up in court, seeing as I'm an outlaw," Robert said. "I hope to glory it won't change the way you feel about my family. But it's something I've been wrong about for a long time, and I'm sorry. And I want you to know, far as I'm concerned, you're a free man."

The meeting in Alec's cabin was still in full swing when Robert got there. It was not just Regulators, he noticed now. There were a lot of men he didn't recognize. Alec said, "Here's the thing, Captain. This town has got nothing against outlaws. I reckon most of us would be just that if we'd stayed east a mite longer. But being an outlaw, you're still fair game for any bounty hunter who happens to look for you."

"Don't I know it," Robert said.

"We want you to be safe here," Bryan Perry said. "That's what we've been trying to figure out how to do. And we ain't hit on it yet."

Robert rubbed the back of his neck, feeling tired. He had known the minute he rode into Sunrising that this was home. He didn't want to keep running. He didn't want to have to kill any more of the governor's men; he hadn't wanted to kill Drake. But he didn't want to get caught again, either.

That brought a glimmer of an idea. He said slowly, "Just one thing I can think of."

"Let's hear it," Mitchell said.

"Alec's right, an outlaw is fair game," Robert said. "Liable to be shot on sight. But once that outlaw is in custody—"

Alec leaned forward, his gaze taking on a keen edge. "I know just enough law to see where you're headed with this."

"What've you got in mind?" Saul demanded.

"Once an outlaw has been caught," Robert explained, "his life is in the King's hands. Which means no one can kill him until the King—or the King's agent, such as the governor—says so." He didn't add how Harrod and Drake had nearly broken that rule in the first panic of the Regulators' attack.

Understanding dawned on Bryan's face and Robert added, "Mayhap I should step outside now, seeing as the fewer details I hear, the less I can say I had to do with it."

"Right on," Alec agreed. "Because this meeting ain't happening, right, boys?"

Robert stepped outside and pulled the door shut behind him. He looked across the street at the inn and thought how fitting it was that it should be called the Dove & Olive. Dry ground couldn't have been more welcome to Noah than that inn was to Robert. He leaned against the door and thanked the Lord that he and his people had been welcomed by a town full of strangers who didn't seem like strangers at all.

He hadn't put an end to unjust taxes. He hadn't changed the world. But his family and his church were safe. No one would bother them here for worshipping as God led them, or for baptizing folks in whatever river was rippling at the edge of town. He pushed off the door and walked out to a rise that looked down on the rushing water.

Just like that, he knew.

This was where he wanted their cabin to be.

As long as the men meeting across from the inn could find a way for him to stay in Sunrising.

Mitchell yelled at him. "Rob, come on!"

Inside the cabin, stoic expressions of law and order did not hide the glint of true Regulator spirit. Alec motioned to a wiry, muscular man and said, "This here's our lawman. He's got something to say."

The man rose and cleared his throat impressively. "Robert Boothe, you are hereby under arrest, by the village of Sunrising, for His Majesty the King—"

He paused. Alec prompted, "To be held in custody—"

"To be held in custody of an officer to be named at a later date, which custody shall extend until such time as a formally identified representative of His Majesty shall arrive in the aforementioned village for the proven and specific purpose of undertaking said custody, or until such time as pardon shall be extended by the Crown or agent thereof."

He paused again. This time Mitchell said, "Until said officer of custody is named—"

"Until said officer of custody is named, the prisoner shall remain in custody of said village and his freedom of movement shall not be infringed. Failure to recognize these terms shall be construed as contempt of sovereignty of the people and shall be subject to such penalty as is deemed appropriate."

The man took a deep breath and spontaneous applause broke out. He bowed and seated himself.

Their shrewdness was plain. Even if a "formally identified representative of His Majesty" should happen to show up in this remote mountain village, and even if he could convince the townsfolk that he was there for the "proven and specific purpose" of taking custody, he would have a hard time dealing with that elusive "officer to be named at a later date." Robert suspected that that later date would never come to pass.

"It's perfect," he said.

"Simon Pembrook there, he used to be a judge," Bryan Perry said, nodding at an imposing man who stood near Robert. "He helped us with the wording and all, once we got it planned out. Says it's good enough for a court of law, long as you don't switch sides on us. He takes a dim view of loyalists."

"Welcome to Sunrising, Boothe." Everything about Simon Pembrook was large. His frame, his voice, even the hand he extended to Robert. It was good, Robert thought, to have a tyrant-hater on his side.

"Remember now, your approval doesn't have a lick to do with it," Alec drawled. "You're under arrest, like it or not. Now go get your wife and daughter and have a look-see around town. There's a nice piece of land up by Button Creek that I think would suit you just right."

They built the meetinghouse first. Three days after it was finished, Alec was baptized in Button Creek. Not because baptism had anything to do with placing his trust in the Lord, but because he wanted to show the whole of Sunrising—especially his wife and brother—what the Lord had done for him in saving him from sin and from himself.

Word soon filtered into town that Governor Tryon had sailed for New York on the thirtieth of June. Malcolm Harrod had gone with him. The church breathed a collective sigh of relief, prayed for New York, and kept building. On the last day of September, the last peg went in on the last cabin. That one was Saul's, soon to be the home of Saul and Elsie McBraden.

The Saturday of the wedding was the grayest, rainiest October day Robert had ever seen in the Blue Ridge. Saul and Elsie clearly did not care. Neither did Caleb, who walked with only a trace of a limp as he gave his daughter away.

"Don't know what we'd have done without you, Pastor," Saul said afterward as he shook Robert's hand, his other arm firmly around his bride. "You've taught us both more than you'll ever know."

"And you too, Mrs. Boothe." Elsie's eyes sparkled. "I know not every day will be as beautiful as today. But now I know who to lean on during the hard times. And that's the most wonderful thing anyone's ever shown me."

Robert did not sleep well that night. He got up while it was still dark and went out and stood on the bank of Button Creek. The dawn was a gray blanket of mist over the bank that rose on the other side of the river. Robert leaned against a tree and stared at the dim edge of horizon.

"Saul and Elsie are so happy, Lord. Maggie and I were just that happy the day we were wed. But darkness is going to come. It will come for them; it will come again for us. Lord, then what? You delivered me this time. What happens if You don't?"

He felt like a traitor to his calling. Good preachers, good Christians, didn't question God. But really, he wasn't questioning God. He was questioning himself.

Behind him Magdalen said softly, "Rob?"

"Over here."

"Are you all right?"

"Maggie, what is it you taught Elsie?"

"Nothing grand." She moved closer. "Only that God has to be enough, whether Saul is there for her or not. Just as He was enough for me when you couldn't be there. They're going to have hard days, Rob. They already have. Trusting God when you can't see is hard. But the Bible talks about walking in darkness. And that's the best kind of faith, because it's been tested."

Robert put his arm around her and held her close. He knew the verse she meant. The fiftieth chapter of Isaiah, right near the end. *Who is among you that feareth the* LORD, *that obeyeth the voice of his servant, that walketh in darkness, and hath no light? let him trust in the name of the* LORD, *and stay upon his God.*

That was it. When darkness came, God's children would trust in Him and keep walking. Because weeping might endure for a night, but joy would come in the morning.

Magdalen squeezed his hand and said, "Rob, the sun's coming up."

This moment was why the town was called Sunrising. The glow exploded over the horizon, crowned the hillside, flashed off the water. Just a tiny glimpse of the glory of the living God. Robert said quietly, "Thank you, Maggie."

She kissed him. And gasped.

"What? What is it?"

She turned, leaned back against his chest, and placed his hands around her waist. Then he felt it. The tiny fluttering kick of new life and joy after months of death and sorrow.

He held Maggie against him and said what he hoped this child would always remember. "From the rising of the sun unto the going down of the same the Lord's name is to be praised."

THREE MONTHS LATER
JANUARY 1, 1772
SUNRISING,
NORTH CAROLINA

# Epilogue

WHEN THE FIRST SNOW OF THE NEW YEAR HAD settled around the cabin on Button Creek, Magdalen sat straight up in bed and said, "Rob, it's time."

A healthy baby boy with a thick shock of dark hair kicked and screamed his way into the world just after Kate McGuiness arrived. Robert and Magdalen named him Ayen John—*Ayen* for the home they had left behind, *John* for the friend Robert had lost at Alamance. Susanna was impressed. She had never known anyone with two names before. She was quite sure Benjamin Woodbridge only had one.

Mitchell stayed in Sunrising and spoiled his nephew rotten for six months. In midsummer he left for the mountain trails with his new circuit-riding partner, Hank Jonas. Hank wanted to learn and grow. He wanted to serve the Lord while he did it. Mitchell's prayer for help had been answered.

Robert was too busy with his new home and his quietly growing flock—he'd baptized Alec's wife and brother within a month of each other—to care what was happening back east. But occasionally Mitchell and Hank ran across friends of friends who passed news along. That was how Robert got the letter Geoffrey Sheridan sent from South Carolina to say he was doing well and had run across Jacob Chauncy in

Cheraw. Sheridan added that he no longer faulted Robert for refusing a preaching license; he had seen firsthand how suddenly the law could turn on a man.

Ayen was ten months old and a roly-poly bundle of mischief when Mitchell and Hank came with another letter. They slipped into the back of the meetinghouse and waited until the service was over before they caught Robert at the door and handed over the message. Susanna stretched on tiptoe to peer over his arm and asked curiously, "Who's it from, Papa?"

Ayen crowed, "Fum!" and stuffed his fist into his mouth.

Robert chucked his son under the chin and flipped the letter open to check the signature. "What do you know, it's from James Hunter."

The men followed him outside and crowded around. James Hunter had led the Sandy Creek Regulators well enough to be branded an outlaw for it. For him to get a message to Robert meant it was important.

"He says Josiah Martin, Tryon's replacement, has called all the county officials to reckon for the mishandled tax funds." Robert scanned the letter. "Sixty-six thousand pounds' worth. He's had it posted in every town."

Ethan Hardy whistled. "Well, we knew it was a lot."

"You boys will like this next part," Robert said. "Hunter says the sheriffs and justices hate Martin as much as we hated Tryon, only they aren't so loud about it."

Saul led three lusty cheers for Governor Martin. It had been a long time since the government had done anything worth cheering for. Robert looked at the last paragraph and something seemed to catch in his throat. "And he says it's safe for the outlaws to come home."

Another cheer would have seemed cheap right then. Magdalen said softly, "Oh, Rob. Praise the Lord."

Hank said, "Y'all can go back, if'n you want to?"

"Yes," Robert said. He looked at Magdalen. "If we want to."

Susanna said in a small voice, "I don't want to."

Ayen pulled his fist out of his mouth and shouted, "No!" He had no idea what the word meant, except that it was said to him a lot, but his timing was exceptional.

"Just what I was thinking," Saul said with a nod at Ayen. "I know Elsie likes it here."

"I don't want to leave, either," Magdalen said. "But Rob, if you—"

"I don't." Robert slipped the letter inside his Bible and reached for his rifle. The two best friends of a Baptist and a Regulator. "I'm where God wants me to be. And where I want to be. The only thing that would make me leave now would be another threat to our freedom."

"The truth holds its own, you say," Alec said grimly. "Freedom, not so much."

"That's why we'll go back down through the valley if we have to." The autumn wind was strong in his face, smelling of fallen leaves and the hope of another spring. "And we'll fight again if we have to. Only next time, *this* is what we'll be fighting for. And next time, we'll win."

# About This Book and Everything In It

This book is a work of historical fiction. Here we separate the wheat from the chaff.

## HISTORY:

-Governor William Tryon and henchman Edmund Fanning.

-The riot act that made a felony of refusing to disperse from a meeting within an hour of an official warning (the Johnston Act).

-The meetinghouse in Rocky River as a Regulator meeting place, and Francis Dorsett as a Separate Baptist pastor. James Hunter is also a prominent figure in Regulator history. His and Dorsett's involvement in chapter 12 is fictional, because the conference is fictional, but if it had actually happened they would certainly have been there.

-The list of Regulator leaders outlawed by Governor Tryon (with the exception of Robert Boothe).

-The bounties placed on select Regulator leaders (again with the exception of Robert Boothe).

-Joseph Murphy, pastor at Shallow Ford, going into hiding to escape arrest, and the migration of many of his church members.

-The loyalist Moravian settlement of Bethabara (pronounced Beth-AB'ra).

-Execution of six Regulators in Hillsborough on June 19, 1771.

-The Anson County oath mentioned by Alec Perry.

-General Hugh Waddell, subordinate officer to Tryon and former protester of the Stamp Act.

-Any Regulator work referenced by fictional characters but carried out elsewhere (gathering of Regulators outside Hillsborough, page 66; disruption of Hillsborough court, page 80; intimidation of Hugh Waddell, page 137; destruction of wagon train in Mecklenburg County, pages

*Alamance Battle Monument*
*(OurBaptistHeritage.org)*

138 and 201). The rescue of Geoffrey Sheridan in Johnson County is fictional.

-The clash at Alamance, including James Hunter's refusal to act as commanding officer; Dr. David Caldwell, Robert Matear (also spelled *Mateer*), and Robert Thompson as Regulator negotiators; Caldwell's address to Regulator leaders; and Thompson's death at Tryon's hands.

-The Regulator pledge in the prologue, known in history as *Regulator Advertisement No. 4*. I modernized spelling and added ellipses for brevity, but otherwise left it unaltered. Scholars disagree on when it was written—March 1767, January 1768, or April 1768. While 1768 is the generally accepted year, my two oldest sources and one of the Regulators' own documents indicated the pledge was written in spring of 1767, so I went with March 1767 (my exact date is just a guess). Incidentally, one of those two sources was completely pro-Regulator, while the other was just as anti-Regulator. Both had the same facts, but the spin put on those facts was extreme in either direction. Some of this can be attributed to sources—Governor Tryon's records or the Regulators' records. Every writer has a bias. It's hard to tell both sides of a story. But my research led me to believe that the truth lies in the middle ground: The Regulators turned to extralegal and illegal means only after their attempts at legal redress failed or brought on more oppression. They weren't banditti. They were frustrated men with very real grievances and no way of rectifying them. Likewise, those on the opposite side were not all cruel or tyrannical. Some did what they could to help the Regulators, up until the point of armed confrontation. Some were simply doing their duty with their local militias, and many went on to serve with distinction in the American Revolution. But some, like William Tryon himself, were too blinded by greed or egotism to have any compassion for the people under them. These were the men the Regulators hated.

# FICTION:

-Robert Boothe and his family, friends, and enemies, except those mentioned above. There *was* a man named Boothe in Regulator documents, but his first name was Charles. Maybe there never was an official who was as much of a creep as Colonel Drake, but if William Tryon and Edmund Fanning are any indication, maybe there was.

-The involvement of Robert's Regulators in any historical event, including the Regulator pledge and the battle at Alamance.

-The towns of Ayen Ford and Sunrising, and the unnamed county in which Ayen Ford is located. The area is Chatham County, but a fictional county seat with accompanying fictional officers was necessary for story purposes. Hunting River Gap is my own name for the crossing through the Brushy Mountains, but all other place names are historical.

As a side note, dialogue would have sounded different in the eighteenth century. As a reader, I find it hard to engage in books that use excessive dialect or stick strictly to the parlance of two centuries ago. I have tried not to use anything blatantly anachronistic, but some idioms may not be completely true to the era, including some traditional Southern expressions that I used for atmosphere or character.

Many parts of this story are based in fact. For example, while Saul McBraden and Alec Perry are fictional and did not actually blow up government supplies, Dixon's Mill was a real place (though there was no supply train there), and as Magdalen reports to Robert on page 138, several young men from two Rowan County Presbyterian churches did blow up a convoy of requisitioned supplies in a different area. Likewise, an instance of a horse being confiscated by officials and then "repossessed" by a band of Regulators gave me the basis for Elsie Thurmond's goods being seized and reclaimed. A breakup of a court session in Hillsborough (which Robert mentions on page 80) and the fear that Regulators would try to free some of their captured leaders gave me historical grounds for the rescue of Alec Perry. I know of no historical evidence for any outlaw being sheltered as Robert was in Sunrising, but to the best of my knowledge, the legal tradition protecting captured outlaws is accurate. James Hunter's fictional letter to Robert in the epilogue, including his comment on how county officials felt about Governor Martin, is based on a letter Hunter wrote to William Butler, another outlaw, around the same time.

Baptists in North Carolina were divided over the Regulator movement. Some churches threatened to excommunicate anyone who took up arms against the government. Others believed it was a Christian duty to right political wrongs. Still others, like Robert's fictional church, simply wanted to protect their own against injustice. Baptists were also divided by differences in belief. Regular Baptists were the most orthodox. Separate Baptists included a wide range of (not all Scriptural) beliefs, from conservative to outright charismatic, but stressed a personal relationship with God through spiritual rebirth. The divide was largely geographical—Regular to the north in and near Virginia, and Separate to the south. A Baptist could be a Regular Baptist by doctrine, but a Separate Baptist by geography. General and Particular were the two other divisions. General Baptists believed anyone could be saved through the blood of Jesus, while Particular Baptists held that certain people were preordained to be saved. Many new converts, often General Baptists, began preaching before taking time to learn solid doctrine, which added to the divisions and often made Particular Baptists appear theologically superior.

Are you confused yet? I certainly was. It took me a lot of research to figure out that if I wanted Robert Boothe to reflect the beliefs that I hold, he would have been considered a General, Separate Baptist—but he would have been rooted and grounded in the truth before preaching it to his people. All historic Baptists held to salvation by grace through faith, baptism of believers by immersion, local and independent churches, separation of churches from the state, soul liberty, and sole and literal authority of the Bible. The struggle of the established church and political elite versus dissenters and the "common people" was fierce and at times brutal. The issue of the vestry tax, or compulsory tithe, was a constant source of tension, as was Governor Tryon's drive to make North Carolina an Anglican colony. As quoted by Charles Drake on page 109, Governor Tryon openly wrote his opinion that the Baptists in North Carolina were "Enemies to Society & Scandal to Common Sense." If his fellow officials shared his views, it's no wonder so many Baptist families left for Tennessee or South Carolina after the Battle of Alamance.

In conclusion: This story's characters and their exploits exist only in my imagination, but the setting is very real—an era in our country when we fought not only for freedom from political oppression, but also for freedom to believe and act according to our convictions.

# Scripture References

All references are from the King James Bible.
Some verses have been paraphrased for dialogue purposes.

(page 1) 1 Corinthians 8:2
(page 16) Proverbs 26:25
(page 25) Romans 3:4
(page 25) 2 Corinthians 5:14
(page 32) Proverbs 3:5
(page 33+) Job 13:15
(page 56) Romans 12:20
(page 70) Matthew 20:27
(page 81) 1 Chronicles 16:36
(page 119) Psalm 11:1
(page 120) 2 Corinthians 6:2
(page 122) John 11:16
(page 140) Joshua 24:15
(page 140) Acts 16:31
(page 145) Ecclesiastes 9:11
(page 150) Matthew 10:23
(page 150) Mark 10:27
(page 150) Matthew 4:7
(page 150) Isaiah 59:1
(page 154) Genesis 12:1
(pages 165, 250, 251) John 8:32

(page 189) James 1:3
(page 214) Matthew 26:42
(page 224) Psalm 23:5
(page 226) Psalm 14:1
(pages 245, 260) Psalm 35:1-2
(page 248) Leviticus 26:8
(page 251) Romans 3:23
(page 254) John 10:11
(page 265) Psalm 56:3
(page 272) John 12:24
(page 273) John 15:13
(page 274) 2 Corinthians 12:9
(page 277) Job 3:25
(page 285) Genesis 2:18
(page 288) Daniel 3:17-18
(page 289) Isaiah 26:4
(page 289) Joshua 1:9
(pages 292, 293) Proverbs 21:30
(page 302) Isaiah 50:10
(page 303) Psalm 30:5
(page 303) Psalm 113:3

# Selected and Annotated Bibliography
## For Those Who Want to Know

Beller, James R. *America in Crimson Red.* Arnold, MO: Prairie Fire Press, 2004. A history of Baptists in America, it provides a brief and moderately reliable overview of Baptist involvement in the Regulator movement, although it's difficult to correctly detail a minute period of history within a work focused on a separate subject.

Fitch, William. *Some Neglected History of North Carolina.* This book, written in 1904, was one of my most valuable secondary sources, though with an extreme pro-Regulator bias. For an interesting contrast, try *A Colonial Officer and His Times*, a biography of General Hugh Waddell, written by one of Waddell's descendants. It describes all Regulators as either banditti or cowards. Ironically, the book lauds Waddell for his part in a militant Stamp Act protest shortly before the Regulator uprising. *A Colonial Officer* did give me some help on a date for my prologue, as again, its facts were solid despite its slanted interpretation.

Kars, Marjoleine. *Breaking Loose Together: The Regulator Rebellion in Pre-Revolutionary North Carolina.* Chapel Hill, NC: The University of North Carolina Press, 2002. This is a detailed look at the Regulator period and its causes and effects. It has something of a "socioeconomic analysis" feel, but the information is comprehensive—from economic causes to the definite influence of "radical Protestantism."

Paschal, George Washington. *History of North Carolina Baptists Vol. 1.* Raleigh, NC: Edwards & Broughton, Co., 1930. As the title suggests, it's a good source on North Carolina Baptists' views and factions.

Powell, William S. *The Regulators of North Carolina: A Documentary History.* A compilation of documents from the Regulator period, this is an excellent primary source, but not light reading!

Troxler, Carol Watterson. *Farming Dissenters.* North Carolina Historical Society, 2011. A general overview of the Regulator period, it highlights the movement's causes and relation to the American Revolution.

*I'd also like to acknowledge historical romance novelist Laura Frantz, whose vivid, well-placed details ignited a desire to make each story richer than the last.*

## Coming Soon
# Patriot by Night
### For Liberty & Conscience ~ Book Two
### A Novel of North Carolina Patriots

It's 1780, and North Carolina is a battlefield—Tory against patriot, patriot against Tory. Rane Armistead, hiding information that could cost him his life, dares to hope he's finally found safe harbor in the mountain village of Sunrising, far from the schemes of royal agent Malcolm Harrod.

Sunrising militiaman Benjamin Woodbridge is looking for a fight. Now that the Revolution has come to the Blue Ridge, it's the perfect chance to avenge his father's death. The last thing Benjamin wants is to take advice from this stranger with a scar and a secret.

But when Loyalist militia takes over Sunrising, both Rane and Benjamin are forced to realize the truth: Fighting for the place they call home means walking straight into a nightmare they've both lived through once. And can't hope to live through again.

### Freedom Fights On

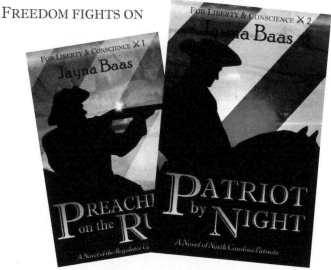

## For Liberty & Conscience
### The truth will hold its own.

### www.booksbyjayna.com

JAYNA BAAS (pronounced as in "baa, baa, black sheep") lives in northern Michigan with a great family of real people and the family of pretend people who live in her head. (Yes, she does know her characters are not real. No, she does not want you to tell them she said so.) She is notorious for working on several projects at once and writing  her series in the wrong order. She hones her craft amid loud southern gospel music and an embarrassing number of composition books, and is convinced God wired her to write—she can't *not* write, even though she believes German writer Thomas Mann was correct in saying, "A writer is someone for whom writing is more difficult than for other people."

*Preacher on the Run* is her first full-length novel, combining her interest in unfamiliar angles of the American Revolutionary period with her interest in America's early "baptized believers." She strongly believes, however, that Baptists don't have a monopoly on salvation. Repentance and faith are the only way to heaven for anyone, and that's really what she wants to write about.

"For whosoever shall call upon the name of the Lord shall be saved." – Romans 10:13